EMMA DARCY

Initially a French/English teacher, Emma Darcy changed careers to computer programming before marriage and motherhood settled her into a community life. Creative urges were channelled into oil-painting, pottery, designing and overseeing the construction and decorating of two homes, all in the midst of keeping up with three lively sons and the very social life of her businessman husband Frank. Very much a people person, and always interested in relationships, she finds the world of romantic fiction a happy one and the challenge of creating her own cast of characters very addictive. Emma Darcy is the author of more than seventy-five novels, including the international best-seller THE SECRETS WITHIN, published by MIRA® books.

Don't miss *The Arranged Marriage*, the first book in Emma Darcy's exciting new trilogy *Kings of Australia*, available in Modern Romance™ this month!

LYNNE GRAHAM

Lynne Graham was born in Northern Ireland and has been a keen Mills & Boon® reader since her teens. She is very happily married, with an understanding husband who has learned to cook since she started to write! Her five children keep her on her toes. She has a very large old English sheepdog, which knocks everything over, and two cats. When time allows, Lynne is a keen gardener.

Lynne Graham also has a book out this month. *The Disobedient Mistress*, part of Lynne's latest mini-series *Sister Brides* is available now in Modern Romance™.

latin liaisons

EMMA DARCY & LYNNE GRAHAM

LATIN LOVERS MAKE RED-HOT HUSBANDS...

MILLS & BOON®

*All the characters in this book have no existence outside the imagination
of the author, and have no relation whatsoever to anyone bearing the
same name or names. They are not even distantly inspired by any
individual known or unknown to the author, and all the incidents are
pure invention.*

Latin Liaisons © Harlequin Enterprises II B.V., 2002

The Secret Mistress and *The Spanish Groom*
were first published in Great Britain by
Harlequin Mills & Boon Limited in separate, single volumes.

The Secret Mistress © Emma Darcy 1999
The Spanish Groom © Lynne Graham 1999

ISBN 0 263 83188 4

126-0602

*Printed and bound in Spain
by Litografia Rosés S.A., Barcelona*

latin liaisons

THE SECRET MISTRESS

THE SPANISH GROOM

THE SECRET MISTRESS

EMMA DARCY

To Lew Pulbrook, whose INCA TOURS of South America inspired this book and provided all of the background material in it. Many, many thanks to Lew and Kristy for sharing their knowledge, while showing me and all 'The Amigos' a fantastic and fascinating part of the world.

CHAPTER ONE

LUIS ANGEL MARTINEZ was feeling good as he rode the elevator up to his hotel suite. He'd completed the business he'd come to La Paz to do, he'd dined well, the current crisis in the city provided him with the perfect excuse for missing his own engagement party, and his mother—widely regarded as the wealthiest and most powerful woman in Argentina—couldn't do one damned thing about it.

He couldn't help smiling.

The two young women who were sharing the elevator—their accents and clothes marking them as tourists from the U.S.A.—turned interested, hopefully inviting eyes on him. Luis instantly killed the smile. Black scorn blazed from his dark eyes, shrivelling their speculation, and his whole body stiffened in proud rejection of whatever fantasies they nursed.

He despised the foreign women who tripped around, looking for sexual adventure, and he most particularly hated being viewed as a possible Latin lover. He might look the part, having the dark olive skin and black hair of his Spanish heritage, with the added attraction of a taller, more powerful physique than the average South American male, but he sure as hell would never get drawn into playing the part.

He'd been burnt once. Once was more than enough for him.

The elevator halted. He glared balefully at the back of the two blonde heads as the women made their exit. Not that their fairness compared in any way to the silky sun and moon mixture of Shontelle's hair, but the minds under the hair probably held the same attitude towards sampling one of the natives for the pleasure of a new carnal experience.

Not me, ladies, he savagely beamed at them before the doors shut and the elevator resumed its upward climb. His mother was right on one score. Best to tie himself to a woman of his own race, own culture, own background. No nasty surprises with that kind of matchmaking. All smooth sailing. Especially with Elvira Rosa Martinez at the helm, steering everything as she saw fit.

Except she hadn't counted on this little squall blowing up in Bolivia, causing him to miss the engagement party she had planned behind his back.

Unavoidable circumstances.

The absolutely perfect excuse.

The thought restored Luis' good humour. He was smiling again as the elevator opened onto his floor and he headed for his private suite. No one could validly question his staying right here. It was literally impossible for him to get out of La Paz without running into trouble.

After yesterday's violent march of the farmers through the streets, Bolivia was boiling up to yet an-

other change of government. The airport was closed.
A curfew had been imposed. The military had taken
over the city.

Safely and comfortably ensconced in the Plaza
Hotel, Luis was not in the least perturbed by these
events. Bolivia was Bolivia, renowned for having
more changes of government than any other country,
five in one day in recent history. The volatile political
situation would eventually blow over and life would
go on as usual.

He entered his well-appointed suite, closed the door
on all the outside problems, and moved to the minibar, deciding one or two more celebratory drinks were
in order.

Of course, a second engagement party would be
arranged, although he'd insist on doing it himself—
his way—next time. This minor reprieve was only a
postponement of the inevitable. He was thirty-six
years old, time for him to marry, time for him to start
a family. It was also time for his mother to step right
out of his affairs.

She'd undoubtedly be stewing with frustration over
this further delay to a public announcement of her
most cherished ambition—the tying of the Martinez
fortune to that of the Gallardo family. Do her good,
Luis thought with intense satisfaction. She was far too
fond of pushing.

She'd picked Claudia Gallardo out for him very
shortly after his brother's death. Luis had scoffed at
the idea—a schoolgirl! She'd be groomed to suit him,

to grace their social position, to uphold all the traditional virtues of a wife, his mother had argued. I'll choose my own wife, he'd tossed back at her at the time, but he really didn't care anymore, not since Shontelle—that green-eyed witch—had chewed him up and spat him out.

He took ice and a lime from the refrigerator, lined up the bottle of *Caipirinha,* and wished he could blot the memory of Shontelle Wright right out of existence. Because of her…after her…he'd wanted more than just a *suitable* wife. He'd wanted to feel…

But maybe he didn't have any passion left in him, so what did it matter if his marriage bed wasn't as warm as he'd like it? Stupid to keep holding out for something he might never experience again. He would make the commitment to Claudia soon enough. She was willing. He was willing. Together they'd beget another line of heirs and heiresses. Surely he'd feel something for his children.

Nevertheless, it was one thing resigning himself to the destiny mapped out for him, another to be relentlessly pressed into it. Although he'd finally put his rebellious years behind him and shouldered the responsibilities that would have been his older brother's, had Eduardo lived, Luis did not want his mother thinking she could rule his life. He was glad—yes, glad—he couldn't fly back to Buenos Aires to keep *her* timetable, however *reasonable* it was.

Claudia would undoubtedly wait submissively.

She did everything…submissively.

Luis grimaced. Sometimes he suspected it was an act, deliberately put on to give him the sense of being on top. Respected. Honoured. King of his kingdom. But, so what? At least he knew where he was with Claudia.

He dropped the wedges of lime into his glass, mashed sugar into them, added the ice and drowned the lot with *Caipirinha*. Sweet and sour—like life, he thought. The telephone rang as he stirred the drink. Carrying the glass with him, he moved to pick up the nearest receiver, cynically wondering if his mother had found a danger-free way out of La Paz for him.

"Luis Martinez," he rolled out carelessly.

"Luis, it's Alan Wright. Please…don't hang up. It's taken me hours to track you down and I desperately need your help."

The quick, taut plea stilled what would normally have been an automatic reaction. Luis had no wish to see, hear, or have any contact with the man whose sister had taken him for no more than a lump of tasty Latin meat. The heat of deeply lacerated pride instantly burned through him.

"What kind of help?" he snapped, angry with himself for even hesitating over cutting off his former friend.

"Luis, I have a tour group caught here in La Paz. We were due to fly to Buenos Aires yesterday. God knows when the airport will be reopened. They're frightened, panicky, and some are suffering from altitude sickness. I need a bus to get them out. I'll drive it. I thought you might be able to provide it.''

A bus.

It conjured up old memories—a much younger, wilder Alan, driving a beaten-up bus through the Amazon jungle to the mining operation where Luis had been sent for safekeeping, away from the troubles in Argentina. Alan had worked there for six months, more or less swapping his mechanical skills for the spare parts he needed to get his bus roadworthy enough to set up his own tour business.

An Australian, in love with South America—nothing was going to stop Alan Wright from selling it to tourists back home. Camping trips to start with, he'd decided. Then gradually he'd build up to the bigger money stuff. Luis had admired his initiative and determination, liked his cheerful good nature, and enjoyed his company. For nine years they'd maintained an infrequent but always congenial contact with each other. If Alan hadn't introduced his sister...

''Is Shontelle with you?''

The question slipped out, unconsidered and loaded with a long, pent-up hostility that hissed down the line.

No denial. Nothing but a fraught silence that emphatically underlined the division of their interests.

''Is she?'' Luis demanded harshly, uncaring of what the other man thought, knowing he had the power to ruthlessly cut their connection without any comeback.

"Goddammit, Luis! I'll pay you for the bus. Can't you just deal with me?" Alan exploded, tension and urgency ripping through every word.

She was with him.

More than pride started burning through Luis Angel Martinez. Every cell of his body was hit by an electric charge. Adrenalin shot through his bloodstream. Even the sense of his sexuality leapt into powerful prominence…sharply revitalised, wanting, needing, craving the satisfaction of wringing something more from the woman who'd dismissed all they'd shared as a brief bout of lust, come to the end of its run.

"Where are you?" he asked.

"At the Europa Hotel," came the quick, hopeful answer. "As luck would have it, just around the corner from the Plaza."

"Very convenient!" Luis smiled. It was a smile that would have chilled the heart of anyone who saw it. "What's the size of your tour group, Alan?"

"Thirty-two, including me."

"I can get you a suitable bus…"

"Great!" A gush of relief.

"…And have it at your hotel, ready to go in the morning…"

"I knew if anyone could do it, you could." Warm gratitude.

"…On one condition."

Silence. On edge again. "What is it?" Wary.

Luis didn't give a damn about Alan's feelings. His

friendship had probably been as self-serving as his sister's association with him. After all, for a foreign tour operator, Luis Angel Martinez was a contact worth having in South America. He could open doors.

And shut them.

"Shontelle will have to come to my suite at the Plaza to negotiate the deal with me," he stated blandly. "The sooner the better, for your purposes."

"You can't be serious!" Alan burst out. "There's a curfew on. Army tanks are trundling around the streets and trigger-happy soldiers are everywhere. A woman alone, breaking curfew...it's too dangerous, Luis."

So was driving a bus out of here, Luis thought. The farmers were in revolt. They'd be blockading all the roads from La Paz. Alan was obviously prepared to take risks to get his people out, probably counting on his skill as a good talker with a dab hand at appropriate bribery. Which he could use tonight, as well, if need be. His plea on Shontelle's behalf left Luis totally unmoved.

"You can escort her from hotel to hotel, if you like. The distance is very short and the road that links us is a cul-de-sac, hardly the place for a tank or soldiers on guard duty," he pointed out.

"I can't leave the group. Shontelle can't, either. The women need her to..."

"There is a side entrance to the Plaza from the steps leading up to Prado 16 de Julio. I'll have a man posted at the door to let her in. Let's say...half an hour from now?''

Luis set the receiver down with firm decisiveness. He smiled again as he jiggled the ice in his drink. A responsibility to others often led to paths one wouldn't take, given an absolutely free choice. Because he was his mother's son, he would end up married to Claudia Gallardo. Because Shontelle was Alan Wright's sister, she would end up in this suite tonight.

With him.

And he would take a great deal of pleasure in stripping her of more than her clothes!

CHAPTER TWO

SHONTELLE saw her brother's jaw clench. He literally gnashed his teeth as he slammed the telephone receiver down. The violent action caused her heart to leap out of the frozen stasis that had held it for the duration of the call. The resulting pump of blood kicked reason into her mind, clearing it of the dark cloud of memories.

"What did he want?" she asked. It was obvious from the conversation that Luis had at least considered procuring the bus. It was certainly possible for him to do so. The Martinez family had fingers in many pies right across the continent; agriculture, mining, cement works, oil and gas, transport...

"Forget it!" Alan's hand sliced the air with negative vehemence. "I'll try something else."

There was nothing else. Shontelle shook her head over the mess of notes on the table. They'd already been down every other avenue. The usual help Alan could tap into was not forthcoming.

She watched him steam around the sitting room of the suite they were sharing, a big man chopping up the space around her, making it feel claustrophobic with the sense of failure. Getting accommodation in The Europa, a relatively new five-star hotel, had been

14

a coup for this tour. Now it seemed like a prison. Everyone in the tour group had lost their pleasure in its luxury, anxieties building with being trapped here. More bad news could make soothing fears and frayed tempers a very difficult, if not impossible exercise.

Alan always fought against imparting bad news to his tour groups, especially when there was no good news to make it more palatable. Normally he was a very cool operator, highly skilled at lateral thinking whenever a crisis arose, as it frequently did in South America. The ability to be flexible was paramount to bringing off a successful tour and Alan was always prepared to come up with an alternative schedule. But this time he'd found himself blocked at every turn.

He was the kind of man who hated being thwarted.

Or found wanting in any way.

So was Luis Angel Martinez, Shontelle remembered.

The two men were very alike in that respect. Kindred spirits. They'd been friends…the type of friendship where time and distance and social standing had no relevance. They might not meet for long intervals but such separations hadn't made any difference, not over the nine years before…

Guilt wormed through Shontelle.

She had ruined it. For both of them. Blindly, wantonly, foolishly. Alan had warned her it wouldn't work between her and Luis. Couldn't. But she had refused to listen, refused to see…until Elvira Rosa Martinez had so very forcefully opened her ears and eyes. Then she'd been too wrapped up in her pride to realise how her exit from Luis' life might have a bitter fallout on his friendship with her brother.

Not that Alan had told her of the consequences of her decisions. She had overheard Vicki, his wife, dryly informing an office associate they were no longer welcome on Martinez territory. The popular day trip from Buenos Aires to the ranch run by Luis' younger brother, Patricio, had been struck from the tour.

When she'd tackled Vicki about it, the forthcoming explanation had been devastating. "Shontelle, did you really expect Luis Martinez to keep up the connection? You and Alan are not only of the same family, you even look alike."

It was true. Alan was ten years older than her but the family likeness was unmistakable. The bone structure of their faces was the same; wide brow, high cheekbones, straight nose, clearcut chin. Alan's top lip was thinner than hers and his eyes were not a clear green—more hazel in colour. The streaky blonde hair of his youth had darkened over the years but the variation in shade was still there. Either one of them was a physical reminder of the other, and that reminder would not be welcome to Luis Angel Martinez.

In her pride, Shontelle knew she had wounded his. It hadn't seemed to matter at the time. But it did. She had the strong conviction it especially mattered now.

"You were talking to Luis about me," she said, drawing Alan's attention.

He flashed her a pained look. "He asked about you," he answered dismissively.

"No. It was more than that." She frowned, trying to recall what she'd heard. The call had ended abruptly, just after Alan had said it was too dangerous for a woman to be out during curfew. "Tell me what he wanted, Alan."

"I said, forget it!" he snapped impatiently.

"I want to know. I have a right to know," she argued. "I'm just as responsible for this tour group as you are."

He paused in his pacing but aggression still pumped from him. His eyes glittered with a fury of frustration. "I will not have my little sister grovel to Luis Martinez for anyone!" he bit out.

More pride.

It was heart-thumpingly obvious that Luis had turned the deal for the bus into something personal. Very personal. Which again was her fault. Shontelle took a deep breath to calm a host of skittish nerves. She couldn't let this pass. It wasn't fair to Alan. Besides which, the tour group was depending on them to rescue them from the situation.

"I'm not little," she pointed out determinedly. "I'm twenty-six years old and I can take care of myself."

Alan rolled his eyes. "Sure you can! Like you did two years ago when you talked me into leaving you with Luis."

"I'm over that. I can deal with him," she insisted hotly.

Too much personal knowledge sliced back at her. "You didn't want to come back to South America. You wouldn't be on this trip but for Vicki getting glandular fever. And you were as nervy as hell while we were in Buenos Aires."

Her cheeks burned. "I came to assist you. That's my job." She pushed her chair back from the table which was littered with the evidence of failed attempts at solutions. Resolution drove her to her feet. "I'll go and talk to him."

"No, you won't!"

"Luis Martinez was your last resort, Alan. Two years ago he would have got you the bus, no problem. I caused the problem and I'll deal with it."

He argued.

Shontelle stood firm.

Nothing was going to stop her; not the curfew, not the danger—which she considered very limited with the Plaza Hotel being virtually next door—not any of Alan's big-brotherly concerns. She'd lived with guilt and shame too long. She'd spent two years being eaten up by memories she couldn't change or bury. Luis Martinez wanted a face-to-face meeting with her. Then let it be. Let it be.

Maybe something good would come out of it.

The bus, if nothing else.

She owed Alan that.

CHAPTER THREE

GOOD intentions were all very fine when made from a safe distance. Shontelle stared at the door which led into the suite occupied by Luis Angel Martinez and her heart quailed. A suite contained a bed...

She wasn't over him. She doubted she ever would be. Luis Angel... She'd even been besotted with his name. Dark angel, she thought now, barely suppressing a shiver. It took all her willpower to raise her hand and knock on the door.

In the next few stomach-knotting moments, Shontelle tried to steel herself against revealing the vulnerability she felt. This meeting would only be a matter of pride to the man she had to face. He undoubtedly wanted to rub in that she was the loser, not him.

Somehow she had to let that wash over her, do a bit of grovelling if need be. Remember the bus, she fiercely told herself. She had to get the bus.

At least Luis couldn't mistake the fact she was dressed for business. Her dark red T-shirt was printed with the *Amigos Tours* logo and her khaki trousers with pockets running down both legs were plainly practical, as were her sturdy shoes. This was strictly a business visit.

The door opened.

And there he was, hot flesh and blood, simmering in front of her. His thick, wavy black hair was brushed away from the beautifully sculpted features of his face, as always, framing them with a kind of dark, savage splendour. His skin gleamed with almost a magnetic vitality. His deeply set eyes, lushly outlined by their double rows of lashes, projected more power than any one man should ever have.

Shontelle stood rooted to the floor, speechless, breathless, mindless, her good intentions instantly zapped out of existence. Her scalp tingled. Every millimetre of her skin tingled. Her fingers curled into her palms, nails biting into flesh. Her toes scrunched up in her walking boots. Her heart swelled, throbbed, its heavy beat of yearning echoing through every pulse point.

She wanted him.

She still wanted him.

''Welcome back to my part of the world.''

His voice jolted her back to the chilling reality of why she was here. She'd loved his voice—its deep, rich, flowing tones—but there was no caress in it now, nothing warmly intimate. No welcome in his smile, either. The full-lipped sensual mouth that had once seduced her with such passion, was curled into a sardonic taunt, and the dark blaze of his eyes held a scorching intensity that shrivelled any hope of reviving good feelings. Or even a workable understanding.

He stepped aside to make room for her to enter,

derisively waving her into his domain. For one nerve-jangling instant, the highly civilised Plaza suite blurred in Shontelle's mind and the Amazon jungle leapt into it—its overwhelming sense of the primitive pressing in on her, vampire bats biting for blood, big black tarantulas hiding in trees, ready to pounce on their prey...

"Scared?" Luis mocked, his eyes raking her with contempt.

It goaded her forward. "No. Should I be?" she tossed at him as she passed by, determined on holding a brave front.

He closed the door behind her.

The metallic click felt ominous.

"Spurned Latin lovers are notoriously volatile," he remarked, still in a mocking tone.

"A lot of water under the bridge since then, Luis," she answered, shrugging off the implied threat and walking on through the sitting room of the suite, aiming for the big picture window on the other side of it.

The spectacular view of La Paz at night was not the drawcard. She desperately needed to put distance between her and the man who'd deliberately raised memories of their affair. And its ending.

"I must say you look as dynamic as ever," she threw at him, forcing herself to attach a conciliatory smile. "I'd say life has been treating you well."

"It could be better," he replied, watching her move

away from him with a dark amusement that raised Shontelle's sense of danger several notches.

"I expect you're married by now," she added, trying to drive a moral wedge between them.

His white shirt was half unbuttoned, revealing a provocative arrowhead of his broad muscular chest, dark skin tipped by a glimpse of the black curls she knew spread across it. His forearms were bare, too, sleeves rolled up, flaunting his strong masculinity. She hated the thought of his wife knowing him as intimately as she had.

"No. As it happens, I'm not married."

The cold, hard words were like nails being driven into Shontelle's heart. Had she made a mistake? A flood of hot turmoil hit her. Fortunately she'd reached the window. She swiftly turned her back on him, hiding her wretched confusion, pretending to be captivated by the spectacular view.

Surely to God he was lying! He'd been betrothed to another woman—the Gallardo heiress—before and during their affair two years ago. He'd lied then, by omission. He'd left Shontelle blindly believing she was the only woman who counted in his life when there were two others who had a longer, deeper claim on him.

How could anyone not count Elvira Rosa Martinez?

More to the point, it had been totally unconscionable of Luis to remain silent about the young woman designated as his wife; the sweet, convent-raised, beautifully mannered Claudia Gallardo.

His silence had spelled out where Shontelle stood in his life—a handy bit of foreign fluff on the side, out of his mainstream, suitable only for fun and relaxation. But then he hadn't made any promises, she savagely reminded herself.

"I assume you're not married, either, since you're travelling with your brother," he drawled, each word sounding closer.

He was coming after her.

"I'm here on business, Luis," she said tersely, wishing she hadn't raised anything personal. He couldn't be believed anyway. He'd undoubtedly say—or not say—whatever suited his purpose.

"Do you have a lover tucked away at home, waiting to serve your inclinations?" His voice had the stinging flick of a whip.

"I'm all out of lovers at the moment," she answered flippantly, disdaining even a glance at him.

"Which is why you came on this trip, mmh?"

The silky taunt hit her on the raw. The urge to swing around and let him have the sting of her tongue almost blew her mind off her purpose here. She gritted her teeth, folded her arms to hold wayward impulses in, and stared fixedly at the myriad of lights beyond the window.

"It looks like a fairyland outside, doesn't it?" she remarked as lightly as she could.

It was true. La Paz was the highest capital in the

world and it appeared to be built in a moon crater. From where she was viewing it from the low downtown area, the lights of the city rose in a great circular curve, going up so high they seemed to be hanging in the sky. Incredible there were actually people living behind them.

"You need a magician to get you out of it," Luis mocked, standing right behind her now.

"We need a bus," she said quickly, fighting her intense awareness of his nearness.

"The curfew doesn't lift until six in the morning."

Her heart skittered. What was he implying? They had all night to negotiate?

"I don't like your hair constricted in a plait," was his next comment, confusing Shontelle further.

Her spine crawled at his touch as he lifted the rope of hair away from her back. She knew what he was going to do but her mind couldn't accept it. He couldn't still love her hair. He couldn't still *want* her!

Or maybe he didn't.

Maybe he was playing some cruel cat-and-mouse game.

She wanted to look at his face but she was frightened to. What if he was waiting to feed off her feelings? Pride insisted she deny him the satisfaction of knowing she was rattled. Could he hear the mad thumping of her heart? Stay calm, stay calm, stay calm, she recited feverishly.

He'd worked off the rubber band and was separating the twisted swathes, seeming to take sensual pleasure in the feel of her hair. Impossible to ignore it. Impossible to stay calm.

"What do you want from me, Luis?" she blurted out.

"What I had before."

Her mind fragmented under the force of her own desire to have him again, and his apparent desire to recall and repeat the passion they'd shared. Some tattered shreds of reason shrieked that he was only playing with her, using his power to make her succumb to him, but she had to know, had to see.

As she jerked around to face him, her arms flew out of their protective fold and lifted into an instinctive plea for truth. "What do you mean?" she cried.

He still held a skein of her hair and he wound it around his hand as his eyes blazed their dark purpose into hers. "I mean to seize the day, Shontelle. Or to put it more graphically…the night. You want a bus. I want one more taste of you."

Shock waves slammed through her.

One more taste…

Only *one…*

Payment for the bus.

"Not such a difficult deal, is it?" he taunted. "Just a matter of giving me what you gave of yourself two years ago…in your desire to get what you wanted of me."

"I didn't get what I wanted then," she protested, her voice thin and shaky under the appalling weight of devastated hopes.

A savage fury flared into his eyes. "Was I not all you wanted of a Latin lover?" His mouth curled with cruel intent. "Well, let me try not to disappoint you tonight. We have many hours ahead of us. I promise you a feast of hot-blooded sensuality."

Hot and hard and ruthless.

The awful part was, Shontelle could not stop her body from pulsing with excitement at what he offered. Only with him had she ever known intense physical ecstasy. She hadn't even felt a twinge of attraction towards anyone else in the past two years. Just the thought of touching Luis again, feeling him…quivers of anticipation shot through her.

But he was treating her like a whore, laying it out that she could only get the bus in return for sex.

Sex…not remotely connected to love. Not even the slightest semblance of love. It was wrong, wrong, wrong! Her heart twisted in torment as he twisted her hair more firmly around his hand and tugged her closer to him. Then his other hand slid over her breasts, his palm rotating caressingly, his eyes glittering their triumphant knowledge of what had pleasured her in the past, and to prove him right, her nipples instantly stiffened into begging prominence.

"Stop it!" she hissed, hating his power to arouse her even as she revelled in the sharp sensation that stimulated a host of nerves, arcing from her breasts to the innermost core of her sexuality.

One black eyebrow arched mockingly. "You no longer like this?"

He was the devil incarnate, tempting her. The truth was, she didn't want him to stop. She didn't want him to ever stop. But he would. This was only to be one more taste. Unless...

Something deeply primitive stirred in Shontelle.

He wasn't married, so he said.

And he still wanted her.

He also wanted a payback for his wounded pride.

Well, so did she. So did she!

"I don't normally go for one night stands," she said.

"But these are special circumstances," he returned silkily.

"Just let me understand you clearly, Luis..."

With her heart thumping to a wild beat, Shontelle flicked open the shirt button over his chest curls and slid her hand inside, seeking and deliberately tweaking one of his nipples. His sharply indrawn breath was music to her ears. She had power over him, too. It wasn't a one-way street.

Her eyes flirted challengingly with his as she spoke through the provocative, physical teasing. "...If I stay with you the night and let you have your..." She lowered her gaze to his mouth, regarding it assessingly. "...taste of me..." She let the words linger for a moment, then flicked her gaze up, raising her eyebrows in pointed questioning. "...I get the bus? Is that the deal?"

"Yes," he hissed at her.

"Then make your calls now, Luis. Let me hear you

arrange the delivery of an appropriate bus to The Europa Hotel as soon as the curfew is lifted tomorrow. When you've done that, I'll call Alan to assure him everything's all right and I'll be staying with you until morning.''

His jawline tightened. His eyes narrowed. He didn't like her calling the shots, but he'd dealt her the cards, made the rules of the game, and Shontelle figured he couldn't fault her over playing them. A sense of triumph poured a burst of adrenalin through her veins. No one was a victim unless they allowed themselves to be.

She pursed her lips into a considering little smile. ''A feast of hot-blooded sensuality sounds good. I do hope you're up to it, Luis.''

The moment the words were out, she felt a swell of danger—a dark and fierce emanation from him swirling around her, sending shivers down her spine. He smiled right back at her as he released her hair— a smile that promised himself a deep well of satisfaction. He plucked her hand from inside his shirt and drew it slowly down, palm against him, fingers splayed.

''Feel for yourself how *up* to it I am, Shontelle,'' he drawled, his other hand gliding up her throat to cup her chin.

He was fully erect, his arousal straining against the barrier of clothes. He guided her into stroking him as he tilted her head and bent his own. ''Just to make sure I do want the taste,'' he murmured, then covered her mouth with his, not giving her any chance of reply.

Shontelle didn't even think of trying to deny him. The urge to taste him, too, was far too strong for any denial. And his mouth was soft, sweetly seductive, at first, his tongue merely flicking over the soft inner tissues of her lips, sensitising them with delicious tingles.

She responded, wanting to know if the passion they had once shared could be triggered again, beyond pride, beyond all the differences between them. Her free arm instinctively curled around his neck to hold him to her and the kiss deepened, pursuing a more erotic, more exciting intimacy.

Her body started clenching with a need it had all but forgotten. She grasped the hard proof of his desire, fingers digging around it, revelling in the feel of him. She was so caught up in her own strong responses, it came as a shock when he abruptly ended their kiss, removed her hand from him and broke out of her embrace.

"You must be hungry for a man, Shontelle," he mocked, lifting the fingers that had been squeezing him to his mouth. He lightly nipped them. "Definitely an appetising taste. Please excuse me while I execute my half of the deal. I look forward to the rest of the night."

He walked away from her, seemingly completely in control of himself. Shontelle was left feeling shattered, her legs trembling, drained of strength, her stomach churning so much she wanted to be sick, her heart aching, her mind zigzagging helplessly through a maze of fierce contradictions.

She loved him…and hated him.

She craved more of him…yet wanted to cut out his callous heart.

Was it to be a night of intense life…or a night of heart-killing desolation?

She didn't know…couldn't decide…couldn't tear herself away from whatever might pass between them.

He picked up a telephone, pressed a sequence of numbers, spoke with the arrogant authority of his name, his position, the power that came automatically with great wealth…Luis Angel Martinez…the only man who'd ever moved her like this…and maybe the only man who ever would.

Was there anything to win by staying?

The bus, her mind answered.

But the bus had no relevance to the question.

She wanted…needed…to win something for herself. So she had to stay and see this night through, even if she lost everything.

One night…one night…unless she could turn it into something more.

CHAPTER FOUR

LUIS was rock-hard and in pain but the shattered look he'd left on Shontelle's face was worth every second of the discomfort. No way was she going to turn the tables on him! He hoped the witch was burning with frustration.

He deliberately kept his back turned to her while he talked on the phone to Ramon Flores who could organize any form of road transport in La Paz. It was local courtesy to speak Quechua, the old Inca language, and Luis did so with perverse pleasure, knowing Shontelle would not be able to follow it. Her grasp of Spanish was good, but she only had a sketchy knowledge of the native dialects.

Let her stew in uncertainty, he thought. She was too damned sure of her power to get what she wanted. Before this night was out she'd learn who was master of the situation, and he'd kiss her goodbye with the same brutal finality she'd shown him two years ago.

"The bus is not a problem, Luis," Ramon said predictably. "But..."

The pause sharpened Luis' attention. "But what?"

"It would be useless to ask any of my local drivers to deliver it. They would be stopped and arrested before the bus got to The Europa. The military edict is no gathering of crowds. They consider three people

31

together a crowd. A local man taking out a bus…it would not be allowed. Too suspicious.''

Luis frowned. He hadn't thought of that. Yet if he didn't deliver…no, he had to. He refused to look weak and ineffectual in front of Shontelle Wright. There had to be a way.

''Your Australian friend…he might get through, being a foreigner,'' Ramon suggested. ''Since he is prepared to risk his tour group in trying to get out of La Paz, tell him to come to the depot and take the bus himself. It will be fully fuelled, ready to go.''

It made sense, but it wasn't the deal he'd agreed to with Shontelle. Her words, not his, he reasoned. He didn't have to toe *her* line. The essence of the deal was the same. The bus would be available for Alan to take. That was all his erstwhile friend had requested.

''Someone will be at the depot to hand over the bus?'' he asked.

''Curfew lifts at six. I'll have a man at the gates at six-thirty.''

''Thank you, Ramon.''

''Your friend is a fool, Luis.''

''His choice.''

''It's our bus. This could bring trouble kicking back to us.''

''I'll wear it. You are simply following my orders, Ramon.''

''As you wish.''

Luis slowly lowered the receiver, his mind engaged in hard reappraisal. This whole enterprise was stupid, inviting trouble. Alan's tour group was safe at their hotel. What was another week or two out of their lives? Better locked away in luxury than dead. It was just as stupid for him to get involved, putting the Martinez reputation for finely balanced political sense on the line.

For what?

A woman who had used him…a woman worth nothing!

Madness to have been tempted into wreaking some sweet vengeance. It was beneath him. He should dismiss her from his suite right now, send her off with a bitter sense of failure. That was vengeance enough.

He turned to do it.

She stood framed by the blackness of the night beyond the window, the twinkling stars of light from the city surrounding her, lending her an air of etherial mystery. Her long hair gleamed like a stream of moonlight and her golden skin glowed, the perfect foil for eyes that shone like emeralds. Her full lips were slightly apart, as he'd left them, waiting it seemed for another kiss, insidiously beckoning him.

He forced his gaze down the long graceful line of her neck to the blood-red T-shirt. She had no heart, he told himself. No heart. But the lush softness of her breasts moved as though to the beat of one, a beat that tugged on him with inexorable and tormenting strength.

How was it possible, he wondered, to feel such desire for a woman…yet hate her with equal ferocity?

"Is the bus assured for tomorrow morning?" she asked, her voice strained.

The conviction swept into Luis' mind. This was no

fun for her. Which was only right and just. She'd had her *fun* last time. It was his turn tonight. He could send her away right now, defeated, but what satisfaction was there in that? He wanted—needed—the same physical satisfaction she had taken from him, over and over again.

"Yes," he said. "You'll get the bus."

Which put their deal on the line.

Luis watched her take that in, and all it implied. Her gaze dropped from the hard challenge in his. Her hands interlocked in front of her waist, as though testing how much strength she had, fingers flexing…and he craved their touch on him again. Her breasts and shoulders lifted slightly as she drew in a deep breath. He found himself holding his own breath, waiting for her decision, willing her to concede to him, his whole body focusing energy on her, determined on drawing her into the ring with him.

She spoke, still with her eyes downcast. "If you have a wife, Luis, this is a rotten game you're playing and I won't be a party to it."

Luis clenched his teeth. It was because of her he didn't have a wife, but he'd rot in hell before she dragged that admission from him.

"If I had a wife, you would have had no access to me, Shontelle," he stated bitingly.

Her lashes slowly lifted, her eyes meeting his with an oddly poignant expression of irony. He caught a sense of fatalism, yet there was no resignation to defeat in it, more a feeling of being ready to ride whatever outcome ensued from the situation. It disturbed him. It wasn't what he expected from her. Not what he wanted, either.

"What time should I tell Alan the bus will be at our hotel?" she asked. "He'll want to have the tour group ready to go."

The hotel! It was on the tip of his tongue to state that Alan would have to collect the bus from the depot. A surge of pride stopped him. If he didn't win his ground with this woman, he would always feel whipped by her. Which was totally intolerable. No way would he give Shontelle Wright any cause to scorn him again.

It might be sheer madness to risk his own skin to balance the scales, madness to risk blotting the Martinez reputation for steering clear of trouble, but he would get the damned bus himself rather than give Shontelle a loophole out of this deal. She had to be his for this one night. Somehow it was a need that drove to the very core of his manhood.

"Seven o'clock," he answered tersely. "Given that it's not stopped by the military. That I cannot control."

A sigh whispered from her lips. She nodded acceptance. "Fair enough! I'll ring Alan now."

Done!

Yet Luis' triumph had a bittersweet taste. She had wrung more from him than she was worth. But she would pay, he promised himself. He would strip her of every bit of power she had over him before dawn came. Then he would be free of her. Finally free of her.

CHAPTER FIVE

SHONTELLE tried desperately to focus her mind on how to tell Alan she was spending the night with the man who'd stolen her heart two years ago and hadn't valued it…a man who'd used her for pleasure…and when she'd taken the pleasure away, had vindictively taken out his displeasure on her brother. There was simply no way Alan was going to understand.

One more night…

With any luck she should at least win something from this encounter. It would either set her free of Luis Angel Martinez…or…give her hope of something more from him, more than she had believed possible.

He *wanted* her…perhaps as badly as she wanted him. It was what she was gambling on. Plus the fact he hadn't married. The Gallardo heiress hadn't got him. And maybe—just maybe—Elvira Rosa Martinez didn't know her son as well as she thought she did.

"The telephone is free for you to use," Luis dryly reminded her, gesturing to it with a casual grace that belied any tension on his part over her decision to stay.

He looked so arrogantly sure of himself.

But he did want her.

Shontelle pushed her legs into action and a wry smile onto her mouth. "This is not going to be an easy call."

He returned a derisive look. "Did you think it was easy, looking like a fool for ordering a bus out in this volatile climate?"

He had a point.

Both of them fools.

For some reason, that thought boosted Shontelle's morale.

Luis did not move away from the telephone to let her speak privately to Alan. He propped himself against the edge of the writing desk, apparently intent on hearing every word. She had no choice but to stand next to him, which heightened her awareness of the strong force field coming from his dominating maleness.

She turned her back on him once the call was put through. She didn't want him witnessing her awkwardness in explaining her decision to Alan. It was bad enough knowing he was listening without him watching her every nuance of expression.

"Where are you calling from?" Alan demanded, the moment she announced herself.

"I'm still with Luis in his suite. He's got you the bus, Alan."

"What did he want for it?"

"It's no problem. You can tell everyone to be in the hotel foyer, ready to leave at seven o'clock, all going well."

"All going well?" Suspicion sharpened his voice. "What's Luis up to, Shontelle?"

"Alan, he's ordered the bus. He can't guarantee the military won't stop it before it reaches the hotel."

She heard him expel a long breath. She also heard Luis straighten away from the desk, moving to stand behind her.

"Right! That's it then," Alan decided. "I take it you've finished talking and you're ready to leave. Give me five minutes and I'll be at the side door into the Plaza to bring you back here."

Hands slid around her waist, distracting her. Luis was standing close behind her, very close, but not touching except for his hands. Her buttocks clenched in sheer nervousness. Her heart leapt into her throat when he started unbuckling her belt.

"Shontelle?"

She dragged her attention back to Alan, belatedly recalling he'd been offering the protection of his escort back to the hotel.

"Uh...no. No, we haven't finished here," she rushed out.

"Just starting," Luis murmured, darkly purred words that set her pulse pounding. The buckle undone, he unbuttoned the waistband and drew down her zipper.

Shontelle held her breath. Her mind blanked out on all active thought, waiting, poised on the edge of an explosion of sensation should he move his hand inside her clothes and...

"What's going on there?" Alan demanded, his voice getting edgier.

She gulped, forced herself to think. An answer was needed. Fast. "I'm going to spend the night with Luis, Alan," she gabbled, almost yelping as her trousers and underpants were pulled down to her thighs.

"What?" Alan squawked.

Her brother's shock was nothing to Shontelle's at being so summarily stripped. Exposed. Vulnerable to anything Luis might choose to do with her. This was going too far, too fast. The urge to drop the telephone and yank up her clothes was muddled by Alan's yelling at her.

"I'm coming to get you right now."

"No!" She jerked around to face Luis, wanting to stop his actions, too. "No!" she repeated for him.

Wild, reckless and wicked intent blazed at her. He ignored her protest, picked her up, sat her bare bottom on the desk, lifted one of her legs, propped her foot against his thigh and proceeded to undo her bootlace. Shontelle lost track of what she should be doing. Luis was undressing her with ruthless efficiency. His powerfully muscled thigh was bent towards her, reminding her of how magnificently perfect his physique was. But shouldn't she stop this…this taking? If she moved her foot up…

"Shontelle…" Alan bellowed in her ear. "…If this is the bargain he's struck with you…"

"Alan, I've done your business," she cut in, frantic to be free of the argument. "This is mine and Luis' business and it's completely personal. Personal! Got that?'' she snapped.

Her shoe and sock were off. Luis was lifting her other leg.

''Are you off your brain? Luis will chew you up and spit you out again,'' Alan thundered at her.

Once both her feet were free, he would remove her clothes and…there was no time for appeasing Alan. Couldn't be done anyway. Just watching Luis' deft, ruthless movements, she was torn between excitement and fear, yet swamping both feelings was a compelling need to know all she wanted to know.

''Let him do it then!'' she cried recklessly.

''Is he holding the deal with the bus over you?'' Anxious now…

Better for her to sound sane…though her trousers and underpants were being tugged down her calves, over her ankles. She struggled for breath, struggled for some final words.

''Do me a favour, Alan, and pack my bags so they're ready to go. I'll come back when the curfew lifts in the morning.''

Luis stepped in between her legs, his eyes glittering at her, exultant, revelling in seizing the moment, the night, her, everything…making it his.

''Shontelle, for God's sake! Will you…''

Luis seized the telephone. ''Stay out of this, Alan!'' he commanded. ''Your sister and I have much to work through and it's very, very personal.''

There was no argument with Luis. He simply didn't

allow it, cutting the connection by slamming the receiver down. Without so much as a pause, he grabbed the bottom of her T-shirt and hauled it off her. Shontelle's arms were still coming down as his hands whipped around her back to unclip her bra. No fumbling. Snap, and her last piece of clothing dangled loose and was swiftly consigned to the pile on the floor.

She was completely naked, dazed by the speed of its happening and the total lack of any sensuality accompanying the stripping of clothes. She stared at Luis' face and saw a mask of hard pride...dark, dark Angel.

He gave her no time to think, speak, question. He gripped her rib cage, hoisted her off the desk and carrying her virtually at arm's length, he strode through the suite to the bedroom. Impossible for Shontelle to find purchase for her arms or legs. They flapped uselessly. She was so stunned at being held like some distasteful object, any sense of coordination was utterly lost. He tossed her on the bed and she bounced into an abandoned sprawl.

"That's where I want you," he said, his voice harsh with the effort expended. He lifted his shoulders back, holding an imperious, superior stance by the bed. "Where you should be..." he went on with savagely mocking emphasis, "...on the playing ground you use so well."

Scathing words, scathing eyes as they travelled slowly over her. They spurred Shontelle into a clear recognition of his fierce drive to pay her back for having regarded him as no more than a good lay. Even lower than that…a transient lay who'd worn out his novelty value. The Latin lover tag had remained a burr under his skin.

But deeper than that…was *she* still under his skin?

He was holding control, determined on keeping the upper hand, but how much feeling for her lay behind his armoured pride? If she could break through…

She moved sinuously, provocatively, arranging herself more comfortably on the bed, looping her hair over one shoulder so it streamed across her breasts. "You were quite a masterful player yourself, Luis," she said with a reminiscent smile, idly moving a tress of hair back and forth over one of her nipples. "A pity you seem to have lost your touch." She deliberately ran her gaze over his body as she added, "Brute strength is rather a sad step down."

A mirthless laugh scraped from his throat. "In your search for variety, I'm sure a bit of rough has featured somewhere." His eyes glittered challengingly at her as he stripped off his shirt. "I thought it might give you a kick since you grew bored with my kind of lovemaking."

"I was never bored with you," she said truthfully. "I thought what we shared was very special."

A flash of derision. "So you left before it got spoiled."

It was spoiled *before she left*. "The writing was on the wall, Luis," she said quietly, remembering how naive she'd been not to even see it until it was pointed out to her. "I got out before it fell on top of me."

"What writing?" he jeered, bending to remove his shoes and socks, his body language clearly contemptuous of any excuse she might offer.

"Your real life in Buenos Aires," Shontelle said, testing for some flash of guilt from him for what he'd kept hidden.

There was no sharp glance at her. He finished taking off his footwear and when he straightened up, his dark eyes gloated over her with unmistakably sexual intent...such burning intent Shontelle squirmed inside.

"I see," he drawled. "Our romantic idyll on the Amazon was over. I had work to do in Buenos Aires so you did not get my full attention there. Rest assured you have it tonight, Shontelle."

He proceeded to unfasten his trousers.

"Why?" she shot at him, frustrated at being relegated to a sexual object. Though that might be all he'd ever thought of her. The urge to sting him as she was stung slid straight off her tongue. "Your other women not delivering any spice, Luis? You need a taste of me to supplement your diet?"

It stung him all right. His mouth thinned for a moment and there was a flare of anger in his eyes, giving her a glimpse of a banked inner rage that promised no quarter given tonight.

"You think you're special, Shontelle?" He left the lilt of mockery hanging while he finished undressing.

Then stark naked, powerfully naked, aggressively naked, he gave her a smile that curled with vengeful satisfaction. "Well, yes you are," he drawled. "A rich, erotic indulgence...so special I think I should make a banquet of you."

And spit me out in the morning.

Shontelle's stomach was suddenly a hollow pit. All the cards looked black in this game—clubs and spades—no hearts, no diamonds. Even so, she could not give up all hope. Not yet.

"Taking a risk, aren't you?" she slung back at him. "People get addicted to rich, erotic indulgences."

He laughed, and despite its being dark amusement, his face was suddenly transformed into the lighter, more lovable Luis she had known, and Shontelle's heart tripped over itself. Her body wantonly buzzed with anticipation as he prowled onto the bed, looming over her, sweeping her hair away from her breasts, raking it into a fan around her head, his eyes simmering with lustful heat.

"A substance has to be readily available for one to become addicted," he murmured, sipping seductively at her lips. "I'll just take all I can get of it tonight."

Readily available...the phrase echoed in Shontelle's ears as Luis fully engaged her mouth with his in a long, devouring kiss, stirring her hunger for him, a hunger that had been starved for two miserable, empty years. If she'd stayed, maybe he would have defied his heritage to keep her. Foolish pride... walking out on him without confronting him with what she'd been told, what he'd withheld. An open choice would have been better, cleaner.

Maybe with this second chance...

She raked her fingers through his hair, revelling in the feel of it, a huge surge of possessiveness welling through her. This man was *hers,* had to be. There was no other like him. And he had to feel the same about her. It had to be mutual, this passionate craving.

Then suddenly her hands were snatched away, slammed onto the bed and pinned above her head as he levered himself up. "It's *my* night, Shontelle."

She looked into eyes seething with dark turbulence.

"And the playing will be all mine."

He bent and licked her lips as though collecting the lingering evidence of her response to his kiss, then trailed his mouth slowly down to the pulse at the base of her throat, pausing there to apply a heated pressure that kicked her heart into wilder pumping.

Satisfied, he moved lower to the taut mounds of her breasts, tilted up by the lifted position of her arms. He subjected them to exquisite torment—teasing tongue-lashing, voluptuous suction, sharp little nips— orchestrating such a varied rush of sensations, Shontelle had no mind to protest the ruling he'd made. She was awash with rippling excitement, too enthralled with experiencing Luis again to care how or why he was feasting on her...as long as he kept doing it.

Even when he took one imprisoning hand from hers, she didn't try to touch him. He was touching...tantalising, circular caresses over and around her stomach, dipping lower, lower, fingers sliding through the silky mound of hair, stroking, parting, slowly seeking the sensitive moist place that yearned for his touch.

And he was so good at it...softly sensual, as though he was acutely attuned to how much arousal her nerve-ends could take at a time, and he matched the rhythm of his stroking to the tug of his mouth on her breasts, building a momentum that held Shontelle utterly enthralled, focused so intensely on what he was making her feel, there was no room for anything else, no time.

All vestige of control over herself slipped away under the sweet onslaught of sensation. Muscles quivered. The ache of need soared into an urgent scream for the ultimate path to be taken. She was more than ready for him. The inner convulsions were starting and he wasn't there yet. Not the part of him she wanted most, the intimate connection that would take her with him on the final climb to ecstasy.

"Luis...please..." The cry burst from her throat, shamelessly begging.

He reacted fast, so fast she didn't even begin to comprehend what he intended to happen. He flipped her body face down, pushed her legs apart with his knees, curled one arm around her stomach and hauled her backwards, her thighs sliding past his as he rocked back on his ankles, her bottom pressing up against his stomach. She felt him position himself for entry, felt her own flesh quiver in eagerness for the promise of him, a totally out-of-control response. The penetration came hard and fast and incredibly deep as he pushed her down on him, taking an angle he'd never taken before, making her feel the passage of every inch of him rushing further and further inside her. Then he arced her body back with his to make her feel it even more intensely.

He rocked her with him—forward, back, up, down—Shontelle was both shocked and shaken by the sheer animal wildness of this coupling, yet acutely aware of sensations she'd never felt before, bombarded by a physicality she hadn't even imagined, and hopelessly distracted by the sheer strength of him both enveloping and invading her.

Every time he drew back he left one strongly controlling arm around her waist, hand splayed across her stomach, pressing in, keeping her hugged tightly to him as he moved almost to the point of losing intimate contact. Then came the hard thrust forward again, the weird, sweet sense of shattering inside her as he drove himself back to the inner centre, and the hand on her stomach held the fullness of him there as though emphasising a claim of absolute possession, relishing it, filling her with the sense of him filtrating every cell of her body.

He repeated the action—Shontelle had no idea how many times. Occasionally when he paused at the innermost point, he slid his other hand over her breasts, cupping them, squeezing them, fanning her nipples, rubbing her hair over them, or he kissed the nape of her neck, making her shiver from the sheer intensity of his *tasting,* while deep within her a storm of ecstatic waves flowed and ebbed, wild, turbulent, impossible to stop.

She didn't care that he controlled everything. The incredible chaos he wreaked on her was beyond anything she'd ever known. It didn't matter when he carried her forward to kneel underneath him, taking the freedom to drive to his own climax in a fiercely pummelling rhythm.

She was so soft and mushy inside, she welcomed the fast stirring of more sensation, the feeling of violent desire being answered by what he found in her, the surging power of it, coming and coming and coming until he spilled the essence of his strength into her and she exulted in receiving it because there was no taking this back. He was hers as much as she was his.

He scooped her to him spoon-fashion as he dropped onto the bed to rest. There was no parting, no letting go. Her head was tucked under his chin, his arms around her. It didn't occur to her that he had used her as his plaything. Her mind was completely fuzzed with the sense of being one with him.

Luis Angel…dark, light…it didn't matter. He was her man. And as he began stroking her again, arousing both of them to a pitch of needful excitement, she thought only that he wanted more of her.

But…he stopped her from making love to him. He

blocked every initiative she started to take. He controlled the moves. He chose how, when and where he tasted her. And Shontelle gradually lost all sense of being one with him. The realisation came like cold claws creeping around her heart, squeezing out the hope she'd nursed.

This was, indeed, his feast. It wasn't mutual. He hadn't meant it to be mutual. She was the food and he was taking it as he liked, sampling whatever appealed to his fancy, sating himself with every aspect of her sexuality. He didn't care what she was feeling, except in so far as it increased his pleasure, his satisfaction, his sense of being master of the situation, master of *her*.

The answer she'd sought was staring her in the face.

There was no future for her with Luis Angel Martinez.

There was nothing for her here.

Nothing.

With that absolute conviction, Shontelle found the strength to fight free of him, jabbing her elbows into his body, kicking and shoving herself out of contact, scrambling off the bed. She heard him curse in Spanish but she didn't stop. Choosing the bathroom as the safest refuge, she sped into it and locked the door behind her.

She was a tremulous mess, a hopeless tremulous mess. Nevertheless, there was one thing she could and would hold firm—the fierce resolution to deny Luis Angel Martinez any further chance of using her as he willed. Regardless of anything he said or did, she would not return to *his* playing ground.

CHAPTER SIX

SHONTELLE'S fast and frantic evasion of him took Luis completely by surprise—a decidedly unwelcome and frustrating one. It came without any apparent reason—compliance suddenly exploding into rejection. However, the slamming of the bathroom door was so jarring, it propelled him into a swift review of what he'd been doing.

She hadn't cried out, hadn't complained or protested. He couldn't have hurt her physically. Every step of the way her body had responded positively, not once baulking at submitting to his pursuit of every desire he'd harboured when thinking of her. No...he shook off the niggle of concern...he had not hurt her.

So why had she cut and run?

He'd certainly stopped her from weaving her seductive power over him. No way would he allow her to treat him as her toy-boy again. He'd made that clear from the start. Though she probably hadn't believed him immune to her charms. More than likely that had finally bit in—no leeway given for Shontelle to get her hooks into him.

He shrugged, dismissing the annoyance of having his game-plan thwarted. Let her sulk in the bathroom. Let her rage. If she thought she was making some stand against his domination of proceedings, she'd soon find out it was impossible to wring any concession from him. Besides, he'd already done what he'd set out to do, and enjoyed every second of it, too. He wasn't about to beg for more.

He smiled with grim satisfaction as he swung his legs off the bed.

She'd begged.

And he'd given it to her.

Right to the hilt.

He hoped she'd remember that to her dying day. Luis Martinez was not a man to trifle with.

The clock on the bedside table read 11:47. Not even midnight yet. So much for Shontelle's agreeing to give him the night. Another cheat from her. All promise…no staying power. Typical.

He collected the hotel's complimentary bathrobe from the cupboard, put it on, wrapped it around his nakedness to ward off the night chill, and headed for the sitting room and the minibar.

As he passed the bathroom he heard the shower running. Trying to wash him off, he thought sardonically. If there was any justice in the world, she'd be no more successful than he'd been in washing her off the past two years.

The lights were still on in the sitting room. Shontelle's clothes were on the floor. Luis viewed the litter of female garments with a sense of black humour as he moved past them to pour himself a drink. Shontelle wasn't going anywhere without dressing herself first. Sooner or later, she'd come out of the bathroom and collect her clothing. That should be an interesting moment.

He heaped more sugar than usual over the slices of lime for his drink. Vengeance was supposed to be sweet, but it wasn't, Luis decided. It reinforced the bitter taste of knowing what was really wanted was beyond reach. Hopelessly beyond reach.

He took his drink over to the picture window and stared out at the lights of La Paz—quite stunningly beautiful, a fairyland, as Shontelle put it. Just like her, Luis thought savagely, a deceptive facade, offering magic, hiding the power to blow him apart.

Tomorrow morning he'd have to face the streets down there, walk them unprotected in order to get to the bus depot. It would be more dangerous once he was behind the wheel of the bus. A stupid deal...all for the sake of one more experience of Shontelle, with him ending up the winner.

Utterly stupid...when there was nothing to win. She'd made that clear last time. No love in her heart for him. Just sex. Sex he'd once believed was entwined with something much deeper...so deep it was still playing hell with him. What joy now in his vengeful drive to expunge that tormenting residue of feeling? He shook his head in self-derision. A brief savage pleasure...leaving him empty.

He sipped his drink and decided he didn't care if he died on the streets of La Paz tomorrow.

He just didn't care.

CHAPTER SEVEN

SHONTELLE switched off the bathroom light, turned the knob as quietly as she could and slowly eased the door open, listening acutely for any sound coming from the rest of Luis' suite. She held her breath. Her heartbeat seemed to be thumping in her ears but she couldn't hear any other movement going on.

Had Luis given up on her and gone to sleep?

Shontelle vehemently prayed it was so. She'd been in the bathroom over an hour, trying to get herself back together, vigorously cleaning off every possible vestige of Luis' tasting, even washing and blow-drying her long hair in a compulsive need to rid it of any touch of him. She would replait it, as well, once she found the rubber band Luis had taken off.

Clutching the top edge of the bath towel she'd fastened around her nakedness, she plucked up a brave front, slid out into the short passageway that linked the bedroom to the sitting room, and headed swiftly into the latter. The lights had been left on. She had no trouble spotting her clothes.

As distasteful as she found having to dress in the same things Luis had stripped off her, there was no other choice in these circumstances. She wanted a barrier established fast, one Luis couldn't fail to recognise, and she'd fight him tooth and nail if he tried to tear it away.

Pants, trousers, bra, T-shirt…she hastily pulled them on, discarding the towel as she donned more protective gear. Rather than waste a second in fully covering herself, she sat on the floor to put on her socks and shoes. Then feeling more in control and less at risk, she climbed to her feet and turned to assess the supposedly comfortable seating near the window, intending to spend the rest of the night there.

Her swinging gaze didn't get that far.

It halted, very abruptly, at the passageway to the bedroom.

Shock ripped through her, throwing her into chaos again; every nerve-end twitching with agitation, every muscle tensing, every logical thought in her head jamming into confusion. Her eyes stayed glued to the man dominating the space she had desperately wanted to stay empty, the man whose presence could only mean more trauma for her, the man who'd systematically destroyed what had once been good between them.

He hadn't just arrived. Shontelle knew instantly he'd been watching her, standing there watching her as she'd scrambled to get into her clothes…another humiliation added to the humiliations he'd heaped on her. It was some relief that he was no longer naked, though the white bathrobe—so pure and clean-looking—formed an ironic contrast to the dark, satanically beautiful face of Luis Angel Martinez. There was no relief, however, to her fear of what was brooding behind it.

There was a less controlled air about him now, hair mussed, wavy strands dipping over his forehead, curling around his ears. The brilliant dark eyes no longer burned with purpose. They were shadowed by his thick lashes but seemed to emit a sardonic gleam— mocking her, mocking himself, mocking the world and everything in it.

"I take it you don't intend to rejoin me in my bed," he drawled.

"You've had your pound of flesh, Luis," she flashed at him, too worked up to temper her words.

He shrugged. "I've lost my taste for it anyway."

She burned under the contempt implicit in his words, contempt for what she had tried to give him, however misled she had been. "Good!" she snapped. "I've lost any taste for you, too."

He waved carelessly towards the door that led out of the suite. "Do feel free to leave anytime you like."

Her fury at his treatment of her sliced straight into bitter scorn. "Oh, sure! So you can welch on the deal."

"Your staying here any longer is now quite irrelevant," he said in a bored tone. "If you're afraid to brave the streets, by all means call your brother. I assume he's prepared to escort you back to your hotel."

"No!" she retorted vehemently, hating him with the same force as she had once loved him. "I'll stay until curfew lifts in the morning, as I agreed. Having been used by you as no better than a whore, I will not give you any loophole to weazel out of paying what you promised.''

She'd hold him to the damned bus if it killed her. He wasn't going to get away with taking her as he had for nothing.

The cold mask of pride resettled on his face. ''I gave you my word.''

''I'll see how well you keep it in the morning.'' Her eyes blistered any worth in his *given word*. ''Since you're finding no more pleasure in my company than I am in yours, I suggest you go back to your bed and I'll settle myself here.''

''Thank you,'' he mocked. ''Do sleep well with your choice of discomfort.''

He strolled off to the bedroom, leaving Shontelle feeling wretchedly deflated. Clearly he now saw her as a waste of his time, not even worth arguing with. For several moments she teetered on the edge of going after him, flaying him with her own contempt for his lies and double-dealing, but what was the point?

He didn't care.

That was the bottom line.

He simply didn't care.

Even if she stayed until the curfew was lifted, it was no guarantee he would follow through on his word, but at least she would have fulfilled her part. If she took nothing else away from this night, she would take her own integrity intact.

Nursing this shred of pride, Shontelle walked over to the window and searched the floor for the rubber band Luis had taken from her plait. Somehow it was important to restore her appearance to what it had been before she'd come here. She looked everywhere without success and finally concluded Luis had pocketed it. Which defeated her.

Defeat all round, she thought despondently, moving back to the writing desk. She picked up the telephone and made a request for a 5:45 wake-up call. It would mean Luis being woken, too, which she'd have to weather, since it served the purpose of letting him know she had stayed the full night.

Reassured of not oversleeping the mark, she proceeded to switch off the lights. The window provided a dim glow, enough to see her way by. She pulled two armchairs together, curled up on one and rested her legs on the other. Hoping fatigue would be her friend tonight, she closed her eyes and prayed for sleep.

But tears welled out of the devastation in her heart. Tears oozed through her lashes and trickled down her cheeks. Silent tears. Lonely tears. Tears that needed to be wept now because tomorrow she had to be strong again. It was a long time before sleep wiped them away and gave her some brief peace.

"Shontelle…"

The sharp call of her name brought her awake. Her

eyelids felt glued together but she dragged them open and looked up blearily.

Luis was standing by her chair, frowning at her.

Her brain was sluggish. Why was he waking her? Then her nose picked up the tangy scent of male cologne and she suddenly realised he was freshly showered, shaved, and fully dressed! Which had to mean she had somehow overslept and he was annoyed at finding she was still here.

She pushed the leg-rest armchair away and scrambled to her feet, crying out, "What time is it?" panicking at the thought of Alan waiting for her, worrying...

"Time enough," Luis answered brusquely. "It's not quite five-thirty. I've ordered breakfast. I thought you might like to refresh yourself before it arrives."

"Breakfast...for me?" she repeated dazedly.

"For both of us."

A knock on the door heralded its arrival and he turned away, moving quickly to let the waiter in. Shontelle stared at his back, flummoxed by this turn of events. He wore a navy shirt, navy trousers, navy Reeboks. What was he ready for this early in the morning?

The question nagged at her as she headed for the bathroom, needing to use its facilities to get herself ready for the day ahead. When she looked at her face in the mirror, she fiercely wished Luis had kept to himself in his bedroom. The whites of her eyes were red-rimmed and the skin around them was obviously puffy. Hating the thought he might have noticed this evidence of prolonged weeping, she did all she could to diminish it, splashing the area copiously with cold water.

Her hair was a flyaway mess but that didn't matter. She finger-combed it into reasonable tidiness. Having straightened up her crumpled clothes and composed herself to face Luis this one last time, she hurried out of the bathroom, anxious to know what his plans were.

Breakfast was laid out on the table in the sitting room. Luis was already seated and helping himself to the food he'd ordered. He glanced sharply at her face as she approached, his dark eyes uncomfortably penetrating.

"I've poured your coffee," he said matter-of-factly.

"Thank you." The reply was automatic, though she hated the reminder of how intimately acquainted they had once been and nothing would induce her to accept anything he offered at this point.

He gestured to the chair opposite his when she made no move to sit at the table. "Don't stand on ceremony, Shontelle. You might as well eat what's here."

"I'm not hungry." Which was true. "I put a wake-up call in for 5:45. I didn't expect you to be up so early."

"I'll be leaving the hotel as soon as curfew lifts," he answered offhandedly.

Alarm jangled through Shontelle's mind. Was Luis skipping out so he couldn't be called to account on the bus? "To go where?" she asked. "La Paz is shut down."

He shrugged. "Personal business."

She watched him crunch into a croissant and her stomach churned over his indifference to Alan's and her urgent concerns. "What if the bus doesn't come at seven o'clock? Where will you be?" she demanded testily.

He gave her a devil-may-care look. "Who knows?"

"That's not good enough, Luis," she shot at him, incensed by his blasé attitude.

His mouth tilted into an ironic curl. "It's as good as it gets, Shontelle. Take it or leave it."

No…she couldn't. She just couldn't. The pain and frustration she'd been holding in reached overload and streamed out over everything else, sweeping pride aside, demolishing any reasonable common sense, demanding an outlet. Her mouth opened and her voice shook with the force of feeling he'd brought her to.

"I never used you as you used me last night. I don't know why you think you have the right to play with me as it suits you, but I will not walk away from your lies and evasions this time."

That jolted his appetite. He stopped eating and glared at her.

Shontelle's throat felt scraped raw but the compulsion to throw down the gauntlet kept the words coming. "I'll follow you when you leave this hotel. I'll haunt you until the bus you promised turns up on The Europa doorstep. I'll…"

"What lies?" he demanded tersely.

"Don't you dare pretend you haven't lied!" His question was like a fire bomb going off in her brain. Old wounds ruptured and demanded to be aired. "Very convenient for you, wasn't it, to forget Claudia Gallardo while you were with me."

"I am not married to her," he bit out.

"*Betrothed* was the word your mother used. Your mother, whom you so carefully screened me from all the time I lived with you in Buenos Aires. Your mother, who explained your *real* life to me."

"When was this?" he snapped.

"The day before I left you. After you excluded me once again from your family life, Luis, evading the invitation your mother extended."

He erupted from his chair, dark menace emanating from him so strongly, Shontelle almost shrank from him. But she would not be intimidated. It was she who had the high moral ground, he who had to answer for his actions.

"You kept this from me," he accused.

"You kept it from me," she retaliated.

"You let my meddling, manipulative mother lay it waste. Without consulting me. You let Elvira have her way without so much as raising a question."

His seething fury rattled Shontelle.

"No heart!" he roared at her. "No faith! No trust! And for *you* I risk my life!"

She stared at him, mesmerised by the powerful surge of energy pouring from him, understanding nothing of what was causing it.

"Your life?" she echoed dazedly.

His chin jerked up. Pride emerged in a fierce blaze. Not cold pride. Not arrogant pride. Shontelle sensed this was his entire manhood on the line.

"Go back to your hotel," he commanded in a tone that brooked no opposition. "Wait with your brother. If I do not arrive with your bus, it will not be for the want of trying."

"You? You'll be driving the bus?"

He'd already turned his back on her, striding towards the door. Her disbelief was unanswered. He did not so much as pause.

"Luis!" she cried, suddenly torn by the feeling she would never see him again and there was too much left unanswered. Far too much.

He opened the door, stepped out, and was gone, the door closed firmly between them.

Shontelle struggled to get her shell-shocked wits together.

Nothing made sense to her anymore.

She didn't know what to believe.

If Luis turned up with the bus...what then?

Go back to your hotel. Wait with your brother.

That command made sense.

Besides, there was nothing else to do here.

Luis was gone.

CHAPTER EIGHT

ALAN was in the foyer of The Europa, obviously watching out for her while keeping an eye on the progress of checkouts at the desk. He was at Shontelle's side the moment she cleared the front door.

"Are you okay?" he asked, sharply scanning her face.

"I'm fine." She kept walking, making a beeline for the elevators, determined on not discussing anything personal with her brother. "Are my bags still in our suite?"

"Yes. I thought you'd want to change clothes."

"I do. I'll need the door key."

He handed it to her.

"Thanks. Won't be long."

"Shontelle..."

"Luis has gone to get the bus," she cut in, blocking what might have been an unwelcome inquiry.

"Luis has?" Stunned surprise.

"He said if it's not here by seven, it won't be for want of trying. Where is everyone?"

Alan was still shaking his head over Luis' personal involvement. "Those not paying their accounts at the desk are having breakfast in the dining room," he answered distractedly. "You'd better grab some, too, Shontelle. Long day ahead."

She pressed the up button on the elevator. Luck was on her side. The doors opened immediately. "Did you get the hotel to pack some food for us?" she tossed at Alan as she stepped into the compartment.

"Yes. Everything's organised. Shontelle…"

"Be down soon," she promised, activating the control panel.

The doors closed, shutting out Alan's frowning face.

Shontelle breathed a sigh of relief. She'd told him everything pertinent to the tour group situation. As for the rest…Luis might have some justification for thinking badly of her…if his mother had lied…and if Claudia Gallardo had conspired with Elvira Rosa Martinez to give a false impression. Where the truth actually lay was impossible for Shontelle to sort out.

Two facts stood out very starkly from all the grey areas. If she had told Luis of his mother's intervention two years ago, there would be no confusion about his feelings now. The blame for that was fairly and squarely on her shoulders. Nevertheless, even granting he had reason to think of her in the worst possible light, Luis should not have treated her as he had last night. That was unforgivable.

So there was no point in agonising over this encounter with him. Any future they might have had together was well and truly dead. It was time to lay the whole affair between them to rest. It was doubtful she'd ever forget her regrets, but she could accept he was gone from her life.

Though if he brought the bus himself…Shontelle felt her nerves tighten. He would only be here for a few minutes, she told herself, just long enough to hand the bus over to Alan. He'd walk away then. No trauma. It would only be a few minutes at most. *If* he came with the bus.

The elevator stopped and opened to her floor as she was frowning over this scenario. It wasn't until she was in her suite and digging into her bag that she attached Luis' claim about risking his life to the procuring of the bus. Yet was it what he'd meant? Was it so dangerous in the streets? Surely Alan wouldn't have decided on this course if the risk was truly grave.

She knew her brother expected to deal with some trouble on the way out of La Paz, but he was confident of steering them through it. Surely with the clout of the Martinez name, Luis could deal with any problem he ran into.

Risking his life for her… It made no sense. Why would a man who felt the utmost contempt for her, put his life on the line to get the bus she'd requested? He could probably snap his fingers and people would fall in to do his bidding. It made no sense at all.

Shontelle found the fresh clothes she wanted and changed into them, glad to feel clean from the inside out. Not that she looked any different, except for wearing a dark green shirt with the Amigos Tours logo, instead of red. She gave her hair a quick brush, plaited it, and felt considerably better, more equipped to handle whatever came.

Having checked the suite in case anything had been left lying around, she took her bags down to the foyer and left them in Alan's care. "Breakfast," she said and zipped off to the dining room. Maybe by tonight she might feel up to fielding sensitive questions, but she felt too raw to start answering them now.

Most of the tour group was moving out of the dining room as she entered it. Time was getting short. She exchanged quick greetings and hurried to the buffet bar, not that she had suddenly found an appetite but sheer practicality dictated she replenish her energy.

Having picked up a fruit juice, a couple of bread rolls, some slices of cold meat and cheese, she headed for an empty table, not wanting to be drawn into conversation with anyone. The ploy succeeded. She was left to eat her breakfast in peace.

At ten minutes to seven she returned to the foyer to help Alan settle the tour group, answering concerns as best she could and preparing them for the long journey ahead. It was ten hours by road from La Paz to Santa Cruz…if nothing went wrong. Once there, it would be possible to catch a flight to Buenos Aires, then home to Australia.

The mood of the group was jumpy. Those suffering from altitude sickness didn't care what other discomforts they might have to suffer, so long as they were getting away from here. Some were fearful of what lay in wait beyond the hotel.

Australians simply weren't accustomed to a military presence. Apart from a formal parade of war veterans on Anzac Day, soldiers did not feature in their lives, and a tank was only seen in a military museum. There were mutterings of never leaving home again. They had a new appreciation of Australia being called "the lucky country."

The minutes ticked by. A nervous bustle started with people rechecking their luggage, making sure they had everything to hand. Having instructed everyone to stay inside, Alan left them to go out to the street where he could watch for the bus which would have to back in to the cul-de-sac.

Shontelle fixed a patient smile on her face, projecting calm confidence to the group. It took quite a lot of concentration. Her stomach was in knots. As more minutes passed, worries mounted in her mind, becoming impossible to set aside. If the bus didn't come, would that mean something bad had happened to Luis?

Despite the deep hurt he had inflicted on her last night, she did not want him physically injured. She certainly didn't want him dead. Though if he was risking his life by getting the bus for them, it wasn't her fault, was it? It was *his* choice. *He'd* made the deal.

Her mind skipped to what Luis had once told her about his older brother, Eduardo. During the political troubles in Argentina, the military police had simply scooped him up off the street one night, supposedly rounding up young dissidents, and Eduardo was never heard of again, becoming one of the disappeared whose deaths were never recorded.

In Buenos Aires, she had seen for herself the Thursday march of the women now called The Mothers of May, protesting the disappearance of their children. It didn't matter how many years had gone by. They turned up each week to parade their banners with photos in front of Government House because they still had no answers. Rumour had it that many of the lost ones had been taken off by helicopter and dropped in the sea.

Shontelle shivered. Could that happen here in Bolivia? No, surely not. This was a land-locked country, no coastal territory at all. Even if Luis was imprisoned for some reason, Elvira Rosa Martinez had the power to have him freed. Eduardo had probably not been identified before he was killed.

Another dreadful thought hit. What if Luis didn't have time to identify himself? What if some trigger-happy soldier...

Alan burst into the foyer. "It's here!"

Shontelle's knees almost buckled in relief.

"Collect your belongings and come outside now," Alan commanded. "Remember what I said—women to board the bus immediately, men stand ready to load the suitcases in the luggage department. The sooner we get going, the better."

Action seemed to buoy everyone's spirits. There was a buzz of excitement as thirty people headed for the door, carrying their bags. Shontelle lingered behind the rest, ostensibly to check that nothing was left in the foyer. She could see the bus being backed into position in front of the hotel and it *was* Luis in the driver's seat.

Her heart lifted. He was safe. He could return to the Plaza Hotel from here and be absolutely safe. The bus came to a halt, the luggage compartment hatches were unlocked, the door was opened, and Luis rose from the driver's seat. He'd go now, Shontelle thought. This was the last she'd ever see of him.

Strange how torn she felt. Absurd after last night. It shouldn't matter to her. Yet her legs moved faster, wanting to get outside, closer to him before he left. She virtually herded the stragglers of the group past the front door.

Luis was rounding the front of the bus. He saw her at the back of the crowd and for one sizzling moment, their eyes locked. Somehow it was as though everything else ceased to exist and there was only the two of them, tied by a bond that went beyond any other reality. The tug on her heart was so strong, her chest felt ready to burst. Then he tore his gaze away and addressed Alan.

Shontelle was so shaken she could barely put two thoughts together. What did that look from Luis mean? He'd shut the door on her before. There was nothing left of what they'd once shared. Couldn't be.

She tried to collect her scattered wits. Her job was to usher the women onto the bus while Alan supervised the loading of the luggage. Somehow that task fell by the wayside. While she was vaguely aware of the women heading into the bus by themselves, she couldn't drag her attention away from Luis and Alan who were clearly having a tense exchange of words. She walked straight over to them and broke into their conversation.

"Thank you for bringing the bus, Luis," she said with genuine sincerity.

Alan shot her a searing look. "He says he's staying with it."

"Sorry..." She showed her confusion to both of them. "What do you mean?"

"He's not handing it over. He insists on driving it," Alan tersely explained.

"To Santa Cruz?" She looked at Luis in bewilderment.

"To hell and back if necessary," he answered with grim purpose.

"But why?" she cried.

His mouth curled. His dark eyes flashed a derisive gleam at her. "Because you'll be on it, Shontelle. And I'm not finished with you."

She should have said, yes, he was. Or at least said *she* was finished with him. But the words stuck in her throat and she just stared at him, feeling the power of his will swirling around her, tying her to him again. It was crazy. Nothing good could come of this.

They'd scarred each other too badly. Yet the feeling coming from him was different now...not contempt, not dismissal or rejection and certainly not indifference.

"Luis..." Alan started in a tone of protest.

"It's my bus," Luis cut in ruthlessly. "Get your people off it if you won't accept my driving it."

The luggage compartments were being slammed shut. The women were already in their chosen seats and the men were proceeding to join them.

"Goddammit, man! Let my sister go!"

Luis' gaze hadn't shifted from Shontelle's. The black resolution in his eyes was not going to be moved by anything. It was either stay here in La Paz where he would be, as well, or take this journey to Santa Cruz with him. Whichever choice was made, Shontelle knew intuitively Luis did not intend to let her escape him until he *was* finished with her. Whatever that meant.

It certainly wouldn't mean more sex, Shontelle thought with fierce determination. Besides which, on a busload of people she wouldn't be alone with him. Better to let him get his "unfinished" business with her over with in the relative safety of numbers, she decided.

"Better to go with Luis than not go at all, Alan. Everyone's on the bus," she said pointedly. "I'll go and do the head count."

"You can't drive a bus as well as I can, Luis," Alan argued as she moved around them.

"From what I've seen on the streets, you'll have your hands full keeping your people calm," came the grim retort. "This is no picnic trip. You can take over the wheel once we're clear of La Paz."

"So you can have time with Shontelle and tear her into more little pieces."

Already on her way around the front of the bus, Shontelle paused, wishing Alan would keep his mouth shut about her.

"I tell you, it's not right, Luis," he went on. "She hasn't picked herself up from her last affair with you."

"Neither have I, my friend," came the cold reply. "Neither have I."

Shontelle frowned. Was that true?

"What's the point, man? You're never going to marry her. I told her so from the start, but she wouldn't listen."

"You, too, Alan?" His voice was ice. "Then some of those pieces can be laid at your door."

"What the hell does that mean?"

"It means stay out of my business on this journey. You don't know a damned thing about what I feel or what I'll do."

Neither did she, Shontelle thought as she moved on to board the bus. It was difficult to focus her attention on completing an accurate head count but everyone had responded to the list of names by the time Alan and Luis had joined them.

Luis took the driver's seat. Alan occupied the tour

guide seat adjacent to it, activating the microphone so the whole group could hear him clearly as he introduced Luis and outlined the planned trip for them. Shontelle settled on the seat left vacant for her, directly behind the driver.

The bus started moving.

She didn't listen to Alan.

The physical trip they were about to take meant nothing to her. It was the journey with Luis that preyed on her mind. What did he want of her now? Where could it lead? How would it end?

CHAPTER NINE

THE streets of La Paz were unnaturally quiet. Traffic was minimal and very few pedestrians were civilians. The eerie sense of moving through a war zone was strong and oppressive. There was no buzz of conversation in the bus. If the passengers spoke at all, it was in whispers.

Shontelle noted that Luis avoided driving along the main thoroughfares, detouring around them through a series of side streets. It was obvious he was highly aware of the danger of being stopped, accelerating past groups of soldiers before they had time to react to a busload of people going by.

Alan instructed the tour group to remain seated naturally, not to duck down or to act in any way which might appear suspicious. Tourists were not targets in the current political conflict. Shontelle hoped her brother was right in his reading of the situation.

They were travelling along what appeared to be a deserted stretch of road, when a tank emerged from a cross-street, directly in their path. Luis had to brake or collide with it. The bus came to a screeching halt and ominously, the tank halted, as well. Slowly, terrifyingly, its turret swung towards them. So did the long barrel of its gun.

Agitation broke out amongst the tour group, screams from the women, shocked cursing from the men.

"Be quiet and sit still!" Alan barked into the microphone.

They settled down but the atmosphere in the bus was thick with fear. The gun did not move. Neither did the tank. Shontelle suddenly realised the barrel was trained directly on Luis. Her mind was jolted into two quick leaps—the driver—who had the colouring of a local man.

She was out of her seat instantly, throwing her arms around Luis' neck, and lowering her head next to his so her fair hair could be seen. She was so clearly not a native South American, it seemed logical that whoever was sighting them from the tank would have second thoughts about attacking them.

"Shontelle…" Alan started to protest.

"Luis is dark, Alan. Could be taken for a Bolivian. Show yourself. Tell them we're tourists and we have sick people on board."

"Right! Open the door, Luis."

Alan waved at the tank to draw attention to himself as he rose from his seat. Luis activated the door. It hissed open.

"Stay near the bus, Alan," Luis sharply advised. "Don't look threatening."

The next few minutes were extremely tense. Alan stood just outside the door, waving and explaining in a quick stream of Spanish. No verbal reply came from the occupants of the tank. Alan kept talking, emphasising Australia and foreign relations.

The gun started to move, swinging back to the direction the tank had originally been taking. Then the tank started to move, proceeding on its route, unblocking their way forward. The relief in the bus was palpable. Alan jumped back on board. Some of the group cheered him, grateful that the crisis was past. Shontelle belatedly realised she was still hanging on to Luis and started to withdraw her arms.

He caught her right hand, his strong fingers wrapping around hers, squeezing, transmitting a quick jolt of electric heat. It lasted only a moment or two before release came. Other actions had to be carried out, closing the door, getting the bus moving again. There was no glance, no word, just that quick squeeze, then total concentration on the job of driving them out of La Paz.

Alan clapped her on the shoulder. "Good thinking," he said with a wide grin, the zest of having won this round beaming from his face.

She nodded and returned to her seat.

Alan gave a morale-boosting speech over the microphone but Shontelle didn't listen to it. She stared down at the hand Luis had gripped, using her other hand to stroke away the feeling of his touch. Her mind fretted over how strongly he could still affect her. It was as though somehow he was imprinted on her—mind, body and soul—and it was an indelible imprint she couldn't wipe out no matter how hard she tried.

He touched her and instantly triggered a chemical reaction through her entire body. How could he do that after last night? And the look he had given her earlier—just one look—and she was drawn to him. Fatal attraction, she thought bitterly.

But she would not let him take her again. If he wanted something more from her it had to be on a very different basis. Respect, for a start. And the truth had to be told from both sides…no more prideful holding back. She recalled Luis' fierce words to Alan…

You don't know a damned thing about what I feel or what I'll do.

One thing he wouldn't do, Shontelle vowed to herself, was seduce her into accepting him as her lover again. Her jaw firmed in resolution. He would not shake her on that.

Then she silently laughed at herself. Unfinished business didn't have to mean sex. It more likely meant getting his facts straight. Then he could move on, satisfied he knew where all the pieces fitted. And maybe the same knowledge would help her put this in the past, as well.

The bus was almost at the top of the long hill that led to the airport, though it was not their destination. They had to go past it to get out of La Paz and on their way to Santa Cruz. However, the area around the airport was sure to be heavily guarded. Alan had anticipated there might be trouble there, if anywhere.

He'd already underestimated possible problems, Shontelle thought, tensing in readiness for more as Luis drove past groups of soldiers who eyed the bus suspiciously. Military jeeps were parked alongside the road but none of them gave chase. It seemed like a miracle when they actually cleared the whole stretch past the airport without being stopped.

The tour group started to relax as the bus travelled on through the settlements on the outskirts of the city. People made jokes to lighten the atmosphere and an air of triumphant jollity started to develop. Alan told a couple of stories about tight spots he'd been in during other tours, making the escapes sound amusing. It really seemed the danger was past—behind them. The bus moved into open country, safely on their journey.

No one was thinking about the farmers' revolt.

At least, Shontelle wasn't. Her gaze was trained on the man sitting in front of her. She saw what Luis saw just as he spoke.

''Alan...ahead of us!''

Large groups of men were milling around what appeared to be a huge speed bump spread across the road.

''They've dug a trench,'' Luis said, no doubt at all about what the hump meant.

Shontelle's heart sank. A speed bump was passable, but a trench?

"Put your foot down, Luis," Alan advised quickly. "We'll have to jump it."

"No telling how wide it is," came the terse warning.

"If you don't want to risk your bus…"

"Prepare your people." It was a grim command.

"Men, up on your feet and put all the overhead hand luggage under seats or on the floor," Alan yelled, clapping his hands to encourage fast action. "The farmers have dug a trench across the road. Our driver is speeding up and we're going to be airborne to cross it. Move, move…we don't want any injuries from flying bags."

The acceleration in speed made the task more difficult but it was accomplished in a wildly lurching fashion. The hump hiding the trench was coming up very fast and looking bigger by the second. Which could mean the gap in the road behind it was too wide. Shontelle started praying it wasn't. This gamble could end in a very nasty accident.

"Sit, sit!" Alan yelled. "Brace yourselves in your seats for impact when we land on the other side…"

If, Shontelle thought darkly.

"…Anyone with a bad back, try to cushion yourself against the thump."

Silence, except for the rustle of adjustments and much heavy breathing. They were hurtling towards the crisis point. Shontelle wondered what Luis was thinking. Why was he risking so much? What was at stake for him?

He stood up behind the wheel, bracing himself against his seat. Could he see beyond the hump? Impossible to stop now anyway. Was he regretting the risk he'd accepted? He'd be the first hit if the trench was too wide. Luis and Alan...*then me,* Shontelle realised. It could all end here and she'd never know...

The thought stopped there.

The bus hit the heaped pile of rubble dug from the trench and lifted, slightly skewing in the air from an uneven take-off. Shontelle looked frantically out the side window. The gap... Oh, God! Oh, God! It was too big...but the bus was soaring, reaching over the threatening maw of emptiness below them. They weren't going to crash into it. As the long vehicle started dipping forward on the other side, it shot through Shontelle's mind that the back wheels weren't going to make it across.

The front of the bus landed at an angle, half facing towards an open field. The left rear end wheel caught the trench but the right side made it onto the road. With a heart-stopping, wrenching manoeuvre, Luis somehow got enough traction to drag the trapped wheel out. The bus careered down the road in a wild zigzag as he fought for control of it, every muscle stretched to the task.

Shontelle was very, very glad there weren't any roadside trees or other obstacles, and no bends to ne-gotiate—just a straight road and unfenced fields on either side. Hand luggage was sliding all over the floor. There were grunts and groans as the passengers were knocked around, but no one screamed. Shontelle felt they were all fiercely willing Luis to pull them through this nightmare.

How long it took she had no idea, but he finally did it, slowing the bus down, gradually easing it to a very ragged halt. The cessation of movement brought a shock of disbelief. It was hard to take in that it was actually over and they'd made it intact.

"Back left wheel's locked up, Alan," Luis muttered.

He jumped up from his seat. "I'll go and have a look."

The door whooshed open as Luis said, "I'll come with you."

Alan flashed him a grin. "Great driving, man!"

"Born to survive," Luis retorted wryly.

"Shontelle, take over in here," Alan instructed.

"Will do." She rose shakily to her feet.

Luis paused, dark eyes sharply scanning hers. He said nothing to her, just gave a curt nod before following Alan outside. *She* should have said something, Shontelle thought crossly. At least thanked him. But the moment was gone and she had no idea what the look and nod from him had meant. Satisfaction that she was more or less fighting fit?

This was no time to concern herself about it. Moving quickly she picked up the microphone and turned to address the tour group.

"Is everyone okay?"

It stirred them all into taking stock of themselves. They reported probably a few bruises but no cuts or other injuries.

"How much more of this can we expect?" the chief trouble-maker in the group demanded.

"I don't know," Shontelle answered truthfully.

"Damned madness! Alan shouldn't have led us…"

"Now, hold it a minute, Ron," another cut in. "Alan gave us fair warning there could be trouble. You were the one who insisted he get us out of La Paz or you'd badmouth his tours when you got home, remember?"

"Yeah!" another chimed in. "Better keep your mouth shut, Ron. You not only asked for this, you roped us all into supporting you. We're here now with no broken bones so far. We've got no complaint. Right?"

"Besides, what an adventure to tell our grandchildren!" one of the women said, awed at having lived through the experience.

"Wish I could have videoed it all," another remarked with rueful humour.

Rebellion over, Shontelle thought with considerable relief. "Well, if you feel up to it," she began cautiously, "it would be a good idea to reorganise the loose hand luggage on the floor while Alan and Luis are fixing the wheel."

"Can they fix it?" someone asked.

"Alan's a highly skilled mechanic. He'll get us going again," Shontelle answered confidently.

The assurance encouraged people to start hunting for their belongings and securing them in a more orderly fashion than they'd had time to do so beforehand. The sound of hammering underneath the back of the bus started and continued while the interior tidy-up was in progress.

Shontelle wondered if Luis and Alan were settling some of their differences as they worked together. She hoped some of the hostility would be eased. Fighting Luis was difficult enough without having to fight her brother, as well.

One of the women suggested opening the thermoses provided by the hotel and having cups of coffee.

Shontelle vetoed the idea. They weren't so far away from the aggressive gathering of farmers to be complacent about time. They had to be off again, the moment Luis and Alan finished the repairs. Apart from which, they were barely an hour's journey out of La Paz. They had nine more hours on the road before they reached Santa Cruz.

No one protested.

At last the hammering stopped. Everyone perked up as Alan and Luis boarded the bus again...everyone except Shontelle. She immediately tensed, glancing warily at the two men's faces. Alan was obviously in high good humour. Her brother seemed to thrive on danger. Luis' expression was more guarded but she sensed a radiation of energy that put her nerves even more on edge.

Alan took the microphone from her. "Any problems?" he asked quietly.

She shook her head and he waved her back to her seat. Luis moved to the instrument panel and activated the closing of the door.

"Okay, we're about to roll again," Alan announced. "We'll travel for two more hours before stopping for..." he smiled "...a refreshment opportunity. If anyone develops an urgent problem before then, let me know. I'll be taking over the driving now. Luis' muscles need a bit of relaxation..."

Shontelle frowned. Had Luis pulled something? He hadn't shown any strain in his movements.

"How about giving him a clap for a fantastic job of getting us this far in one piece?" Alan suggested, starting off the applause.

Everyone joined in enthusiastically. Luis turned around and acknowledged them with a casual salute and a dry little smile. Alan set aside the microphone and took the driver's seat. The two men had a brief, private discussion. Then Alan gunned the motor and the bus started moving, in a straight line, much to Shontelle's relief. The back wheel problem had obviously been fixed.

She expected Luis to take Alan's seat, but he didn't. Without so much as a by-your-leave, he stepped back and settled himself onto the twin passenger seat beside her.

Every nerve in Shontelle's body jangled. Her hands clenched. She almost cringed away from him in fear of being touched. Which was ridiculous, she fiercely told herself. What could Luis do to her here in front of a busload of people? She was safe from any unwelcome touching. Alan was directly within call, too. Not that she wanted to involve him. She could cope with Luis by herself. Of course she could.

"Are you hurt?" she asked brusquely, not quite able to bring herself to look directly at him.

"No," he answered.

"Then why aren't you driving?"

"Because I want time with you."

Her heart squeezed tight. "Did Alan agree to this?"

"Yes."

Two hours, she thought, staring at the back of her brother's head. Was he listening? No, concentrating on the road, she decided. The drone of the engine was probably filling his ears, as well. The cushioned backrests of their seats closed them off from the passengers behind them. This was probably as good a place as any for a private talk.

Shontelle steeled herself to look at the man who had given her so much torment. Slowly she turned her head, met his waiting gaze, and at point-blank range, asked, "Why?"

The dark eyes had a black intensity of purpose that sent shivers down her spine. "Tell me about your meeting with my mother."

The words "my mother" were edged with acid.

Shontelle wrenched her gaze away, deeply disturbed by the force of energy he emitted. ''Why dig around in the past?'' she cried. ''What point is there now?''

''As far as I'm concerned, the past is the present. And I shall deal with it,'' he stated with ruthless intent.

Shontelle shook her head, not wanting to relive the pain of Elvira Martinez's disclosures. ''You deceived me two years ago, Luis,'' she accused bitterly.

''No. I didn't.''

The rebuttal was instant and powerfully stark.

Shontelle closed her eyes. She couldn't bear it if he was telling the truth. She just couldn't bear it.

''Start talking, Shontelle,'' he commanded. ''Tell me every detail of your experience with my mother.''

Again the acid emphasis on ''my mother'' as though he was barely suppressing a violent flow of bitterness.

The truth, she thought. However much it hurt, whatever it might mean to her, she had to know it, too. So she cast her mind back to that fatal day…the day Elvira Rosa Martinez broke her heart and changed the course of her life…and started to recall it in all its painful detail.

CHAPTER TEN

Two years had not faded the memory of her meeting with Elvira Rosa Martinez. Shontelle had tried to seal it into a hidden compartment in her mind, but once the locked doors were opened up, it flooded out so vividly, it could have been yesterday…visually, emotionally, physically.

"You said it was the day before you left me," Luis prompted.

"Yes. But it didn't really start then," Shontelle answered slowly, remembering back to the weeks they'd spent together, living in Luis' apartment which was wonderfully well situated in the Barrio Recoleta. This was considered the most chic neighbourhood in Buenos Aires and Shontelle had been more than happy to call it home. Except Luis kept his life there strictly separate from his *family* home which was only a short distance away from the apartment.

"My mother had contacted you beforehand?" he asked sharply.

"No. But you avoided introducing me to her. You also avoided introducing me to any of your friends or social acquaintances in Buenos Aires." She turned to search his eyes. "Why was that, Luis?"

He held her gaze unflinchingly. "I didn't want to share you."

"Did you ever plan to?"

He shrugged. "It would have become inevitable if you'd stayed."

"Were you ashamed of me?"

He frowned. "Whatever for?"

"Not measuring up in some way."

His eyes flashed black venom. "Are these my mother's words?"

"If you had not decided to keep me to yourself, her words wouldn't have had any power, Luis."

She turned her head away and stared blindly out the side window, remembering how she'd filled in all those days he'd spent at the Martinez company offices, working long hours. She'd filled them alone. No companions. Just waiting out the time until Luis came back to her.

Admittedly it had not been difficult. There was so much to do and enjoy; roaming around the famous and fascinating Recoleta cemetery where Eva Peron had finally been laid to rest, wandering around the plazas, watching the mime artists, listening to mini-concerts by street buskers, looking through galleries. Buenos Aires was called the Paris of the Americas for good reason. Even the architecture was fascinating.

She hadn't been bored.

Not at all.

But she had been alone. In a strange country. In a

strange culture. Even so, she hadn't felt really *foreign* until the day with Luis' mother. And Claudia Gallardo.

"You know…one of the hardest things to bear that day was her sympathy," Shontelle dryly remarked. "How sorry she was that I'd been so blind about what your relationship with me meant. How very wrong it was for her son to have deceived me about my place in his life."

"What place was that…according to my mother?"

"Oh, good for satisfying the desires men have. Not good enough to marry, of course," she answered flippantly. "Women like me get *used* so the fine men of Argentina can behave themselves with the properly brought up virgins they marry."

"You believed I had so little honour I would use a woman—any woman—*let alone the sister of a friend,* for such a purpose?" he bit out scathingly.

She swung fiercely condemning eyes on him. "You used me as a whore last night. Are you going to deny that?"

"You had a choice," he retaliated, hard black eyes denying any shame in his actions. "You chose the role. The same role you put me in two years ago. Someone to be used for sexual satisfaction."

"You were never that to me," she cried. "I only said so because…"

"Because my mother's words meant more to you than all we'd been to each other?" he interpreted savagely.

"Not just *words*, Luis," she retorted just as savagely. "I met your bride-to-be, Claudia Gallardo."

"Ah…" His eyes glittered. "Did Claudia actually say she was my fiancée?"

"Betrothed was the word used."

"By Claudia?"

Shontelle frowned. She couldn't recall Claudia actually saying she was betrothed to Luis, yet everything she said and did had certainly implied it. "*When I am married to Luis*…it was a kind of refrain she tossed at me over lunch, prefacing her plans for the future with you," she related, determined on being accurate in her recollections. "It was your mother who used *betrothed*. Before Claudia arrived."

"Where was this lunch?"

"At your family home in the Avenue Alvear."

His jaw visibly tightened. His lips compressed into a thin line. She felt an emanation of wild, destructive violence before he brought it under control.

"How did this come about?" he demanded, his voice thick with the unresolved conflicts inside him.

"Your mother came to the apartment that morning," she replied quickly. "It was about nine-thirty. She introduced herself and invited me…" A wave of nausea shot bile up Shontelle's throat. She swallowed hard and turned her head away from the sickening lack of sympathy in Luis' eyes. "…To learn more about you and your life," she added dully.

This was hopeless…hopeless… No good was going to come from raking over the past. She tried to focus on the present, the journey they were on now. Alan was driving fast across the high Andean plateau. At least the weather wouldn't hold them up, Shontelle thought. It couldn't be a finer, sunnier day.

Like the day Elvira Rosa Martinez had walked into her life.

Alan had told her Luis' family was very wealthy. He had listed off their assets when he had grown concerned over her involvement with his friend. Though all the time she had spent with Luis, his wealth hadn't really seemed relevant to her. He hadn't pushed it in her face.

The boat he'd hired for their trip down the Amazon was more like *The African Queen* than a luxury cruiser. His apartment had certainly been comfortable, but not what she'd call showy. It wasn't until she'd opened the door to the woman who introduced herself as his mother that she saw serious wealth being flaunted.

Beautifully coiffeured black hair was artfully winged with white. The deep mulberry-coloured suit was very smartly trimmed with black, its classy elegance marking it as an Italian design, most probably Cerruti. Shoes and handbag were black with a mulberry trim, obviously made to complement the clothes.

Having toured the H. Stern workshops in Rio de Janeiro, Shontelle recognised the work of the famous jeweler in the fabulous geometric design of the woman's necklace and earrings; hexagonal wine-red rubellites set in yellow and black gold, costing a small fortune. The rings on her hands were equally fabulous.

Shontelle had instantly felt like a waif from the streets, wearing merely a loose button-through cotton dress designed more to hide a traveller's pouch for money and passport than to flatter her figure or give her a bit of style. The sandals on her feet were for practical comfort.

However, since her touring wardrobe did not contain fancy clothes, she had to accept her own appearance as being as good as it could be in the circumstances. Luis had never once criticised it. Though she'd thought afterwards he liked her best naked, anyway.

The plush chauffeur-driven car she'd been led to had made her feel even more self-conscious. The distance they travelled was easily walkable, a matter of a few blocks, but Shontelle was acutely aware that walking the streets with the common people was not the done thing in Elvira Rosa Martinez's world. They drove right to her front door, a semicircular driveway guarded by huge iron gates allowing this private access.

Front door was a misnomer for the huge, elaborate portico that embellished the entrance to a home which was far more than a home. It was probably impossible to explain to Luis, who'd grown up with it, how overwhelming that virtual palace in Alvear Street had been to her, the almost obscene wealth evident in every room she'd been shown, furnishings and furniture imported from Spain, Italy, France. The ballroom had featured all the unbelievable richness of the hall of mirrors in Versailles, reflecting over and over again how hopelessly unsuitable Shontelle looked in such a place.

Naturally, Elvira Rosa Martinez was far too gracious to say so. She didn't have to. Pointing out family heirlooms and portraits, recounting the achievements of Martinez generations in Argentina, she'd made it subtly clear to Shontelle that Luis had the responsibility of carrying on a heritage—an integral part of him no foreigner could even begin to comprehend.

Beside her, Luis stirred from his tense stillness, thrusting out his hand in an impatient gesture. "So tell me the judgment you made...of my *real life*."

Shontelle sighed at his persistence. "You know it better than I, Luis."

"A conducted tour through the mausoleum must have been quite an experience for you," he went on sardonically. "All my forebears framed on the walls, the accumulated treasures of centuries of plunder and exploitation on ostentatious display. I'm sure my mother didn't spare you anything."

His disrespectful tone startled Shontelle. She glanced sharply at him. "Don't you value what's yours?"

His eyes mocked the value she'd placed on it. "It

cost too much. Did Claudia join you for the grand exhibition?''

''No.''

Shontelle scooped in a deep breath as that memory billowed into her mind—the perfectly presented Claudia wearing a spectacular silk dress in glorious autumn tones, highlighting her lovely, glowing olive skin, a lustrous fall of black curly hair, and dark velvet eyes. Fine gold chains and a gold filigree necklace and earrings added their rich touch to her young vibrancy. It was all too obvious she belonged to the same class that the Martinez home portrayed so tellingly.

''Claudia arrived about midday,'' she added, anticipating Luis' next question and deciding she might as well satisfy his curiosity and have done with it.

''Were you introduced to her as my secret mistress?''

A surge of hot blood scorched up her neck and flooded into her cheeks. She shook her head, trying to get rid of the painful flush. ''Your mother tactfully explained about your friendship with Alan and simply introduced me as Alan's sister who was staying in Buenos Aires for a while.''

''Tactful!'' Luis snorted derisively. ''That was for your benefit, Shontelle, not Claudia's. Who was clearly in on the game of getting you out of my life.''

Was that true? Even if it was, didn't Claudia have good reason to want to be rid of the woman sharing Luis' bed...his *secret mistress?* Having just returned from a tour of Europe, it must have been galling to hear that her man had been playing fast and loose with another woman.

Though the comments she had made over lunch about her future with Luis had seemed quite natural, artless. Impossible to tell if they were or not now. They had certainly robbed Shontelle of any appetite…any appetite for food, for staying with Luis, for remaining in Buenos Aires any longer than it took to get a flight home to Australia. The feeling was so sickeningly strong that she didn't belong with these people and never would.

She remembered staring at the centrepiece on the dining table, a magnificently crafted artwork in silver. It was a tree rising from a mound of grass and roots where three deer lay at rest. At the top of the trunk was a holder from which spread a beautiful array of fresh red roses, forming the foliage of the tree. Similarly, silver branches held other, smaller holders, containing more bunches of roses. The effect was stunningly sumptuous and the scent of the roses dreadfully insidious. Red roses for love. Shontelle had hated red roses ever since.

"Was Claudia wearing a ring on the third finger of her left hand?" Luis asked.

"No. Though she talked about what she fancied. An oval yellow diamond surrounded by two rows of white diamonds."

Louis muttered something vicious under his breath.

The Spanish was too fast or too colloquial for Shontelle to pick up the meaning.

"Yet even hearing all this," he said tersely, "you were still there for me in the apartment that evening."

"I didn't want to believe you'd used me like that. I thought there was a chance you had changed your mind about marrying Claudia," she explained ruefully.

"Then why did you not speak of this?"

Because it was too shaming if it was true. Because she still wanted him. Because she simply couldn't face it…until after the telephone call.

She heaved a sigh to ease the burden of all she'd felt, and still felt. "Your mother called you that evening. At the apartment. She said she'd call at eight o'clock. And she did, didn't she, Luis?"

"Yes."

"With an invitation for you to bring me to her next Sunday lunch."

"No," he answered vehemently.

"Luis, I heard the excuse you made. In fact, you sounded extremely vexed and impatient with her for suggesting it."

"She wanted me to be Claudia's escort at a welcome home party. It had nothing to do with you, Shontelle. Nothing!" He gave a derisive laugh. "Or so I thought at the time. I actually thought you were still safe from her. Safe! ¡Madre de Dios!"

Confusion swallowed up Shontelle's understanding

of the situation. Was Luis afraid of his mother? How much power did Elvira have over him?

"My mother planned this call with you…as a test of my intentions?" he probed in a hard ruthless tone.

She gave him her vision of the situation because she had nothing else to give him. "I thought it was a woman to woman thing. A kindness to show me where I stood with you."

"So when you heard my negative reply, you assumed this meant I was keeping you as my secret mistress…yes?" he snapped.

"Yes," she acknowledged.

"And the fire of your love for me went out that night."

She'd cravenly given herself one last night with him, but had found it impossible to respond to his lovemaking, impossible to block Claudia out of her mind, impossible to feel Luis really loved her.

"I felt…used," she repeated wearily.

"So you made me feel *used*."

"Yes."

"For you, it was marriage or nothing."

He had no right to leap to that conclusion. Her love had been freely given, no strings attached. "We hadn't got that far, Luis," she angrily reminded him.

"No, we hadn't. Which was why I did not throw you into the ring with my mother who had her own plans for me."

"You must have known of them," Shontelle argued. "There was too much…too much evidence."

His hands sliced the air in a contemptuous scissor movement. "Talk. Deliberate, divisive talk. If you had spoken to me...but no, you decided I would marry Claudia and there would be nothing for us."

"Back then...your marriage to Claudia meant there was nothing for *me,* Luis," she fiercely corrected him. "Nothing I could feel happy with."

"Claudia Gallardo will never get her yellow diamond from me! Not from *me!* Never!" he declared passionately. "I see now she is every bit as manipulative as my mother and I will not be caught in either of their webs."

Shontelle retreated into silence. She had never been part of this *power* side of Luis' life. From what he'd said, it seemed now that she'd been a victim of it, but it was all beyond her experience.

The old saying...*power corrupts*...slid into her mind. It had never applied to her personal life. She didn't want it to, either. It felt dark and ugly. Luis had accused her of having no faith, no trust, but how could anything be trusted or believed in Luis' world if his own mother plotted behind his back?

The truth—if that was what she had now—did not give her any satisfaction. Only sadness.

Alan had been right.

Her relationship with Luis had been doomed from the start.

Love didn't always find a way.

Not when there was too much stacked against it.

CHAPTER ELEVEN

LUIS closed his eyes. He felt like a drowning man whose whole life was passing before him. And there was no rescue to be had. No going back to a more promising place. He'd killed any possibility of that last night.

The rage inside him was futile. What was done could not be undone. Shontelle—the Shontelle who had brought love and joy and laughter and the sweetest of pleasures into his life—was forever lost to him. No point in blaming her for it. She'd been an innocent, mangled by the forces that had ruled his world, forces he'd known all too well and had wanted to ignore with her. To be free of them with her.

Fool! he thought savagely.

He might have won her back last night. Instead, he'd driven her further away. Beyond reach now. He could feel the shield she'd wrapped around herself, blocking him out. And why not? He was pain…pain in all its forms.

He'd done wrong by Alan, too. Another innocent party. While the guilty ones had almost reaped the benefits of their self-serving conspiracy. Tonight, if there'd been no trouble in La Paz, he would have presented Claudia with the yellow diamond ring, and his mother would have beamed triumphant approval over the proceedings.

How the coin of Fate turns, he thought with an acute sense of irony. But for Alan's need for a bus, his mother would have succeeded in her drive to link the Gallardo and Martinez fortunes. He would have let her succeed, and in doing so, would have provided her with justification for sacrificing the one great love of his life. For that, there was no justification. None that Luis would ever accept.

Everything Shontelle had said to him last night made sense now. If he hadn't been so blinded by bitterness he might have picked up on her repeated references to marriage, questioned more closely.

No...on reflection, there'd been no chance of his being sensitive to what was going on in her mind. The damage had been well and truly done two years ago. Old scars didn't suddenly clear up. But those who'd delivered the wounds could and would still pay for the injuries.

The beautifully polished, submissive Claudia, offering her cold comfort, hiding a Machiavellian heart...she could kiss goodbye to whatever ambitions she'd nursed as an outcome of their marriage merger. The sly bitch hadn't turned a hair at making Shontelle bleed, delivering her poisonous little cuts. He could see her delicately picking through her lunch, sticking her knife in with sweet, loving smiles. She, who didn't know a damned thing about love. Not the kind of love Shontelle...

His heart cramped.

Forget it, he railed at himself. Alan was right. Let it go. God knew there were other things that had to be dealt with. Like his mother…

If only Eduardo had not been taken…Luis could mark the change in his mother from that terrible grief. Not even his father's death, five years before Eduardo's, had touched her so deeply, so traumatically. Perhaps because there'd been no body to bury, no answers to be drawn from anyone.

It was then that the woman she was today had emerged. Control had become everything. The more wealth she acquired, the more power she had, the more control she wielded. Loving anyone was a weakness that left one vulnerable. Better not to love. Better to hold what you had with an iron fist and never risk it, never allow even the possibility of risking it. Protect. Shore up the walls so they were impregnable. Keep a constant watch.

She didn't put her philosophy in such stark terms, but that was what it boiled down to. Luis had fought it for years, to no avail. She'd hung his heritage—Eduardo's heritage—around his neck like an albatross, and wouldn't listen to any point of view that differed from hers. He'd understood—to a degree—what drove her. He'd tried to fill the void she feared—within reason. But for her to take Shontelle out of his life with such ruthless efficiency, uncaring of the pain she gave to either of them…

She had to be stopped.

So forcefully she would never interfere in his life again.

Better still, if she could be made to realise how far she'd gone along a road that was intolerable to him, maybe she could be turned around. Shutting her out of his life was not the answer. She'd find a way to intrude, to interfere. She had to be faced with consequences she couldn't change.

But how to do it? How to hammer it home?

He knew what he wanted to do, what he'd love to do, but he also knew in his bones Shontelle wouldn't agree to it. She was probably longing for him to move away from her right now, have nothing more to do with him.

Yet he couldn't let the idea go. It was the perfect act of justice. No secret moves. No sly manoeuvrings. An act no one could stop, a public act in the spotlight of his mother's own choosing, an undeniable act that declared Luis Angel Martinez his *own man* against any force that could be rallied against him.

But he needed Shontelle's cooperation. Would she listen? Would she see it was an act of justice for her, too? Her response would almost certainly be she wanted no more to do with either him or his family. But it was worth a try. It was very much worth a try. It might just balance the scales so that Shontelle would look at him and see a man she could love again, a man who was free to love.

CHAPTER TWELVE

ALAN made good time to Caracollo, their first stopping place. To have achieved this distance without further mishap put everyone in a good mood.

"You have twenty minutes maximum," Alan warned. "Don't wander away. Use the facilities you'll find across the road, then come back to the bus. Shontelle and I will have coffee and cake and soft drinks ready for you."

The tour group alighted from the bus looking both relieved and happy. Shontelle was grateful for the opportunity to move away from Luis and get about her business of helping Alan with the refreshments. To her frustration, Luis offered his assistance, as well, hovering around her until everything was set up. She refused to look at him, knowing it would only upset her. She was tense enough as it was, feeling him watching her.

Maybe the message that his presence was unwelcome finally got through to him. He drew out a compact mobile telephone that had been clipped to his belt and walked away to make whatever calls he wanted to make in private. Shontelle insisted to herself she was not curious about them. Luis' life was no business of hers anymore. She was better off out of it.

"Are you okay?" Alan asked.

"Yes," she answered shortly.

"I was wrong about Luis, Shontelle. Sorry for thinking I knew better."

"Don't worry about it. We were all wrong. About a lot of things."

"Did you sort it out?"

"Yes."

"And?"

"And nothing. There's nowhere to go."

Alan frowned, not liking the answer, but people were trailing back to the bus and his attention was claimed by them. Shontelle's attention, too.

Cochabamba was their next stop, then the long stretch through the lowlands to Santa Cruz, hopefully arriving there by early evening. Alan had booked them into a hotel for the night, and on a flight to Buenos Aires tomorrow morning. All going well, they would arrive there in time to make the prebooked flight home to Australia. All going well...which it rarely did in South America. Keeping schedules ran on hope, never certainty.

A downpour of rain could block roads, holding up traffic for hours. Flights were cancelled or delayed with no apology or explanation. A gunfight had broken out in Rio on this trip, causing them to take a long detour around the trouble spot. Then a political upheaval in La Paz. Hopefully that problem was behind them, but who knew what they'd run into next?

On the other side of the ledger, was the sheer magic of this continent, so many incredible wonders: La Paz itself, with its fantastic Moon Valley, the Inca history in Cuzco and the strange, eerie atmosphere of the abandoned city of Machu Picchu, the splendid primaeval spectacle of the Iguazu Falls, the awesome Amazon Valley, the beauty of Rio with its Sugarloaf Mountain and the majestic statue of Christ the Redeemer, Buenos Aires...where the Martinez family lived.

Shontelle tried to sigh away the pain.

Whatever discomforts their tour groups ran into on tour, the trip was always worthwhile, the journey truly memorable. Especially this one, Shontelle thought wryly as they herded everyone back on the bus. She suggested to Alan she do a tour commentary over the microphone during this next leg of the trip.

"It will keep them entertained," she pressed, wanting to avoid sitting with Luis again.

Alan surprised her by replying, "I'll do it myself. Luis said he'd take the wheel to Cochabamba. We'll get along faster and more safely with us both coming fresh to driving after a spell."

So Luis *was* letting it go.

It was the inevitable outcome, Shontelle told herself, as they got under way again. She sat alone, which should have relieved the stress of being constantly aware of him, but now she found herself staring at the back of his head, wishing she could read his thoughts. The stress didn't diminish at all. She gradually sank into a black pit of depression.

No heart…no faith…no trust…

The words Luis had hurled at her earlier this morning kept pounding through her mind, making her head ache. She ached all over. The plain truth was she hadn't believed enough in his love for her. She'd let her own sense of inadequacy swallow it up, then spit it out. She had trusted his mother instead of Luis, put her faith in women she didn't know against the man she did know. He was right. Where was the heart in that?

Broken, she thought. Smashed. Bleeding to death.

And there was no cure for it. None at all.

Eventually they reached Cochabamba and stopped for lunch. Luis went off by himself, the mobile telephone in his hand ready to make more calls. Probably shuffling his business affairs around, Shontelle thought. She and Alan led the tour group into a hotel where a buffet spread provided instant self-service. Once everyone was fed and watered, it was back to the bus.

The next stretch of their journey to Villa Tunari was very picturesque and again Shontelle offered to carry on a commentary, aware that Alan would be doing this drive.

"Better to keep quiet and let them doze after lunch," he argued. "Let's save it for when they get restless later on."

Which meant she had to sit with Luis.

More torture.

She shrank into herself as best she could as he settled beside her. Anticipating a long journey of tense silence, she was surprised when he spoke to her, the moment Alan had the bus moving.

"Will you accept an apology for my behaviour last night, Shontelle?"

She glanced sharply at him, drawn more by the low intense tone than the question. There was no mockery in his eyes, not one trace of contempt for her, just deep unfathomable darkness. His face looked strained, absolutely serious. Shontelle's heart skittered nervously. Had she been wrong about his decision to let it all go?

"We've both acted regrettably, Luis," she answered stiffly. "I'm sorry, too, for the pain I caused you."

His mouth twisted into a rueful grimace. "Saying *sorry* isn't enough, is it?"

She shook her head. "There are too many other factors."

"Yes," he agreed.

They were in tune with each other on that score, Shontelle thought, sliding back into bleak despondency.

"My mother is holding a grand reception tonight," he remarked. "The guest list includes the most prominent people in Argentina. The Gallardo family will certainly be there. In strength."

Shontelle fiercely wished he'd keep his family business to himself.

"I would be very honoured," he went on, "if you'd be my partner to this highly glittering occasion, Shontelle."

Shock addled her brains. He couldn't mean it. She was either dreaming or he'd taken leave of his senses. Yet he still looked perfectly serious.

"Why?" she blurted out, needing to sort through the ambivalence of such a suggestion.

His mouth curved into a whimsical little smile. "It is, perhaps, one thing I can right, out of all the wrongs I've done you."

"How could that make anything right?" she cried.

"Two years ago, I made you feel less than you were, Shontelle," he said quietly. "It was unintentional, but a very grave error on my part. I would like, at least, to correct that error. I'd be very proud to present you as my partner in front of my mother and all of Argentina."

Shontelle squirmed in anguish. "It's too late for that, Luis."

"No. It's never too late to give due respect. To restore pride and self-esteem. I shall do it tonight, if you'll allow me."

"It doesn't matter. These people are not part of my life. They never will be."

His face hardened. "It doesn't matter that they lied to you? That they lied about me to make you feel like *nothing?* You can forgive and forget that, Shontelle? Or will it not always burn a hole in your heart?''

''It's in the past, Luis.''

''No.'' His eyes blazed with passionate intensity. ''The past is never in the past. It lives with us. Always. I need...please, I beg you...let me give you justice.''

She wrenched her gaze from his, feeling the power of his will tugging on hers, intent on drawing her with him again. For what? Justice was a cold repast. It could never give back what had been taken. At best, all it did was balance the scales.

Nevertheless, there was an insidious attraction about turning up at a grand reception given by Elvira Rosa Martinez, being flaunted as Luis' chosen partner for the evening, right under his mother's and Claudia Gallardo's snobbish noses. Yes, there would be some satisfaction in that...robbing them of their mean triumph over her.

But it would also mean more time spent with Luis...time filled with painful might-have-beens. He'd be touching her, stirring memories, putting her through a make-believe situation, pretending all was right between them when it wasn't. She couldn't do it.

Besides, how did he expect to get to this reception? ''Have you forgotten we're in the middle of Bolivia, Luis? We'll be lucky to make it to Santa Cruz tonight.''

"A company jet will be waiting there to fly us on to Buenos Aires."

She looked at him in astonishment. "You've already made arrangements?"

"For me, yes. I hope you will accompany me."

His calls on the mobile telephone, Shontelle thought, and wondered when he had started planning this proposition. As early as before Caracollo, or had the idea grown on him while he drove to Cochabamba?

"Shontelle, I owe you this," he said softly. "You owe it to me, as well."

She stared at the steadily burning purpose in his eyes. "How do you work that out?" she challenged.

"You let them picture me falsely. Because they got away with it, they will go on picturing me falsely to others whenever it suits their purpose. That must be stopped, and the most effective way of stopping it is for you to bear witness for me in a court where it will count, in front of people who count to them. Together we can throw their game back in their faces."

She shivered at the ruthless intent behind his words. "As you did with me last night, Luis?" she said, reminding him of that wretched outcome.

"No. That was not justice. It was the vengeance of a man whose love had been robbed of all value. And it will always haunt me as a shameful act on my part. But there is no shame in seeking justice, Shontelle. Only shame in not pursuing it."

He was right in a way. It was wrong to let Elvira

Rosa Martinez and Claudia Gallardo get away scot-free with what they'd done. Justice…it gave a kind of closure to a crime. And it had been a crime…the premeditated murder of love.

It wouldn't take much, she argued to herself. Just one more night. For his pride. For her pride. But how could she carry it off? "I don't have anything suitable to wear, Luis. They'd all look down their noses at me and think you mad for bringing me into their midst."

"I'll provide you with appropriate clothes. I'll have a selection delivered to my apartment. With the finest accessories." He flashed a wicked smile that jiggled her heart. "Believe me, you will not be underdressed for this occasion."

Wealth, Shontelle sternly reminded herself, was one of the divisive factors she could not overlook. Obscene wealth. Luis could probably order anything to appear at the snap of his fingers. Or a telephone call. Though there were some things one couldn't buy… like love and trust and happiness.

"Is it worth it to you, Luis?" she asked. "Even if we manage to get to Santa Cruz by seven o'clock, it's then a three hour flight to Buenos Aires. Add on the hour time difference, plus time to dress ourselves appropriately. I doubt we could make it to the reception before midnight."

"Yes, it's worth it," he asserted strongly. "And I consider midnight perfect timing. Everyone will be there by then and no one would have left. It would be seen as rude to leave such an elite gathering before

3:00 a.m.'' Another flash of wickedness. ''We shall make quite an entrance, you and I.''

He relished the idea. And suddenly Shontelle did, too. Why not? ''You intend to turn the pumpkin into a princess at the stroke of midnight?'' she half mocked.

''You were never a pumpkin,'' he shot back at her, anger flaring from his eyes. ''Do not ever regard yourself in such a demeaning light. You are…'' His lips compressed, shutting off the line of thought he'd been about to give voice to. He shook his head in an anguished roll. ''It is wrong to hate one's mother. But I do hate much of what's she's done.''

The torment so clearly expressed moved Shontelle more than anything else he'd said. She thought of her own mother who was always there for her, ready to give any help or comfort, always looking to answer her needs without ever forcing anything. For all the wealth at his disposal, it had not been an easy life for Luis, always feeling the load of responsibility he'd inherited through his older brother's death.

She remembered all the things he'd confided to her when they'd been most intimate. He had never openly criticised his mother for the way she had ordered his life so he could take Eduardo's place, but she had sensed he sometimes felt trapped in a role that had been thrust upon him. Once he had said he envied Alan's freedom to choose his own path.

''I have to break the chains that have bound me for so long,'' he muttered. Then his hand reached across and took hers, interlacing their fingers in a tight, forceful grip that throbbed with intense feeling. "Be my partner tonight, Shontelle. I will see that you catch your flight home to Australia tomorrow. But tonight is ours…one final stand together…for justice."

"Yes," she agreed, barely aware of giving her consent.

She was overwhelmingly aware of the physical link he had just forged. Except somehow it was more than physical. It was like a current flowing from him and flooding every cell of her body. She stared down at their hands, not understanding, only knowing she ached with a terrible need to stay joined to him.

She forgot the other factors.

Suddenly they were meaningless.

If only Luis would hold on to her, she would stand with him to the end of time.

CHAPTER THIRTEEN

"THE red," Luis said decisively.

"Are you sure?" Shontelle asked, her gaze clinging to the safer, black lace creation.

She still couldn't quite believe the array of beautiful designer clothes and accessories laid out for her to choose from in the main bedroom of Luis' apartment. It was difficult enough, coping with being hit by the familiarity of a room they had shared so intimately. Besides which, the prospect of returning to the Martinez mansion had her nerves in a jangling mess, despite having the promised security of Luis' arm to support her. She was afraid of looking wrong.

"Melding into the crowd is not what tonight is about, Shontelle," Luis dryly reminded her.

Not the black then. "The gold one is very elegant," she pointed out.

"Wear the red." No doubt, no reservation in his voice.

"Luis, it hardly has any back to it," she protested worriedly. The gown dipped right down to waist level, apparently supported by a silver Y-strap running down her spine and two shoestring red straps that joined it to hold the bodice firmly across her breasts.

"You have a beautiful back."

The soft, thick words raised goose bumps all over her skin. Her heart thumped erratically. She knew she could still arouse desire in him. Last night had proved that. Even when he'd hated her the sexual chemistry hadn't waned. But tonight wasn't about answering those needs, was it? He'd given no indication of it.

"That doesn't mean I should bare it," she said, keeping her gaze fixed firmly on the dress, as though studying its potential to embarrass her.

Her mind was jagging off in wild directions. This togetherness project was bound to push them into more intimacy as the night went on…holding, dancing, continual linking with each other. What if it led back to this bed? What if they ended up making love? Would he ask her to stay with him…or would he stick to his promise to have her at the airport tomorrow in good time to join Alan and the tour group for their flight home?

"Your hair will veil most of it," he said, his voice even more furred with sensual overtones.

"I thought I'd put it up. It's more sophisticated," she almost gabbled in helpless agitation.

"No. Wear it loose. And wear the red, Shontelle." She heard his breath hiss out on a long sigh. "I will leave you to dress. The bathroom is free for your use."

His footsteps moved to the spare bedroom. Its door clicked shut. He was giving her complete privacy, removing any sense of lurking intimacy she might feel. And did feel. One night…for justice, he'd said. Did she dare reach for more? Was *more* possible?

Dear God! Hadn't she hoped the same last night? She'd be totally mad to lay herself on the line again. Just get on with what's been planned, she savagely berated herself, and grabbed the make-up that had been supplied to complement the red dress. The bathroom was free and there was no time to waste.

Nevertheless, as she took a quick shower and set about adding glamour to her face, she couldn't stop her mind from wandering over Luis' manner to her since she had agreed to his plan. Apart from the one strong hand grip, he hadn't touched her, nor said anything suggestive of a sexual interest or any interest in her beyond tonight.

Unfinished business, he'd told Alan when he'd asked they be dropped at the Santa Cruz airport before the tour group was driven on to their hotel. Alan had simply asked her, "Is this your choice, Shontelle?" and when she'd answered, "Yes," he'd set the scene for her and Luis' departure, explaining to the group that Luis had supplied them with the bus as a special favour to the Amigos Tours Company and they were returning the favour in helping him to make an important business connection on time. Shontelle's accompanying him to Buenos Aires on a private flight would place her there to deal with any problems arising tomorrow.

No one had protested.

On their arrival at the airport, it had been all business. The moment the bus pulled up, a man from the Martinez company had been on the spot to escort them to the company plane. He'd handed Luis an attaché case which Shontelle had deduced contained important company documents, then taken charge of her luggage. The tour group gave them a rousing farewell, happy that their journey was almost over, Alan wished them well, and their escort whisked them away.

There was no delay in taking off. Once safely in the air, they were served dinner, after which Luis had urged her to get some rest and moved to another part of the plane, presumably to work on the papers in the attaché case. She'd actually slept for most of the flight, the toll of a long day's travelling following a wretched night of distress finally wearing out her too active mind. Luis woke her as they were about to land, awakening her senses, too, as she breathed in the cologne he'd splashed onto his freshly shaven face.

His shaving on the flight had probably been done to leave his bathroom free for her, she thought now, but right then, in her drowsy state, she'd almost reached up and touched his face, only just halting the movement and redirecting her hand to scrape an errant strand of hair off her own face. But the impulse had rattled her. She shouldn't still want him so... wantonly. She knew it was foolish.

The subsequent drive from the airport to this apartment had been fraught with tension on her part. They didn't talk. It was a company car with a chauffeur doing the driving. The silver-grey Mercedes with its plush interior was clearly executive class. The power of wealth was being demonstrated in full, ever since she'd agreed to standing with Luis tonight.

A final stand…

Final!

She had to get that through her head.

Tonight was the end, no chance at all of a new beginning.

Having emphasised her eyes with subtle earth tones and put a glow on her skin with the clever cosmetics designed for that purpose, Shontelle outlined her mouth with the red pencil provided and filled in the curves with a vivid scarlet lipstick, the perfect match for the dress Luis had insisted upon.

The thought occurred to her she'd certainly be a scarlet woman tonight to at least two people. Or a flaming sword, cutting their lies down and laying them waste. Which was what those wicked lies deserved, defaming Luis and deceiving her with such devastating results.

Justice…

Satisfied she'd at least done justice to her face, Shontelle put the lipstick down, unbraided her hair, and brushed it into a cloud of rippling waves. The plait had crinkled it and there was no time to wash and dry it into a straight fall, but it was still clean and shiny from last night's washing. Luis had always preferred it loose. She hoped it didn't look too untamed and casual to other eyes.

Wrapped in a towel, she collected her things and dashed back to the bedroom. Luis was nowhere in view. She hurried through the nervous business of dressing herself to the standard expected of a guest at a Martinez grand reception.

The red gown was spectacular. The fabric was soft and slinky and woven through with silver thread, creating a kind of oriental design of meandering vines and leaves that shimmered exotically on the scarlet background. It clung to every curve of her body, only flaring slightly from the knees so she could walk comfortably.

The silver shoulder straps extended down the outside curve of her breasts and joined underneath them, creating a bra effect with the fabric stretched above and between them. Shontelle worried over the cleavage on display until she added the fine filigree silver chains and necklaces that cascaded from her throat, filling in the expanse of bare flesh and adding that indefinable sense of class to sexiness.

Beautiful silver strappy high heels and an elegant little silver handbag gave the perfect touches of completion. Shontelle couldn't help staring at her reflection in the mirror, amazed by the transformation that could be wrought, given no expense spared for anything. Fine feathers certainly made fine birds. Even to herself she looked stunning. Which gave her a much-needed boost in confidence.

She quickly put the scarlet lipstick, a couple of tissues and some emergency money into the tiny evening bag. The bedside clock read 11:43. Luis' estimate of a midnight arrival at the reception was going to be very close, assuming he was also ready to leave now. Time to find out, she told herself, taking a deep breath and hoping the flutters in her stomach didn't get any worse.

He was waiting for her, just standing in the middle of the living room, nursing a drink in one hand. The sheer impact of him, dressed in formal evening clothes, brought Shontelle to a halt. His black dinner suit had the expensive sheen of silk, and its black satin lapels and matching bow tie added a sensual touch against the crisp whiteness of his finely pin-tucked shirt. He looked utterly superb and so handsome, Shontelle could hardly breathe, let alone walk.

The perfect man, she thought—tall, dark, handsome and loaded with a brooding, male animal appeal that was all the more enticing for being encased in the clothes of sophisticated civilisation. Her heart was going haywire, frantically signalling that *he* was the man for her, and if she let him go, she would be losing the mate of her life. But how could she make it right between them? How?

''The sun and the moon and the stars...''

The soft murmur from Luis seemed to feather down her spine. His eyes glowed the kind of warmth she'd all but forgotten, stirring memories of beautiful times together, times of tenderness and deep, inexpressible joy. Hope leapt into her mind and danced through her veins. Then his thick lashes lowered, shadowing the look that belonged to an idyll of blissful togetherness, and his mouth curved into an ironic little smile.

"You'll outshine them all tonight. As you should. Though I would have been proud to present you whatever you wore, Shontelle. I don't suppose you'll believe that, but it's true."

"I want to do you proud, Luis," she answered, feeling he was making light of the power of first impressions. Not that he'd care…if tonight was the end. First impressions would only be important to him if she were to stay in his social circle. But just this once, Shontelle wanted to feel acceptable in his world, and see acceptance in others' eyes. It was important to her that she didn't fail this test.

His brows drew together in a quick frown. "If you feel…not right…" He gestured an apologetic appeal. "I should not have pressed you to wear anything you prefer not to."

"No. I like the red on me," she quickly assured him.

His concern broke into a grin of sheer, wicked pleasure. "Good! It is absolutely perfect for you in my eyes. I shall enjoy being the envy of every man at the reception."

He set his glass down on a table as he moved to open the door with a flourish, his grin still alight with devilish anticipation. "Come, Cinderella. It is time to go to the ball."

A nervous laugh bubbled out of her throat as she forced her legs to move. Elvira Rosa Martinez wasn't exactly the wicked stepmother and Claudia Gallardo couldn't be described as an ugly stepsister, but Shontelle couldn't help hoping they'd get the shock of their lives when they recognised who had the Prince's arm tonight.

The silver Mercedes was waiting for them. The chauffeur saw Shontelle settled on one side of the back seat while Luis rounded the car and took the other side. They were closed in together for the final act.

Five more minutes and the players would be on stage, Shontelle thought, wondering just how many people would be shocked by her appearance with Luis Angel Martinez, the heir to a fortune, who was undoubtedly expected to be paying court to the heiress of a fortune. A worriesome thought struck her and she turned sharply to Luis as the car moved off.

"What about the Gallardo family? Will this make bad business between you?"

"I don't care, Shontelle. What will be, will be," he said quietly, firmly.

Reckless?

She studied him for a moment, but his expression was difficult to read in the shadows of the night. He sat back, apparently perfectly relaxed, yet she could feel the harnessing of power and purpose in him, the determination to sweep all before him, to stamp his own will on everything that happened.

"Don't fear anything on my account, Shontelle," he said softly. "Whatever the consequences of tonight, I would rather be known as my own man than have others think they own me."

"It's strange to me...this Martinez side of you... the public position you hold in Argentina. You never really showed it to me."

"I preferred you to know the private person."

"I don't think you can separate yourself out like that, Luis."

"It was wrong," he agreed. "You have made me, see that very clearly, Shontelle. For which I am deeply grateful. A man cannot live another's life. He must be true to himself."

Shontelle suddenly perceived tonight wasn't so much about justice to Luis. It was about freedom. Which made it a far more momentous occasion than she had realised. He was seeing this as a major turning point in his life...and *she* had done this?

A shiver ran down her spine.

No, she argued frantically. I'm only the catalyst. He wasn't happy. He probably hadn't been happy for many, many years. Even in his mind, his love affair with her had been time stolen from a life he found oppressive, time for himself. Which was probably why he'd been so frustrated and embittered when she'd ended it.

Had he ever really loved her? Or had she represented something he'd needed...a rebellion against the structure he'd been born into...an outlet for feelings he couldn't normally express...a refuge from pressures that seemed ultimately inescapable?

There were so many layers to him she didn't know. She had loved him instinctively. Still did. Impulsively she reached over and lightly squeezed his arm. "I'm with you tonight, Luis. Whatever you want to achieve, I'm on your side."

Before she could withdraw her hand he caught it, trapped it, transmitting a burst of energy that zinged up her arm and raced through her whole nervous system. "Is that a promise, Shontelle?" he asked, and even in the darkness his eyes blazed with an intensity that shot quivers through her heart.

"Yes," she whispered.

"Then the sun and the moon and the stars shine on me tonight," he said, and laughed, tilting his head back and giving vent to a peal of joyous, devil-may-care laughter.

Even as Shontelle stared at him in startled wonder, he lifted her hand to his lips and pressed a warm kiss across her knuckles. His eyes sobered, but a winsome smile lingered on his mouth as he said, "Thank you. Though I will not hold you to such an all-encompassing promise, Shontelle. I would not want you to rue it. You are free to choose whatever is right for you."

Free...her heart sank, taking with it the foolish hopes that had persisted in fluttering, despite a strong dose of common sense. He did not want her to tie herself to him. This partnership was mutual in so far as they had a common purpose in seeking justice, but there the mutuality ended. He could not have spelled the position out more clearly.

The car slowed, turned, and the huge black iron gates that guarded the Martinez mansion caught her eye.

They were here!

The impressive Graeco-Roman edifice with its massive columns and elaborate cornices was stage-lit from the gardens on either side of the driveway. Music drifted from the opened doors to the second-story balconies which led off the ballroom. The grand reception was clearly in full swing.

The Mercedes stopped at the flight of steps which was framed by a portico that would have done a temple proud. It was a temple, Shontelle thought with painful irony, a temple to all Elvira Rosa Martinez held dear. The question tonight was…which did she hold more dear, her son or his heritage? The choice was almost upon her.

Luis released her hand to alight from the car, quickly skirting it to lend his arm to Shontelle's emergence on the other side. The chauffeur held her door open. She gathered her skirt up carefully to avoid any problem with it as she stepped out.

Red…the colour of danger.

Too late to retreat now.

She'd given her word.

Luis took her hand again, and as she straightened up beside him he tucked her arm around his in a proprietary gesture that proclaimed their public togetherness.

"Ready?" he asked, his eyes gleaming some deep, personal satisfaction.

"Yes," she answered, resolved on facing the people who had brought her—brought both Luis and her—to this final act.

Arm in arm, they moved up the steps.

And somewhere in the distance, a clock tolled midnight.

CHAPTER FOURTEEN

"SEÑOR MARTINEZ!" The surprise on the elderly manservant's face was echoed in his voice as he ushered them into the foyer. "It was not expected…" He looked in confusion at Shontelle, who was undoubtedly even more unexpected.

"I had some luck getting out of La Paz," Luis explained.

"Your mother will be…" He choked on whatever word he might ordinarily have used—pleased, delighted, ecstatic—staring at Shontelle in a kind of dazed horror.

"May I introduce my companion, Miss Shontelle Wright. Shontelle, this is…"

"Carlos," she broke in. "We've met before." She smiled at the elderly retainer whose skin had gone quite sallow. "You served me with lunch here, two years ago, though you may not remember me."

"Sí, Miss Wright," he answered faintly, then swallowed hard. "I shall go and announce your arrival."

Luis reached out and stayed the man before he could move. "Let's pretend I let myself in, Carlos. I wish to surprise my mother."

"But, Señor…"

Steely authority instantly emerged. "I'd advise you

to look the other way, Carlos. Do I make myself clear?''

"Sí, señor."

He backed off and Luis swept Shontelle onto the grand staircase which led to the long gallery bordering the ballroom; the gallery of gold-framed portraits and priceless objets d'art that had so overwhelmed her on her last visit here.

They mounted the stairs, meeting no resistance from other household staff. The music was louder now, an orchestra of master tango musicians playing traditional *porteno* arrangements on violins and the unique Argentinian version of squeeze-boxes, *bandoneons*.

''Remember dancing the tango with me?'' Luis murmured.

She glanced at him, flushing at the memories he'd evoked; the wildly erotic movements they'd practised in private, teasing each other with a pretence of discipline and control, throwing themselves into the beat of the music for the sheer dramatic fun of it…and always ending up making passionate love to each other.

His eyes caught hers, and she saw he was thinking of those times, too. ''It was good,'' she answered huskily, her pulse beat speeding up at the simmering look he returned.

''Poetry and fire…it is a dance of the soul, yes?''

She nodded, unsure what he wanted from her. Historically, the tango had evolved from a *darkness*

of soul, more an expression of tragic pain than anything else...men without women, dancing alone,
working off their despair with life. Was Luis feeling
some parallel with that history now?

"Will you dance it with me tonight?" he asked.

A last tango? Her legs quivered at the prospect. To
her the dance was associated with very raw, uninhib-
ited desire. Was it sensible to tempt fate when there
was no future in it? An unaccountable surge of reck-
lessness overrode wisdom.

"If you think it's appropriate," she said.

"I find poetry and fire particularly appropriate in
this instance."

Dante's *Inferno* slipped into Shontelle's mind.
Were the devils in hell dancing tonight? Luis seemed
intent on using every bit of firepower to blow his
mother's ambitions for him apart. *I'm his torch,* she
thought, and wondered if there'd be anything other
than ashes left over when all the burning had been
done.

He'd mockingly named this place a mausoleum,
she recalled, as they stepped past the marble arch that
marked the entrance to the gallery. It might contain
treasures of the dead but Shontelle was made instantly
aware of very alive people occupying it. Groups of
guests were viewing items of interest or just chatting
amongst themselves, taking a break from the ballroom.

The late appearance of Luis Angel Martinez with
an unknown woman in tow was swiftly noticed. Con-

versation stopped. Heads craned. Shontelle was acutely sensitive to the wave of shock rolling down the entire showroom, and it was her presence causing it, or rather her being partnered by Luis. Eyes busily assessed her appearance. Whispers started. Shontelle imagined people hastily asking... *Who is she? What does this mean?*

One man broke away from his circle of companions and hurried towards them. Shontelle's heart did a little skip as she recognised him as Luis' younger brother, Patricio. He looked bewildered, unable to believe his eyes, yet driven to ascertain what the situation was.

"*¡Dios!* This is some entrance, Luis!" he muttered, deliberately blocking their way.

His physique was shorter and leaner than his older brother's but there was a tensile strength about him that made him a formidable opponent if he wished to be. His moustache gave his handsome face a rather dashing, playboy air, which was deceptive. Shontelle knew him to be an exacting and shrewd businessman who managed the Martinez agricultural interests with a very astute reading of marketability. He occasionally showed off his brilliant horsemanship to tour groups who visited the main ranch outside Buenos Aires, but Alan had told her that was the only playing Luis' brother indulged in.

"Move aside, Patricio," Luis commanded in an equally low voice.

"You're supposed to be in La Paz," came the confused protest.

"Get out of my way," Luis warned. "And please give Shontelle the courtesy of a greeting. You have met Alan's sister."

"Shontelle?" He did a double take, staring at her with suddenly enlightened eyes. "I did not recognise you. And this…" His long Spanish nose lifted haughtily as he glared back at Luis. "…This I do not understand."

"You don't have to," Luis tersely informed him.

"You yourself declared any member of the Wright family persona non grata," Patricio retorted fiercely.

"The betrayal of trust was not theirs. I did them an injustice I am bound to correct."

"There's a time and place for everything, Luis. This isn't it," Patricio argued.

"There is none better in my opinion."

"Are you mad? The Gallardo family is here in full force. You cannot flaunt another woman in Claudia's face."

"Oh, yes I can."

The venom in Luis' voice jolted Patricio. He turned a beetling frown on Shontelle. "I mean no offence to you, Shontelle, but this is a situation of some delicacy. My mother intends to announce…"

"She will not," Luis cut in. "I informed her it was not possible when I called about the situation in La Paz. I told her I would select a time of my own choosing."

Patricio shook his head. "Your supposed absence was not going to stop it, Luis. You gave your tacit approval before you left for La Paz. When the orchestra finishes their performance…''

''So she would force my hand…even to this,'' Luis grated. His face was thunderous as he shot out an arm to hold Patricio at a distance while he steered Shontelle around him with such alacrity, she almost tripped trying to keep up.

Patricio fell into step beside him, urgently pleading. ''Luis, this is tantamount to committing harakiri in public.''

''She leaves me no choice.''

''Let me take care of Shontelle. You can ride this through and…''

''No.'' Luis instantly secured Shontelle's hold on his arm by clamping his free hand over hers, deliberately emphasising their togetherness as he moved relentlessly forward. ''There will be no more riding anything through at my mother's will,'' he seethed at his brother.

''Luis, what is this about?'' Shontelle pleaded, agitated by the turbulent currents in the conversation. ''You said it was a glittering occasion but if it has some important meaning…''

''His engagement to Claudia Gallardo is about to be announced,'' Patricio shot at her.

''What?'' she cried in horror.

''No!'' Luis denied vehemently. ''It will not happen. I will not allow it to happen.''

Shontelle's feet faltered as she was hit by the enormity of what he had kept from her. ''But you knew…

Oh, my God! You brought me here, knowing…and last night…"

He halted to face her, his eyes blazing into hers. "*I* have not given Claudia a commitment, Shontelle."

"You let them think it was on the cards," Patricio sliced in, moving to close them into a private little circle.

"The cards got reshuffled today and they will never be the same again," Luis fired at his brother. "I am reclaiming my life. Wear Eduardo's shoes yourself if all this means so much to you. They probably fit you a lot better than they do me."

Patricio recoiled a step, his face reflecting intense inner turmoil. "I don't want it, Luis."

"Then don't shovel it on me."

"Luis…this is wrong…you didn't tell me how it was," Shontelle cried, plucking at the hand holding hers, hating the feeling of being used.

"Did Claudia care for you? Did my mother let us be?" he flashed at her with such violent feeling, it shook Shontelle from her bid to detach herself from him. "You said you would stand by me," he went on passionately. "Can I count on no one?"

His eyes burned with a terrible need that sucked relentlessly on Shontelle's heart, draining it of resistance to what he was asking of her. She was part of the pattern of deceit that had riddled his life and that guilt still remained, twisting inside her. Yet two wrongs didn't make a right and he had let her believe—led her to believe—there was no relationship with Claudia worth talking about.

"You repeat your own error in holding things from me, Luis," she reminded him, unwilling to let his fault pass without comment.

"The issue of justice was the same," he insisted.

Was it? Somehow the imminent engagement muddied everything. The thought of him courting Claudia, kissing her... "Have you made love to her?" she asked, riven by the stark memory of what he'd done last night with no love at all.

"*¡Cristo!*" Patricio expostulated. "She has no right..."

"*¡Silencio!* It is you who has no right!" Luis snapped, then swung his gaze back to Shontelle, urgently begging belief. "I was never even tempted to make love to her." His look of repugnance reinforced his claim. "There was absolutely no intimacy between me and Claudia Gallardo."

"Then how could this engagement come about?" she cried in torment.

"It was a matter of indifference to me whom I married. Claudia pursued it. My mother pushed it. *You* had left me to them."

Her fault? Was this justice or vengeance? A last tango with him...dark, dark angel.

"Luis, the music has stopped," Patricio warned.

"Shontelle...am I alone?" he pressed, still searing her soul with his eyes.

The tug was stronger than ever, despite the dreadful

confusion swirling around it. She gave up the fight to understand. If it meant so much to him—that she stand by him now—using her to gain his freedom— then why not do it? At least it would expunge her guilt over how she'd scarred his life.

"No," she whispered. "I'm with you."

He released a long shuddering breath and quickly acted on her consent, walking them both on. She could hear people gathering behind them, following them, drawn by the promise of scandal. The scarlet woman indeed, Shontelle thought, beginning to feel quite light-headed.

As they rounded the corner of the gallery to the shorter section which opened into the ballroom, Patricio slipped behind Luis and stepped up beside Shontelle so she was flanked by both men. The three of them walking abreast drew attention from the people they were approaching. More stares. Buzzing speculation.

"Better peel off, Patricio," Luis advised.

"No."

"This is my fight."

"I don't know what the hell is behind this, Luis, but if you're vacating Eduardo's shoes, she's not going to put me into them. I'll stand with you."

"This a highly personal affair, Patricio."

"Better we present a united front."

"A bit late for that, given your attempt to stop me."

"Not too late for the main event."

Stubborn resolve from Patricio, reckless resolve from Luis. Between them, Shontelle felt carried along towards some kind of Armageddon, a clash of power that promised the end of an era of domination. And here she was, dressed like a princess to be a pawn in the battle. No, not a pawn, she decided. A symbol. A weapon. A flaming sword for truth and justice.

She smiled at that thought...definitely light-headed. The words of the song—*Don't Cry For Me, Argentina*—flitted through her mind as they entered the ballroom. The aristocracy was all around her now, very distinguished-looking men, women lavishly be-jewelled. She was being inspected by them. Shontelle held her head high—Cinderella at the ball, escorted by the Martinez princes.

Then from the other end of the ballroom, a voice rang out over a microphone, a voice Shontelle instantly recognised as belonging to the woman reputed to be the wealthiest and most powerful woman in Argentina.

"My friends...thank you for coming this evening. It gives me much pleasure to see you all here, to join with me in celebrating a very special event. Unfortunately, my son, Luis, has been trapped in La Paz, due to..."

"No, *Madre*... Luis has come," Patricio called out.

It was as though he had pointed a staff like Moses. The sea of people in front of them parted, fell back, and a clear path opened up down the length of the dance floor to the dais where Elvira Rosa Martinez stood like an all-powerful pharaoh in command of her world.

She looked magnificent, dressed in shimmering royal blue, with a fabulous collar of gold around her throat, gold falling from her ears and circling her wrists. The hand holding the microphone sparkled with ornate rings. But her handsome face lost its winning smile as she realised what was facing her.

Not Luis alone.

Not Luis with his younger brother.

Not Luis, miraculously arriving in time to pledge himself to the woman his mother had ordained he marry.

On his arm was another woman, possessively secured there by a hand that proclaimed her his in no uncertain terms.

Shontelle had no idea if Elvira recognised her but the message being telegraphed was unmistakable, to everyone looking on. This was a parade of proud defiance of what anyone thought. This was a statement of arrogant independence. The gauntlet had been thrown in front of every high-ranking person in the country and there was no turning back from it.

CHAPTER FIFTEEN

A SILENCE fell, and it seemed to Shontelle there was a freezing of time in the Martinez mansion. The huge gilt-framed mirrors in the ballroom reflected a scene that had stopped moving. Overhead the many-tiered chandeliers were brilliantly alight, glowing with a life of their own. Below them, she and Luis and Patricio walked in unison, a pace measured by dignity...no haste...no falter.

The sound of their footsteps on the parquet floor was eerie...isolated...echoing in a weird emptiness. Luis and Patricio were stepping into an unknown future, Shontelle thought, and risking all they'd had in the past for it. Was it worth it to them? Was it? She didn't know what it was like to be shackled by a heritage such as theirs. Impossible for her to weigh the prizes and penalties of great wealth.

Elvira...staring at them, her expression oddly glazed.

Open rebellion facing her.

Would she act to stop it?

Did she sense there was no stopping it?

Shontelle's nerves prickled as Elvira's gaze focused on her, her eyes suddenly sharp with recognition. Yes, she thought fiercely. Look at me. Look at your victim of yesteryear and feel the wheel turning. It's right that it should.

Elvira's head turned slightly, her gaze shooting to a group of people gathered to the right of the stage. And there was Claudia Gallardo, presumably surrounded by her family. Claudia, dressed in pure virginal white, a bridal beacon, masking the calculating mind that had sacrificed integrity in her ruthless push to an altar of greed. Claudia, staring at them in disbelief, not receiving whatever mental message her co-conspirator had tried to send.

Frustrated and aware of the electric curiosity aroused, Luis' mother sought to distract, as well as soothe the escalating tension, using the microphone to draw attention back to her. "Well, this is a wonderful surprise! It appears nothing—not even a revolution in Bolivia—could keep Luis from joining us tonight. Please forgive a short delay while I welcome him home."

She turned and gestured to the violinists to play. They quickly struck up a tune. Elvira set the microphone on its stand and moved regally to the left-hand side of the stage, away from the Gallardo family, a blatant directive to Luis to accommodate her wish to have a private word with him before he committed himself to what she undoubtedly saw as ultimate folly.

Luis did not oblige her.

Without hesitation, he aimed the three of them straight towards the Gallardo family. Patricio needed no signal. He adjusted his step to keep the united front. A march into the face of enemy lines, Shontelle thought, seeing a bristling start to run through the family who had expected to seal an important liaison this night.

Did they know what had been done in pursuit of it? The Gallardo men were older than Luis and Patricio. Much older. Had they viewed Luis Angel Martinez as a bunny to be taken for what he was worth?

Well, meet the rabbit in the hat, Shontelle thought with wild irreverence for their fortune-melding. She locked her eyes onto the dark, dazed gaze of the heiress who'd cut Shontelle's faith in Luis' love into irredeemable fragments, and all her grief boiled up into a blistering challenge.

How do you like it, Claudia, being faced with a partnership you thought you'd destroyed? Being faced with the woman you lied to? Seeing the future you'd hoped for dashed into dust?

The answer was not long in coming.

There was a sudden snap of recognition…the realisation of what Shontelle's appearance with Luis had to mean…then fury…sheer black fury. No broken heart in those eyes as they slashed down Shontelle's dressed-to-kill gown and whipped up to the man she'd almost won with the connivance of his mother. The fury switched to a haughty contempt. No way was Claudia Gallardo going to be bowed in defeat.

"I see you've taken up with your foreign trash

again, Luis,'' she attacked first, just as they halted directly in front of her.

Shontelle's hackles rose. It was difficult to treat such an insult with disdain, but she did her best to project unassailable confidence in her right to be at Luis' side. Apart from which, this was his fight. He proceeded to answer his erstwhile fiancée with icy control.

"I leave it to you to explain to your family why I do what I do now, Claudia. And may I suggest you curb your malicious spite. It will not serve you well."

"Explain to *me!*" the elderly man beside Claudia demanded brusquely. "You serve us with a public humiliation. It is not to be forgiven, Luis."

"Esteban, your daughter and my mother contrived to destroy the most precious thing in my life. Do not speak of forgiveness to me. I will see justice done first."

For a moment, Shontelle's heart swelled painfully. Hearing Luis call the love they'd shared *the most precious thing in his life* made the loss all the harder to bear.

"What justice?" the old man spluttered. "Patricio…" he appealed, "…is this an act of honour?"

"You cannot divide me from my brother, Esteban," came the hard warning. "We will have truth tonight and there is no dishonour in truth."

"We had an understanding!" Esteban protested fiercely.

"Built on deception," Luis accused.

"You can prove this?"

"Ask your daughter," Luis repeated with steely force. Then with a harsh edge of suspicion, he added, "If you don't already know of the lies she spun to engage me with your family."

The Gallardo patriarch flushed in anger. "To what are you referring?"

"Clean your own house, Esteban...as I now clean mine."

Luis inclined his head slightly, a token respect to the old man, then wheeled their small procession towards the other side of the stage where his mother was waiting.

"Foreign trash," Claudia sniped again.

"Hold your tongue, girl, and put your best face forward," Esteban commanded tersely. "You will not shame me in this company."

Luis Angel Martinez was no bunny and would never be taken by any of these people as anything but a man to be reckoned with, Shontelle thought with intense pride. She savagely wished she had given him the chance to stand up for her two years ago. She knew now, beyond a shadow of a doubt, he would have done it, would have challenged his mother then and there and fought to keep what was *precious* to him.

Tears pricked her eyes. She'd been so stupidly gullible. Yet looking at the woman—Luis' formidable mother—who had played her hand with such subtle but devastating force, Shontelle knew she'd had no defences against such cleverly harnessed power. She had needed a champion, such as Luis had shown himself to be tonight.

Stand by me…

Was he drawing strength from her support?

She willed back the moisture threatening to film her eyes. People were watching. Elvira Rosa Martinez was watching. To cover the snub by Luis, she had moved on to the group of people closest to the other side of the stage, smiling, chatting, as though there was nothing amiss—

"The sister of a very enterprising tour operator. An old friend of Luis'," Shontelle imagined her explaining. "They must have been in La Paz, too. They've obviously managed to get out together. Heaven knows how…"

But Elvira needed space to confront the only truth that mattered to her. She excused herself to meet her sons, and there could be no misreading the battle light in her eyes. The queen was not amused at having her act upstaged and sabotaged.

Shontelle braced herself. Elvira would certainly consider her the weak spot, the most vulnerable to attack. It was vitally important to show no weakness whatsoever. Luis was counting on her to play her part through. If this was a courtroom, the jury was all around her, judging her performance. She had to prove worthy of being championed by both the Martinez men.

"Could you not have faced me first, Luis?" she lashed at him in fury.

"You did not face me at all two years ago, Mother," he retorted.

"It was for your own good," she retaliated. "Which, if you had any sense, you would recognise."

"And for my good, you would wed me to a cold, lying bitch! Step aside, Mother."

"No. I will not let you throw all I've worked for away."

"Your needs are not mine. Accept me for the man I am or *you* throw it away. Who else have you got, Mother?"

The challenge could not be borne. She fixed a commanding gaze on her younger son. "Patricio…"

"No." His rejection was sharp and immediate. Then with quiet and resolute force, Patricio stated, "I will not carry the load you demanded of Luis. I am content with what I am."

Thwarted, she raked Shontelle with bitter scorn. "This woman…how can she be worth bringing us down?"

"Down from what?" Luis mocked. "The prison you have made for me out of Eduardo's death?"

She flinched. "How dare you…"

"How dare you abrogate my rights to my own life?" His voice vibrated with outrage.

Elvira's chin lifted in arrogant pride. "She is not even Argentinian."

Foreign trash…

"She is the woman I love, Mother."

Love? Shontelle's heart stopped. Had she heard right? Did Luis mean it or...

"You could try to remember how that feels," he went on with hard, driving passion. "The intense joy of it, Mother. The sheer exhilarating splendour of it. Look into the cold little coffin you call your heart and dredge out what you felt for my father. Or even more, for Eduardo."

"Stop this!" Her face was drained of colour.

"Just once. Do it! I'm your son, too. As is Patricio."

"It's because you are, I've done what I've done to protect you," she argued.

"We are men. We do not need or want your protection."

"Eduardo would not have died..."

"Eduardo is gone. And I shall lead my own life...with or without you. Your choice, Mother."

"Luis, you can't..."

"Watch me! Shontelle?"

The call of her name and the slight tug on her arm jolted Shontelle out of her absorption in the deep conflict between mother and son. She looked up at Luis, unsure what had been said in truth or for telling effect.

"It is your turn now," he said, his eyes burning with a purpose she didn't comprehend.

Did he mean her turn to say something to his mother? Surely he realised it was irrelevant.

"Patricio…" He glanced over her head at his brother. "…The stage is mine."

"We will stand by and watch," he replied. "Won't we, *Madre?*"

Shontelle didn't see or hear a response from Elvira. Luis swept her around his mother, heading for the steps at the side of the stage. "What do you plan to do?" she whispered urgently.

Surely there was nothing left to be achieved. The announcement his mother was to have made had been stopped and rendered impossible. Was Luis going to make some kind of public relations speech to cover the breech?

He bent his head closer to hers. "Shontelle, you are free to choose as you wish." His voice was low, intense, his eyes scouring hers. "Have I done enough?" he muttered, seemingly to himself.

His words made no sense to her. "You've set everything as right as you can," she assured him.

"No. I stripped you down to nothing last night. I know it is something you will never forget. But, Shontelle, I offer you now the chance to do the same to me. You can reject all I am in front of everyone, and I will not blame you for it. It is your just due."

"Luis…" He was frightening her. "I don't want this…this atonement."

"Then accept my gift for the spirit in which it is given."

"What gift?"

"You will see…and I hope…understand."

Already he was drawing her up the steps to the stage. Bewildered and apprehensive, Shontelle could barely respond to the smile he flashed at her as he unhooked their arms and caught her hand. He signalled to the violinists to stop playing, which they very promptly did.

The sudden cessation of music was like a clarion call to the crowd, galvanising attention on the stage which had been vacated by Elvira Rosa Martinez and now starred her son, Luis Angel, and the woman in red.

The general hush was loaded with fascinated anticipation. The Gallardo family had not walked out. Elvira Rosa Martinez stood with her younger son, Patricio, apparently at ease with this curious development. An announcement had been promised. A celebration was supposed to ensue. When Luis took hold of the microphone, one could have heard a pin drop in the ballroom.

Shontelle found herself holding her breath and forced herself to relax. As far as she was concerned, justice had been carried out. Whatever Luis did now was for himself. She had no further axe to grind.

Only his declaration of loving her remained a private torment. She wished it was true. But his reminder of last night's wretched travesty of intimacy…how could that equate with love?

He squeezed her hand, transmitting a bolt of tingling warmth, distracting her from her feverish thoughts.

She looked at him, craving all that his touch had once meant.

As though he'd been waiting for her gaze to lift to his, he smiled at her, a brilliant heart-tugging smile that mesmerised her into smiling back. And for that one incandescent moment, there was no darkness between them. None at all.

Then he turned to face the crowd and began to speak.

''Ladies and gentlemen...''

CHAPTER SIXTEEN

SHONTELLE hoarded that one lovely moment with Luis in her heart as she looked out at the elite gathering in front of them—*the ladies and gentlemen*—Elvira's guests, people who were important to the smooth running of Martinez interests, people of influence, people who mattered if Luis was to hold his stake in the family company. Their faces seemed to run together in a stream of avid curiosity.

She heard Luis take a deep breath before continuing, and tension screamed along her nerves again. Had he listened to her? Enough to put aside whatever plan he had to even the score for treating her badly? She didn't want some public humbling. She'd hate it. Please…let him satisfy these people and be content with his stand for personal integrity, she prayed with desperate fervour.

His deep, resonant voice seemed to boom through the ballroom. "…I am very proud to introduce to you, a woman of great heart and courage, Miss Shontelle Wright…"

Shontelle squirmed inside at the heightened interest he was stirring…spotlighting her. What was the point?

"Her brother, Alan, is a long-time friend of mine,"

Luis went on. "He worked with me at the Martinez mine in Brazil and has since built up a highly successful business, running tours of South America, using Buenos Aires as his base city." He gestured encouragement for approval as he added, "And, co-incidentally, bringing a lot of tourist money into our country."

There was a buzz of appreciation from the spectators. Shontelle relaxed a little. She could see the need to publicly explain her connection to him.

"Last night, Shontelle braved breaking the curfew in La Paz to acquire a bus for Alan's tour group, some of whom were suffering seriously from altitude sickness."

The sympathetic murmurs around the ballroom did not soothe the alarm jabbing through Shontelle's mind. Luis wasn't going to reveal personal details, was he? She darted a sharp glance at him, eloquently appealing for discretion.

He smiled as though sharing something good with her, with everyone. "Today," he said, giving a time-frame which relieved her of her worst fears, "this amazingly resourceful lady saved me from one of the military tanks cruising the streets, just as I was looking straight down its gun barrel. Her beautiful fair hair provided the right distraction."

His blatantly admiring comments evoked a lighter humour in the crowd. There was a ripple of laughter as people visualised the scene he'd drawn for them.

Luis' smile widened to a grin. "I returned the favour later by jumping our bus over a trench which the farmers had dug across the road. It was a rather bumpy ride, but we survived it.''

Outright laughter, this time, and a burst of applause for their daring in getting out of La Paz. Shontelle found herself smiling, glad that Luis was turning what had been a nightmare into a tale to be enjoyed by others. It also neatly covered why they were together tonight, making his partnering her perfectly acceptable in the light of today's events.

The noise died down, the desire to hear more rising uppermost. Again Shontelle glanced at Luis, wondering where he would take them next. His expression had sobered. When he resumed speaking it was in a quieter, more confidential tone.

''I am happy to say there was more than survival involved in our long journey here to be with you tonight.''

He paused, galvanising everyone's attention.

''Two years ago, because of difficult, personal circumstances, Shontelle decided, much against my wishes, that she could not share her life with me.''

Oh, my God! He couldn't…he just couldn't reveal his mother's and Claudia's scheming in public! Shontelle could feel all her insides knotting up.

''Today, when both our lives were in danger, those circumstances no longer held any meaning,'' he went on.

How could he say that? Shontelle thought frantically. Their whole purpose here was to exact justice for those *circumstances!* And they'd done it. So what was he leading to now?

In sheer agitation she scraped her nails against his palm. He threaded his fingers through hers and gripped more tightly. It increased her agitation a hundredfold. She didn't know what he was tying her to.

He turned to look at her and all she could think of was…dark Angel…dark Angel… She sensed him reaching out through some critical mass, unsure of his way but bent on fighting every obstacle and suddenly the words he had spoken this morning burst into her mind—*for you I risk my life*—and she wanted to scream… *No!*…but her throat was too constricted to utter anything.

Then he spoke.

"To all of you I announce…this is the woman I love…and will always love."

The words vibrated through her, creating chaos. Impossible to sort out truth from need—either his or hers. Tears misted her eyes. She couldn't even see him clearly, let alone perceive what he meant by this public announcement.

"Shontelle…" His voice was husky. He poured more strength into it. "…Will you do me the honour of marrying me?"

Understanding came in a burst of anguish… *marriage or nothing.*

This was his offer…in atonement for last night…perhaps even in atonement for never having made their love public when it would have counted.

She wasn't *foreign trash* to him. He had paraded her as his partner into the highest of Martinez circles. Now he was offering her his name in front of these people…if she wanted it. And if she didn't…if she refused it publicly…he was prepared to have his pride sacrificed, just to give her the satisfaction of knowing he had paid her the highest compliment he could pay any woman.

To lay himself on the line like this…risking everything…as she had done last night, though differently, privately…was it an expression of abiding love…or an extreme expression of balancing the scales?

Panic coursed through her. He was waiting for her answer. Everyone was waiting. But the answer wasn't simple. Except…she was utterly incapable of humiliating Luis in front of these people. So there was no choice. And she had to speak.

"I…" Her mouth was hopelessly dry. Perversely, her eyes were awash with tears. She nodded to Luis as she tried to work moisture around her tongue, signalling the consent he had to want, for whatever reason he wanted it. Then in an explosive rush, she said what she had to say. "Yes, I will." Somehow it didn't seem enough, coming belatedly, so she quickly added, "I will marry you, Luis."

The words carried through the microphone for everyone to hear and they seemed to echo and echo, haunting her, until someone started clapping. The sound came from the side of the stage where they'd left Patricio and Elvira. Impossible to know who it was, slapping their palms in approval, but the action caught on and was repeated by others, more and more, building such a momentum, the ballroom seemed to thunder with the noise.

Luis released her hand and curved his arm around her shoulders, hugging her closely to him. Shontelle concentrated fiercely on blinking back tears, pasting a smile on her face. Unbelievably, she was being approved as Luis' wife-to-be and she still had to do him proud, regardless of her own tearing confusion.

"Gracias. Muchas gracias."

Maybe it was a distortion of the microphone but Luis' voice sounded thick with emotion. Shontelle reasoned it was huge relief that his public proposal had produced this result. Even she was stunned by this overwhelming acceptance of his choice. Was he a popular personage in Buenos Aires? Or had his presentation of a crossed love, revived in the face of possible death, struck some deep appeal?

Romance...

A fairy tale...

Cinderella claimed by the prince.

She was getting light-headed again, her mind dizzied by too many whirling thoughts. It was just as well Luis was holding her because her knees were trembling.

"In the hope..." he started again when the prolonged applause died down. "In my quite desperate hope...that Shontelle would agree to sharing her life with me..."

There was so much warm pleasure in his tone, Shontelle couldn't stop her heart from going mushy. If he really meant what he was saying...but what of his promise to have her at the airport tomorrow? How did that gell with this?

"...When we stopped on the road at Villa Tunari, this afternoon, I called ahead to Santa Cruz. As you know, Bolivia produces some of the finest emeralds in the world and there are some very fine jewellers in Santa Cruz. I wanted to present Shontelle with a ring tonight, an emerald to match her eyes."

He had been planning this...all those hours ago? From the moment she had agreed to accompany him to this reception? Shontelle's mind boggled. He'd been so...so businesslike in getting them here.

"So I had a selection brought to the airport..."

The attaché case!

"...And while Shontelle slept on the flight to Buenos Aires, I chose the one I now give her, as a token of my love, my commitment to her, and my belief in our future together."

Luis thrust the microphone into her right hand. In a helpless daze Shontelle watched him take the ring from his coat pocket, pick up her left hand, and slide onto the third finger the most amazing ring she'd ever seen—huge glittering emerald, set amongst an abstract cluster of baguette diamonds—like a perfect green pool surrounded by a pile of irregular rocks.

It won't fit, she thought wildly, but somehow it did, as though her finger had been measured for it. And it looked...totally incredible. She was still staring down at it—a fortune of precious stones displayed on her hand—on her engagement finger!—as Luis took the microphone again.

"I think I have surprised her," he said with such happy humour, people laughed indulgently.

Surprise was not the word for it, Shontelle thought, trying to struggle through a maze of shockingly unanswered questions.

"Since most of you have not yet met my wife-to-be," Luis raved on, "may I inform you Shontelle speaks fluent Spanish, probably knows more about our country than we do, and can dance a superb tango. Which I feel in the mood to demonstrate right now."

He waved to the orchestra to take their places on the stage in readiness, then appealed to the guests who were obviously enjoying his showmanship. "I invite you all to join us on the dance floor in celebration of a night to remember."

So now the tango, Shontelle thought, feeling helplessly entangled by decisions she had no hand in making. As Luis set the microphone back on its stand— the microphone that had made his proposal so terribly public—it struck Shontelle that he'd used it to virtually blackmail her.

Forcing his will?

Was this engagement really, truly what he wanted?

Nothing to do with justice?

Luis turned to her, his face alight with the exhilaration of having carried all before him, his eyes sparkling and his mouth almost dancing with a smile of wicked pleasure. He lifted her newly beringed hand to his lips, gave it a cavalier kiss, then slid his arm around her waist and swept her off the stage and onto the dance floor.

They were still very much on show, the guests

waiting for them to lead off, or watching to see if Shontelle could, indeed, dance a superb tango. Luis certainly exuded confidence as they positioned themselves in front of each other. Shontelle's heart was hammering, confusion still rife in her mind, but pride demanded she perform with all the skill she could muster, which meant she had to get her jelly-like legs in strong, agile order very fast.

It helped when she and Luis lifted their arms and settled into the initial embrace. Somehow his confidence flowed into her and his sheer arrogance in staging all this, sparked a gush of volatile energy. He might be the leader, she the follower in the sophisticated interrelation of steps in this dance, but the urge to challenge him with a few intricate improvisations of her own, tripping up his comfort zone, was very, very tempting.

The orchestra had chosen a 1950's song, setting a distinctive style and mood with its dramatic passion, which suited Shontelle's need for a little individual creativity. Luis had had a fine time manipulating her movements. He deserved to be pushed into meeting her initiatives.

"Just remember this dress doesn't have the mobility of a slit up the side," she warned him.

He laughed, his eyes very hotly wicked. "My control will be masterly."

It was a goad that fired Shontelle's blood. Luis Angel Martinez had taken far too much control upon himself. It was time to show him she had rights, too, including the right not to be boxed into a corner.

"Ready?" he asked with a cock of his eyebrow.

"You had better be...this time," she retorted with a mocking little smile.

He grinned and started them into the traditional *salida,* the basic walking pattern. Shontelle gave him his head for a while, following his perfectly executed figure eights, turns, twists, sweeps, but after he threw in a masterful drag, making himself very much the leader with her trailing in a feet-together slide, she started challenging him with subtle little embellishments to the hooks and kicks, forcing him into very fancy footwalk.

He growled at her, his eyes taking on a very animal gleam as he engineered a *sandwich,* catching her thigh against his, leaning into her, arching her back, his arm circling her so his hand was virtually cupping the underswell of her breast.

"Taking again, Luis?" Shontelle fired, seizing the advantage of close range.

"Giving. Giving with all I've got," he answered, and the raw desire in his eyes had nothing to do with justice.

He really did want her!

Still!

Maybe always?

Excitement sizzled through Shontelle.

The controlled elegance of their tango swiftly acquired a slinky sexuality, a stalking sexuality, and Shontelle deliberately kept it simmering with artfully provocative wiggles and shakes.

No point in pretending she didn't want him. He had a lot of answering to do, but if this night could lead to sharing their lives in an acceptable way, Shontelle was not going to turn her back on the possibility.

Luis swept her into double-time steps, moving into a high lift and a dexterous curl around him, re-establishing his dominance. She countered with a full body downward slide that left her in no doubt of his state of excitement.

They indulged themselves in the dramatic rhythm of the music, communicating heat that became so steamy, Shontelle felt herself in danger of melting on the floor. Only the wild exultation of more than matching Luis kept her feet twinkling, her body sensuously supple, and her head proudly held.

They were breathing hard when the music ended, her breasts heaving against his chest, their lower bodies entwined in the traditional aggressive/resistant pose, her arms held back, hair still swinging, and Luis' face hovering over hers.

But this wasn't the end, Shontelle thought in wild elation. Not in Luis' eyes. And the hopes that had seemed so foolish, danced their own irrepressible tango through her heart.

CHAPTER SEVENTEEN

HAD he done enough?

The question gnawed at Luis' mind as he watched Shontelle dancing with Patricio—a waltz, not the tango. No way would he allow any other man to dance the tango with her. A waltz was bearable…just. He itched to have her in his arms—only his—though he knew it was appropriate she dance with his brother; obvious evidence of family support, reinforcement of approval.

His plan had worked…so far. Shontelle was still carrying through the role he'd thrust upon her, but what she was feeling…what she was thinking…he couldn't even begin to be sure of that until this reception was behind them. The words she'd spoken during the tango kept haunting him—*Taking again, Luis?* Could his giving tonight make up for the way he'd treated her in La Paz? Was it enough?

He had done all he could here, Luis decided. His need to have Shontelle to himself could no longer be suppressed. He had to know if she'd been co-operating with everything for his sake—saving him from social disaster—or giving him the chance to show he meant what he said. If it was the latter case, there was hope.

A check of his watch showed it was close to three o'clock, not too early to leave.

"Impatient, Luis?" one of his friends asked, a knowing grin on his face.

"Who could blame him?" another remarked. "Such a woman would heat any man's veins. She is magnificent, Luis."

"She is, indeed," he agreed, smiling to cover his gut-twisting need to keep her in his life.

He signalled to one of the household staff and requested a message be immediately taken to Carlos— their car and driver to be summoned and waiting at the door for them.

Most of the guests looked set to party on and might well remain until dawn, but Luis had no doubt that indulgent understanding for his and Shontelle's early departure would be readily given. After all, it had been a long and highly eventful day and they had clearly won the popular vote tonight. Benevolence was still running strongly.

The Gallardo family had effected a tactful exit during the past hour, Esteban undoubtedly exercising his patriarchal authority to ensure there was no open rift between the families. If there was any accounting to be done, it would be done in boardrooms, not here. Saving face was just as important as holding profitable business connections. Luis had banked on that. Esteban Gallardo was a very pragmatic man.

Shontelle could no longer harbour any fear of being ostracised or snubbed by Argentinian society. On the contrary, over the past few hours, she had been show-ered with admiration and genuine good wishes. At least this much had been achieved, Luis thought with satisfaction.

The public response to *his* announcement had been all he could have wished. Not that it had been criti-cally important, but it was helpful—one less issue to argue, once he and Shontelle were alone. *If* they got as far as argument.

Her acceptance of his proposal had been so long in coming, he certainly couldn't count on its lasting be-yond the doors of this house. She'd promised support and she'd given it, right down the line. Though he'd felt there'd been more than support in the fire of her tango dancing. Surely she couldn't have been quite so excitingly sensual if she felt no desire for him. Unless it had been an angry tease.

Yet if she was nursing anger, there'd been no hint of it since then. She'd been warmly gracious through all the introductions, her apparent ease in bantering with him, smiling, laughing, giving him every en-couragement to believe their partnership was real. Or was she simply acting out what she thought he ex-pected of her?

It was possible her manner stemmed from a need to prove herself a match for him, whether she saw any future in it or not, but Luis fervently hoped it was motivated by more than personal pride.

The waltz ended.

Luis moved aside from his friends, compelled by

the urge to gather Shontelle to himself as soon as Patricio escorted her from the dance floor. *Magnificent* was an apt description, he thought, watching her walk towards him, the red and silver dress enhancing her glorious femininity, her hair flowing like a river of light, her face alive with vibrant personality. Everything she was called to him...body and soul, and the primitive caveman inside him was severely testing his control.

I have to win...

The thought—the need—burned through his mind, through his entire body. He held out his hand to her. Without hesitation she placed hers in it, though she bestowed her smile on his brother, making Luis' stomach clench with uncertainty.

"*Gracias,* Patricio," she said huskily.

"We'll leave now," Luis announced, the inner caveman insisting on it. He couldn't share any part of her with anyone anymore, not even his brother. "I appreciate your support, Patricio," he forced himself to add, sincerely grateful for his brother's stalwart defence of both their positions.

Patricio's eyes twinkled with understanding. "I could do with more warning next time you're intent on bearding lions, Luis. Though I must concede you do it with style." He lifted Shontelle's left hand, which he'd retained while they spoke, and bowed over it with excessive gallantry. "Forgive my trepidations, Shontelle. I am truly delighted to welcome you into the family. You do my brother proud."

"It's kind of you to say so," she replied, leaving Luis acutely aware there was no commitment in those words.

Having finally released Shontelle, Patricio gave Luis an earnest look. "Don't go without speaking to our mother. It was she who began the applause after Shontelle accepted your proposal of marriage."

It surprised him. "I thought it was you."

"I very quickly joined in but she led."

"Face saving," Luis interpreted sardonically.

Patricio shrugged. "A public step into your camp. It could mean more than you think."

"We shall see," Luis said noncommittally. "Goodnight, Patricio."

"Buenos noches."

Luis waved to the friends he'd been waiting with while Shontelle danced, then drew her down the ballroom towards the exit to the gallery, mentally crossing off another confrontation with his mother. Why risk her saying something unpalatable to Shontelle? He needed every advantage on his side.

"I take it *court is adjourned,*" Shontelle remarked dryly.

His heart contracted. Had it all been an act on her part? "I hope you feel justice has been done," he answered, willing her to look directly at him.

She flicked him a derisive glance. "It could have been a bit tricky there, if you'd produced a yellow diamond."

Tricky…yes, she could certainly accuse him of that.

Though, to him it had been a gamble, pure and simple. The biggest gamble of his life. And still he didn't know if the outcome was positive.

"Was an emerald the right choice for you?" he asked, almost begging for a hint.

Her mouth curved as she lifted her left hand and gazed down at the ring he'd put on her finger. "It's a very extravagant gesture, Luis," she said with a wry twist. "And it certainly served to persuade everyone you meant what you said."

She didn't believe him.

Shock rattled his confidence. What more could he do or say? Had his plan been futile from the start? *¡Dios!* He ached for her. He could not let her go. Frantically he counted the hours before he had to take her to the airport. Thirteen. Another two before the flight boarded. He had to make every minute work for him.

"I do mean it, Shontelle," he stated quietly. "I thought it was the only way to prove you could trust my word. In the circumstances…it seemed to me that actions would be more convincing than speech."

He felt the fingers that had been resting lightly within his grasp, curl into her palm with knuckle-tight intensity. Her left hand dropped to her side. Her head lowered. Shutting herself off from him, Luis thought, and frenziedly searched for some opening which might turn her towards him.

His mother intercepted their path to the gallery.

He silently cursed her interference. If she'd kept out of their lives two years ago...

"Luis, Shontelle...are you leaving?"

"I trust you're not going to stand in our way," he answered tersely, in no mood for political appeasement.

Her eyes looked sick, her face strained, yet neither sign of stress touched him. The damage she'd done went too deep. She touched his arm, a tentative reaching out which was uncharacteristic of her. Still he could not respond to the gesture. Two years...two years of being twisted around at her behest, and if he lost Shontelle now...

"I'm sorry. I was wrong," she acknowledged, her gaze sliding to Shontelle in bleak appeal, finding no softening in his for the admission that had been wrung out of her. "Shontelle, I beg you...don't take Luis from me."

Shades of Eduardo... Luis gritted his teeth against a savage wave of resentment. Couldn't his mother comprehend his need to be free of that blight on her life?

"I would never have done that, Señora Martinez. Nor will I now," Shontelle answered gently.

No, she would just walk away and leave him, as she had before, Luis thought bitterly.

"You...shame me."

Such humbling made him restive. He stared at his mother, unsure if this was some ploy to regain favour or a genuine expression of regret. Her face looked older, seamed with lines he hadn't noticed before—tired, sagging lines. It struck him forcefully that the indomitable arrogance was gone.

"I hope you can find it in your heart to forgive me…in time," she said haltingly, as though treading an unfamiliar path where the end could not be seen.

"Patricio said you started the clapping after I accepted Luis' proposal," Shontelle said with a slightly quizzical air.

Ascertaining the truth? Luis wondered. Why would it matter, if she didn't care?

"It was…something I could do," came the rueful reply. "I didn't know…no, I didn't allow myself to think…that Luis would…or could…love you so much." She looked back at him, openly pleading his forgiveness. "Please believe now…I wish you both…every happiness."

Virtually against his will, Luis found himself moved. Maybe an understanding could be reached with his mother if she was finally comprehending he was not her tool.

"Thank you," Shontelle murmured.

Polite to the end?

Luis tried to shake off the doubts plaguing him. "We'll talk…another time," he promised brusquely. "If you'll excuse us now?"

Elvira Rosa Martinez re-emerged. She nodded graciously and moved aside.

"Call Patricio to her, Luis," Shontelle whispered.

He frowned at her, hope warring with disbelief. Her

beautiful green eyes were filled with caring—sympathy, the wish to make things better. It stunned him.

"Now. Before we leave. Please?" she urged.

He looked back to where they'd left Patricio and found him watching them. Luis nodded towards his mother. It was enough. His brother raised a hand in a salute of understanding and started walking.

He met the query in Shontelle's eyes with a crooked little smile. "Done," he assured her.

His smile was returned. "She *is* your mother."

"And you? Are you my fiancée, Shontelle?"

Her lashes fluttered down. The slight curve of her lips disappeared as she sighed.

Luis held his breath.

"Let's get out of here, Luis."

It wasn't a no!

"I've already ordered the car. It should be waiting at the door."

She slid him an ironic look. "So efficient."

He laughed out of sheer relief that she hadn't handed him an outright rejection. Then he tucked her arm around his and swept her out of the ballroom, a full complement of newly vitalised energy coursing through him.

The reception had served its purpose.

Shontelle *wanted* to be alone with him.

He had thirteen hours to win her over.

CHAPTER EIGHTEEN

FIVE more minutes, Luis told himself as he settled into the car beside Shontelle. The desire to reach out and haul her onto his lap and hug her tightly to him, washing away whatever doubts she had with a passionate rain of kisses, was pumping through him. But *taking* might not be a good idea, particularly not in the car. The chauffeur would get them to his apartment soon enough. Then he wouldn't have to stop. Unless Shontelle…

He took a deep breath and looked at her, craving some sign that she felt the same urgent desire for him. Her gaze was turned back at the house, remaining fixed on it even as the chauffeur drove towards the exit gates. Worried that the whole wretched Martinez heritage it represented might still be a barrier between them, and determined on smashing all barriers, Luis seized Shontelle's hand to draw her attention to him.

Her head snapped around, her eyes meeting his, but with a faraway look in them that screwed up his gut again. His fingers dragged over her palm, the need to get under her skin burning through him. Her expression changed, inviting him into the rueful reflection in her mind.

''We've never had a tragedy in our family, Luis.

I'm sorry I didn't understand…didn't appreciate the toll it can take.'' She squeezed his hand. ''However hard it was, I'm glad it was faced tonight. I think it was good for all of you. And for me. It showed me things aren't always what they seem on the surface.''

Relief surged through him. There was nothing negative in that little speech. ''What things?'' he prompted.

She shrugged. ''I put your mother's rejection of me down to snobbery and I didn't think that would change. But it wasn't snobbery. It went much deeper…''

''It had to do with power, Shontelle,'' he supplied.

She nodded. ''Yes, I see that now.'' Her eyes searched his in anxious concern. ''Will there be a backlash from the Gallardo family?''

''I doubt it. In any case, there's little they can do to really hurt the Martinez company. It's not vulnerable to attack. There could be deals that won't now be made, but overall, it's not a make or break situation.''

With a satisfied sigh, she looked down at her lap where her left hand rested. Even in the dimness of the car the emerald and diamond ring glittered as she stretched out her fingers, apparently studying his gift to her.

Once again Luis was racked with uncertainty. Had he chosen wrongly? Was she preparing to take it off and return it to him?

''I thought…last night…it was all gone…what

there'd been between us,'' she said quietly, still gazing down at the ring as though unsure whether to believe what it stood for.

He winced, fiercely wishing he could turn back the clock and do it all differently. She might have told him the truth last night if he'd given her any leeway, shown her…what? His love for her had been buried under so much bitter fury and frustration, there was no way it could have been expressed. So why should she believe him now?

Despairingly he sought for an answer she might accept. His mind was a blank. The urge to just pull her into his arms was barely containable. Words were no good. He had to show her…make her feel all the positive flow inside him. Not like last night. Completely different.

''You'd better tell me,'' she went on, catching back his attention, pausing the wild train of thought. ''Was tonight…'' She hesitated. The corner of her mouth turned down into a grimace. ''Well, it served many purposes, didn't it?''

''No.'' The word burst from him with passionate vehemence, the built-up tension reaching breaking point. ''¡Dios! Look at me!''

She did, her eyes wide and questing and seemingly reflecting his own desperate need.

''I hated you last night, Shontelle. I hated you because for two damnably empty years I'd wanted and needed and craved the love I'd felt we'd shared. Then when I realised today we *did* share it…'' That dreadful moment of revelation rushed back on him, choking him momentarily. He swallowed hard and pushed out the truth. The only truth that counted. "I'd do anything to have it again. *Anything!* Do you understand?"

The car stopped.

Luis couldn't bear to wait another second. Shontelle was just staring at him in a kind of awed daze. He was out of the car and around it to her side before the chauffeur had alighted. He easily beat the man to opening Shontelle's door. Without a pause, he scooped her off the seat and swung her up against his chest, one arm under her knees, the other cradling her close, the caveman inside him rampaging straight through any other considerations…his woman, *his!*

"Don't say no!" he heard himself wildly muttering as he carried her to the door of his apartment.

Her warm breath fanned his ear as she wound her arms around his neck. "Can I touch you tonight?" she asked huskily.

"Yes," he hissed. "Touch me all you like. Anywhere. Everywhere."

"No holds barred?"

Was that a teasing note in her voice? He wasn't sure. Didn't care. "None. None at all," he repeated gruffly. "Hang on to me. I've got to get the door key."

He felt like kicking the door in but some grain of sanity told him it was too solid. Shontelle didn't seem to mind him hoisting her over his shoulder as he fumbled in his pocket. She started to laugh. Laughter was good, wasn't it? His heart was thumping so hard he could hardly put two thoughts together.

He jammed the key in the door and one more barrier gave way. They were inside. A satisfying kick closed out the rest of the world.

"Put me down, Luis," Shontelle said in a breathless gurgle.

"Soon." He charged for the bedroom.

"Not on the bed," she managed more emphatically.

"Not?" It seemed a very good place to him.

"On my feet. Now!" she commanded, wriggling to break his hold.

It was against every raging instinct, but…somehow he managed enough control to pull himself back from falling onto the bed with her. He set her on her feet, though it was quite impossible to pluck his hands away from her waist. A hold was a hold and releasing her altogether was unthinkable.

"I don't want you to tear my dress," she said.

"I'll get you another."

"No, this one is special. Put the light on, Luis."

"Light," he echoed, telling himself "special" was good. It was okay to let go. For a few seconds. He did it to switch on the light.

She was grinning at him, her beautiful green eyes sparkling, dancing, teasing with wicked delight. "It's my turn to undress you," she said pointedly. "All touching permitted."

And the driving urgency inside him shattered into a brilliant burst of happiness. It was all right. Just like it used to be between them. The freedom of it bubbled through him…glorious, exhilarating, exultant freedom.

"Yes," he said, and he knew her grin was on his face…exactly the same…sharing…no barriers, no inhibitions, nothing coming between them except clothes. "How about one each? My tie, your necklace, my coat, your dress…" He cocked an eyebrow at her. "It'll go much faster."

She laughed and started undoing his bow tie, her eyes flirting deliciously with his. "I don't want it to go fast, Luis. I want to revel in every moment."

And suddenly, so did he, though there was one thing he needed to hear. "You do still love me." It came out more a statement than a question because he just couldn't accept a question, not with her hands on him, the look in her eyes, the pleasure humming through him.

She sighed. "Looks like I'm stuck on you, for better or for worse. Which reminds me, naked is fine, but if you think you're going to get this ring off me…"

"I want you to say it, Shontelle," he cut in, the yearning to hear the words too needy for playfulness.

She slid his tie out from his collar, linked her hands around his neck and raised her lashes, revealing the windows to her soul. "I love you, Luis Angel

Martinez. There never has been anyone else for me. And never will be.''

She carried that promise on her lips to his and Luis' heart seemed to pump liquid fire through him as they kissed, and kissed, and kissed, hungry for the giving of each other, the knowing, the certainty, the lifting of every last shadow on a love that should never have been shadowed.

He was so beautiful…so intoxicatingly beautiful… the feel of him, the smell of him, the sight of him…Shontelle felt as though her whole body was effervescing with happiness, her skin tingling like champagne.

Her man…her mate in every sense there was… and when they did move to the bed, it was to-gether…together in all the ways she had craved last night, the giving and taking so excitingly, blissfully mutual, the sheer ecstacy of loving and feeling herself loved, the intense pleasure of touching, not just phys-ically, but knowing how deeply it went, the wonder-ful, awesome flow of becoming one again, one in heart and mind and soul.

It was so incredibly special…this filling of all the empty spaces that had blighted two years of their lives…the unanswered needs and desires and hopes and dreams. It was as though everything they'd felt for each other had been waiting, trapped in a time-warp, and the release of it was heaven.

And when he entered her, slowly, both of them

treasuring the magical sensation of ultimate intimacy, his face hovering above hers, their eyes mirroring the rapture they shared...that was heaven, too, and she heard it in his voice as he murmured, "Shontelle..." and tasted it in his mouth as he kissed her, making the melding complete, and in her mind beat the one beautiful word... Angel...Angel...Angel.

It was goodness and light and joy and it moved into a rhythm that celebrated the life they would have together. She wrapped her legs around him in exultant possession and lifted herself to him, urging the feast of sharing that would always be theirs...the feast of love...free to soar into any future they decided upon, because the form didn't matter. This was the substance of it, the essence of it, the fusion of their lives.

Then there was no thought...only feeling... powerful waves of feeling, obliterating everything but the sense of their oneness, peaking into a sublime climax, a pulsing flow that lingered on and on, permeating their embrace as they lay together in the harmony of utter fulfilment.

"Thank you," Luis whispered, his voice furred with deep emotion. "Thank you for being you and loving me."

"It was meant to be," she murmured, feeling that as a deep, unalterable truth. "I felt only half alive without you, Luis."

"And I without you." He raised himself up on his elbow to look into her eyes. His were dark velvet, glowing with lovely soft warmth. "Where would you like our future to be, Shontelle? If you want me to move to Australia…''

''No!'' She was shocked he would even think of it. ''Your life is here, Luis. I'm happy to be here with you.'' Besides, she had more or less promised his mother she wouldn't take Luis away. She couldn't compound the tragedy of Eduardo's loss by removing Luis from all Elvira held dear.

''Away from your family?'' he softly reminded her.

Shontelle hesitated a moment, knowing she would miss them, wishing they were not so far away. But by air it was only a day's travel. ''We could visit them, couldn't we?'' she appealed hopefully.

He smiled. ''As often as you like, my love. And, of course, I shall fly to Australia to meet your parents and discuss our marriage plans with them.''

''Okay, master planner,'' she happily teased. ''What is your schedule for that?''

He grinned. ''Well, since I have to put you on the plane with Alan all too soon…''

He intended to keep his promise, which was only right, but it gave them such little time together just now when…

''…I thought I could follow next week.''

Relief and pleasure instantly swamped the little jab of disappointment.

''Which gives you time to prepare your family,'' he went on purposefully, ''and me time to deal with mine.''

"I thought your mother was…well, accepting tonight," she reminded him.

He nodded. "I just want to make sure everything's ironed out before you come back with me."

She smiled, joy bubbling through her. "So you're flying out to Australia to fetch me, are you?"

His eyes sparkled. "One week alone I can manage. But only with the promise I don't have to spend any more of my life without being able to reaffirm this."

He kissed her, long and lovingly.

"I promise," she murmured, moving against him with languorous sensuality, happy to have absolutely everything reaffirmed as much and as often as Luis liked.

Which was how they spent the hours leading up to their departure for the airport, hours well used, deliciously used, and when they joined up with the tour group at the terminal, the glow of their love for each other was like a neon light to Alan and everyone else.

No one asked Shontelle to do anything. She and Luis were left alone to talk the talk of lovers soon to be separated, but knowing it wouldn't be for long. The promise was real, as real as the emerald and diamond ring on her finger, and every bit as lasting as all the precious stones in the world.

"One week," Luis said with passionate longing when he finally had to let her go to board the plane.

"I'll be waiting at Sydney airport for you," Shontelle promised.

"I'll call you every day," he vowed.

"Yes, yes."

She had to go. One quick last kiss and she ran to catch the others, her feet yearning to dance a wild and wonderful tango because she was coming back to Luis, coming back to Argentina, coming back to the love of a lifetime.

Nothing was banished forever.

Marriage was the final act.

CHAPTER NINETEEN

"I NOW declare you man and wife."

At last, Luis thought, a sense of triumph soaring through him. The commitment of marriage was sealed. Three months he'd waited for this, three months of wanting it every day, craving the security of knowing with absolute certainty that nothing could stop it. Now he could breathe easily. He and Shontelle were publicly, legally wed. Their future together was assured.

Brimming with elation, he turned to lift the veil from his bride's face. Shontelle's beautiful green eyes were shiny with tears, just as they'd been when he'd asked her to marry him in front of the very same people who now filled the church. But there was no doubting the emotion behind these tears.

Love...love and joy and sparkles of sheer blinding happiness.

"You may kiss the bride."

He took her in his arms. Heart of my heart, he thought, and kissed her, feeling a glorious sense of completion. Husband and wife—one in name—one in everything—and they would cherish each other for the rest of their lives, cherish all they were to each other.

"I love you, Shontelle," he whispered as he lifted his mouth from hers.

"I love you, Luis Angel Martinez," she answered with a wealth of feeling, rolling his name off her tongue as though it was the most magical name in the world.

"Well, *Señora* Martinez," he rolled back at her, grinning from ear to ear. "Ready to face the world as my wife?"

"Anytime," she declared, sharing his grin.

Anytime… It was music to his ears. Shontelle at his side, standing by him, right down the line. Faith, trust, love, loyalty, boundless support…he had no doubt she would give them unstintingly, just as he would to her. All that was needed was to be honest with each other and that lesson had been learnt. Too painfully to recollect it now. Today there was no pain and he fiercely hoped it was forever in the past.

This was the real beginning of their lives together.

As they turned for the walk down the aisle, he tucked her arm around his, feeling a huge surge of love and pride. Patricio and Alan ranged up beside him. Alan's wife, Vicki, and his own young cousin, Maria, fussed over the train of Shontelle's beautiful bridal gown.

His mother rose to her feet from the front pew, looking very much the impressive figure she'd always been. Luis still found it difficult to forgive the two years she'd taken from him and Shontelle.

You see? he beamed at her with all the positive

energy pulsing through his mind. This is right. This is good. This is how it should be between a man and his woman.

She smiled and nodded, accepting his choice, and the scarring on his soul faded under a flow of contentment. He knew there would still be skirmishes over her way and his, but the war had been won. Elvira Rosa Martinez had conceded there was a power beyond her grasp. Wealth and influence could not buy love. He hoped she kept remembering that truth.

But it was irrelevant right now.

He and Shontelle were married.

Irrevocably married.

If problems arose they'd work them out. If they had differences of opinion, they'd talk them through. Nothing was ever going to tear them apart again.

His gaze was drawn to her parents rising from their pew, their blessing having been given to this marriage without any reservation at all. Their daughter loved him. And he silently vowed to them he'd return her love a hundredfold.

The organ began to play, filling the church with its rich, resonant sound. Luis hugged Shontelle's arm closer to him and of one accord they stepped forward, heading down the aisle to the exultant lilt of the last piece of ceremonial music, heading towards the life they would forge together.

A shining future, Luis thought, watching Shontelle bestowing a brilliant smile on all the guests they passed. She dazzled them, just as she dazzled him…always had, always would.

With her there was no darkness.

She was the sun and the moon and the stars.

Shontelle…his wife.

He'd won.

They were married.

Luis Angel Martinez smiled, too.

THE SPANISH GROOM

LYNNE GRAHAM

CHAPTER ONE

CÉSAR replaced the phone, his lean, strong face taut, wide, sensual mouth compressed. So Jasper's health was failing. Since his godfather was eighty-two, the news should not have come as a shock...

Rising restively from behind his desk, César crossed his spacious office—a contemporary triumph of glass and steel, wholly in keeping with a minimalist building much mentioned in architectural digests. Formed round a series of stylish atriums embellished with lush greenery and tranquil fountains, the office block César had commissioned to house the London headquarters of the Valverde Mercantile Bank was as elegant and impressive as its owner.

But César was indifferent to his surroundings. His thoughts were on Jasper Dysart, who had become his guardian when he was twelve. He was a true English eccentric, a bachelor bookworm who had made rare butterflies his lifestudy, and the kindest old man imaginable. César and Jasper were mental poles apart. Indeed César and Jasper might as well have come from different planets, but César was fond of Jasper, and suddenly grimly aware that the only thing Jasper had ever wanted him to do remained undone and time now seemed to be running out...

A knock on the door heralded the entrance of his executive assistant, Bruce Gregory. Normally the very epitome of confident efficiency, for some reason Bruce chose to hover, a sheet of paper rather tensely clutched between his fingers.

'Yes?' César prompted impatiently.

The young blond man cleared his throat. 'The random security check has turned up a member of staff with financial problems.'

'You know the rules. Getting into debt is grounds for instant dismissal.' César frowned at the need to make this reminder when that warning appeared in all staff employment contracts. 'We deal with too much confidential information to take the risk.'

Bruce grimaced. 'This…er…person is a very minor cog in the bank, César.'

'I still don't see a problem.' The brilliant dark eyes were cool, unemotional, the hallmark of a hugely successful financial genius with neither time nor sympathy for those who broke the rules. César was contemptuous of weakness, and ruthless at exploiting it in business opponents.

'Actually…it's Dixie.'

César stilled. Bruce studied the wall, not wanting to see César smile at that information. Everybody know how César felt about Dixie Robinson, currently the equivalent of an office junior on the top floor. Dixie, quite simply, irritated the hell out of César.

She had not one single trait which *didn't* grate on her cool, sophisticated employer. In recent weeks, César had been heard to censure her sloppy appearance, her clumsiness, her friendly chatter, her constant collecting for obscure charities…and, it had to be admitted, a degree of incompetence at business skills that had raised her to the level of an office mascot. César, alone, was deflatingly untouched by the compensatingly warm and caring personality which made Dixie so universally well liked.

But then on a level playing field, Dixie Robinson would never have got as far as an interview at the Valverde Mercantile Bank: she had no qualifications. Jasper Dysart had *asked* César to give her a job. Personnel had jumped to the task, only to find themselves seriously challenged by Dixie's inability to cope with technology. Passed on from one department to another, Jasper's protegée had finally arrived on the top floor, a fact which had delighted her elderly sponsor but which had unfortunately brought Dixie into César's immediate radius.

César extended a hand for the computer printout. Bruce passed it over with perceptible reluctance.

Scanning down the sheet, César slowly elevated a winged ebony brow. Evidently Dixie Robinson led a double life. The list of her dissatisfied creditors included a well-known interior designer and the kind of bills that indicated some serious alcoholic partying. César was tickled pink, his even white teeth flashing in a derisive grin of satisfaction.

So her resolutely innocent front *was* a façade, just as he had always suspected it was. For a split second he thought how appalled Jasper would be—Jasper who broke out with a modest sherry only at Christmas and who fondly believed that Dixie Robinson was a thoroughly decent, old-fashioned girl with homely tastes.

'Obviously she's been really stupid. But if she's sacked, she'll sink like a stone,' Bruce pointed out gruffly. 'She doesn't handle anything confidential, César—'

'She has access.'

'I don't really think she's bright enough to use that kind of information,' Bruce breathed tautly.

César gave him a look of grim amusement. 'Got you fooled as well, has she?'

'Fooled?' Bruce's brow furrowed.

'Now I know why she always looks half asleep—too many late nights.'

In desperation, Bruce shot his last bolt in Dizzy's defence. 'I guess Mr Dysart will be upset not to find her here on his next visit.'

'Jasper's not well. It's unlikely that he'll be in London in the near future.'

'I'm sorry to hear that.' Bruce studied his employer's coolly uninformative face warily. Well, that was that, he acknowledged. He couldn't say he was surprised either. César was not a soft touch. And proof of such foolish extravagance had merely increased his contempt. 'I'll pass the information concerning Dixie on to Personnel.'

'No. I'll deal with this personally,' César contradicted without warning.

Bruce wasn't quite fast enough to hide his dismay.

'I'll see Miss Robinson at four,' César completed.

'She'll be very upset, César.'

'I think I can handle it,' César drawled, in the sort of tone that made the younger man flush and go into retreat.

Alone again, César studied that list of creditors, a smouldering look awakening in his narrowed gaze. Jasper was very fond of little Dixie Robinson. In fact, superficially Dixie was exactly the kind of young woman Jasper longed to have César produce as the future Mrs Valverde, the sort of girl who didn't intimidate an innocent old bachelor totally out of step with a world approaching the Millenium.

So there it was, out in the open. The admission that he *had* disappointed his godfather, César conceded with exasperated reluctance. Jasper's deepest and most naive hope had always been that César would marry, settle down and have a family. And live happily ever after, of course, César affixed, scornfully recalling his late parents. His volatile Italian mother and equally volatile Spanish father had between them stacked up half a dozen failed marriages before dying young and anything but happy.

Wincing at the very idea of marital togetherness with any woman, but with his conscience still causing him rare discomfiture, César brooded on the problem of Jasper's disappointment. Experience had taught César that there was no such thing as a problem without a solution. When shorn of the inhibiting factors of emotion and morality, the impossible could almost always become the possible…

No doubt Jasper fondly imagined that his veiled hints about what a wonderful wife Dixie Robinson would make some fortunate male had been too subtle to be recognised for what they were. In point of fact, Jasper had the subtlety of a sledgehammer, and when César had first picked up on his godfather's pointed comments on the subject of his protegée he had been anything but amused.

But now César grimly acknowledged that were he to announce that he *had* got engaged to Dixie Robinson, Jasper would be overjoyed. César visualised Dixie with something less than joy, but Jasper thought the sun rose and set on her. And, as pleasing Jasper was César's only goal, there would be little point in persuading any other woman into playing his temporary fiancée. What Jasper wanted, César decided there and then, Jasper deserved to receive.

As he pictured how he might sensibly stress the need for a lengthy engagement between two such disparate personalities as himself and the office klutz, César began warming to the exercise. It would make Jasper happy. And Jasper, who could spend hours just choosing a single book, would scarcely expect his godson to leap straight from an engagement into matrimony.

And Dixie Robinson? Dixie was between a rock and a hard place. She would do as she was told. Around him, she was quiet and cowed, which was just as well because César was convinced he would strangle her if she behaved any other way. He would slim her down, smarten her up, do whatever it took to ensure that the fake engagement appeared credible. He would be nothing less than thorough…

'At f-four?' Dixie stammered, pale as milk as she stood over the photocopier, striving somewhat hopelessly to conceal the 'inoperative' sign flashing above a pile of discarded photocopies printed with impossibly tiny type. 'But why would Mr Valverde want to see me?'

Already conscious that his attempt to speak up on her behalf had taxed César's patience, Bruce did not dare utter a word of warning.

'Is it about that Arab guy whose call I cut off?'

Bruce tensed. 'He doesn't know about that.'

'That file I accidentally took out?'

Bruce paled at the reminder. 'You got it back from the bus company.'

Dixie gulped. 'I've been trying so hard to stay out of Mr Valverde's way…it's just he keeps on popping up in the most unexpected places.'

'César likes to be visible. What sort of unexpected places?' Bruce could not resist asking.

'Like the kitchen…when I was icing the cake for Jayne's leaving party last week. Mr Valverde went through the roof,'

Dixie recounted, half under her breath, shuddering at the recollection. 'He asked me if I thought I was working in a bakery and I ended up spelling her name wrong. Then yesterday he walked into that little room the cleaning staff use and found me asleep…he gave me the biggest fright of my life!'

'César expects all his employees to make a special effort to stay awake between nine and five,' Bruce responded, deadpan.

Currently working two jobs just to keep a roof over her head, Dixie gave him an abstracted look, her eyes, so dark a blue they were violet, strained with anxiety and tiredness. Fear emanated from her in waves. Small though she was, she seemed to grow even smaller as she hunched her shoulders and bowed her head, the explosive mop of her long curly dark brown hair falling over her softly rounded face. She was terrified of César Valverde, had become acquainted with every hiding place on the executive floor within days of arriving there.

But then she had started out on the wrong foot, hadn't she? Her big mouth, she conceded glumly. While covering for the receptionist during her afternoon break, Dixie had begun chatting to the gorgeous blonde seated in the waiting area. In an effort to make entertaining conversation, she had mentioned the world-famous model, Mr Valverde had entertained on his yacht the previous weekend. And then her employer had strolled out of the lift…

And without the slightest warning all hell had broken loose! The blonde, who it later transpired had actually been waiting for César Valverde, had risen to her feet to throw a jealous fit of outrage and accuse him of being a 'love-rat'.

Dixie's co-workers had very decently acknowledged that that charge might well have some basis in fact, but it was not an allegation César had expected to face within the hallowed portals of the bank because one of his own staff had been recklessly indiscreet. Indeed what César had had to say about Dixie's gossiping tongue had been, as one of the directors had frankly admitted while trying hard not to smile, unrepeatable. Since then she had been banned from manning Reception.

'Is César dating any nice girls at present?' Jasper always asked hopefully in his letters to Dixie, not seeming to appreciate that at the threat of what his godfather deemed a 'nice girl' César Valverde would undoubtedly run a mile. It was a well-worn joke in the bank that César's answer to commitment was escape.

But Dixie's troubled face softened at the thought of Jasper Dysart. He was a dear old man, but she hadn't seen him in months because he lived in Spain most of the year, having found the hot climate eased his arthritic joints.

Dixie had met Jasper the previous summer. She had been walking down the street when a thuggish bunch of youths had carelessly pushed him aside when he didn't get out of their way fast enough. Jasper had fallen and cut his head. Dixie had taken him to the nearest hospital. Afterwards, she had treated him to tea and buns in the cafeteria, because he had looked so poor and forlorn in his ancient tweeds and shabby old overcoat.

They had been firm friends from that moment on. She hadn't once suspected that Jasper might be anything other than he appeared: an elderly academic living on a restricted income. So she had been quite honest about being unemployed, sharing her despair at not even being able to get as far as an interview for a clerical job. She had also told him how horribly guilty she felt about being dependent on her older sister Petra's generosity.

They had arranged to meet up again, and Jasper had escorted Dixie to his favourite secondhand bookshop, where they had both promptly lost all track of time browsing through the shelves. The following weekend she had returned the favour by taking him to a library sale, where he had contrived to buy a very tattered copy of an out-of-print tome on butterflies that he had been trying to find for years.

And then quite casually Jasper had announced that he had fixed her up with an interview at the Valverde Mercantile

Bank. 'I put in a word for you with my godson,' he had informed her cheerfully. 'He was very happy to help.'

She hadn't had a clue that Jasper's godson was the chief executive. And she had been utterly appalled to be confronted by César Valverde that first day, and coldly interrogated about exactly how she had met his godfather. He had made little attempt to conceal his suspicions about her motives in fostering such a friendship with an elderly man, and had coolly enjoyed informing her that Jasper would be returning to his home in Spain at the end of September. Dixie had found that encounter deeply humiliating.

'César always had a head for figures…very clever chap with that sort of stuff,' Jasper had conceded vaguely when Dixie had later gently taxed him with his failure to tell her that his godson *ran* Valverde Mercantile and was, in fact, a super-rich and very powerful legend of thrusting success in the financial world. 'It's in his blood.'

Jasper was a genius at understatement. The Valverdes had been in banking for generations. César was the last of the dynasty, and reputedly the most brilliant. He also had very high expectations of his staff. All Dixie's colleagues had a university degree in financial management, economics or languages, and thrived on the cracking pace of a high-powered mercantile bank with an international list of hugely important clients and companies.

Dixie knew that she was a fish out of water at Valverde Mercantile, only fit, it sometimes seemed, to run messages, ensure the coffee machines stayed filled and perform the most humble of tasks. She worked really hard at keeping busy, but the kind of lowly work she did rarely produced results that other people could appreciate.

And Bruce Gregory's announcement had thoroughly shaken Dixie. The threat of a face-to-face meeting with César Valverde kept her stomach churning throughout the day. What had she done? What had she *not* done? Well, if she had made some awful mistake or oversight, she would have to grovel on her knees and promise to do better in the future; she had no choice.

Right now, the only thing keeping Dixie going through exhaustion was the knowledge that she had a steady salary coming in as well as what she earned working as a waitress several nights a week. That long talk she had had with the helpful lady at the Citizens' Advice Bureau had suggested that as long as she could prove an honest intent to pay back those creditors in instalments, her offer to do so should be acceptable, and would hopefully protect her from the threat of legal proceedings.

And, in the meantime, there was always the hope that her sister Petra would phone to say that she was back in funds again and able to send the money to clear her debts. Petra had always had terrific earning power as a model, Dixie reminded herself bracingly. All she herself was really doing was holding the fort until her sister could pick up the financial slack. Petra *had* been upset when Dixie called her to tell her about the bills she had neglected to pay before she flew out to Los Angeles in the hope of starting an acting career.

In the cloakroom, minutes to go before the encounter, Dixie freshened up and morosely surveyed her reflection. Plain and wholesome, that was her. The loose beige top and long grey cotton skirt at least concealed the worst of her deficiencies, she told herself in consolation. But as always it seemed particularly cruel to Dixie that she should have been endowed with hatefully large breasts and generous hips but only a height of five feet two inches.

As often happened at times of particular stress, Dixie drifted off into her own thoughts. Was it any wonder that Scott saw her as a good sport and a mate, rather than a possible girlfriend? Scott Lewis, handsome, extrovert and the love of Dixie's life. Momentarily, self-pity filled her to overflowing. And then she scolded herself for being so foolish. Hadn't she always known she didn't have a hope of attracting Scott?

She had met Scott at one of her sister's parties. Having just moved into a new apartment, he'd been giving a comic description of his less than successful efforts to get organised on the domestic front. His frank admission that his mother had spoilt him rotten had impressed Dixie, and before she had even thought about what she was doing she had found herself offering to come round and give him a hand...

When Dixie presented herself for her appointment, César Valverde's secretary, a svelte brunette in her thirties, gave her a pained look. 'It might have been a good idea to be on time, Dixie.'

'But I am on time.' Dixie checked her watch and then her face fell. Once again time had run on without her.

'You're ten minutes late.' The other woman didn't wince but she might as well have done.

Sick with apprehension, Dixie knocked on the door of her lofty employer's office and walked in, a band of tension tightening round her head, her mouth bone-dry and her palms damp.

César Valverde spun lithely round from the wall of glass which overlooked the City skyline and studied her. 'You're late,' he delivered icily.

'I'm really sorry...I just don't know where the time went.' Dixie studied the deep-pile carpet, wishing it would open up and swallow her and disgorge her only when the interview was safely over.

'That is not an acceptable excuse.'

'That's why I apologised,' Dixie pointed out in a very small voice without looking up.

There was really no need to look up. In her mind's eye she could still see César Valverde standing there, as formidable and unfeeling as a hitman. And close to him she always felt murderously awkward, not to mention all hot and bothered. Yet he was physically quite beautiful, a little voice pointed out absently inside her head.

He had the lean dark face of a fallen angel, blessed with such perfect bone structure that at first glance he knocked women flat with his spectacular sleek Mediterranean looks. Hair thick and glossy as ebony. Eyes the same colour as dark bitter chocolate, which blazed into the strangest silver in strong light. Mouth mobile, wide and sensual. A sensation-

ally attractive male animal, but at second glance he had always chilled Dixie to the marrow.

Those stunning eyes were hard and cold, that shapely
mouth rarely smiled, except at someone else's misfortune,
and those sculpted cheekbones stamped his features with a
quality of merciless unemotional detachment which intimidated. He might radiate raw sexuality like a forcefield, but
Dixie still prided herself on being the only woman in the
whole building who was repulsed by César Valverde. The
guy could give a freezer pneumonia just by arching one satiric brow.

Belatedly conscious of the dragging silence, Dixie
emerged from her own reflections and glanced nervously up.
Her pupils dilated, her heartbeat quickening as she stared. A
decided frown on his striking dark features, César Valverde
was strolling in a soundless circle round her, his piercing
gaze intent on her now shrinking figure.

'What's wrong?' she breathed, thoroughly disconcerted by
his behaviour and the intensity of his scrutiny.

'*Dio mio*…what's *right*?' His frown deepened as her slight
shoulders drooped. 'Straighten up…don't slouch like that,'
he told her.

Flushing, Dixie did as she was told. She was relieved when
he positioned himself against the edge of his immaculately
tidy glass desk.

'Do you recall the terms of the employment contract you
signed before you started work here?'

Dixie thought about that and then guiltily shook her head.
She had had to fill in and sign an avalanche of papers at
speed that first day.

'You didn't bother to study the contract,' César gathered
with a curled lip.

'I was desperate for a job…I would have signed anything.'

'But if you'd read your contract, you would have known
that getting into debt is grounds for instant dismissal.'

That unexpected revelation struck Dixie like a sudden
blow. She stared at him in horror, soft full lips falling apart,
what colour there was in her cheeks slowly, painfully drain-

ing away. César studied her the way a shark studies wounded prey before moving in for the kill. In silence he extended a computer printout.

With an unsteady hand, Dixie grasped at the sheet. Her heart felt as if it was thumping at the foot of her throat, making it impossible for her to breathe. The same names and figures which already haunted her every waking hour swam before her eyes and her tummy flipped in shock.

'Security turned that up this morning. Regular financial checks are made on all staff,' César informed her smoothly.

'You're sacking me,' Dixie assumed sickly, swaying slightly.

Striding forward, César reached for a chair and planted it beside her. 'Sit down, Miss Robinson.'

Dixie fumbled blindly down into the chair before her knees gave way beneath her. She was waiting for him to ask how such a junior employee could possibly have amassed debts amounting to such a staggering total. Indeed, in that instant of overwhelming shock and embarrassment, she was actually eager to explain how, through a series of awful misunderstandings and mishaps, such a situation had developed through no real fault of her own.

'I have not the slightest interest in hearing a sob story,' César Valverde delivered deflatingly as he lounged back against his desk again, his impossibly tall, lean and powerful length taking up a formidably relaxed pose.

'But I *want* to explain—'

'There is no need for you to explain anything. Debts of that nature are self-explanatory. You have a taste for living above your means and you like to party—'

Cringing at the knowledge that he knew about those shameful debts in her name, and her equally shameful inability to settle them, Dixie broke back into speech. '*No*, Mr Valverde. I—'

'If you interrupt me again, I won't offer you my assistance,' César Valverde interposed with icy bite.

Struggling to understand that assurance, Dixie tipped back

her wildly curly head and gaped at him. *'Assistance?'* she stressed blankly.

'I'm prepared to offer you another form of employment.'

In complete confusion, Dixie blinked.

'But if you take on the role, it will entail a great deal of hard work and effort on your part.'

Sinking ever deeper into bewilderment, but ready to snatch at any prospect of continuing employment like a drowning swimmer snatches at a branch, Dixie nodded eagerly. 'I'm not afraid of hard work, Mr Valverde.'

Obviously he was talking about demoting her. Where did you go from office junior? Dixie wondered frantically. Scrubbing the floors in the canteen kitchen?

César sent her a gleaming glance. 'You're really not in a position to turn my offer down.'

'I know,' Dixie acknowledged with total humility, suddenly starting to squirm at the reality of how much she had always disliked him. Evidently she had completely misjudged César Valverde's character. Even though he had a legitimate excuse to sack her, he seemed to be willing to give her another chance. And if that meant scrubbing the canteen kitchen floor, she ought to say thank you from the bottom of her heart and get on with it.

'Jasper hasn't been well.'

The switch in subject disconcerted Dixie. Her strained face shadowed. 'By what he's said in his letters he still hasn't quite got over that chest trouble he had in the spring.'

César looked grim. 'His heart is weak.'

Dixie's eyes prickled. That news was too much on top of all her other worries. Her stinging eyes overflowed and she dug into the pocket of her skirt to find a tissue. But the horrible news about Jasper did make sudden sense of César Valverde's uncharacteristic tolerance, and his apparent willingness to allow her to remain in his employment by fixing her up with another job. He might not approve of her, or of her friendship with Jasper Dysart, but clearly he respected his godfather's fondness for her. Presumably that was why he wasn't going to kick her when she was already down.

'At his age, Jasper can't hope to go on for ever,' César gritted, his unease with her emotional breakdown blatant and icily reproving.

Fighting to compose herself, Dixie blew her nose and sucked in a deep, steadying breath. 'Will he be coming over to London this summer?'

'I shouldn't think so.'

Then she would never see Jasper again, she registered on a powerful tide of pain and regret. The struggle to stay abreast of the debts Petra had left behind made a trip to Spain as out of reach as a trip to the moon.

'It's time we got down to business,' César drawled with perceptible impatience. 'I need a favour, and in return for that favour I'm prepared to settle your debts.'

'Settle my debts…what favour?' Dixie echoed, all at sea as to what he could possibly be talking about and stunned by the idea of him offering to pay off those appalling bills. A favour? What sort of favour? How could her staying employed in any capacity within the Valverde Mercantile Bank be any kind of a favour to César Valverde?

César moved restively away from the desk and strode over to the window, the clear light of early summer glittering over his luxuriant hair and hard, classic profile. 'In all probability, Jasper doesn't have long to live,' he spelt out harshly. 'His dearest wish has always been that I should marry. At this present time I have no intention of fulfilling that wish, but I would very much like to please him with a harmless fiction.'

A harmless fiction? Dixie's bemusement increased as she strained to grasp his meaning.

'And that is where you come in,' César informed her drily. 'Jasper likes you. He's very shy with your sex, and as a result he only warms to a certain type of woman. *Your* type. Jasper would be overjoyed if I announced that we had got engaged.'

'We…?' Dixie whispered weakly, certain she had missed a connecting link somewhere in that speech and beginning to stand up, as if by rising from the chair she might comprehend something that she couldn't follow while still sitting.

César wheeled round, a forbidding cast to his lean features.

'Your job would be to pretend that you're engaged to me. It would be a private arrangement between us. You would play the role solely for Jasper's benefit in Spain.'

A curious whirring sound reverberated in Dixie's eardrums. Her lungs seemed suddenly empty of oxygen. Disbelief paralysing her, she gazed wide-eyed across the room at César Valverde. 'You can't be serious... *Me*,' she stressed helplessly, 'pretend to be engaged to...to *you*?'

'Jasper will be convinced. People are always keen to believe what they *want* to believe,' César asserted with rich cynicism.

As yet uncertain that this weird conversation was actually taking place, Dixie moved her head in a negative motion. 'But nobody would believe *that*...that you and I...' A betraying tide of colour slowly washed up her throat into her cheeks. 'I mean, it's just so *un*believable!'

'That's where your upcoming hard work and effort will pay off.' Once again César studied her with that curious considering frown he had worn earlier. 'I intend to make this charade as credible as possible. Jasper may be naive, but he's no fool. Only when I've finished transforming you into a slimline, elegant Dixie Mark Two will Jasper be truly convinced.'

It crossed Dixie's mind that César Valverde had been at the booze. A slimline Dixie Mark Two? She snatched in a short, sustaining breath. 'Mr Valverde, I—'

'Yes, I expect you're very grateful,' César dismissed arrogantly, a scornful light in his brilliant dark eyes as he surveyed her. 'In fact I imagine you can hardly credit your good luck—'

'My good luck?' Dixie broke in shakily, wondering how any male so famed for his perception could be so wildly off course when it came to reading her reactions.

'An image makeover, a new wardrobe, all your debts paid *and* an all-expenses-paid trip to Spain?' César enumerated with cool exactitude. 'It's more than good luck...from where you're standing now, it's the equivalent of striking oil in the desert wastes! And you don't deserve it. Believe me, if I had an alternative choice of fiancée available you'd have been fired first thing this morning!'

'I was the *only* choice, wasn't I?' Dixie gathered in a wobbly voice. '*Your* type,' he had said minutes ago, the only woman liked by Jasper that César Valverde knew. A slimline Dixie Mark Two? How dared he get as personal as that? Didn't he even appreciate that she had feelings that could be hurt? But then why should he care, standing there all lean and fit and perfect, probably never having had to watch his appetite once in his entire spoilt rotten life!

'That's irrelevant. By the way, I want this arrangement of ours to stay under wraps.' César scanned her with threatening dark eyes. 'Do you understand the concept of keeping a secret, Dixie?'

Locked to those spectacular dark eyes, Dixie felt oddly dizzy and out of breath. 'A secret?'

'It's quite simple. If you open your mouth to another living soul about this deal, I'll bury you,' César Valverde murmured with chilling bite.

Dixie blenched. 'That's not very funny.'

'It wasn't meant to be. It was a warning. And you've been in here long enough. As soon as you walk out of this office, you can clear your desk and go home. I'll be in touch this evening so that we can work out the finer details.'

Dixie lifted her chin, her rarely roused temper rising at the arrogance with which he simply assumed that she would do whatever he told her to do, no matter how immoral or unpleasant it might be. 'Whatever decision I make, I can now consider myself sacked...isn't that right?'

'Wow, quick on the uptake,' César derided smoothly. 'Too dumb to safely operate anything with a plug attached, but reads Nietzsche and Plato in her spare time. According to Jasper, you have a remarkable brain. And yet you never do anything with it. You certainly never dreamt of bringing it into work with you—'

Her lashes fluttered over huge violet eyes. 'I beg your—?'

'But then that's because you're a lazy, disorganised lump,

who contrives to hide behind the front of being a brick short of the full load! Only around me you won't get away with that kind of nonsense!'

Disbelief roared through Dixie as she reeled from the full impact of that derisive attack, even though on another level she longed to question him about Jasper having said that she had a remarkable brain. However, anger abruptly overpowered that brief spark of surprised pleasure and curiosity. 'If I can consider myself sacked, then I'm free to tell you exactly what I think of you too!'

César gave her a wolfish half-smile of encouragement. 'I'm enjoying this. The office doormat suddenly discovers backbone. Make my day… Only be warned—I will respond in kind.'

Teeth almost chattering with the force of her disturbed emotions, Dixie drew herself up to her full unimpressive height and hissed, 'You have to be the most unscrupulous, selfish human being I have ever met! Doesn't it even occur to you that I might have some moral objection to cruelly deceiving a sweet old man, who deserves better from a male he loves like a son?'

'You're right. That thought didn't occur to me,' César confessed, without a shade of discomfiture or remorse. 'Considering that you're currently on the brink of being taken to court for obtaining goods and services by fraudulent deception, I'm not remotely impressed by the sound of your moral scruples!'

Dixie shrank and turned white. 'Taken to c-court?' she stammered, aghast, her eyes nailed to him in the hope that she had somehow misunderstood.

CHAPTER TWO

'*DIO mio…*' César raised a winging ebony brow to challenge Dixie's stricken expression. 'Didn't you read that printout I gave you either? The interior designer, Leticia Zane, has instigated proceedings. Did you expect her to be sympathetic towards a client who took advantage of her services without the slightest hope of being able to pay for them?'

Numbly, Dixie shook her pounding head, her stomach curdling. 'But I haven't got any more money to give Miss Zane…I've already offered instalments.'

César Valverde shifted a broad shoulder in an unfeeling shrug. 'The lady may well have decided to make a public spectacle of you to deter other clients who are reluctant to settle up. You're a good choice—'

'A good choice?' Dixie parroted, scarcely believing her ears.

'You don't have socially prominent friends likely to take offence on your behalf and damage her business prospects.'

'But…but a court prosecution.' Dixie squeezed out those words, breathless with horror, utterly appalled by what he was spelling out to her. Her own naivety hit her hard. She stared down at the printout, belatedly reading the small type beneath the debt to Leticia Zane's firm. 'Prosecution pending', it said. Her blood ran cold with fear and incredulity. The interior designer knew very well that all the work on her sister's apartment had been done at Petra's behest. Dixie had merely been the mouthpiece who'd passed on the instructions.

'Delusions of grandeur have a price, like everything else,' César Valverde sighed.

'I can't think straight,' Dixie mumbled sickly.

'Sharpen up. I haven't got all day to wait for an answer

that is already staring you in the face,' César breathed with callous cool.

Dixie gave him a speaking glance from tear-filled eyes and fumbled with the crushed tissue still clutched between her shaking fingers. 'I just couldn't deceive Jasper like that, Mr Valverde. I couldn't live with lying to him. It would be absolutely wrong!'

'You're being selfish and shortsighted,' César drawled crushingly, dealing her a look of hostile reproach. 'Getting engaged to you is the one thing that I can do to make Jasper happy. What right have you to say that it would be wrong or immoral?'

'Lies are always wrong!' Dixie sobbed helplessly, and turned away from him in embarrassment.

'Jasper won't ever know it was a lie. He'll be delighted. I plan to leave you with him in Spain for a few weeks... assuming he's well enough for me to leave, even temporarily,' César adjusted flatly.

'I couldn't...I just *couldn't*!' Dixie gasped strickenly, already plotting a weaving path towards the door, barely able to see through her falling tears but determined not to be swayed by his specious arguments. 'And it's wicked of you to call me selfish. How can you *do* that?'

'For Jasper's sake...easily. I'll call on you tonight to get your final answer. I think you'll have seen sense by then.'

Dixie hauled open the door with a trembling hand and shot him an angry, accusing glance. 'Go to hell!' she launched thickly as she walked out.

Only as she shut the door behind her did she notice the little clutch of staff standing with dropped jaws further down the corridor.

'And you OK, Dixie?' Bruce Gregory enquired kindly.

One of the directors put his arm round her in a very paternal way to walk her away. 'We'll get you sorted out with a job some place else.'

'Not in a bank,' someone whispered ruefully.

'Ever thought of cooking for a living?' another voice asked brightly. 'You're a great cook.'

'A restaurant kitchen could be very stressful, though.'

'And I drop things,' Dixie muttered, a sense of being a total failure creeping over her.

'Imagine you telling César to go to hell!' the director remarked bracingly.

'But he'll never let Personnel give her a decent reference now,' Bruce groaned as the older man slotted her into a seat in the office she shared with a couple of the secretaries. Just about everybody on the whole floor seemed to crowd around her then.

'He tried to blackmail me,' Dixie mumbled sickly.

'Say that again…' someone breathed.

Dixie reddened, and then turned very pale with fright at what she had almost revealed in her distress and buttoned her mouth. 'Don't mind me…I don't know what I'm s-saying,' she stammered fearfully.

And she registered then that her brain was in a state of complete flux. What César Valverde had suggested already seemed completely unreal, a figment of her own fevered imagination. A fake engagement to please Jasper? A fantasy slimline Dixie Mark Two, united even in pretence with César's icy sophistication? Did blue moons come up in pairs?

'I don't know what we're going to do for a laugh around here now,' someone lamented.

'You'll have to get your goldfish out of the fountain… wasn't the ideal environment for them anyway. César raised Cain when he saw you out there feeding them,' Bruce reminded her ruefully.

'There's only one now, and I don't even have an aquarium!' Dixie sobbed, because it felt like absolutely the last straw. To take her goldfish out of the fountain below César Valverde's office and never, ever come back into the building? Suddenly she felt completely bereft and cut adrift.

Across the room, her desk was being cleared for her. One carrier bag grew into three as books, knitting, fish food and sundry items were removed from the crammed drawers. Tissues were supplied and a glass of water was pressed on her.

'We're all going to really miss you, Dixie...so we had a bit of a whip round.' She was mortified when a large fat envelope was thrust by Bruce into her shoulder bag. She realised then that everyone had known even before she did that she was getting the sack, and had been waiting to comfort her.

'I'll give you a lift home with your bags,' Bruce volunteered.

The chipped china jardinière was filched from beneath the dying cactus on her desk, and the goldfish she had found abandoned at the bus stop in a plastic bag removed with some difficulty from the fountain and temporarily rehoused.

'I just can't get over how kind everyone's been,' Dixie confided as she climbed into Bruce's car in the basement car park.

She clutched the planter with careful hands, gazing down at the single handsome goldfish she had secretly christened, César. He had eaten his original companion, and even the one she'd actually bought for him, fearing that he would be lonely. César the fish was up near the surface, patrolling with fast flicks of his tail. Dixie gave him a loving and abstracted smile.

'César can be a real bastard. But the guy's a complete genius. You can't expect him to be human too. Try not to think about it. Go round and do Scott's washing...or whatever,' Bruce advised, striving to be upbeat. 'That always seems to give you a lift.'

Yes, it did, she acknowledged ruefully, only this evening she would be waiting tables. But doing anything for Scott gave her the feeling that she had some small personal stake in his busy life. And in the right mood, if Scott didn't have a hot date or wasn't eating out, he might suggest that she cooked some supper and stayed to eat with him. She *lived* for those infrequent invitations.

'You were in with César a very long time,' Bruce commented abruptly.

'We talked a little about Jasper.'

'Dixie...why did you say César tried to blackmail you?'

'I must've been trying to make a silly joke…'

Bruce sent her scared face a covert appraisal. 'He never did approve of your friendship with the old man. Can't think why.'

As soon as Bruce had carried her bags upstairs for her, he left to speed back to the office, long hours being a feature of his highly paid employment. Dixie unlocked the door of her bedsit. She transferred César the fish into a large glass mixing bowl and fed him, setting him next to the window in the hope that a view of the pigeons on the roof opposite would keep him entertained.

Locking up again, she went down the street to call in on a neighbour she often babysat for at weekends. In return the older woman kept her Jack Russell dog, Spike, during the day.

She took Spike for a quick walk in the park, and then nervously carried him back up to her bedsit for the night. She wasn't allowed to keep pets, but she had never had any bother sneaking Spike in after it got dark. Now that the light nights had arrived, she was really scared that she would be seen.

How on earth had her life got into such a terrible, frightening mess? she asked herself in a daze as she watched Spike wolf down his dinner. The future had looked so promising when she had first come up to London to share Petra's spacious apartment, certainly a lot brighter than it had seemed for many years beforehand…

Dixie's mother had died when she was five and her father had remarried the following year. It was hard to recall even now that Petra wasn't really her true sister but actually her stepsister—the daughter of her father's second wife, Muriel. Already a teenager, Petra had had little interest in a child seven years younger, but Dixie had always longed for a big sister and had adored blonde and beautiful Petra. At seventeen, Petra had left home on her first modelling assignment.

A year later, Dixie's father had died of a heart attack, and the year after that Muriel had shown the first symptoms of what was to prove to be a long, debilitating terminal illness.

Dixie had never managed to pass any exams because she had
been forced to miss so much school. Whenever Muriel's
health had been particularly bad, Dixie had had to stay at
home to see to her needs. She had left school at sixteen.

Over the following four years, Petra had sent money home
regularly but the demands of a career which took her all over
the world had made it impossible for her to visit much. A
year ago, Muriel Robinson had passed away, and Dixie had
more or less invited herself up to London to stay with Petra.
Used to living alone, Petra had understandably not been too
keen on the arrangement at first, but had soon appreciated
that Dixie could look after her apartment when she herself
was abroad.

For her own convenience, Petra had opened a household
account in both their names, and paid in sufficient money to
cover her bills, so that Dixie could easily pay them for her.
And when, soon afterwards, Dixie had started work at
Valverde Mercantile, she had had her entire salary paid into
the same account.

Dixie had frequently ordered expensive food and alcohol
for Petra's lavish parties. In the same way she had dealt with
Leticia Zane, after the interior designer's initial meeting with
Petra, ensuring that all the costly redecoration was done in
exactly the way her sister wished.

And then, about three months ago, Petra had suddenly announced that she was leaving the UK. Giving up the lease
on her apartment, she had packed her bags and flown to Los
Angeles. Dixie had moved into the bedsit. But within weeks
the demands for payment had begun rolling in from her sister's creditors. Dixie had discovered that the joint account
was not only empty of her own savings but also overdrawn.
Only after the deputy bank manager had patiently explained
it to her had Dixie understood that she herself could be held
liable for Petra's unpaid bills.

She had immediately phoned her sister. After admitting
that she was broke, but promising to help as soon as she
could, Petra had rather drily reminded Dixie of all the money
she had generously sent over the years that Dixie had been

nursing her mother, Muriel. And Dixie had felt really guilty, because tough as those years had been they would have been intolerable without Petra's financial assistance.

But the next time Dixie had phoned that same number she had been told that Petra had moved on without leaving a forwarding address. That had been two months ago, and since then she hadn't heard a word from her sister.

The awful fear that Petra had not the slightest intention of getting in touch again, or of trying to satisfy her creditors, was now beginning to haunt Dixie. She felt so disloyal, thinking about Petra that way. Yet in her heart of hearts she was facing up to the harsh fact that her glamorous stepsister invariably put her own needs first.

And Dixie was terrified of being taken to court and appalled by the reality that she had no way of settling those dreadful bills. That was so unfair to the creditors concerned, and César Valverde *had* offered to pay them…

'Can I just run over this again?' Dixie asked the table of customers anxiously. 'That's one cheeseburger with pickles, one without dressing, a double—'

'How many times do we have to go over this?' one of the teenagers groaned. 'A double hamburger *with* pickles, a single cheeseburger *without*…'

Pink with embarrassment, Dixie hurried to amend her notebook as the girl ran through the entire order again. Beneath the jaundiced eye of the manager, Dixie thrust the order over the counter.

'Get those tables cleared,' he urged impatiently.

Scurrying over to her section of the busy café, Dixie began to load up a tray. She was so tired that she could feel her knees wobbling whenever she stood still. Wiping her damp brow with the back of her hand, she lifted the heavily laden tray. As she straightened, she could not help but focus on the tall, dark male blocking her view of the rest of the cafe. Dixie froze in shock and dismay.

César Valverde stood six feet away, emanating the kind of lacerating cool which intimidated. Brilliant dark eyes entrapped her evasive ones. As he lifted one ebony brow at her frazzled appearance and coffee-stained overall, Dixie simply wanted to curl up and die. Oh, dear heaven, how had he found out where she worked? And what did he want now, for heaven's sake?

But then had she really believed that César Valverde would take no for an answer? He wasn't accustomed to negative responses. His naturally aggressive temperament geared him to persist and demand in the face of refusal, she reminded herself. A workaholic, he thrived under pressure and lived for challenge. When César Valverde set himself a goal, he went all out to get it. She should feel sorry for him, she told herself. He really didn't know any other way to behave.

An exasperated male voice demanded, 'Where's our food?'

'It's coming…it's coming!' Dixie promised frantically, rudely dredged from her reverie. She fled without looking where she was going, as to look would have brought César Valverde back into focus again.

A shopping bag protruding from beneath a table was her undoing. Catching her foot, Dixie tipped forward, and the tray shot clean out of her perspiring hold. Eyes wide with horror, she watched pieces of food, coffee dregs, crumpled napkins, plates and cups go flying up in the air and fall in all directions. The noise of smashing china was equalled if not surpassed by the shaken exclamations of customers lurching from their seats in an effort to escape the aerial bombardment.

A deathly silence fell in the aftermath. Feverishly muttering incoherent apologies, Dixie bent down to scoop up the tray. The manager removed it from her trembling hands and hissed in her ear, 'You had your final warning yesterday. You're fired!'

Only yesterday, three entire meals complete with accompanying drinks had landed on the floor, because in an effort to speed up Dixie had overloaded a tray and then stumbled. Tears of mortification and defeat stinging her eyes, Dixie scuttled into the back of the café. Ripping off the overall, she reached for her cardigan and bag.

When she emerged again, the manager stuffed a couple of notes into her hand. 'You're just not cut out for waitressing,' he said ruefully.

A long, low and expensive sports car hugged the pavement outside the café. The driver's window whirred down. César surveyed Dixie with an enquiring brow.

'It's your fault I dropped that tray…you spooked me!' Dixie condemned unevenly.

'If you hadn't been so busy trying to ignore me it wouldn't have happened.'

'You are so smug and patronising. I hate you!' Dixie gasped truthfully, studying his staggeringly handsome dark features with unconcealed loathing. 'You always think you're right about everything!'

'I usually am,' César pointed out, without skipping a beat.

'Not about deceiving Jasper…so go away and leave me alone!'

Walking on past, Dixie struggled to swallow the aching thickness of tears in her throat. The car purred in her wake but Dixie was oblivious. In the space of one ghastly day a security that had at best been tenuous had come crashing down round her ears. Jasper was dying, she thought wretchedly, and she was going to end up being prosecuted like a criminal.

'Get in the car, Dixie!'

Having totally forgotten about César Valverde while she pondered her woes, Dixie nearly died of fright. She glanced round and saw the flash car only feet away. Sticking her nose in the air, she prepared to cross the road to the bus stop.

'Get…in…the car,' César framed as he climbed out, six foot three inches of towering bully.

'I don't have to do what you tell me any more!' Dixie flung chokily.

A policeman crossed the road. 'Is there some problem here?'

'Yes, this man won't leave me alone!' Dixie complained.

'I saw you kerb-crawling,' the policeman informed César thinly. 'Are you aware that kerb-crawling is an offence?'

'This woman works for me, Officer,' César drawled icily.

'Not any more, I don't!' Dixie protested. 'Why won't you just leave me alone?'

'I don't like the sound of this, sir.' The policeman appraised the opulent car and then the cut of César's fabulous dark grey suit with deeply suspicious eyes.

'Look, that's my bus coming!' Dixie suddenly gasped.

'Settle the misunderstanding, Dixie,' César commanded in a tone of icy warning.

'What misunderstanding?' she enquired in honest bewilderment.

'This gentleman was kerb-crawling and employing threatening behaviour. I think we should all go back to the station and sort this out,' the policeman informed her as he radioed in the registration of César's car.

César looked at Dixie. Eyes like black ice daggers dug into her. It was like being hauled off her feet and dropped from a height. She blinked, and then warm colour flooded her drawn cheeks. 'Oh…you actually think…my goodness, are you kidding?' she pressed in a strangled voice. 'He would never bother *me* like that…I mean, he would never even *look* at me like that!'

'Then what was this gentleman doing?' the policeman asked wearily.

'He was offering me a lift home…and we had a slight difference of opinion,' Dixie mumbled, not looking at either man in her mortification. This policeman had *genuinely* suspected that César Valverde had been kerb-crawling with an intent to…?

'And now she's going to get in my car and be sensible,' César completed stonily.

Dixie slunk round the sports car and climbed in. 'It's not my fault that policeman thought you might've been making improper suggestions,' she muttered in hot-faced embarrassment.

'Oh, don't worry about that. That *wasn't* what he was

thinking. He thought I might be your pimp,' César gritted not very levelly, half under his breath, his accented drawl alive with speaking undertones of raw incredulity.

Dixie nestled into the gloriously comfortable bucket seat and decided that silence was the better part of valour. Flash car, flash suit. In this particular area César probably had looked suspicious.

'How *dare* you embarrass me like that?'

'I'm sorry, but you were annoying me,' she mumbled wearily.

'*I*…was annoying…*you*?'

He seemed to find that very difficult to understand. But then an enormous amount of boot-licking went on in César Valverde's vicinity, Dixie reflected, struggling to smother a yawn.

People shouldn't worship idols, but they did. Expose the average human being to César's intellectual brilliance, immense wealth and enormous power and influence, and they generally behaved in all sorts of undignified ways. They toadied, they talked a load of rubbish in an effort to impress, and went to ridiculous lengths to please and be remembered by him.

As for the women—that constant procession of gorgeous females who paraded through his life, Dixie reflected sleepily. Well, he had the concentration span of a toddler, always on the look-out for a new and better toy. And he invariably had a replacement lined up before he ditched her predecessor. But he was never available during working hours, and those women who tried to breach that boundary lasted the least time. Possessive behaviour was a surefire way to make César stray.

César shook her awake outside the building where she lived. 'As a rule, women do not fall asleep in my company.'

'I don't fancy you,' Dixie mumbled, barely half awake, and then aghast at the sound of what she had just said.

'Then you won't develop any ambitious ideas while we're in Spain, will you?'

'I'm not going to Spain.'

'Then you can send Jasper cute "glad you're not here" postcards from prison.'

Dixie sat up, full wakefulness now established, and turned aghast eyes on him.

César gave her a faint smile. 'It's your first offence, but who knows? Women often get weightier sentences than men when they transgress.'

Her tummy tying itself into petrified knots, Dixie whispered shakily. 'Maybe we should talk this over.'

'I think we ought to,' César agreed smoothly. 'A female who said she was your landlady cut up rough when I knocked on the door of your bedsit earlier and a dog started barking. She came upstairs to investigate.'

Dixie sat bolt upright, horror now etched on her face. 'Oh, no, she heard Spike and now she knows he's there!'

César released an extravagant sigh. 'And pets aren't allowed. I gather it's going to be a question of moving out or getting rid of the dog.'

Dixie shook her head in anguished disbelief. This was truly the very worst day of her entire life. 'Why did you have to knock on the door? You must've frightened Spike! He's usually as quiet as a mouse.'

'I think Spain's beckoning,' César remarked lazily. 'You have one very angry landlady waiting to pounce.'

'*Oh, no…*' Dixie groaned.

'Life could be so different,' César drawled smoothly. 'All those debts settled…no nasty hanging judge to face in court…relaxing trip to Spain…Jasper happy as a sandboy and the comforting knowledge that you are responsible for giving him the best news he's ever heard. *Wrong?* I don't think so. I don't think anything that could give Jasper pleasure at this trying stage of his life could possibly be wrong.'

Hanging on every specious word, Dixie watched him with a kind of eerie fascination. He was so damnably clever, so shockingly good at timing his verbal assaults. Here she was, her whole life in ruins and on the very brink of being thrown out on the street because she couldn't possibly give up Spike, and a living, breathing version of the devil was holding out temptation without shame.

'I couldn't…'

'You could,' César contradicted softly. 'You could do it for Jasper.'

Dixie's soft full mouth wobbled as she thought of Jasper dying and never, ever seeing him again. Her eyes began to prickle and she sniffed.

'You can pack right now. It's *that* simple,' César stressed in the same low-pitched deep, dark tone.

He sounded mesmeric. Dixie couldn't peel her wet eyes from him either. In the dusk light, his bronzed features were half in shadow, dark eyes glimmering silver beneath the sort of long, incredibly luxuriant black lashes that would drive any sane woman blessed with less to despair.

'My dog, Spike…' she muttered uncertainly, so very, very tired it was becoming an effort even to string words together, her mind a confused sea of incomplete thoughts and fears.

'Spike can come too. One of my staff will pick up the rest of your possessions tomorrow. You won't have anything to do,' César asserted gently.

At that moment, the concept of not having anything to do impressed Dixie like the offer of manna from heaven. 'I…I—'

César slid out of the driver's seat, strolled round the bonnet and opened the door beside her. 'Come on,' he urged.

And Dixie found herself doing as she was told, all the fight drained out of her. 'A harmless fiction', César had called it. A pretend engagement to make Jasper's last days happy. And it *would* make Jasper happy. She knew how much Jasper longed to see César on the road to creating the family circle that Jasper had never managed to create for himself. Maybe lying wasn't always wrong…

Her landlady emerged from her small flat on the ground floor. As she broke into angry, accusing speech, César settled a wad of banknotes into her hand. 'Miss Robinson will be moving out. I hope this takes care of her notice.'

* * *

A phone was ringing somewhere horribly close to Dixie's ears. Struggling to cling to sleep, she sighed with relief when the shrill buzz stopped, but her eyes slowly opened on the dawning realisation that she didn't have a phone in her bedsit.

Her brain in a fog, Dixie surveyed her unfamiliar surroundings. For a moment she couldn't even remember where she was. Then her attention fell on the suitcase lying open with miscellaneous garments tumbling untidily out of it. And whoosh, everything came back in a rush; she was in César Valverde's London home.

The phone by the bed started ringing again. This time Dixie reached for the receiver. 'Hello?' she said nervously.

'Rise and shine, Dixie.' César Valverde's rich, dark drawl jerked her bolt upright in the bed. 'It's half-six and I want you in the gym by eight, dressed appropriately and fully awake.'

'The gym?' Dixie was aghast at the news that she was expected to be up before seven in the morning, particularly on a Saturday. Even Spike was still asleep in his basket. He was as fond of having a lie-in as his owner.

'I've engaged a fitness instructor to put you through your paces,' César completed drily, and rang off.

A fitness instructor? Dixie stared into space with wide eyes, picturing some giant, suntanned musclebound male standing over her like a bullying sergeant-major, bawling instructions liberally splattered with abuse. She shrank. Maybe the instructor would be nice and break her in gently. She tried to imagine César hiring someone nice. Hope dwindled fast. The fitness instructor would be tough and pitiless. César was, after all, the male who had called her a lazy lump.

Scrambling out of bed, Dixie roused Spike and left the bedroom. A short corridor beyond led out to a small enclosed courtyard.

On her arrival the night before, Dixie had been handed over to César's butler, Fisher, like a unwelcome parcel. The comfortable *en suite* bedroom she had been assigned on the ground floor was former staff accommodation. Dixie had understood the distinction being made. She was not going to be treated like an honoured guest in César Valverde's palatial Georgian mansion.

Having attended to Spike's needs, she went for a shower. Appropriate clothing? Dixie had never been in a gym in her life. A baggy pair of sweat-pants and an oversized T-shirt were all she had to wear. The unflattering combination made her look as wide as she was tall. A slimline Dixie Mark Two? But what if the exercise routine *worked*? a more seductive voice asked, and she dawdled by the mirror then, imagining Scott suddenly recognising her as a member of the female sex…

Her stomach growling with hunger, she was about to go off in search of the kitchen when a quiet knock sounded on the door.

Fisher appeared with a tray bearing a tall glass filled with some strange greyish green liquid. 'Miss Stevens faxed your diet plan to Cook yesterday,' the butler explained. 'I believe this is the lady's own personal recipe for an early-morning energy boost.'

'Oh…' In bewilderment, Dixie accepted the glass. *Diet plan?* She didn't like the sound of that. She was willing to exercise, but diet? And who on earth was Fisher talking about?

'Miss Stevens?' Dixie queried with a frown.

'Gilda Stevens, the fitness instructor,' Fisher supplied expressionlessly. 'Her instructions regarding your menus were most precise.'

At that point, Dixie's tummy gave an embarrassing gurgle. So her fitness instructor was a woman. Taking a sip of the noxious brew, Dixie tried not to grimace. A cruel woman. The drink tasted like dishwater with bits of floating weed, but, remembering her manners, Dixie drank it down and waited eagerly to be told when she might receive her first meal of the day.

'Mr Valverde will be in the gym in five minutes,' the butler informed her as he retrieved the glass and returned to the door.

'What about breakfast? Do I eat later…or something?'

'That *was* breakfast, Miss Robinson.' At her aghast look of disbelief, the older man averted his eyes.

'A drink…a drink is all I'm allowed on this plan?' Dixie breathed shakily.

In silence, the older man nodded.

Fisher gave her directions to the gym. On her way there she caught tantalising glimpses of magnificent paintings, marble floors and wonderful rugs. She was not surprised to walk into a superb purpose-built gymnasium worthy of the most élite health club.

At the far end of the spacious room, César was lounging elegantly back against a piece of machinery that looked like an instrument for torture. He was talking to a brunette wearing less clothing than Dixie wore in bed. Presumably Gilda Stevens. A tiny white crop top adorned the lady's dainty bosom. Skintight white shorts hugged her impossibly slender hips. Every inch of visible skin was tanned and satin smooth.

Oh, no, why does she have to be so gorgeous? Dixie thought, cringing from such a cruel comparison, such an impossible peak of feminine perfection.

Tall and supremely authoritative in a dark designer suit, sunglasses dangling from one brown hand, César spoke without turning his dark, arrogant head. 'Don't skulk, Dixie. Come and join us. Gilda's done us a very special favor in agreeing to devote her personal attention to you at such short notice.'

The very thin brunette studied Dixie critically as she walked towards her.

Dixie flushed, her soft mouth tightening with embarrassment. César swivelled round, as light as a dancer on his feet in spite of his size. His winged brows pleated as he took in her appearance with frowning dark deepset eyes. 'Haven't you got anything more suitable to wear?'

'Dixie would probably feel too self-conscious in more revealing garments. I've seen this so many times before,' Gilda Stevens informed them both. 'Fortunately, diet and exercise can work real miracles—'

'Look…' Dixie began. 'I'm not an inanimate object you can discuss—'

'I'll send out for some gear for you,' César cut in, lean bronzed features already distant as he strode towards the door.

Gilda gave Dixie a cool, assessing appraisal from glassy blue eyes, and a panicky sensation twisted Dixie's empty tummy. Before she could even think about what she was doing, she raced in César Valverde's wake. Suddenly he felt like her only friend.

'César!' she gasped strickenly.

At the door he wheeled round, brilliant eyes glittering with impatience.

'César…she's not a normal woman,' Dixie whispered almost pleadingly. 'When she stands sideways on she's only about six inches wide! I didn't know anybody could be that thin and still live…and of course I look enormous to her, but I can't help the shape I was born with!'

After a stunned pause, César threw back his arrogant head and burst out laughing.

'It's not funny,' Dixie hissed in severe mortification. 'When you talked about hard work and effort, you didn't mention depriving me of food and putting a stick-insect in charge of me. Did you see how she looked at me? Like I was the size of an elephant and she wanted to skin me?'

César pivoted round to the wood-panelled wall and braced one lean hand against it as he struggled to contain his mirth. Turning his head back to her, silvered dark eyes still vibrant with reluctant amusement, he murmured drily, 'It's the deal, Dixie. Gilda has an international reputation in the fitness field.'

'I'm hungry,' Dixie mumbled tightly, but, disorientatingly, she found that she couldn't take her eyes off him. With laughter dying out of his lean, strong face and his cool, dark brooding air of detachment banished, she glimpsed a different César Valverde. A devastatingly masculine male with megawatt charisma, she recognised in some shock. Colouring with discomfiture, she dragged her eyes from him and stared at the wall instead.

'Tough…no pain, no gain,' César rhymed without pity.

'Have you ever been on a diet, César?' Out of the corner of her eye she could see his classic profile, and she found her head easing round towards him again without her own volition.

'I'm too disciplined to over-indulge.'

Dredging her attention from a profile worthy of a Greek sculptor, Dixie decided it would be safer to study the natural wood floor.

'Don't *do* that…it always winds me up!' César imparted with startling abruptness. 'Look at me when I'm speaking to you!'

Blinking in hot-faced bewilderment that he had actually noticed she almost never looked directly at him, Dixie glanced up.

César's aggressive jawline eased only slightly. 'That's only one of your most annoying habits.'

As he turned away, Dixie cleared her throat awkwardly. 'What did you tell Miss Stevens to explain *why* you are hiring her for my benefit?'

Complete surprise flared in his stunning eyes. 'I don't explain my actions to anyone. Why should I?'

Why should I? The baseline on the way César Valverde lived his entire life, Dixie registered. He was so self-contained, so unapologetic about guarding his privacy. Naturally he wouldn't have the slightest inhibition about snubbing people who exercised their curiosity.

'Dixie…we'd better get started,' Gilda Stevens called. 'We'll begin with a weigh-in.'

Dixie hadn't been on the scales since she was sixteen, and inside herself she simply cowered.

'I'll see you tomorrow,' Gilda told Dixie.

Face-down on a mat, perspiring freely, Dixie tried to nod, but even that took muscle power and she decided not to bother. After all, at some stage she would have to get up, walk…well, maybe crawl, she decided. She was beyond caring about putting a proud face on her exhaustion.

'You're out of condition,' her torturer sighed as she took her leave. 'But now I've shown you the ropes you'll be able to follow through on your own every day.'

Every day. Dixie suppressed a groan but she forced a grateful smile. Gilda might be tough, pitiless and completely lacking in the humour department, but she had worked out alongside her and had been tireless in her efforts to ensure that Dixie did every single exercise correctly. Horribly, hatefully tireless.

Left alone, Dixie slowly slid into a comfortable doze. The sound of footsteps made her stir. Tipping back her head, she focused sleepily on Fisher's polished shoes.

'Where would you like to eat lunch?' the butler asked.

'Here will do.'

A tray was set on the floor. A plate piled high with salad greens and raw slivers of vegetable awaited her.

'I never liked salad,' Dixie confided guiltily.

'It's a detoxifying diet, I believe,' Fisher commented. 'You do get a whole grapefruit mid-afternoon.'

Dixie's tastebuds shuddered, but she was so hungry she munched at a piece of celery. 'I like starchy food. I like meat, pasta with lashings of cheese…chocolate fudge cake,' she enumerated longingly, mouth watering as she fantasised.

Another pair of shoes appeared in her field of vision. Italian leather casuals with handstitched seams. She froze.

'But you're not allowed to cheat,' César Valverde drawled.

'I thought you were at the bank,' Dixie said accusingly.

'I intend to keep an eye on this project. Just as well,' César condemned. 'Gilda's gone, and here you are lazing about like you're on holiday!'

'I'm so weak I can't move!' Dixie gasped in disbelief.

César crouched down to her level with athletic ease. Hard dark eyes assailed her dismayed orbs in a head-on collision. 'I checked your staff medical. You're healthy. There's no reason why you shouldn't follow a structured fitness regime.

Why didn't you change into one of the exercise outfits I had sent over?'

They had all looked so incredibly small, and Dixie hadn't fancied struggling to squeeze herself into figure-hugging garments with Gilda around.

'You're over-tired because you let yourself get far too hot.'

'I need to eat to have energy,' Dixie muttered self-pityingly.

César dealt her a chilling glance of reproof. 'Your attitude to this is all wrong. In fact your attitude to life in general is your biggest flaw. You're so convinced you're going to fail you won't even bother trying!'

'I'll follow the schedule…OK?'

'That's not good enough. I want one hundred and five per cent commitment from you.' As César studied her with fulminating intensity, his jawline squared. 'Keep in mind what this is costing me. The sum total of your debts was considerable. And if you haven't learnt it yet, learn it now. There is no such thing as a free lunch.'

Having paled during that crushing speech, Dixie could no longer meet his ruthlessly intent gaze. 'I…I—'

'I paid for the right to expect you to stick to your side of this deal. Start slacking and you'll have me standing over you with a stopwatch! And if you think Gilda's bad, you ain't seen nothing yet!' César swore in unapologetic threat.

That evening, Scott's welcoming, 'Am I glad to see you!' was balm to Dixie's low self-esteem when she arrived on his doorstep.

Shyly pushing her heavy fringe off her brow, Dixie smiled up at him. Tall, slim and fair-haired, Scott responded with a matey punch that hurt her shoulder, and showed her straight into his kitchen.

'I had some friends staying for a couple of days. What a mess they left this place in!' he complained.

'I'll soon have it sorted out,' Dixie told him eagerly.

On his way back out again, Scott glanced at her and then frowned slightly. Pausing in the doorway, he stared at her.

'Have you done something to your hair or changed your make-up or something?'

Dixie tensed. 'No…I don't wear make-up.'

'It must be the colour in your cheeks. You look almost pretty.' Scott shook his handsome head over this apparently amazing development, frowned as if he was rather surprised to have noticed the fact, and departed, leaving her to the mounds of dishes stacked on every available surface.

Almost pretty. In real shock at the very first compliment Scott had ever deigned to pay her, Dixie hovered in the centre of his filthy kitchen with a dreamy look on her face. Colour in her cheeks? It was the effect of the exercise, it *had* to be! Maybe the detoxifying diet was starting to work already! Scott had finally noticed that she was female…

Suddenly feeling like a woman on a mission that might just miraculously transform her life, Dixie swore to herself that she would be up early the next day and into the gym to work out. Humming happily, she washed dishes, scrubbed the floor and cleaned the cooker.

'I don't know how you do it!' Scott exclaimed appreciatively as he paused by the kitchen door in the act of donning the jacket of a smart suit. 'What would I do without you, Dixie?'

Like a starved plant suddenly plunged into water and sunlight, Dixie blossomed and beamed at him.

'I'm off out now, but there's no need for you to hurry home,' Scott assured her. 'And if you could find the time to run the vacuum cleaner round the sitting room, I'd be really grateful.'

'No problem,' Dixie hurried to tell him. 'Is the washing machine fixed yet?'

'No, the mechanic's coming on Wednesday.' Scott grimaced. 'He says I must have one of those rogue machines.'

Dixie followed him to his front door with the aspect of someone walking on hallowed ground. 'Hot date?' she asked with laden casualness.

'Yeah. A real stunner too,' Scott chuckled. 'See you, Dixie!'

'See you,' she whispered, closing the door in his wake.

It was after ten when Dixie and Spike got back to César Valverde's imposing home. She had to use the front door and press the bell to gain entry. She just hadn't been able to bring herself to leave Scott's apartment sooner, not until she had polished every piece of furniture and vacuumed every inch of carpet. As Fisher said goodnight to her, Dixie gave him a vague smile and drifted away.

She was ludicrously unprepared for César Valverde to stride out of one of the reception rooms off the lofty ceilinged hall and demand harshly, 'Where the hell have you been?'

'I…I b-beg your pardon?' Dixie stammered.

'I expected a report on your progress at six and you'd already gone out,' César imparted grimly.

'Oh…I was with Scott.' Dixie studied him vaguely, as if she couldn't quite manage to get him into focus. In fact, she was striving to superimpose Scott's beloved features onto César, to make him more bearable, but for some strange reason the attempt wasn't working. And instead she somehow found herself making all sorts of foolish comparisons between the two men…

César was much taller, more powerfully built, his skin a vibrant gold where Scott's was fair. César's luxuriant black hair was perfectly cut to his well-shaped head, not endearingly floppy like Scott's…oh, heavens, what was she doing, and why was she studying César Valverde like this, noticing every tiny thing about him where once she had been afraid to look at him?

An odd shivery sensation Dixie had never experienced before ran through her when she collided with those striking dark eyes of his…so piercing, so brilliant, so *alive*. A definable five o'clock shadow roughened his jawline, accentuating the wide, sensual shape of his mouth, the perfect whiteness of his teeth. And he still looked so incredibly, impossibly immaculate, she reflected in growing wonderment. How did he *do* it? Here she was, with wind-tousled damp hair, a stain of cleansing fluid on her T-shirt and shoes spattered from puddles.

'How do you do it…how do you look so perfect all the time?' Dixie heard herself ask wistfully, desperate for the magic secret, the miracle formula which might transform her appearance as well.

'Are we on the same planet?' César enquired with satiric bite.

'I don't think so.' Dixie reddened with sudden discomfiture.

'Who's Scott? A boyfriend?' César demanded with a chilling edge to his dark, deep-accented voice.

'Oh, I don't have a boyfriend… Scott's just…Scott…well, Scott…' Suddenly Dixie was having some difficulty in quantifying her relationship with Scott, because tonight she had rediscovered hope, and to write Scott off as merely a friend now felt like acknowledging defeat again.

'Scott?' César queried with an impatient flare of one ebony brow.

'Scott Lewis…' Her blue eyes became even more abstracted. 'I love him, but he hasn't really noticed me that way yet, but I think he might be on the brink—'

César clenched his even white teeth. 'I'm getting closer to the brink too—'

Dixie heaved a sigh, shoulders down-curving. 'So I suppose I still have to say that Scott's just a friend.'

'Dixie…I asked a straight question. I didn't request an outpouring of girlish confidence,' César informed her with withering cool. 'I hope you're more circumspect with him than you are with me. I don't expect to find out that you've confided in him about our private arrangement.'

'Scott and I don't have those kind of conversations.' Inexplicably the happy shine on Dixie's evening was now beginning to drain away, leaving her feeling rather down on the dumps. 'Nothing deep—'

'He's got his head screwed on, then, hasn't he?' César sent her a winging glance of burning exasperation. 'You're not grounded enough for a deep conversation. Inside that flighty, vacant head of yours, you're up in the bloody clouds with the angels most of the time!'

But then there was no room for magic or love in César Valverde's world. He was so grounded in reality he didn't know what it was to dream. Well, he was missing out on an awful lot, Dixie decided, determined not to be affected by his censure.

Without warning the door of the room César had emerged from opened again. A gorgeous blonde in an elegant strappy black dress peered out and frowned at Dixie. 'Staff problems, César?'

Taken aback by the appearance of the other woman, Dixie stiffened with discomfiture.

César dredged his frustrated attention from Dixie and turned with a slashing smile. 'Nothing that need concern you, Lisette.'

Lisette. Frisky name for a frisky lady, Dixie thought nastily, and then was genuinely shocked by her own bitchiness. Lisette was probably a very nice woman, and was undoubtedly far too good for César Valverde. He was a real rat, the kind of guy who didn't phone, always put work first, cancelled dates last-minute and strayed without conscience the instant he got bored. Poor Lisette. She was more to be pitied.

Dixie went to her room and settled Spike into his basket. She fed César the goldfish, still feeling guilty about him being alone in his bowl. But he obviously preferred being alone. He was an aggressive fish. But possibly the two companions he had eaten had been the wrong sex, she reflected with a considering frown. Maybe he would be transformed by the arrival of a female fish… Could she risk adding to the body count?

As Dixie pulled on her shortie pyjamas, she struggled against the conviction that if she didn't eat some proper food soon her stomach would meet her backbone. After all, now she had a goal, a *real* goal. Scott was worth that one hundred and five per cent commitment César had demanded from her. She would throw herself heart and soul into Gilda's fitness schedule.

But hunger kept Dixie tossing and turning, unable to sleep. At one in the morning she rolled out of bed in sudden de-

46 THE SPANISH GROOM

cision. An apple, a slice of toast, a cup of tea with the merest drop of milk…surely such a meagre snack wouldn't show on the scales?

As Dixie crept with a fast-bating heart towards the kitchen, the entire house was in darkness. She stubbed her toe on the edge of the kitchen door and went hopping round on one leg in the gloom, silently screaming until the worst of the pain receded. Then she folded down on her knees in front of the giant fridge. Tugging open the door, she sat there gently massaging her aching toe and contemplating the immensity of the temptation now available.

One little sin, she urged herself circumspectly. Just one… A sandwich…she wouldn't butter the bread, she bargained with herself. Or what about a thin slice of cheese on toast with a dash of that salsa…or possibly…?

'Just what do you think you're playing at?'

At the sound of that raw-edged icy demand coming out of nowhere at her, Dixie almost had a heart attack.

CHAPTER THREE

WITH a strangled cry of fright, Dixie twisted round on her knees, her heart pounding so fast she couldn't breathe.

The lights beneath the units flipped on, framing César, barefoot and bare-chested, only a pair of close-fitting jeans hugging his long, powerful legs as he stood there surveying her with complete scorn.

'I only wanted a little snack,' Dixie whispered tremulously. 'I didn't think I'd wake anybody up!'

'When I go to bed, I switch on the alarm system. If anything moves down here, I know about it.'

Abstractedly still rubbing at her throbbing toe, Dixie studied him with huge violet eyes. Clothed he was intimidating; half-naked he was…he was *awesome*. The instant that thought occurred to her, she reddened with mortification and twisted her head away, terrified that he might read her face and somehow *know* what she'd been thinking. But in her mind's eye she still saw César. Wide brown shoulders, sleek strong muscles flexing beneath smooth healthy skin as his hand dropped back from the light switch, a magnificent torso with curling black hair hazing his pectorals, and a stomach as taut and flat as a washboard.

A frisson of strange heat curled in Dixie's stomach and then seemed to dart down somewhere infinitely more private and sort of twist in pleasure-pain. Her mouth felt as dry as a bone and she didn't know what was the matter with her. Spooked by his descent, and dying with embarrassment at being caught in the act of trying to cheat on her diet plan, it was all too much at once. Dixie parted her lips to explain herself, but to her utter horror a choky little sob escaped instead.

47

'Porca miseria!' César glowered at her in disbelief. 'You can't be *that* hungry!'

Seeing him through a haze of mortifying tears, Dixie dragged herself upright and turned away, struggling to get a grip on her seesawing emotions and hide her face.

She didn't read anything into the silence that followed, merely pictured him gripping his whiplash tongue between his teeth sooner than risk provoking her into a real crying jag. And she felt so hatefully childish. She had never been a crybaby, but he always made her feel so awkward, useless and silly.

'Madre di Dio…' César Valverde breathed incredulously. 'Who ever would have believed it? You've got the body of a men's magazine centrefold!'

Dixie's damp eyes slowly opened wide with bewilderment. Not even crediting that he could possibly have said what she thought he had said, she whirled round. She connected with stunned dark eyes engaged in a shockingly intimate appraisal of her lightly clad length. Having until that instant completely overlooked the fact that she was only wearing a pair of shrunken shortie pyjamas, Dixie crimsoned under that raking scrutiny and crossed her arms over herself.

'Don't!' César ejaculated forcefully, his seemingly mesmerised attention nailed to the proud swell of her full breasts so clearly delineated by the clinging cotton jersey.

His transfixed gaze came to a halt at her tiny waist, and at that point keeping a distance became more than he could apparently bear. Striding over to her, he turned her round with one impatient hand. Like a male quite unable to believe the evidence of his own eyes, he scanned the highly feminine curve of her hips and the surprising length of her shapely legs.

'What…for heavens' sake…*what are you doing*?' she gasped in helpless confusion at his behavior as she attempted to coil away and conceal as much as possible of the body she loathed.

'I assumed you were overweight. I thought you were hiding a multitude of sins beneath those shapeless sacky clothes you wore. I didn't even know you *had* a waist! And *Dio*, all the time…all the time,' César slowly repeated in a roughened and dazed undertone that sent a curious quiver rippling down her taut backbone, 'You were covering up the kind of lush curves that keep teenage boys awake and fantasising at night!'

'I don't know what you're talking about!' Dixie pulled away, hugging herself with her arms, shaken and mortified by what he was saying and convinced that he was being sarcastic. But, whatever, it was obvious that in his eyes she wasn't anything like as overweight as he had evidently believed she was. So maybe she could now risk letting her breath out, because holding her stomach in was becoming painful.

César backed off a soundless step, brilliant dark eyes veiled, faint colour highlighting his slashing cheekbones. A shuttered look wiped all expression from his stunning dark features as he continued to survey her. 'I know you don't. And while obviously you have no idea how to maximise what you've got, *I* have,' he stressed with unconcealed satisfaction. 'We'll be in Spain within a few days.'

'Within a few days?' Dixie parroted in astonishment. 'But that doesn't give me enough time to—'

'You don't need time. All you need is the right clothes and something done with that hideous untidy mop of Raggedy-Ann curls.' César strolled gracefully over to the fridge, flipped the door wide and cast her a satiric glance. 'Eat your heart out! And go easy on the exercise. Conserve your potential. I intend to exploit every luscious inch.'

And with that smooth invitation, light gleaming over his thick dark hair and smooth brown back, César sauntered back out of the kitchen, exuding in waves the kind of self-satisfied aura that he usually reserved for closing a major deal.

Every luscious inch? In a total daze of disbelief, Dixie squinted down at the much despised bountiful bosom which had caused her such agonies of mortification during her teens. Both her stepmother, Muriel, and Petra had been naturally thin, and only minimally endowed in that department. Both had fully entered into Dixie's conviction that such generous curves were gross and only worthy of concealment.

And school had been a nightmare for Dixie. She had started to develop at an age when her classmates were still flat-chested. The cruel, thoughtless teasing from the girls and the crude comments of the rowdier boys had devastated Dixie's confidence in her own body. Her pronounced hourglass shape had made her a target for ridicule. Times without number she had come home from school and gone up to her room to cry her heart out.

Muriel had bought her a big sloppy sweater which she could pull down over her hips, ensuring that the size of her breasts became instantly less likely to attract attention. And ever since then Dixie had relied on the same remedy and dressed accordingly.

And yet César Valverde had, incredible as it seemed to her, actually looked at her figure with stunned appreciation. No, not any kind of *personal* appreciation, she hurriedly adjusted, wondering how on earth she had contrived to pick up such an exaggerated false impression from him. He had only been acknowledging that she had the sort of over-generous curves that teenage boys liked, and that was certainly not news to Dixie. His appreciation had been of the entirely dispassionate variety. But what she had always considered a great disadvantage and a flaw, César somehow saw as an asset.

And suddenly he didn't think she needed to lose weight, or even exercise too much. But had she really stood there, letting him look her over when she was, if not quite half-naked, certainly only minimally clad? A hot tide of painful color swept up Dixie's throat at that belated awareness. He had taken her so much by surprise. Now she felt sick with chagrin, and all desire to eat had ironically evaporated. Slamming shut the fridge door, she returned to her room.

So César Valverde didn't think she was quite as unattractive as he had believed. Hadn't he noticed her tummy or the surplus flesh on her thighs and ribcage? She peered over her shoulder at the pronounced swell of her hips and slowly shook her head, his staggering change in attitude still a complete mystery to her. But then César Valverde treated her like a piece of meat, to be properly packaged for sale in a butcher's window, and after all, the only living person she had to impress was Jasper Dysart...

César walked into the sunlit gym with Gilda the next morning and then stopped dead. His sunglasses dropped out clean of his hand. Sheathed in a fitting one-piece dark green leotard, Dixie was doing her warm-up exercises.

She paused and connected unexpectedly with César's shimmering dark eyes. She fiercely resisted the urge to wrap her arms round herself like a self-conscious schoolgirl. The leotard was less revealing than a swimsuit, she reminded herself. As she gazed across the gym, unwittingly entrapped by that piercing silvered stare of his, so bright in that dark masculine face, she began feeling light-headed, and without even realising it slowly fell still.

A wave of startling heat slowly engulfed her from head to toe. Her eyes widened, her pupils dilating as for the first time she became aware of her own body in the most extraordinarily unsettling way. Her skin felt too hot and tight to encase her bones. Her breasts felt strangely heavy, stirring in their cotton casing with her every shortened breath and making her nipples ache with oversensitivity.

Gilda picked up César's sunglasses and extended them to him. With a slight frown he slowly dredged his attention from Dixie, and momentarily studied the sunglasses as if they didn't belong to him.

'I got up really early this morning.' Dixie blinked rapidly, like a sleepwalker rudely awakened. She folded her arms tightly above her waist, face burning as she strove to work out what had happened to her there for a few seconds while seriously hoping it never, ever happened again because she had felt really peculiar.

'That's the spirit!' Gilda applauded in the incredibly tense silence.

Without comment, César strolled over to one of the tall

windows, effortlessly elegant in pale, beautifully cut chinos and an aqua silk short-sleeved shirt. Dixie's gaze abstractedly followed him, taking in the tense set of his wide shoulders, the aggressive jut of his set profile and the dusting of darker colour delineating one carved cheekbone. He was so incredibly perfect, she conceded absently, still having a problem getting her brain into gear while she could not help but wonder what was bothering him. Business, no doubt, or perhaps irritation at her unwelcome presence in his home and the disruption of his own workaholic schedule.

Two days later, Dixie appraised her new hairstyle in fascination. Her mop of curls had been tamed by the talented stylist. Sleek, feathery layers curved back from her face, fanning down into casual waves just clear of her shoulders. Shorn of the chunky overhang of hair she used to hide behind, her cheekbones now lent fresh definition to her features.

The beautician was waiting for her in another part of the salon. Dixie had given up on make-up because she had always seemed to buy the wrong colours and had never been satisfied with the look she ended up with. But with an expert adviser on hand to select the right shades, she was delighted with the subtle effect contrived with a few light cosmetics.

Clutching a beauty case crammed with items, as per César's explicit instructions, she finally emerged and walked back to the waiting area. She was astonished to see César there, talking into a mobile phone while glancing broodingly at his watch and studiously ignoring the many languishing female glances coming his way from both staff and customers.

Dixie's steps slowed. Look at me, she suddenly wanted to shout. *Notice* me! The shock of that instant desire to impress was profound, but she soon explained it to her own satisfaction. Five minutes after she had arrived for her appointment at the salon, César had descended without warning. So wasn't it only natural that he should now be keen to see the end result, and equally natural that she should expect to be noticed?

After all, hadn't he told the stylist exactly what he wanted him to do with her hair? Hadn't he warned the beautician that he didn't want her covered in what he had bluntly described as 'a two-inch deep layer of goop'? She smiled helplessly at the memory.

'You've got to have a tongue in your head in a place like this,' César had informed her drily before he departed again. '*You'd* give them a free hand, but they need limits.'

And Dixie hadn't been the slightest bit embarrassed while César was domineeringly engaged in setting those limits, because two most unexpected compliments had indirectly come her way. No, Dixie would not require highlights, lowlights or any other kind of lights in her dark brown hair. Dark brown hair was elegant, César had stated, and also, since Dixie had flawless skin, why cover it up?

Now, when she was about six feet away from him, César's smooth dark head turned in her direction. He stilled, appraising her with unreadable dark-as-night eyes. Her breath fluttered in her throat, her heartbeat quickening as she waited for his reaction.

'Major improvement,' César commented as he retracted the aerial on his mobile and strode towards the exit, having awarded her little more than an assessing glance.

The wobbly smile of anticipation on Dixie's lips fell away as she rushed to keep up with him. 'Yes, it is, isn't it?'

'What?'

'An improvement?' Dixie reminded him wistfully, encouragingly, as they emerged on to the crowded street outside. 'I can't believe I look so much smarter.'

'Only from the neck up. Your wardrobe is still a disaster area,' César pointed out, thoroughly deflating her as he stood back for her to step into the rear of his chauffeur-driven limousine.

'No, you first,' she urged uncomfortably, still very conscious of what she felt to be his superior status.

'Move, Dixie,' César gritted in her ear.

In haste, Dixie scrambled into the limousine, sending a file sitting on the back seat flying. As documents spilled out,

Dixie groaned and bent down to clumsily gather them up again. 'I didn't expect you to take the trouble to come into the salon this morning,' she admitted, squinting down at the documents and realising that there was no way she could even try to put them back in order when they were written in a foreign language.

'I didn't expect to have to take the trouble either,' César confided almost to himself, his attention lingering fixedly on the mess of confused papers now being apologetically slid on to the seat between them. 'I was in the middle of a board meeting before it dawned on me that I couldn't trust you alone in a place like that. You might go overboard and emerge looking totally unrecognisable—'

'I've always sort of wanted to be blonde,' Dixie mused absently, now engaged in hurriedly cramming the documents out of sight within the file. 'My sister's blonde—'

'—or you'd sit there in a total daydream and let them do whatever they felt like doing to you. It was too big a risk.'

'I'm sure this has all been very inconvenient for you,' Dixie muttered ruefully.

'You're not joking, but we'll get the clothes problem sorted today too. We're flying out to Spain the day after tomorrow.'

'That soon?' Dixie sighed. 'Spike's going to miss me terribly.'

'The dog? I haven't laid eyes on that dog since the night you moved in,' César remarked, with belated awareness of that surprising fact.

'Oh, you have, you just haven't noticed him. Spike hides when there are people around. He was very badly treated by his first owner. The lady he used to stay with during the day was a volunteer at the animal refuge, but he'll have to stay in your house while I'm away because I couldn't ask her to keep him for so long.'

'Couldn't…er…Scott keep him?'

'Spike is terrified of men. Anyway, Scott's at work all day, and often out at night as well. I'm going to miss him too… Do you think I'll be in Spain long?' she asked rather guiltily.

'What does Scott do?' César enquired, without answering that question.

'He's a stockbroker with a City firm called Lyle and something…'

'Makes sense,' César said softly.

'What does?'

'That the smartass who has you acting as an unpaid skivvy would be a broker. Brokers are wheeler-dealers. He saw you coming.' César flicked her a narrowed glance of complete exasperation.

'You don't know what you're talking about…Scott is *not* a smartass!' Dixie had turned very pink, highly disconcerted as she was by that uninvited opinion coming from such a source.

'He knows that you're infatuated with him and he uses it to his own advantage.'

'I didn't ask you what you think and I don't want to know either!' Her hands tightly linked on her lap, Dixie stared unseeingly out the window at the heavy traffic. 'How did you find out that I help out with his housework anyway?' She suddenly had to know.

'I heard two of the secretaries talking about what an idiot you were weeks ago.'

Dixie trembled. It took that much effort to hold in the surge of angry humiliation now eating her alive.

'You don't seem to know any of the tricks other women are *born* knowing. Doing the guy's washing doesn't seem to be getting you very far,' César said with scathing cool.

'I hate you…do you know that?' Dixie jerked round to look at him, violet eyes pools of angry, hurt reproach.

'For telling you the truth? If you had any decent friends they'd have broken the news and given you a few useful hints long ago.'

For a split second meeting those stunning dark eyes on the level deprived Dixie of both breath and concentration. Her lashes fluttered in confusion and her head whirled. She sucked in oxygen and hurriedly turned her head away again, her heart slamming hard against her breastbone. She felt really shaky in the aftermath of that exchanged glance, and blamed it on her overtaxed emotions.

'You think I'm wasting my time, and yet you don't know Scott and you don't know me. What sort of "useful hints" do you think I need?'

'*Dio*…I'm not an agony aunt,' César drawled, boredom oozing from every honeyed accented syllable.

'Jasper spoilt you terribly…' Dixie's chagrined reaction to that snub leapt straight on to her tongue. 'That's why he worries about you so much. He feels responsible for the way you've turned out!'

The silence that rewarded that startling speech positively reverberated in her ears. Realising that she had been inexcusably blunt on the worst possible subject, Dixie glanced up in stricken apprehension.

Outraged dark eyes filled with rampant incredulity were trained to her.

'I'm sorry. I was too personal…but it's just you can be so very rude, and it doesn't seem to bother you that other people have feelings that can be hurt,' Dixie completed shakily.

'Is that a fact?' César drawled, with a sardonic smile that utterly dismissed her comments.

But Dixie was not fooled. She had drawn blood. His fabulous bone structure was rigid, his eyes glittering hard as diamonds. Dixie bent her head, shaken that she had spoken up to censure him and conscious that she had struck a very low and inappropriate blow in revealing that his godfather had actually discussed such very personal concerns with her.

She was thoroughly ashamed of herself. How could she have been so thoughtless? How could she have betrayed Jasper's confidence? And even though he had never been known to show them, César *had* to have some feelings! Naturally she had hurt César by voicing Jasper's guilty conviction that he had made serious parenting mistakes while he was his guardian.

Jasper had told her that César had always inhabited another plane from his peers. Intellectual brilliance had set him apart at an early age and made him intolerant of those less able.

That whiplash tongue had made people very scared of César Valverde. If they weren't super-careful they lost face in César's presence; scorn was infinitely more humiliating than a straightforward rebuke or criticism.

'I should never have said those things,' Dixie whispered valiantly, desperately needing to try and put right any damage she might have done, particularly to Jasper's standing in César's highly critical eyes. 'And you mustn't get the idea that Jasper discussed you with me—'

'Where would I get an idea like that?' César countered, with such tacit scorn that she paled with even greater dismay and guilt.

'But it wasn't like that!' Dixie protested frantically. 'You remember all the publicity there was about that actress you dumped last summer? The one who was rushed into hospital with an overdose—?'

'Not an overdose. Alcoholic poisoning.'

'Oh…w-was it really?' Dixie floundered at that immediate contradiction.

'I dumped her because she was never sober,' César returned icily.

'Jasper didn't kn-know that, and he was upset at all the furore in the papers,' Dixie stammered. 'And that was when he said just a few things *unthinkingly*,' she stressed feverishly, 'about the way he had brought you up not having been the best—'

'*Accidenti!* I only knew the woman a few weeks.' Black eyes assailed hers in remorseless challenge. 'She had a problem long before I met her, but I persuaded her to accept professional help *and* I arranged for her to stay in a special unit where she received all the counselling and support she needed.'

'J-Jasper would've been so relieved to know all that,' Dixie mumbled weakly, treading now on ground she wished she had never dared to set a single toe upon.

Indeed, now squirming with embarrassment over her own clumsy misapprehensions, Dixie felt ten times worse. When she climbed out of the limo in César's imperious wake, she put an anxious hand on his sleeve. From his lofty height, he studied her small hand as if it was a gross invasion of his personal space.

Her nerveless fingers slid off his sleeve again as though she had been burnt. 'I didn't mean to hurt your feelings.' Sincere concern shone from her scrutiny.

'Hurt my feelings?' César echoed in disbelief. 'Where the hell do you get the idea that—?'

'You're a not very easy person to apologise to...are you?' Dixie was appalled to see bitter anger flaming in his burnished dark eyes. 'I just seem to keep on digging myself into a deeper hole with you. Every time I open my mouth, I put my foot in it.'

'A vow of silence would be welcome,' César spelt out grittily.

She got on his nerves, she conceded, her shoulders slumping.

'Don't slouch.' A lean hand squared over her spine to brace her upright again.

He really disliked her, Dixie thought morosely. Everything she did and said irritated him. She wasn't used to being disliked. Presumably that was why she felt so absolutely awful all of a sudden. Her usually sunny nature reacted to the endless night of his like oil on water. They were such incompatible personalities. He was so cold, so unfeeling, so critical, and that made her more nervous, more likely to say and do the wrong thing. She had always found it totally impossible to concentrate around César Valverde. It was as if her brain went on holiday.

César stole an undeniably apprehensive glance down at her tremulous lip line.

'I'm not going to cry...I'm *not*!' Dixie swore.

'You're not convincing me.'

Her wide eyes shimmered.

'*Dio*...you have really stunning eyes,' César breathed in an abrupt and roughened undertone, staring down into her face as if she was the only woman in the universe.

In severe shock, Dixie gazed back up at him, even her

breathing arrested. That deep, sexy, accented drawl rippled down her sensitive spine and made her shiver in reaction. Locked into the dense darkness of his amazing eyes, it was as if the world had stopped turning for her, sentencing her to paralysis. Not a single thought filled her blank mind. And yet on another level she dimly recognised the desperate yearning surging up inside her like a hungry, terrifying beast. That sensation scared the living daylights out of her, but still she couldn't have moved, couldn't have spoken, couldn't have broken the spell that held her fast.

César did that. While she gazed at him, her heart beating so fast it felt as if it was about to burst from her chest, his spiky glossy black lashes lowered, setting her free from the cage of her own suffocating excitement. And as she watched, trembling, utterly disorientated by what was happening to her, she saw him breathe in very slowly and deeply, like a male tasting life-giving air after a long time asleep. A black frown line indented his brow, his striking features broodingly tense for a split second.

'I just got this really creepy feeling,' Dixie confided helplessly, tottering away from him to cannon blindly into a group of shoppers and stop to splutter unsought apologies while still blocking their path.

'Really…creepy…feeling?' César framed expressionlessly as he reached out a lean brown hand and tugged her out of harm's way and back towards him.

'I'm not feeling very well.' Her body still running alternately hot and cold like a broken boiler, her head spinning, her legs weak as matchsticks and her breasts throbbing in the most mortifying and uncomfortable way, Dixie focused on his burgundy silk tie with big bewildered eyes. 'I hope it's not the flu…or maybe I'm upset because I'm not likely to see Scott again for ages.'

A vague frown of recall on her flushed face, she looked up at César, surprised by the intensity of his piercing gaze. 'Why did you say that about my eyes?'

'I was trying to distract you. It worked like magic.' His eyes were as remote and icy as the Himalayas.

Distract her? From what? Oh, the tears. He had thought she was about to burst into tears and embarrass him in public. Naturally the bit about her eyes being stunning had been a whopper. It was a wonder he had managed to keep his face straight while he said it.

César urged her through the gilded doors of the hugely impressive store they had been standing outside. One step inside the doors, he abandoned her. The silence of an élite clientele and very expensive merchandise intimidated Dixie.

Her attention stayed with César, now in close conversation with a svelte older woman who appeared to have been awaiting their arrival. César had the most weird effect on her, she mused. That almost sick sensation of excitement she could only equate to her never-to-be-forgotten terror on a roller-coaster ride as a child. And he had treated her like an over-wrought child.

He strode back across the floor to her, looking every inch what he was. A very, very rich and powerful man, a highly sophisticated male, superbly elegant in a formal pinstripe suit that accentuated every powerful line of his lean, magnificent length. He stopped a good four feet from her, rather as if he was in the presence of potential contagion. His expression was cold and hard as stone.

'Mariah will select your clothes. Regard them as props and don't question her judgement. She knows what I want.'

And with that icy assurance he took his leave. Dixie stared after him with a perplexed frown. What had she done to deserve the deep freeze treatment? Just been herself, she decided glumly. Tactless, clumsy and embarrassingly emotional. Three flaws that César would never suffer from.

The evening of the following day, Dixie cast a dubious glance at herself in the bedroom mirror. Was that really her? The blue chambray skirt and fitted jacket showed an awful lot more of her body than she was used to seeing. As for the silk T-shirt she wore beneath, every time she looked down she was confronted by a view of her own cleavage. The strappy stiletto shoes had perilously high heels and she found it hard to walk in them.

The phone by her bed buzzed and she answered it.

'I want to see you in the drawing room in ten minutes,' César drawled coolly.

'Gosh, you nearly missed me. I was just on my way out to Scott's,' she confided cheerfully.

'It's going to take me a while to get the hang of these heels,' she carolled as she stumbled in the drawing room doorway and had to snatch at the doorhandle to steady herself.

In the act of lifting a brandy goblet to his lips, César froze. Dixie froze too. He was wearing a white dinner jacket that fitted him like a glove, the light colour throwing his vibrant golden skin and black hair and dark eyes into exotic prominence. He looked so devastatingly attractive Dixie's soft mouth fell open.

And for some reason César was staring at her too. Suddenly self-conscious, and mortified by the way she had gaped at him, Dixie got all hot and bothered. 'Is this going to take long? I don't want to miss Scott.'

'*Dio mio*…he's unlikely to miss you.' Brilliant dark eyes scanned the fit of the T-shirt, the skirt outlining her tiny waist, then dropped to the shapely legs on display outside the gym for the first time. 'That bloody stupid woman!' he grated abruptly. 'You look like a bimbo! That neckline's too low. That skirt is too short.'

In frank dismay and surprise, Dixie gazed back at him. 'The skirt's only three inches above my knee—'

'Totally inappropriate for Jasper…and even more inappropriate for doing Scott's washing,' César completed with withering bite.

'I wanted him to see my new look.' Dixie's face had fallen like a disappointed child's.

César elevated a winged ebony brow, and suddenly such a desire seemed pathetic on her part. She flushed miserably.

Feeling both over and under-dressed, Dixie relinquished the colourful fantasy of Scott taking one look at her and instantly realising that she was the woman for him. She would put on her usual clothes and remove the make-up. Suddenly she was grateful that César had spoken up. She didn't want to make it obvious to Scott that she was trying to attract him. That might wreck their friendship and scare him off altogether, mightn't it?

'A jeweller is coming to show us a selection of engagement rings.'

'Oh…' Dixie said.

'Whatever you pick you can keep,' César informed her carelessly.

'No. When I get a *real* engagement ring, I'd like it to be my first. I'll just look on this one as being on loan.'

The jeweller arrived. By then, Dixie was hunched on the sofa, looking very self-conscious. She so wished she had had time to get changed. César was a real sophisticate, and if he thought she was showing too much flesh obviously he had to be right. She was ashamed that he had had to tell her what she should have realised for herself. And yet she had seen loads and loads of perfectly respectable young women wearing what she had assumed were similar clothes.

But now her jacket was buttoned to her throat, to conceal the offending T-shirt, and her restive fingers were constantly tugging at the hem of the skirt which felt indecently short.

'So choose,' César invited in the increasingly tense silence.

'Diamonds are very cold,' Dixie sighed. 'Pearls and opals are unlucky. Some people say green isn't very lucky either. I don't know anything bad about rubies, *but*—'

'So pick a ruby.'

The jeweller, who was keeping his head down, hurriedly extended the appropriate tray.

'Rubies are supposed to stand for passionate love,' Dixie completed in an apologetic undertone. 'A diamond might be more suitable.'

César breathed in very deep. With an unerring eye, he reached down to select the most opulent diamond ring. 'We'll have this one.'

The cluster was so big it looked like a fake out of a

Christmas cracker. Dixie was relieved that she didn't like the ring. She felt it kept everything on a comfortingly impersonal basis.

As soon as the jeweller had checked the size of her finger, Dixie was on her feet. 'Can I go now?'

'Please don't let me keep you,' César drawled acidly.

Thirty minutes later, Dixie rang Scott's doorbell. She was totally taken aback when the door was answered by an unfamiliar man.

'Looking for Scott?' he said helpfully.

Dixie nodded.

'We work together...he said I could use this place while he's in New York.'

'New York?' Dixie stressed in a shaken tone, certain she must have misunderstood.

'Temporary secondment. Scott only got the offer yesterday. A chance like that, he didn't waste any time. He flew out this morning.'

Dixie was in shock. 'How long is he likely to be away?'

'A couple of months, I should think.'

CHAPTER FOUR

'MR VALVERDE is waiting,' Fisher informed Dixie with suppressed urgency.

Tears welling up in her eyes, Dixie settled Spike into his basket.

'Cook's going to bring Spike into the kitchen every day. He doesn't mind her,' the older man told her kindly. 'We'll spoil him rotten if he lets us.'

Nodding, because she didn't trust herself to speak, Dixie focused on the aquarium sitting on the chest. César the fish was at one end, his new lady companion, Milly, at the other. Neither seemed to venture into the other's territory. A bit like her and César Valverde, she conceded ruefully. She lived in his house but saw him only by rare and reluctant invitation.

'I'll take the aquarium down to the kitchen too,' Fisher promised.

'I talk to them every day.'

'Cook could talk the hindleg off a donkey.'

César was pacing the front hall. Lean, mean and magnificent in a lightweight charcoal-grey suit, burgundy shirt and silver-grey silk tie, he surveyed Dixie with glittering dark eyes of enquiry.

'I've kept you waiting…I'm sorry.'

As his attention lingered on her, Dixie smoothed an uneasy hand down over the skirt of her chic green summer dress.

César fixedly studied the ragged, uneven hem of the garment from which several stray threads still hung. 'What have you done to that dress?' he demanded.

Dixie had hoped he wouldn't notice. 'After what you said last night, I thought it might be a bit too short too…so I let the hem down, but it didn't go down the way I thought it would—'

'So why didn't you wear something else?'

'Fisher had already taken away my case.'

In thunderous silence, César gritted his even white teeth. Crossing the hall, he proceeded to hunker down and pluck away the hanging threads with impatient fingers.

'You see, I needed something to occupy me last night. Scott's been sent to New York for a while…I didn't even get to say goodbye…' Her voice trailed away as she absently watched a shard of sunlight glance over César's gleaming blue-black hair and then marvelled at the incredible length of his inky black lashes as she gazed down at him.

'Life's little cruelties toughen one up,' César advised with an outstanding lack of sympathy as he vaulted back upright. He pressed her towards the front door. 'And now, while you're in Spain, you won't have the distraction of thinking of Scott being back here in London.'

'I guess not…and it's a great opportunity for him.' Dixie gave a determined smile. 'Scott's boss must think very highly of him to offer him such a chance.'

César turned to her once inside the limo. 'You have blue shadow on one eyelid and green on the other.'

'Is it noticeable?'

'It's screaming at me.'

Dixie nodded, dug a tissue out of her bag and removed the shadow without resorting to a mirror. She then dug out a paperback and proceeded to read. This obvious solution to coping with César, who would sooner she was seen but not heard, had occurred to her the night before. If she dug her nose into a book he wouldn't feel he had to talk to her, and she wouldn't find herself inadvertently trying to chat to him.

An hour and a half later she hurried up the steps of his private jet, her excitement unconcealed. 'I've never been on a plane before,' she told the flight attendant without hesitation. 'I've never been abroad before either!'

'Sit down and behave like a grown-up,' César growled in her ear from behind.

Reddening, Dixie dropped down into the nearest seat.

'You sit with me.' César had the embattled air of a male restraining his temper with the greatest of difficulty.

Dixie wondered what she had done wrong. She hadn't spoken to him once, not once, and she'd assumed he would be delighted to be able to forget her existence. She'd had a great chat with his chauffeur on the way through the airport, and then there had been that lovely old lady she'd got talking to in the VIP lounge. Yet far from appreciating the space and privacy she had awarded his natural reserve, César had become tenser and colder by the minute.

As the jet taxied down the runway, Dixie started getting nervous at the prospect of her first take-off. In an effort to distract herself, she turned to look at César, where he sat to her right, a file open in one lean hand. 'What did I do that annoyed you?'

His hard profile clenched. He looked at her broodingly, shimmering dark eyes glinting from below semi-lowered lids. 'You're everybody's best friend. You have no dignity, no normal reticence. You told my chauffeur about Scott—'

'He told me about his daughter's marriage breaking up.'

'That's the point. He's an employee. I didn't even know he *had* a daughter!' César condemned as the engines whined and the jet began to race down the runway.

Dixie turned a whiter shade of pale and clutched at the arms of her seat with protruding knuckles. 'Oh, golly, I feel sick… I'm scared…this is really frightening… I don't think I want to fly *anywhere*!' she suddenly wailed, jerking loose her seatbelt and starting to rise.

She was tugged back safely into her seat by a restraining hand. As she attempted to catch her breath, César took one look at the sheer panic etched on her face and, meshing lean fingers into her hair, held her fast and kissed her.

Dixie forgot she was on board a jet. She forgot she was afraid. She even forgot to be afraid of *him*. In shock, she felt the hard male heat of his mouth prying apart her lips. Like lightning suddenly unleashed inside her, that kiss zapped out every sane thought and burned her up with excitement. Without realising it, she clutched at him. As the tip of his tongue expertly invaded the moist sweetness of her mouth she shuddered, as if she was in a force ten gale, and pushed the fingers of one hand ecstatically into the springy silk of his hair.

He felt so good she wanted to sink into him and lose herself for ever in the frantically seductive tide of physical sensation assailing her. She was wildly, madly aware of every throbbing cell in her own body. Fierce energy and urgency was penned up inside her, fighting for release. She never passed the point of temptation. She got one taste of temptation and simply succumbed.

Without warning, César jerked away, long fingers dropping to her forearms to set her back from him. Dixie opened her eyes, blinked, and focused on his lean strong face, the feverish glitter in his brilliant dark incisive eyes. She couldn't see his anger, yet somehow she could *feel* his anger, silently striking out at her in the unbearably tense atmosphere.

'Did I do that wrong as well?' she asked, struggling to come to grips with the devastating reality that César Valverde had actually kissed her.

His incredible lashes dropped down over his eyes. He released her, but the silence continued to seethe.

'Of course you only did it because I started to panic about flying.' Dixie twisted her head away and tried to stop shivering.

'Even Jasper is likely to expect an engaged couple to exchange the occasional kiss,' César imparted very flatly.

Dixie swallowed hard on that assurance. She would have thought Jasper would be shocked rigid if they exchanged a passionate kiss in front of him. *Passionate?* No, not for César, she decided, her tummy muscles tightening with sudden extreme discomfiture. For César it had obviously just been a casual kiss, something in the nature of a reluctant rehearsal. He was probably affronted that she had thrown herself into that kiss as if they were Romeo and Juliet.

'You think I enjoyed you kissing me too much.' Looking anywhere but at him, Dixie was extremely embarrassed but determined to clear the air. 'You took me by surprise... I guess with your experience you're used to that kind of over-board response, but it was more of an experiment for me—'

'I think this may well be one of those deep conversations better shelved.'

Unexpectedly, Dixie turned back to face him, a sunny smile of anticipation slowly curving her reddened mouth. 'You don't understand. If *you* can make me feel like that, I can hardly wait to find out how Scott can make me feel!'

The silence refused to break. Indeed, the silence sat there like a huge brick wall barrier.

César stared steadily back at her, dark eyes black as a stormy night, not a revealing muscle moving on his strong dark features.

As the tension crackled sky-high, Dixie frowned in bewilderment. 'I just wanted to reassure you that I wasn't being silly and feeling attracted to you or anything like that... I mean I just *couldn't* be attracted to you...you're so...' She faltered to a halt in the pin-dropping quiet greeting that impulsive explanation.

'So...*what*?' César invited, with the most lethally intimidating smile.

Dixie gulped, an odd, thrilling chill running down her taut spine, as if she was dicing with death on the edge of a precipice. 'So...so far removed from me—'

'That's not what you were about to say.'

'I was getting too personal again,' Dixie back-tracked in haste.

'*So what*, Dixie?'

Mesmerised by the full onslaught of his dark stare, she whispered, 'So cold, so self-absorbed, so inhuman...'

'And you are so refreshingly, dangerously...honest,' César murmured.

Dixie had stopped breathing without understanding why. Then at that moment the bright voice of the flight attendant broke the spell. 'The captain wondered if Miss Robinson would like to visit the flight deck, sir.'

César rested his arrogant dark head back. 'I should think

Miss Robinson would be delighted. Don't touch anything, Dixie…don't fall against anything either.'

The flight attendant giggled.

Dixie went pink as she rose from her seat, well aware that César hadn't been joking.

By the time Dixie got out of the jet at Malaga, her cheerful outlook had vanished. Reality had dug in and dug in hard.

Until now she had cravenly avoided thinking about the masquerade that loomed at journey's end. She had concentrated her thoughts on simply spending time with Jasper again. That was in itself a most pleasurable prospect. She was intensely fond of Jasper and refused to dwell on the idea that he might be seriously ill. What could not be cured had to be endured. Dixie had learnt that lesson at an early age.

Only now, as she wandered in César's purposeful wake through the airport, was she becoming miserably, guiltily aware that she was about to take part in a deception which went against every principle she had been raised to respect. She had been in the depths of despair when César had approached her with his proposition. Sick with worry about Petra's debts, and exhausted by the strain of working two jobs, she had been further devastated to learn of Jasper's failing health…

And she remembered sitting in César's Ferrari later that same evening, listening against her will to his silver-tongued assurance that their pretend engagement would be the best news Jasper had ever heard. César had made it all sound so simple, so harmless. He had even made her feel that to refuse would be selfish and cruel.

But the imminent prospect of lying to an old man as sincere and trusting as Jasper made Dixie feel sick with nerves and guilt. She stumbled round a baggage trolley and stood gazing into space. How could she look Jasper in the face and lie?

'*Dixie!*' Striding back to intercept her for about the fourth time, César snapped an imprisoning hand over her shoulder to turn her in the right direction again. '*Accidenti!* Didn't you even notice you'd lost me?'

'No…'

Outside, César pressed her into a chauffeured limo with the driven aspect of a male who had valiantly herded an entire flock of wandering and wilful sheep through the crowded airport.

Dixie emerged from her uneasy thoughts to find César doing up her seatbelt. Jawline hard as a rock, he tightened it the way a medieval jailer might have tightened a chain on a prisoner likely to try and escape. 'Now just stay there…don't move.'

Lashes fluttering, Dixie gazed up at his lean, dark, devastatingly attractive face in total bemusement. 'Where would I move to?'

'And you can ditch that miserable expression. Agonising over Scott is forbidden!' Grim dark eyes scanned her startled face without remorse. 'You have a part to play, and although I don't expect your performance to qualify for an Oscar, I *do* expect you to look reasonably happy.'

'But I wasn't agonising over Scott. If you must know, I was worrying about lying to Jasper—'

'Leave the lying to me.'

'Yes, you'll be so much better at that than I could ever be,' Dixie conceded reflectively.

Flames of gold flared in César's incredulous gaze. 'I don't know how I've got you this far without strangling you,' he confessed in a shaken undertone. 'I have reserves of restraint I never knew I had.'

Dixie snatched in a stricken breath. 'That's a horrible thing to say…what could I possibly have done to deserve that?'

César spread the fingers of his two clenched brown hands very slowly. 'You want to know…you *really* want to know?'

He was truly angry, Dixie realised in shock and perturbation, violet eyes very wide.

'One…' César gritted, like a male about to embark on a very long speech. 'You have the attention span of a flea. Two…you wandered through the airport like a headless chicken. Three…you're still acting like the office junior. Exactly when are you planning to psych yourself into the role of my fiancée? While you were giggling like a schoolgirl with my cabin staff and trying on their hats, I heard you refer to me three times as *Mr* Valverde. Four…you're emotionally manic—'

'M-manic?' Dixie parroted tremulously.

'Either you're acting euphoric or you're on the brink of tears! There is no happy medium, no nice quiet level of normality.'

'My life hasn't *been* very normal recently,' Dixie pointed out, her throat thickening.

'Point five,' César growled rather raggedly as her violet eyes shimmered in helpless reproach, 'I do not like being ignored.'

Like a spoilt child, convinced that the entire world revolved around him, was Dixie's first thought. Fortunately she didn't say it out loud, but she was tempted to remark that she didn't recall him showing any sign that he wished to speak to her himself. Surely he didn't expect her to sit beside him in total silence, like a glove puppet waiting for an empowering hand?

'I wasn't ignoring you. I thought you preferred me to keep a low profile—'

'A *low* profile?' César echoed in a tone of rampant disbelief.

Dixie reddened and clasped her hands tightly together on her lap. 'You have so many hang-ups—'

'Hang-ups?' César ejaculated rawly.

'You're not a people person. And just having fun is beneath you. That brain of yours just never stops ticking and dissecting things…you are so deadly serious all the time. It's unnerving.'

'I find you equally unnerving,' César imparted after a staggered pause.

Involuntarily, Dixie collided with eyes that were silvered by a stray shard of sunlight filtering into the car, eyes that were dazzlingly beautiful in that lean, dark, brooding face, and her heart jumped and her tummy twisted and her conscience smote her all at once. In confusion she turned her head away, but in her mind's eye she was now seeing the unhappy, far too bright and knowing little boy whom Jasper had once sadly described to her. A cynic at the age of five, with a deep distrust of adults.

A wealthy young mother's fashion accessory only while he was still at the cute baby stage, César had been the pretty much unwelcome result of an impulsive and short-lived marriage. His parents had parted before he was even born. His playboy father had wanted his estranged wife to terminate her pregnancy, and when she'd failed to follow his advice had considered himself absolved of any further responsibility, other than financial, towards his son.

Finding a toddler's needs more of a nuisance than she had envisaged, César's youthful mother, Magdalena, had regularly left him with an ever-changing succession of nannies for weeks on end. As soon as she could she had put César into an English boarding school, and had often found it more convenient to simply leave him there during the long vacations.

'Magdalena was very immature. Her own parents were dead, so she had no support. She often had good intentions but she was hopelessly selfish,' Jasper had explained heavily. 'Forever promising to visit César at school but always letting him down. One of his stepfathers encouraged her to make more effort for a while, but he was soon out of the picture again.'

So it was no wonder that César was a complete loner, Dixie conceded tautly, already deeply regretting her censure. She had been unjust and unkind. César couldn't help being the way he was. By the time Jasper had got hold of him, at twelve, the damage had been done. César had walled up his emotions. He had never had a real home, never had a proper family or even siblings to tease him, never been loved just for himself...except by Jasper.

'Why are you looking at me like that?' César demanded

in sheer frustration as the limo drew up at a private airstrip where a helicopter awaited them.

Shaking her head in mingled emotion and embarrassment, Dixie made no response. But she had suddenly appreciated that César might talk about Jasper in that cool, offhand way of his, but that Jasper Dysart was probably just about the only person in the whole world whom César actually cared about.

And if anything happened to Jasper, César was in all probability going to be absolutely devastated. Jasper was César's one weakness. And suddenly the extravagant lengths César was prepared to go to in his determination to make Jasper happy struck Dixie as the most touching, telling thing ever…and the tears welled up.

'OK…' Tensing, César raised expressive lean brown hands in an attempted soothing motion that did not come naturally to him. 'You don't fancy the helicopter, but the alternative is hours of driving through the mountains and spending the night in a hotel.'

Dixie tore her shimmering gaze from César and said chokily, 'Actually I was thinking about you.'

'Don't think about me. I really do not *want* you thinking about me.'

Dixie nodded jerkily.

César reached for her knotted fingers, straightened them out and threaded on the opulent diamond engagement ring.

'I'll do the best I can to convince Jasper…I promise!' Dixie swore feverishly. 'I'll act just the way he would expect me to act if I was in love.'

'What's that likely to entail? No, no, make it a surprise,' César advised as he edged her by subtle motions out of the car.

'I'll try to think of you the way I think of Scott…' Dixie confided very seriously.

'That could be dangerous. You might fall in love with me instead.'

Dixie sent him an arrested look full of such astonishment that César stared back at her, hard black eyes narrowing and glinting, fabulous bone structure tautening. Quickly her mind went empty, and it was suddenly so hard to breathe, so impossible to look away.

Abruptly, César removed his intense gaze from her. 'I may be a cold bastard, but I don't want this charade to cause any lasting damage. A woman who cries her heart out over a cannibalised goldfish has to be more than usually vulnerable. In fact when I saw you leaning over that fountain asking the survivor how he could have stooped to eating his only friend, I decided you were totally off this planet.'

'I get very fond of my pets, but there is no danger that I would *ever* get fond of you!' Dixie retorted in fierce self-defence, and she scrambled into the helicopter without a backward glance.

For the duration of the flight over the snow-capped sierras of Andalusia, Dixie was deep in her own thoughts. She was reliving that whirling other-worldly sensation that overwhelmed her whenever she met César Valverde's eyes. It was terrifying, embarrassing, and yet weirdly thrilling. And she had finally worked out what was the matter with her...

César was gorgeous. Undoubtedly she was reacting to his intense sexual charisma. It was not that she was mentally attracted to him, she reasoned, it was that she was *bodily* attracted to him. Like when she was peckish and the vision of a tempting dessert formed inside her head. Foolish, harmless and meaningless, she told herself, resolving to keep a tighter rein on herself now that she understood the problem. And putting César on a level with chocolate fudge cake made her feel a lot less threatened and self-conscious. She would soon get over such silliness.

When the helicopter began to descend, it was dusk. As the craft tilted, Dixie gazed down into a thickly wooded hidden valley, a silvered road snaking like a ribbon through it into the distance. A beautiful hacienda clung to the steep forested slopes. The seemingly endless stretch of pale walls and red-tiled roof glimmered in the fading light. The helicopter set down on a helipad within the perimeter walls.

César sprang out and stretched in a hand to assist her.

Dixie grasped his fingers, her eyes brimming with surprise. '*This*…is where Jasper lives?'

'What did you expect? A little cottage complete with butterfly net in the foothills?'

Dumbly, Dixie shook her head. It was a simply huge house, with all the elegant opulence that only the very, very rich take for granted. As they crossed an exquisitely landscaped courtyard, with a softly playing fountain to the side entrance, César reached down and closed his hand over hers. 'Let's get the big announcement over with.'

A smiling middle-aged woman awaited them in the vast tiled hall. As she spoke, a frown instantly indented César's brow.

'What's wrong?'

'Jasper's not here.' César dropped her hand again—there now being no necessity to pretend he wanted even that small amount of physical contact with her, Dixie assumed. 'His housekeeper hasn't a clue where he is either. Typical Jasper! And in his state of health what on earth is he doing running about the countryside?'

'Maybe you should have phoned him to tell him we were coming.'

'I wanted to surprise him.' César sent her an impatient glance. 'Out of character for me, but exactly the kind of impractical impulse that Jasper would expect from a newly engaged couple!'

Dixie stared at him, not quite grasping the connection.

César's wide, sensual mouth twisted. 'I thought the very sight of me arriving with you unannounced would make us look more convincing…like I couldn't wait to show you off!' he pointed out in exasperation as he strode back to address the hovering housekeeper in fluent Spanish again. 'Ermina will show you up to my room. I'll need to make some calls to run Jasper to earth!'

An older man laden with their luggage was already heading up the ornate wrought-iron and stone staircase. Dixie followed the housekeeper up to the first landing, briefly stilling with an uncertain frown. She flushed. No, she must have

misheard him. César couldn't have said '*my* room'. He
couldn't possibly be expecting her to share his bedroom!

But minutes later Ermina showed her into a very large and
luxuriously furnished bedroom, where her luggage and
César's sat together like a statement. Dixie surveyed the bed,
with its massive intricately carved headboard. It was an extremely big bed. No, she was being ridiculous. This was
some silly misunderstanding. After all, Jasper was very old-
fashioned, and rather fond of muttering about the appallingly
lax moral habits of modern youth.

Tilting her chin and striving to suppress her discomfiture,
Dixie went downstairs again to find César. She located him
in a magnificent library, and for a split second her awed and
eager appraisal of all those tempting shelves of books made
her still in wonderment.

César was on the phone, talking in Spanish. His dark, deep
drawl sounded so...so sexy, Dixie reflected dimly, listening
to all those fluid rolling vowels with instinctive appreciation,
a curious little quiver fingering down her spine. She studied
him. Even after hours of travelling, César retained his incredible elegance, and he paced the room with the prowling
sure-footed grace of a leopard.

Turning his arrogant dark heard, César finally chose to
acknowledge her presence in the doorway. 'If you're hungry,
Ermina will fix you some supper.'

It was her cue to depart again. Staying put took courage.

'There's been a bit of a mix-up.' Dixie shuffled her feet
restively. 'They've gone and put my stuff in with yours...in
the same room, I mean, and I don't have the Spanish to
explain that...well, you know—'

'No, I don't know.' César elevated one satiric black brow
with daunting cool. 'Naturally we have to share a bedroom.
Jasper's not an idiot. If we slept apart he would never believe
this engagement was for real!'

CHAPTER FIVE

OPEN-MOUTHED, Dixie stared back at César, heated colour rising in a slow tide beneath her pale skin. 'You really expect me to share your room?' she whispered in disbelief.

César cast aside the cordless phone. 'Where are you coming from on this? Clarify the problem for me.'

The weighted silence pulsed.

Recognising the chill hardening his brooding dark features, Dixie drew in a sustaining breath. 'I couldn't possibly sleep in the same bed. I didn't bargain on anything like that when I agreed to this arrangement.'

'Didn't you? You sold your immediate future to me for a price. I've paid that price. You were up to your throat in debt, and scared witless of being dragged into court to answer for your dishonesty. You are not in a position to call the shots here,' César warned with icy bite, studying her as if she had crawled out from beneath a piece of furniture and was in dire need of being thoroughly squashed. 'And you are *far* from being the little innocent you like to pose as for Jasper's benefit!'

That full frontal attack came at Dixie out of nowhere and she was quite unprepared for it. She gaped at him. 'I'm not dishonest, and—'

'You *are* dishonest. You ran up debts you hadn't a prayer of paying. You are no better than a thief.' César's eloquent mouth curled with contempt. 'You should've faced up to that by now. And when you start trying to pretend to be something you're not with me as well, it's time to call a halt to your fantasies!'

'Fantasies...?' Dixie repeated weakly.

'The big parties? The ludicrously expensive trappings for a rented apartment? What else but fantasies? Maybe you were

77

trying to buy friends. But I don't have the slightest pity for you,' César informed her without hesitation. 'I know you have a brain, and I *know* you had to know exactly what you were doing—'

'But those parties weren't mine…and neither was the apartment!' Dixie broke in helplessly.

'I think you assumed that Jasper might pick up the bills for you. What a shock it must've been to learn that Jasper is as poor as a church mouse!' Brilliant dark eyes like lasers probed her shattered expression for a betraying response. 'Did you really think I wouldn't work that possibility out?'

Pale as milk and trembling, Dixie was appalled by his suspicions. 'I honestly don't know what you're talking about, and if you'd let me explain about those debts in the first place, you'd have known that—'

'You worked your way into Jasper's soft heart and stupidly assumed he was loaded?' César incised with stinging scorn. 'I'm not a fool. First the friendship, next the extravagant spending spree, and then no doubt you wrote to Jasper, anxiously confiding that you had got into some financial hot water—'

'No…no, that's crazy!' Dixie was falling into deeper shock by the second.

'And then possibly Jasper wrote back saying how much he would've liked to be able to help you…but unfortunately, since his trust fund was embezzled by a crooked accountant over ten years ago, he has been wholly dependent on me!'

'I wouldn't *do* anything like that…wouldn't have dreamt of worrying Jasper with my problems!' Dixie's eyes were stricken as she moved her head in a negative motion. 'You have such a hateful opinion of other human beings, César. You're always looking for the bad, never, ever the good.'

Unimpressed by that pained condemnation, César continued to survey her from his towering height, eyes as cold as black ice. 'Oh, I acquit you of real evil, but I'm certain that at some stage you must've attempted to fish yourself out of trouble by approaching Jasper for a loan.'

'Then perhaps you ought to ask him for my letters,' Dixie

countered with as much dignity as she could muster. She lifted her head high, her mouth tightly compressed with the effort self-control demanded of her. 'And perhaps you ought to get your facts right too.'

'And where could I possibly have got them wrong?' César traded very drily.

'My sister threw those parties—'

'You don't have a sister. You don't have a single living relative.'

'I'm talking about my *step*sister, Petra Sinclair. She's made quite a name for herself as a model. The apartment was hers. When I first came to London I lived with her, and because she was away so much she opened this bank account so that I could settle her bills. Then everything went wrong... *somehow*!' Dixie shook her aching head again, her forehead furrowing, as if she was still trying to come to grips with how everything had gone so very wrong.

'Petra...*Sinclair*?' César queried, with the oddest stress and a look of surprise.

While sensing something not quite right, either in his intonation or in his narrowed stare and hardening jawline, Dixie was far too involved in telling her story to let his curious reaction to her sister's name register with her for more than a second.

'Petra decided to go to Los Angeles and become an actress, and she's still over there...I don't know where. Well, you see, the deputy bank manager...who was just incredibly *nice*,' Dixie stressed, and then fell into a somewhat erratic explanation about the joint account and the way she had often ordered goods and services on Petra's behalf.

'If you're telling me the truth, Leticia Zane would've been well aware that *Petra* was her client.'

'Of course she was,' Dixie confirmed wearily. 'But once Miss Zane realised that Petra had left the UK she was furious. I don't think she believed me when I told her that I didn't have an address for Petra—'

'Probably not. I can check all this out,' César warned her, but for some reason the warning emerged almost as an afterthought, the suggestion being that he had already decided that she was telling the truth.

'Go ahead. I've got nothing to hide.'

He asked her several more probing questions. The set of his mouth grew more grim. 'I take back what I said about your brain,' he breathed. 'It's weak on survival skills and common sense.'

'You don't understand. Petra was terribly upset about the whole thing too, but by then, with the expense of moving to LA, she was really broke. If you only knew how terrific she was when my stepmother was ill—'

'She *was*?' For some reason César sounded very surprised to receive that assurance.

'Petra was absolutely wonderful, and I was very grateful. She really is a great person—a little thoughtless sometimes, but very generous and kind with everything she's got…when she's got it, I mean,' Dixie concluded rather limply.

'Generous…kind,' César echoed, as if he had never heard the words before, his deep, forceful drawl having for some reason sunk to the level of a constrained whisper.

Dixie looked up worriedly, drained by that outpouring.

César was studying her as if she was some strange life-form he had never come across before. An uncharacteristic mix of reluctant fascination and suppressed disbelief mingled in his brooding dark features. 'I imagine you're extremely *fond* of Petra?'

Dixie nodded in confirmation. She wasn't blind to César's incredulity, but, unlike him, she believed in taking people as they were. Petra's faults did not detract from Dixie's affection for her stepsister. Nor had Dixie ever resented the lack of hands-on help she had received during her stepmother's long illness. Petra and her mother had never got on, and Petra could not have coped with that caring role. In contrast, Dixie had loved her stepmother very much, and had wanted to do everything she could to repay the woman who had taken her into her heart as if she were her own child.

César stared steadily down into Dixie's clear blue eyes, opened his mouth and then finally closed it again. Then curiosity seemed to get the better of him, and he breathed, 'For how long did you take care of your stepmother?'

Dixie told him.

César braced a taut hand on the edge of the handsome library table beside him. 'Quite a slice of your life,' he remarked grimly.

'It's not something I'll ever regret.'

César expelled his breath in a slow hiss and glanced away from her. 'Even I can now accept that you would never have tried to coax money out of Jasper,' he conceded heavily. 'I got the wrong idea. I thought you'd been leading some kind of double life. Now I know that what you see is what you get with you...and that is spooky.'

'Spooky?'

'Let's just say that we don't have a great deal in common.' César flashed her a veiled look. 'Only very rarely am I forced to appreciate what I have by a terrifying glimpse of an alternative lifestyle and outlook.'

Recognising that he no longer believed that there was any truth in those dreadful suspicions he had cherished, Dixie sagged with relief.

'I owe you an apology,' César stated grittily.

'It's not important. You were sure to come up with a really nasty scenario. You can't help the way your mind works,' Dixie said forgivingly. 'Have you had any luck finding Jasper?'

'No...for all I know he's out camping somewhere under the stars!' César's profile tautened with a concern he couldn't hide.

Dixie cleared her throat awkwardly, deciding that now that César was more approachable she should return to the prickly question of sharing a bedroom. 'César, I really do think Jasper would take a very dim view of coming back home to find us in the same bedroom—'

'Don't be ridiculous,' César countered with careless cool. 'We're not living half a century ago.'

'Jasper has very strong Christian beliefs,' Dixie pointed out very gently, conscious that César was sure to believe that he knew best where his godfather was concerned. 'He lives very much in his own little world, and it dates back more than half a century. I honestly believe he would be very shocked and offended at us sharing a room under this roof.'

César dealt her an impatient frown. 'You haven't a clue what you're talking about. Jasper has never questioned what I do in my private life.'

Did you bring your private life into his home? she badly wanted to ask, but couldn't bring herself to that controversial brink. César's notoriety as a ruthless womaniser was a source of very genuine concern and mortification to Jasper. But possibly Jasper had never dared to admit that to César. Indeed, it was hard to picture Jasper standing up to César, of whom he stood in considerable awe.

César swept up the phone again, indicating that the subject was closed.

'César...I'm just not comfortable with this bedroom arrangement,' Dixie persisted valiantly, her mind boggling at the prospect of sleeping in the same room as César, never mind the same bed.

'Quit while you're ahead, Dixie. Allow me to know my own godfather better than you do. Act like I'm Scott,' César suggested with a satiric glance of finality as he strode out of the library.

Dixie made a beeline for the books. An hour later, she climbed upstairs with a towering pile of rather dusty hardbacks, it having proved impossible for her to make a smaller selection. Her cases had already been unpacked for her. Eager to get to bed now that she had her books, she went back downstairs, found the kitchen and helped herself to a glass of milk. Then, back in the bedroom, she located one of the ridiculously glamorous new nighties she had been endowed with and hurried into the beautifully appointed bathroom with its fleecy towels. Stripping off on the spot, she got under the shower.

She was far too strait-laced, she told herself then. César would never dream of making a pass at her! They would each sleep on their own side of what was admittedly a very generously sized bed. There was an adjoining dressing room and with a little mutual care and consideration it needn't be that embarrassing an exercise.

Five minutes after reaching that seemingly sensible conclusion, Dixie was tucked up in bed in the enthusiastic hold of a weighty tome on eighteenth-century philosophy, her shapely figure fetchingly sheathed in palest green silk. When César walked through the bedroom door she was mental miles away, and she didn't hear him.

So when she groped out blindly for her milk, and then was forced to tear her attention from her book and actually look for the glass, she was quite transfixed to suddenly notice César casually peeling off his shirt about ten feet away.

She took in that magnificent expanse of golden brown male flesh and flexing muscles and just gaped.

'Ignore me,' César drawled with supreme casualness, a strange silvered challenge in his dazzlingly bright eyes, his expressive mouth twisting.

Barely breathing, Dixie ducked her head down again, heartbeat racing, mouth dry. The printed page swam. She could see nothing but César, could hear nothing but the rushing in her own eardrums and, preternaturally loud, the soft rasp of a trouser zip. He does this all the time, a dry little voice said inside her head. He's used to sharing a bedroom, a bed. Don't embarrass yourself by reacting in any way. She could breathe if she tried, *couldn't she*? Well, possibly, if she cleared her disobedient brain of wanton images of César Valverde completely unclothed.

Warmth like heated honey pooled in the pit of Dixie's stomach and made her quiver. She wanted to watch him undress. That awareness shook her rigid, but it still took real physical restraint not to lift her head again and peek.

When the bathroom door closed behind César, she drank in oxygen in great needy gulps, her face hot as hellfire with shame. Was this what sexual curiosity felt like? She couldn't ever remember being tempted to spy on Scott. Thank heaven, she thought, genuinely loathing the secret burn of guilty excitement which César's mere presence now unleashed in her.

Continued exposure to César's deeply unsettling aura of raw animal sex appeal had finally decimated her natural defences.

César strolled back out of the bathroom. Without the will to stop herself, Dixie peered surreptitiously out from behind her book, glimpsed long powerful thighs lightly dusted with dark curling hair, what might have been the hem of a pair of black silk boxer shorts, and felt as if she was about to have a heart attack.

'I see you hit the library hard.' With easy grace, César swept up a book and glanced through it.

In studious silence, Dixie nodded without looking at him. She didn't trust herself to look at him any more. She was really ashamed of herself. Out of the corner of her eye, she saw him pull back the sheet and slide into bed.

'To think I assumed you would cover yourself from head to toe to share this bed with me,' César confided, in a low-pitched murmur that was terrifyingly intimate.

Her tension shooting up to megawatt heights, Dixie slowly turned her head to register shimmering dark eyes lingering on the ripe curves cradled by sheer silk. A heady surge of colour blossoming in her cheeks, Dixie pressed her book against the swell of her full and now tingling breasts. 'I never thought—'

'There's too many things you never think about...' César mused in a thickened undertone that growled through the beating silence like a warning.

Already fiercely preoccupied with the mortifying throb of her tightening nipples, Dixie was striving to sink herself beneath the more decent concealment of the sheet that had fallen to her waist. Yet colliding head-on with silvered eyes as mesmerically bright as stars in that lean, dark face, she stilled, paralysed by the sudden greedy burst of excitement flaming through her disobedient body.

'Whereas *I* never stop thinking, except in bed, where other more natural instincts take over,' César imparted in a whisper as rich as thick velvet. 'So cold, so inhuman, but *not* in the bedroom, *cara*.'

Dixie found herself leaning over him slightly without even

recalling the move that had sent her into that dangerous and inexplicable change of direction. It was like being drawn by a force stronger than she was, to the heart of a fire that might burn but still blazed a cruel attraction for her. 'César...?' she queried shakily, her tongue cleaving to the roof of her dry mouth.

In an almost involuntary motion César lifted a lean brown hand, hard colour accentuating the feverishly taut slant of his high cheekbones. And still Dixie was held there by those stunning silver eyes, fighting to get a grip on a mind that had shut down even as César dropped his hand again, clenching his long fingers into a fist in the humming, dragging quiet. Her soft pink mouth opened, the tip of her tongue creeping out to moisten her generous lower lip.

And with a sudden, driven groan of surrender, César reached for her with two powerfully impatient hands and dragged her down hungrily into his arms. Lightning struck between one second and the next. One moment Dixie was hung on the agonising brink of a craving she did not even fully comprehend, and the next she was lost without hope of recovery.

Her whole body exulted in the ferociously hard demand of César's sensual mouth crashing down on hers. Anything softer would have been cruel disappointment. As he rolled over and pinned her beneath his weight, his tongue stabbing into her mouth to plunder the sweetness within, she was overwhelmed by the rawness of his passion and the shockingly aggressive surge of emotion rising within herself.

Her wondering fingers glossed over his broad, smooth shoulders and then speared convulsively into his luxuriant black hair, to curve to his skull and imprison him. Welded to every sleek muscle in César's big powerful frame, she felt the hot hard thrust of his all-male arousal against her quivering stomach. The responsive heat that burned up inside her reduced her to a mindless jelly.

'Why does this feel so incredibly good?' César ground out accusingly against her reddened lips as they fought in concert to get breath back into their lungs.

César was holding Dixie so tightly that breathing remained more of a challenge than a likely possibility. Hazily studying her own fingers, which were now possessively welded to his cheekbones, Dixie parroted weakly, *'Good?'*

One hand meshed into her thick silky hair, César gazed down at her, brilliant eyes lambent silver pools of fierce frustration. 'This is not the time to think of me as a trial run for Scott—'

'Scott?'

As if he couldn't concentrate long enough to listen, César let one questing hand smooth down over the swell of one full breast. As every skin cell in her shivering body jumped in electrifying reaction, any hope of sanity reasserting itself was quickly lost. Dixie gasped out loud, eyes dilating, head tipping back to expose her throat as she trembled with a hunger as fierce as it was ungovernable.

César breathed something rough and fractured in Italian, his entire attention melded to his own hands as he lifted them to her slight shoulders to brush down the straps that concealed her from his almost reverent gaze. A husky, sexy hiss that was almost agonised escaped him.

'You are *so* gorgeous…' he gritted not quite evenly as the glistening sheer fabric slid down the proud upper slope of her full breasts, catching on prominent pink buds already swollen with excitement.

And in the same self-conscious moment that Dixie tried to cover her wanton flesh, César touched her where she had never been touched before, and the entire world vanished in the violent surge of her own overpowering response. 'César…' she moaned.

'Madre di Dio.…' César husked, with the self-absorption of a male wholly bent on seduction.

He shaped her tender flesh, his thumbs glancing over the sensitised rosy peaks, making her jerk and squirm helplessly. And then he bent his dark head to a straining pink bud and laved it with his tongue, with the kind of sensational expertise that sent her temperature rocketing to fever-point and wrung strangled sounds from low in her throat.

Her back arched, a tight maddening ache spiralling up between her thighs, sending every inch of her mad with uncontrollable desire. Shuddering in the circle of her arms, César closed his hungry mouth over hers again. She didn't hear the door opening, wasn't aware of anything before Jasper's well-bred voice, raised in a tone of delighted surprise and welcome, interrupted them. 'My dear boy, *when* did you arrive?'

César jerked his head up and Dixie looked past his shoulder in sudden horror and confusion. Jasper was hovering like a small portly Santa Claus suddenly told that Christmas had been axed. Dixie was too shocked even to be grateful for the fact that César was blocking all but her face from Jasper's aghast look of recognition.

'We'll discuss this downstairs, César,' Jasper announced in a deeply shaken and pained tone of censure as he turned on his heel.

CHAPTER SIX

PARALYSED by Jasper's swift entrance and even swifter exit, and the situation she now found herself in, Dixie studied César, who was still staring at the space Jasper had briefly filled, his bemusement doubtless the result of being addressed as though he was a misbehaving teenage boy.

'Porca miseria!' Suddenly coming back to life, César pulled free of Dixie's loosened hold, thrust back the rumpled sheet and sprang out of bed. 'Jasper looked at me as if he hated me!' he exclaimed with the glancing rawness of shock, pushing a not quite steady hand through his wildly tousled black hair, dark, deep-set eyes full of fracturing emotion.

Frantically engaged in righting the bodice of her nightdress, a sob of distress in her voice, Dixie whispered jaggedly, 'I t-told you Jasper wouldn't approve!'

'I wasn't expecting him to return this late and walk right in on us! This is scarcely how I planned to make our announcement. But when I tell him that we're engaged, he'll calm down,' César forecast with frowning conviction.

Unable to look at him any longer, and wishing she shared his confidence, Dixie rolled over on her stomach and stared at the headboard with strained eyes full of deep regret and shame. What had she been doing with César? What had he been doing with her? Her wretched body ached from the severance of his. Cold little shivers of reaction now rippled through her, but deep down inside herself she was hatefully aware that the physical craving which had reduced her to such a level still lingered on like her worst enemy.

'Jasper chose an opportune moment to interrupt us,' César continued with meaningful cool as he banged through the storage units in the adjoining dressing room, evidently in search of clothes. 'Next time you get into bed with me, cover yourself from head to toe.'

'There won't *be* a next time,' Dixie responded in a chagrined undertone. 'I wasn't expecting anything like that to happen.'

'But now you have reassuring proof that I *am* human. Throw a sexually active male into bed with a scantily clad woman putting out provocative signals…and he'll fall from the path of rectitude so fast your head will spin!' César slashed back with defensive bite.

Dixie rolled over and sat up. 'I wasn't provocative,' she protested in dismay and bewilderment at such a charge. 'I was reading my book…I was minding my own business! You just pounced on me!'

Emerging from the dressing room, only halfway into a shirt, César sent her an incredulous look, eyes splintering a silvered challenge. 'You were *begging* for it!'

'I don't even like you…I wouldn't beg you for anything!' Dixie flung back in increasing turmoil.

'No? Very much against my will and my intelligence, I am sexually attracted to you.' As he made that grudging acknowledgement César slung her a brooding look, his darkly handsome features rigid as stone. 'It's really getting on my nerves, but unlike you I'm prepared to be honest about it…I'm not telling the whole world every hour on the hour how much I'm in love with someone else!'

In a complete daze in the aftermath of that gritty confession, Dixie surveyed César with very wide eyes. He was attracted to her? *Personally* attracted to her? Since when? A rosy blush slowly lit her cheeks. 'You're attracted to me…?' she parroted, suddenly feeling very short of breath.

'It's lust, Dixie…pure naked *lust*.' César stressed in sizzling contradiction. 'A complication we can do without…and do without it we will.'

As his brilliant eyes glittered like ice shards, Dixie was mortified. Bowing her head, she pulled her knees up under the sheet and hugged them. She got the distinction, and the message he had gone out of his way to make. Nature was playing the cruellest kind of joke on them both. The sexual chemistry was there, but nothing else, and César was relieved that Jasper's arrival had concluded their intimacy. Dixie was still feeling too embarrassed to feel relieved. Indeed, she could never recall experiencing such intense emotional turmoil.

Anger, resentment, pain, regret. The extent of her own confusion destroyed her ability to think straight. César had left the room before it occurred to her that she ought to go down to see Jasper as well. One didn't avoid dear friends, no matter how awkward the situation might be. Jasper had been embarrassed, and that was her fault. She shouldn't have allowed César to overrule her misgivings about sharing a room. And now it was her duty to soothe and reassure alongside César. It was time to act like one half of a couple...

As she hurriedly pulled on a light cotton robe, she thought fiercely about Scott. She knew Scott so well. His faults, his strengths. He might take her for granted, but she knew he genuinely liked and respected her as a friend. Beneath the city slicker image he worked so hard to maintain, Scott was a country boy with a love of home cooking. He was always very even-tempered and cheerful. And she did love him, she really *did*, had known the very first night she met him that he was the man for her. Scott's image finally glimmered into being inside her mind's eye. True, his features were a little blurred, but she let her breath escape with relief.

César was right. She hadn't appreciated his bluntness but he had been right, she told herself urgently as she ran a brush through her hair. Those mindless dislocated-from-planet-earth feelings she got every time she looked at César were sheer lust. And staggeringly beautiful looks and magnetic sex appeal were all César had to recommend him. He was impatient, quick-tempered, manipulative, sarcastic, critical and essentially cold...except in the bedroom.

Satisfied by that summing up, Dixie left the room. Of course, she then acknowledged, César was impatient because he liked everything perfect. And he was sarcastic and critical because he was so much cleverer than most people, and it had to be frantically frustrating always having to wait for others to catch up with his reasoning. Being so very rich and powerful had spoilt him, but he couldn't really be blamed for that either, could he? And if he was cold, well, he had endured the most heartbreakingly loveless childhood, and he was extremely fond of Jasper—indeed had seemed positively shattered in receipt of what could only have been a disapproving frown from Jasper...

Hearing the dull murmur of distant voices when she reached the main hall, Dixie followed them and found herself outside an ajar door. She was just about to sound a light knock and announce her presence when she heard Jasper speak in a grim voice she had never heard or even imagined she might hear from so gentle a man.

'So you gave my poor little Dixie a ring to seduce her,' Jasper was saying with harsh distaste. 'Here she is, compromising her own most deep-felt beliefs and doubtless innocently trusting that you *will* eventually marry her! But I don't share her faith, César.'

'*Dio*, I—'

'You tell me you're engaged to her, but not one word do you say about *loving* her,' Jasper broke in stiffly. 'Nor is there any mention of when this hypothetical wedding is to take place!'

'We've just *become* engaged,' César stressed in a driven undertone, sounding just a little desperate and equally unlike himself.

'You finally met a woman who wanted no part of your kind of loose living. You couldn't take no for an answer, so you offered her an engagement ring. A couple of months from now, when you've lost interest in Dixie, you'll throw her back out of your life again without any consideration for the damage you've done,' the older man condemned curtly.

'*Accidenti!* You've got completely the wrong idea—'

'I *know* you and I *know* Dixie,' Jasper contradicted heavily. 'I imagine she's hopelessly in love with you—and I should've seen this coming. For months she's been telling me about everything you do in her letters. Why couldn't you have left her alone, César? It will be a long time before I can forgive you for this. Dixie's very dear to me. She's gentle and caring and kind…yet you didn't even have enough respect for her not to embarrass her in this house!'

'Let's sit down and talk this over calmly, Jasper,' César replied fiercely.

Outside the door, Dixie slowly retreated. Shocked and distressed by the bitterness of Jasper's censure, she could not immediately see what she could do to sort out such a ghastly mess. This was not the sort of discussion she could play a part in. Jasper would not speak freely with her present, and César would certainly not welcome her interference. And after what Jasper had witnessed in that bedroom it would be difficult to confess the truth about their fake engagement.

'No, I've already told you how I feel,' Jasper was saying tightly. 'I want you to leave this house right now, César. I'll send your clothes after you. If you're going to break Dixie's heart, get it over with when I'm here to look after her.'

'OK…I'll set a date for the wedding,' César drawled flatly.

'Next year?' Jasper suggested, audibly unimpressed by that offer.

'Next *week*!' César suddenly gritted explosively. 'Dixie and I will get married next week!'

Dixie almost fell over her own feet. In her disbelief, she stared wide-eyed at the door.

Complete silence had fallen between the two men. She imagined Jasper was as shocked by that startling announcement as she was.

'That puts quite a different complexion on matters, doesn't it?' Jasper sighed with perceptible relief. He sounded much more like himself, but very weary and oddly breathless. 'So you do love her, even though you can't show it… Well, can't have everything…couldn't make a better choice than Dixie…'

'What's wrong, Jasper?' César exclaimed with raw abruptness. '*Jasper!*'

Reacting instantly to the current of alarm in César's exclamation, Dixie pushed open the door. Jasper was lying unconscious in a chair, looking terribly small and old and ill.

César was bending over him, frantically trying to revive him.

'Get a doctor!' Dixie urged.

César strode across the room to snatch up the phone. He was ashen pale beneath his bronzed complexion, and his dark eyes were blank with shock. He made the call, but for its duration he watched Jasper with appalled intensity, drawing in a shuddering breath of unconcealed relief when he saw his godfather begin to revive and mutter.

'Eduardo Arribas is a friend…he lives just outside the village,' César imparted as he replaced the phone.

Jasper was still confused and rather dizzy. César wanted to carry him up to bed, where he would be more comfortable, but Dixie thought it was better not to move him before the doctor's arrival, and she sent César to get a glass of water for him instead. She patted Jasper's hand soothingly.

'Heart, you know,' he complained weakly. 'Never passed out before…'

'You're tired…that's all. You should've been in bed hours ago.' Dixie reached for the glass César extended, noticing in some surprise that César couldn't hold it steady because his hand was shaking. She pressed the glass gently to Jasper's lips.

'Glad you're here,' Jasper mumbled. 'Both here… Suppose I'll have to face that wretched operation after all—'

'What operation?' César broke in with a sudden frown.

'I'm a silly old duffer…never liked hospitals,' Jasper muttered. 'Eduardo says I need one of those pacemakers fitted.'

Dr Arribas came very quickly. The two men helped Jasper up to bed, and Dixie then sat with him until he fell asleep, quietly reflecting on what she had overheard outside that room downstairs before Jasper's collapse gave all of them something rather more important to worry about.

César had actually promised to marry her next week! César, usually the most rational and cool of males, had been so shaken by his godfather's angry demand that he should leave that he had made a really crazy promise sooner than explain that the situation was not quite as it might have appeared. But then telling his godfather the truth would have been a considerable challenge after Jasper had seen the two of them sharing the same bed. Had César then admitted that their engagement was a complete fake, Jasper would have been even angrier.

Well, fortunately for César Jasper's state of health would protect César from being expected to keep to that insane undertaking to immediately marry her. Jasper would now be scheduled for surgery as soon as possible, and when he was convalescing no doubt César would confess that their supposed engagement had been a well-meant but foolish pretence. And César would just have to brace himself to explain that nothing whatsoever had really happened in that bedroom. *Nothing*, Dixie stressed for her own benefit. Nothing she need ever think about again, she told herself urgently. A moment's weakness, best forgotten.

When Dixie emerged from Jasper's room, she was surprised to find César waiting outside in the corridor.

'You should've come back in after seeing Dr Arribas out...' Her voice trailed away as she met César's haunted dark eyes and registered the strain which had indented harsh lines between his nose and mouth. 'Did Dr Arribas give you bad news of some kind?' she asked anxiously.

'No,' César said stiltedly, turning his head away, his strong profile clenching hard. 'In fact the prognosis is very good. Jasper may have told me that his heart was failing but I gather that was something of an exaggeration. Apparently he was just very much afraid of the idea of having this pacemaker fitted.'

'I can understand that. He's never had to go into hospital before.'

'When Eduardo first diagnosed his condition last year, Jasper buried his head in the sand and refused to consider surgery. He also told Eduardo that under no account was I to be informed,' César shared in a constrained undertone, digging his balled fists into the pockets of his well-cut trousers and moving restively away from her, a powerful tension etched into the taut set of his wide shoulders. 'Jasper *knew* that I would put pressure on him to have the operation...'

'Of course you would've. It's the only sensible option.' Dixie was bewildered by the depth of emotional reaction which César was visibly struggling to contain and conceal from her.

'He was afraid I would bully him into it,' César breathed with suppressed savagery.

'That faint Jasper had tonight has done the trick for you,' Dixie said consolingly. 'He's accepted now that he needs surgery.'

'But he'd never have had that attack tonight if it hadn't been for me!' César suddenly raked back at her, every syllable of that roughened assurance raw with stark guilt and self-loathing. '*Madre di Dio*...I damn near killed him!'

Really shaken by that outburst, Dixie protested instantly, 'That's not true, César. Dr Arribas himself said that this could've happened at any time—'

'*Accidenti!*' César's striking dark features were set with bitter self-condemnation. 'Don't feed me that sentimental bull! Jasper was extremely upset tonight...I've never seen him that upset about anything! Who caused that needless distress? *Me!* Me and my smartass ideas!' he completed savagely.

Shimmering dark eyes raw with angry pain and regret, César spun on his heel and strode away without another word, leaving Dixie standing with a deeply troubled frown.

She breathed in deep and swallowed hard. Every natural urge prompted her to follow César and reason with him. He was being far too hard on himself. She would never have allowed anyone else to walk away in such a state without trying to offer some comfort. But she forcibly restrained herself from such a move.

César, who let his guard down with nobody, had just let his guard down on a positive flood of self-recrimination. A few hours from now he might well look back on that emotional outburst and despise it as an act of weakness. He would, very probably, be most annoyed that she had witnessed that brief loss of self-discipline. He *was* a very private man. And he didn't like it when she got too personal, wouldn't thank her for her interference, she reflected, pained by that knowledge, suddenly finding herself hating the awareness that she couldn't reach out to César.

César was a perfectionist. He had started out with good intentions, buoyant in his confident belief that their fake engagement would delight Jasper. And then it had all suddenly gone horribly wrong. Jasper had been shocked and upset. Jasper had revealed a very hurtful lack of faith in his godson. César must have been shocked enough by that. He certainly hadn't needed to see Jasper collapse in front of his eyes as well.

She slipped back into Jasper's room and sat by his bed watching him sleep. At about three in the morning, his housekeeper, Ermina, came in, her kindly eyes full of concerned affection as she gazed down at her elderly employer and indicated that she would like to take Dixie's place.

Dixie wandered back to the bedroom she had vacated earlier and found herself pacing the floor while she anxiously wondered where César was. Had he simply moved into one of the guest rooms? In the frame of mind he had been in, Dixie didn't think it very likely that César would simply have gone back to bed.

After a certain amount of hesitation, she left the room again and went downstairs. There was still a light burning in the elegant sitting room where César and Jasper had had their unfortunate confrontation earlier. Dixie opened the door. César was slumped in an armchair. He had been drinking. A half-empty brandy decanter sat on the sofa table beside him, and he still had a glass clasped in one taut-fingered hand. He looked at her with curiously unfocused dark eyes.

'*Dio…*' César slurred with brooding wit. 'It's everybody's best friend!'

Dixie's soft heart still went out to him. She was tempted to tell him that he was his own worst enemy. He just could not cope with what had happened tonight. He was trying to drown the nasty unsettling effect of his own emotional turmoil in alcohol. And, since alcohol was a depressant, it had only made things worse.

'You'll feel much better tomorrow if you get some sleep now.'

'Proper little ray of sunshine aren't you? Tell me, how does it feel to know that you got it right and I got it *all* wrong?'

'Got what right?' she prompted uncertainly.

'You said lies were always wrong. You were right. You said I'd be so much better at lying than you. You were *wrong* about that,' César gritted, thrusting long fingers roughly through his black hair. 'When Jasper confronted me, I completely blew it—'

'His attitude upset you…you weren't prepared for it.'

'He hates my guts now.'

Dixie knelt down by his feet and looked up at him with concerned blue eyes. 'Of course he doesn't. It was a storm in a teacup.'

'A storm in a teacup,' César repeated unevenly, gazing down into her wide eyes and blinking slightly.

'You take everything far too seriously. Jasper was taken aback…the bedroom bit was very unfortunate, and then, instead of reassuring him, I bet you got on your high horse—'

'My high horse…?'

Dixie gently removed the glass from his hold and then linked her fingers with his. 'César…look on the bright side.'

'The bright side?'

'All right, I use a lot of clichés but clichés are often spot-on,' Dixie pointed out as his hand closed round hers. 'Here you are, feeling really miserable—'

'Guilty,' César contradicted harshly.

'But when we came here you thought Jasper was dying. Now you know that he has every hope of making a complete recovery.'

'True…' César frowned, as if he hadn't quite absorbed that message yet.

'He'll probably live until he's at least a hundred,' Dixie

added bracingly. 'And staying away from him now has only made you feel worse.'

'The sight of me might have upset him again,' César breathed darkly. 'That's why I kept my distance.'

'There you are again, thinking the very worst. Jasper loves you,' Dixie scolded softly. 'He just isn't as naive as you assumed. Because he was so surprised at the idea of us being engaged, he suspected that—'

'I had dishonourable intentions?' César grimaced.

Dixie slowly stood up and tugged suggestively at César's hand, in the hope of getting him upright.

'What are you doing?'

'You need to go to bed.'

César rose with something less than his usual inbred grace, and swayed ever so slightly. Dixie smiled at him. Shorn of his icy reserve, he had such tremendous humanity. His ridiculously long lashes swept down, closing her out for a split second, and then he looked at her again and gave her an almost boyish smile that made her heart give a violent lurch.

'You're so nice—you make me feel very bad sometimes,' César shared.

Dixie's smile died. 'I irritate you.'

'No…it's more like meeting my conscience face to face. I'm getting used to it.'

Dixie's smile glimmered again as they reached the bedroom door and she opened it. 'Do you feel better now?'

'Not so as you'd notice.'

'You were only trying to make Jasper happy. You had good intentions,' Dixie assured him warmly.

César gazed down at her with those stunning silvered eyes, a curious stillness freezing his facial muscles as if some sudden revelation had struck him. As he studied her with bewildering intensity, Dixie entirely forgot the rest of what she had intended to say. He slowly lifted one lean hand and stroked a long forefinger very, very gently along the generous curve of her mouth. Her heart jumped and her breathing arrested, a trail of fire tingling where he had touched.

'Never trust my intentions,' César husked, the accented

words velvet-soft. 'I invariably calculate everything right down to the final full-stop.'

'You probably can't help yourself…'

Dixie found it impossible to concentrate when she looked up into that lean, dark fallen-angel face of his. Instinctively she hovered, without acknowledging either her own fierce reluctance to be parted from him or the fact that César had actually tightened his grip on her hand. Indeed, all of a sudden it was as if the world was standing still, and in the interim every sense magically sharpened. She was incredibly aware of each breath that she drew, of the surging pulse of her own blood through her veins…

'I feel…I feel like I'm tipsy,' she confided.

'Least it's not a "really creep feeling" this time…' César muttered almost dazedly as his dark head slowly, steadily lowered to hers.

And she stopped breathing, sanity drowning in his brilliant magnetic gaze. As his mouth found hers, with a sweetness that was almost unbearable, she felt her knees start to give. He caught her up into his arms and cannoned backwards into the door to close it. 'Stay with me…I don't want to be alone tonight,' he confessed raggedly.

And then he kissed her again, hard, hungry, drugging kisses that blew her mind and melted her to liquid honey. He might have spoken again. But every time he tried to stop kissing her Dixie held him fast. The wanting had escaped like a damburst inside her, carrying all before it. So powerful was that need she could not resist it.

With an erotic expertise she was defenceless against, César let his tongue delve deep, emulating a far more intimate possession. Sealed in his arms, she trembled violently, heartbeat racing, pulses thrumming. Bringing her down on the bed, he knelt over her, releasing the tie on her robe, tugging it down out of his path as he pressed his mouth hotly to the sensitive skin at the base of her throat, and she jerked and whimpered out loud.

That betraying sound made César jerk up his head. He gazed down at her then, and stilled, tension snaking through every muscle of his lean, powerful body. 'No, I'm not so-ber...this shouldn't be happening, *cara*,' he began with breathless urgency. 'I'm not in control.'

'Why should you be?' Dixie asked helplessly.

Disconcerted by that unexpected response, César stared down into her starry eyes, and he dragged his hands from her slender forearms like a male fighting himself every step of the way. A long shudder racked him. 'Stop looking at me like that,' he urged unsteadily.

Dixie was fascinated. 'Like what?'

With a stifled expletive, César closed his eyes and snatched in a jagged breath of restraint. *'Accidenti!'* he groaned. 'I want you so *much*...I've never wanted a woman as desper-ately as I want you right now!'

That acknowledgement of her feminine power was like a shot of adrenalin in Dixie's veins. It was a power she had never dreamt she might possess. There was no rational thought in the manner in which she reached up to César and found his wide, sensual mouth again for herself. An intoxi-cating sense of joy surged up inside her, lending a fevered edge to the fierce pulse-beat of desire thrumming wildly through her.

César reacted to that invitation by flattening her to the bed. As he connected with her shapely curves he growled deep in his throat with all-male pleasure. They exchanged searing, scorching kisses while Dixie tried stubbornly to unbutton his shirt without disconnecting herself from him.

César made one last attempt to get a grip on the situation. 'We *can't*...' Resolution failing as she spread her hands ap-preciatively over his magnificent torso, he raised her up in his powerful arms and struggled as clumsily as a teenager to extract her from her nightdress, while letting the tip of his tongue dip between her parted lips before he groaned in be-lated completion, 'Can't do this...'

'Shut up...' Dixie sealed her lips wonderingly to a smooth, hard shoulder. Like an addict, she drank in the scent and the hot salty taste of his bronzed skin. Everything about him felt so good, so right, so perfect. She started to work steadily

downwards, in love with every sensation she shared with
him, overwhelmed by a glorious sense of freedom.

'Say my name...' César breathed jerkily.

'César...'

'Again,' he purred, like a big hungry cat, trembling as she
reached the flat, taut muscles of his stomach.

'César...César...César,' Dixie sighed voluptuously, engaged in following her every sensual instinct, smoothing ex-
ploring fingers down over his long muscular thighs, discov-
ering the distinctly shocking bulge of his pronounced arousal,
but only for a split second.

With a broken hiss of impatience, César wrenched at his
zip and started kissing her breathless again. Her heart sang;
her whole body blazed. As he fought his way out of his
clothes he found her breasts, and it became even more of a
struggle to undress and make love to her at one and the same
time. Dixie had never even imagined such explosive passion
could exist, and she revelled in it. She couldn't get close
enough to him. He couldn't get close enough to her.

'You were made for me, *cara*...' César closed his mouth
reverently to a rosy pink nipple and laved the straining bud
with his tongue.

Her spine arched and she panted with helpless pleasure,
hands biting into his shoulders. The illusion that she was in
control was gone by then, but she didn't care. He dragged
her down into a frantic hot well of excitement, where all she
could do was feel and react to the incredible intensity of
sensation. Her skin felt as if it was burning over her bones,
super-sensitive to his every caress, and she just couldn't stay
still.

'You meet my passion with your own,' César muttered
with intense appreciation. 'You make me burn for you, *cara*.'

He traced the length of a slim trembling thigh, and the
throbbing ache at the heart of her suddenly surged to screaming proportions. As he sought out the moist heat of her most
sensitive flesh, she flung her head back and writhed. The
surging excitement was almost intolerable. Her temperature
was rocketing, her body electrified.

'I can't bear it...I can't bear it!' she suddenly gasped wildly.

César crushed her reddened lips under his again and made her bear it, hot, timeless moments of bittersweet pleasure that drove her crazy. And then he shifted over her, sliding between her thighs, pushing up her knees. In her fevered state, she understood only that at last the unbearable ache of emptiness might be satisfied.

'*Dios*... I can't wait any longer,' César growled.

And she opened her eyes and looked up at him, absorbing the feverish flush on his high cheekbones, the silvered intensity of his eyes, the sheer hunger all for her, and it made her feel that she was flying as high and free as a kite.

As he arched over her, the hot, hard surge of his hungry invasion took her by surprise. The sensation was so new to her she froze in astonishment, and then he thrust deeper, and a sharp, piercing pain dragged a startled cry from her lips.

César stilled in bemusement. 'I'm the first...?' he exclaimed, thunderstruck.

As the pain receded she shifted helplessly beneath him, unable to think, not wanting to speak, longing only to luxuriate in the incredibly intimate feel of him inside her. And that one tiny movement of hers destroyed whatever shred of self-control César had gained from his shock at her innocence. With a ragged groan he thrust deeper still, with passionate urgency, no more able than she to detach himself from the driving demands of his own body.

All awareness of self fell away as he engulfed her in his stormy rhythm. Wild and mindless pleasure controlled her. Her heart thundering against her breastbone, she rode that storm with him. All that mattered was that he shouldn't stop, shouldn't deny the remorseless craving he had unleashed within her. And he drove her to a frenzied climax that made her cry out in ecstasy, her body convulsing in what felt like a thousand pieces as he slammed into her one last time.

Afterwards she felt as if she was falling and falling, down

into endless layers of soft cotton wool. And although later she would dimly recall César trying to rouse her to speech, she just couldn't stay awake in the hold of the most seductive contented peace she had ever known.

CHAPTER SEVEN

DIXIE woke up only when a maid pulled open the curtains. Blinking sleepily, she began to sit up, only then realising that she was no longer in César's bedroom.

'Lunch will be ready in one hour, *señorita*,' the smiling maid informed her in perfect English. 'Señor Valverde asked me to wake you.'

A Technicolor replay of what she had been doing shortly before dawn with César assailed Dixie. Shock reeled through her in waves. She could not understand how a mere few hours ago making love with César could have seemed so right, so natural and so inevitable.

César had been drinking, far from his usual unemotional and rational self. But even in that state César had attempted to call a halt. In fact he had tried to be the voice of reason more than once, Dixie remembered. With a sinking heart she recalled ripping him out of his shirt. Colour ran like a banner of shame into her cheeks. She had taken advantage of César...

How could she have done that? He had kissed her first, hadn't he? He had started it...but he had also tried to stop it. But she had wanted him, craved him, shamelessly clung. High on the discovery of the power a woman could have over a man, she had discarded every inhibition. Oh, dear heaven, was there the remotest possibility that she could ever look César Valverde in the face again?

As the maid carried in her clothing and proceeded to hang each garment in the built-in wardrobes, Dixie was frozen by ever-deepening panic to the bed. She was picturing César as he had been in the early hours, César as she had never seen him before. César, unusually vulnerable, knocked for six by Jasper's collapse and his own guilty conscience.

In kissing her, he had surrendered to a moment's temptation. And she had entirely misread the situation. César had
really just been seeking the reassuring warmth of human contact, but, being César, he had expressed that need in the form
of a sexual invitation. What she should have done was give
him a hug or talk to him…or something.

It was all *her* fault. How could she blame him? According
to the magazines she read, men weren't good at withstanding
temptation. The average single male was programmed to say
yes every time. No way could César be held accountable for
what she had wantonly encouraged him to do!

He had been so shocked when he'd realised that she was
still a virgin. Dixie groaned. She had even gone to sleep
while César had presumably been trying to talk to her about
what they had just done and why they shouldn't have done
it! Within five seconds that speed-of-light intelligence of his
would have homed in on the fact that he had made a major
mistake. Suddenly she was very grateful that César had
shifted her out of his room and slotted her into a guest room
bed.

Sliding off the bed, she went for a shower. Then she put
on an elegant blue skirt and matching sleeveless top. With
every passing minute her inner turmoil simply increased.

Why *had* she cast away every principle and just seized
César along with the moment? She hadn't thought of Scott
once! But then she had never got past friendship with Scott.
And clearly she had a more physical nature than she had ever
appreciated. That was obviously why she had lost control
with César.

Last night's events had upset her equilibrium as well, but
she hadn't recognised her own vulnerability. She had succumbed to what César had earlier bluntly described as 'pure
naked lust'. She winced at the label, but there it was. César
had awakened the sexual side of her nature.

Better to face that mortifying fact head-on rather than
make silly sentimental excuses for herself and begin imagining that she was now falling in love with César! Hadn't
that stupid thought been in the back of her mind as she'd

drifted blissfully off to sleep in his arms? Yes, it had been. Her subconscious already trying to provide a more acceptable excuse for her behaviour.

But she was *not* falling in love with César. She loved Scott…or did she? She was no longer so sure of that fact. From the moment César had come close she had begun thinking less and less about Scott. Suddenly she didn't know what was going on inside her own head any more. But she badly wanted to see Scott again, and reinforce her feelings for him. Loving Scott from afar was safe; loving César would be emotional suicide. How many times had César already warned her not to get too keen on him?

As she sat at the dressing table, feverishly brushing her hair, a light knock sounded on the door.

In the mirror, she saw César's tall dark figure. Paralysis set in instantaneously.

In beautifully cut chinos the colour of toffee and a black polo shirt, César looked drop-dead gorgeous. All bronzed and dark and dangerous. Her heart lurched and she quivered in dismay.

'Let's not talk about earlier,' she heard herself say tautly. 'We should forget it ever happened.'

'Dixie, I—'

'Please don't say any more,' Dixie broke in at frantic speed.

'I can't forget it ever happened.' The assurance was harsh.

'Work at it…you'll be surprised. I always think mistakes are forgotten the quickest, but maybe you don't make enough mistakes to know that the way I do,' Dixie muttered rather limply, fiddling with the hairbrush, avoiding even his reflection now, because even his reflection sent her heartbeat crazy. 'How's Jasper?'

'He slept late. I haven't actually seen him yet, but I gather he's fine. It was Ermina who told me he would be coming down to lunch,' César proffered with audible impatience. 'We *have* to talk about this, Dixie. I need to know what you're trying to say to me.'

Paling, Dixie breathed in deep. 'It was an awful mistake.

We were both upset. You'd been drinking. I was concerned, trying to comfort you...things just got out of hand. What more is there to say?'

'Are you telling me that you went to bed with me because you felt *sorry* for me?' César prompted with wrathful incredulity.

Dixie moved her head in a helpless gesture of confusion. 'I don't know... Apart from the obvious, I don't *know* why I did it!' she finally confessed.

'"Apart from the obvious"? What does that cover?' César demanded suspiciously.

'The lust bit,' Dixie whispered, marvelling that he hadn't grasped that for himself. 'I just get really carried away when you kiss me.'

The thunderous silence pulsed.

César settled his lean hands to her shoulders, raised her upright and turned her round. His stunning eyes locked into her mortified gaze like guided missiles. He bent his arrogant dark head and kissed her. Stars exploded in the darkness behind her lowered eyelids. Fireworks blazed up in a shower of sparks inside her. Her legs went hollow; her mind went blank.

César held her back from him, retaining a steadying hold on her slight shoulders. Deceptively indolent dark eyes surveyed her bemused expression. 'It's the sort of problem we need to work on together, Dixie.'

'I thought you'd be furious with me for taking advantage of you when you weren't quite sober,' she admitted in bewilderment.

César tautened, lashes dropping very low over glinting eyes. 'I'm not remotely sexist, and I'm remarkably resilient.'

Still struggling to understand why he had kissed her, Dixie tensed when he reached for her hand. He slid the diamond engagement ring on to her finger. 'You left it in my bathroom. Jasper will be expecting to see it.'

And only then did she realise why he had kissed her and why he wasn't furious. They still had to pretend to be engaged for Jasper's benefit. So when César closed a seemingly

possessive hand over hers on the way downstairs she wasn't
surprised. It was all part of the act.

'I didn't like to mention it before,' she confided. 'But I
overheard you and Jasper talking—'

César glanced at her enquiringly. 'How much did you
hear?'

Dixie looked awkward. 'Enough to know that it was going
badly. You let Jasper back you into a corner—'

'I did...did I?'

'Well, you know you did,' Dixie pointed out ruefully.
'Telling Jasper that you'd marry me next week could've got
us into a very difficult situation!'

Dark colour sprang up over César's spectacular cheekbones. He opened his mouth as if he was about to say something really cutting, and she stiffened. Then something
strange happened. He looked at her. He sealed his lips again,
veiled his eyes and simply shrugged a shoulder, expressively
conceding the point.

'We'll have to tell him the truth when he's recovering from
his op,' Dixie sighed. 'I think he'll understand why we did
it.'

César's lean fingers gripped hers rather more tightly.
'Slight change of subject here, before we join Jasper,' he
murmured smoothly. 'When we made love—'

Dixie bristled like a cornered animal, suddenly finding the
hunter on her trail again. 'I thought we weren't going to
discuss that again!'

'Just this once...' César studied her with broodingly intent
and incisive dark eyes. 'I had this weird and wonderful idea
that it might be something *more* than lust.'

Dixie reddened, humiliated by what she read into that admission but determined to assure him that she was not so
foolish. 'You really don't need to worry about that, César.'

'I...don't?'

Dixie stared miserably down at their linked hands, thinking
what a joke they were. 'I'm not silly enough to think that
being physically attracted to someone is the same as being

in love. Scott's still the only guy for me,' she swore vehemently.

César dropped her hand and bit out a sardonic laugh. 'You were with *me*, not him!' he derided.

'I'm pretty ashamed of that,' Dixie mumbled chokily.

'So you should be,' César confirmed in a suddenly savage undertone. 'Let me tell you, if you were in love with me I'd have an armed guard on you at all times. I wouldn't trust a woman as dippy and disloyal as you out of my sight!'

'But I don't even have a relationship with Scott yet,' she protested in her own defence.

'And if *I* have anything to do with it you never will!' César shot back at her chillingly.

Bemused by that assurance, Dixie finally worked up the courage to look up. César looked outraged. She was nailed to the spot by silvered eyes as piercing and threatening as knives.

'You used me,' César condemned fiercely. 'I don't let anybody do that.'

'How did I use you?' she gasped strickenly, seriously out of her depth and fighting to comprehend how she had angered him to such an extent.

'*Santo cielo*…like a bloody dry run for Scott! And to think I was worried about the fact that I hadn't taken any precautions!' César sent her a glittering look of what could only be described as pure loathing.

'Precautions?' Dixie was still working through the astonishing concept of César being some sort of sexual experiment, and not doing very well.

'Of course you're already on the pill, prepared for Scott,' César assumed with even greater scorn. 'The last thing you were going to risk was an accidental pregnancy, and I'm grateful…don't think I'm not! But when this fiasco is over I want you out of my life like you were never there in the first place!'

Dumbfounded by the number of contradictions, unexpected attacks and freewheeling assumptions coming her way, and hopelessly confused, Dixie watched César stride off, aggression radiating from every taut line of his lithe, powerful frame. She followed at a slower pace. She *wasn't* taking the contraceptive pill. The risk of a pregnancy hadn't even occurred to her. Confronted with that daunting reality, she went into even deeper shock.

Without warning, César wheeled round and strode back to her. Closing his hand back over hers again, he released his breath in a fractured hiss. Grim dark eyes gazed down into hers. 'I'm sorry...I had no right to attack you like that.'

Shaken by the gruff apology, Dixie muttered in a stifled voice. 'It's OK. I understand.'

'I don't think you do,' César said flatly.

But she did, she thought wretchedly. Over the past twelve hours everything had gone haywire. Sudden intimacy had brought down the barriers between them, and now the barriers had to be raised again. But no wonder César had been so on edge when he was worrying about whether or not he might have got her pregnant. Right then she decided to let him continue believing that he didn't need to worry about that possibility. She told herself that it was unlikely that one rash act would lead to the conception of a child, and stamped down hard on her anxiety. This morning she had to smile like a woman in love and newly engaged. Not one hint of the divisions between them could be revealed in Jasper's presence.

Jasper was waiting for them in a sunlit courtyard beneath the shade of a giant casuarina tree. With a wide smile on his creased face, he rose to his feet. 'Now don't tell me that I should've stayed in bed. Father Navarro is joining us for lunch.'

In the act of settling Dixie into a chair behind the beautifully set table, César stilled. 'Father Navarro?'

'So that we can set a date for the wedding. I gave him a call this morning. We haven't got time to waste. Eduardo wants me into that clinic within the next two weeks!' Patently unaware of the bombshell he had dropped on them both, Jasper sank back down into his seat, exuding an air of happy complacency.

CHAPTER EIGHT

As Jasper cheerfully suggested that César pour the wine, Dixie struggled not to visually betray what a shock she had just received.

'Don't look so disapproving, César,' Jasper scolded gently. 'One glass of wine won't do me any harm. This is a very special occasion.'

'Jasper…I seriously doubt that you need the excitement of a wedding night now.' César filled the crystal glasses with an admirably steady hand.

'Nonsense. I don't want you both feeling that you have to put things off until *after* my op! I'm fit enough for a quiet family affair.' A slight frown of strain formed on Jasper's worn features as he studied them both. 'Oh dear, have I taken too much of a liberty in contacting Father Navarro?'

César gave him an amused smile that impressed Dixie to death. 'Of course you haven't.' He glanced fleetingly at Dixie. 'Jasper and the village priest are old cronies, *cara*. He was sure to share our news with him first.'

Jasper relaxed again. 'You'll throw a big reception for all your friends once you're back in London, but a private ceremony here is much more your style, César. You won't be bothered by any paparazzi in this neck of the woods.'

Dixie suddenly grasped two things. Jasper was throwing himself into this wedding idea to take his mind off his coming surgery. He was also very much afraid that he wasn't going to survive the operation.

'You'll be fine. Apart from this little heart thing, you're in great condition for a man of your age,' she told him, as if he had spoken his fear out loud.

'Dixie reads me like a book,' Jasper told César rather smugly.

'You think a lot alike,' César remarked, without any expression at all.

And then the village priest arrived. For the two older men it was a jovial meal. Dixie kept on finding her mind drifting off the dialogue. She watched César, in awe at his self-control, his ease of speech, his ability to hide his horror at the situation in which they now found themselves. She kept on waiting for him to casually produce some clever reason which would regrettably make such a wedding out of the question in the near future, but César made not the slightest attempt.

Indeed, throughout that meal she could not drag her attention from César. That lean, strong face, the shard of sunlight that gleamed over his blue-black hair every time he threw his well-shaped head back, the warmth in the beautiful dark eyes she had once thought so cold when he looked at his godfather. He was putting on the show of the century for Jasper's sake.

By the time Father Navarro took his leave, a date only five days away had been settled on for the ceremony. Jasper went indoors for a nap. As his quiet footsteps receded, Dixie suddenly rose from the table and walked away, dragging in great gasps of the hot, still air as her tension slowly drained away, only to leave her in a state of disbelief.

Standing by the wall bounding the courtyard, she looked beyond the gorgeous terraced gardens spread out below to the magnificent view of the lushly wooded mountains. And she thought, Now César is about to tell me that we have no choice but to get married.

César paused several feet away, studying her with veiled dark eyes. 'You're furious with me.'

Dixie turned a strained profile to him, shaken reproach in her troubled blue eyes. 'You got us into this. Somehow I assumed you'd magically get us out of it again.'

'If I'd argued Jasper would've suspected I was having second thoughts about marrying you, and then he would've been upset. I couldn't risk it.'

'I care very much about Jasper, but I don't want to go to

the lengths of a church wedding to placate him!' Dixie admitted starkly.

'We can get an annulment later.' César moved soundlessly closer, his brilliant eyes silver-bright slivers beneath his lush ebony lashes. 'I know you didn't bargain on this, and I'm not about to try and browbeat you into it. I realise that I'm asking you for a really huge favour.'

Her attention locked to his strikingly serious features, the stark tension etched into his fabulous bone structure, and something inside her just began to melt like butter left out under the sun.

'César, I—'

'*Please*...I need you to do this for me,' César breathed with roughened sincerity.

Dixie collided with his eyes, and a wave of such physical craving consumed her that it was a literal agony not to be in his arms. Shocked by that awareness, she trembled and twisted her head away. 'OK...it'll just be for a few weeks. Then we'll be back in London and we can just tell Jasper that it didn't work out.'

'I swear you won't regret this decision.'

Involuntarily, Dixie stole a glance at him. A slashing charismatic smile had driven the tension from his startlingly handsome features. As a burst of heat ignited in the pit of her stomach she lowered her gaze again, appalled by the power he had to disturb her. A power he wasn't even trying to exercise, a natural power he had simply been born with.

'There's just one thing you could do to make things a little easier,' she heard herself say stiffly.

'Name it.'

'Could we try and avoid each other as much as possible?'

For a split second César looked stunned.

Conscious that she had been clumsy, Dixie dropped her head and added, 'I just think it would make us both more comfortable.'

'You didn't seem particularly uncomfortable over lunch,' César remarked very softly. 'In fact you never took your eyes off me once.'

There he was again, seeking reassurance that she wasn't getting keen on him, Dixie reflected in mortification, her cheeks flaming. 'I was acting.'

'I should've thought of that. So you were imagining I was Scott?' he prompted in a roughened undertone.

Too embarrassed to look at him, Dixie interpreted that fracturing intonation as one of immense amusement. 'What else?'

Dixie's reflection in the tall cheval mirror took her breath away. Three days earlier César had had a selection of wedding dresses flown in, complete with a seamstress to make any necessary alterations on the spot. Just another prop for Jasper's benefit, Dixie had gathered. But seeing herself in full bridal regalia now, on her wedding day, was somehow something else entirely…

Jasper had insisted on loaning her a diamond tiara that had belonged to his mother. The jewels glittered like a wreath of stars in her upswept hair. And the gown? The gown was a perfect dream. Ivory silk enhanced by delicate embroidery skimmed her breasts, hugged her tiny waist and fell softly down to feet sheathed in gold embroidered shoes straight out of *Cinderella*.

Over the past five days Dixie had scarcely seen César, except in Jasper's presence. On César's side, keeping up an act had demanded little more than an impressive air of concerned interest in her wellbeing, and circumspect walks in the grounds after dinner.

'Jasper doesn't trust us to be alone,' César had gritted with a flash of outrage while his godfather strolled about in the courtyard above them like an eagle-eyed chaperone. 'What does he think I'm about to do? Drag you under the trees like a randy teenager?'

Recalling that incredulous outburst the previous evening, Dixie could not help smiling as she was ushered out of her room by Ermina, who had insisted on helping her to dress. Dear Jasper, she thought fondly. He didn't trust César an inch on the moral restraint front. Her smile slowly ebbed. Jasper really had nothing to worry about. That fateful night of passion would never be repeated.

Jasper watched Dixie come down the stairs with immense pride. 'You look superb, my dear.'

He handed her out into the waiting car as if she was a queen, and the run down the steep mountain road to the tiny church on the outskirts of the village slumbering in the heat of midday took only minutes. Jolted by the appearance of a photographer, to record her entrance on Jasper's arm, Dixie was a bundle of nerves when she mounted the shallow steps clutching her beautiful bouquet.

As the ceremony began, César finally turned to look at her. His dark, deep-set eyes flared silver, and he didn't turn away again. Eduardo Arribas, standing up as best man, had to give him a suggestive nudge when it was time to put the ring on her finger. Dixie was conscious of nothing but the quiet words of the service and César, devastatingly tall and sensationally attractive in an elegant charcoal-grey pinstripe suit.

She was leaving the church before she remembered to remind herself that it was all just a masquerade and not real at all. The photographer made them pose, and when they finally climbed into the car that would waft them back to the house for the wedding breakfast, she expected César to say something very cynical along the lines of, I'm glad that charade's over!

'You look absolutely incredible in that dress,' César breathed huskily instead.

'You don't have to pretend when we're on our own.'

'I'm not pretending—'

'Yes, you are. You know you are…like when you told me I had really stunning eyes,' she reminded him ruefully. 'You can switch off the act until we have to get out of the car again.'

In receipt of that dauntingly prosaic assurance, César murmured almost aggressively, 'You *do* have gorgeous eyes.'

Dixie sighed. 'Why are you carrying on like this?'

César met her frankly reproachful gaze with shimmering

dark eyes that blazed a heat trail of intense sexual awareness through her. Dixie quivered. The atmosphere was suddenly so raw with leaping tension she couldn't breathe. Her mind filled with wanton imagery of their brief intimacy only days earlier. The hot, drugging glory of being in his arms. The wondrous, incredible sensation of that lean, powerful body moving over hers. In the grip of such memories, Dixie shifted on the seat, stabbed by guilty excitement.

And when César curved a lean-fingered hand to her waist and drew her close memory and reality converged, and there was not a thought in her head that she shouldn't do what she so desperately wanted to do. He crushed her soft mouth under his with devouring hunger. With scant ceremony, Dixie speared her hands possessively into his thick black hair and pulled him to her. Her thundering heartbeat merged with his and slowly, very slowly, they disappeared below the level of the car windows until they were lying full-length on the back seat.

Some timeless period later, after a bout of fevered kissing that left them both struggling for oxygen, César raised his head. 'The car's parked,' he remarked with a slight frown. 'The driver's gone.'

As César raised himself, taking her with him, Dixie surfaced, almost senseless from the depths of an all-encompassing passion and with her tiara askew. With deft hands César eased the tiara free, straightened her tumbled hair and slotted the tiara back into place.

'I think we'd better make our entrance…you can't have a wedding breakfast without the bride and groom, *cara mia*.' A heartbreaker of a smile curved César's wide, sensual mouth. As her heart gave a violent lurch, that smile set Dixie back at least five minutes in the recovery process.

César handed her out and smoothed down the folds of her gown as if they had all the time in the world. Then, before she could even catch her breath, he bent down and swept her up into his arms. 'What—?'

'Tradition, *cara*. Relax,' he teased, reading her anxious face with instant understanding and amusement. 'If you ever went on a diet, I'd forcefeed you with chocolate fudge cake every night.'

Dixie had never heard that teasing intonation from César before. It poleaxed her. And she was even more taken aback by the revelation that César could do something as distinctly uncool as kiss her breathless in the back of a car while their few guests waited for them to emerge.

In a decided daze, she let him carry her into the house, for all the world like a real bride on her wedding day. Hovering in the imposing shaded entrance, Jasper watched them approach with unconcealed contentment.

As they drew level he smiled, and said in a cheerful undertone, 'Bruce flew in with your mail, César. He also brought an unexpected visitor, whom I'm sure will be very much appreciated. I haven't shared your news yet. I love to surprise people!'

And indeed, as César strode into the comparative dimness of the hall, Dixie's beautiful ivory gown trailing across him like a banner, Jasper certainly succeeded in his wish to see people surprised.

César's executive assistant, Bruce Gregory, moved forward first, focused on Dixie in her wedding dress and fell still with a dropped jaw.

'Close your mouth, Bruce,' César murmured gently to the younger man. 'You look like one of Dixie's fish.'

The unexpected visitor pushed past Bruce. A very glamorous blonde wearing an eye-catching leopard print skirt and matching crop top that exposed her exotically jewelled navel. She let her breath escape in a startled hiss when she saw the bride and groom. Momentarily, her beautiful face was a study of complete disbelief.

'*Petra?*' Dixie exclaimed in delighted amazement. 'César, this is my sister, Petra!'

Brilliant dark eyes narrowing, César came to a halt and surveyed the now brightly smiling blonde. 'Hello, Petra,' he drawled smoothly. 'What a shame you had to miss the ceremony by such a narrow margin!'

'Petra…this is César…César Valverde,' Dixie announced,

with considerable pride in her ability to introduce her famous sister to someone she felt to be worthy of her notice.

'Everybody knows who César Valverde is,' Petra Sinclair remarked with a patronising look of amusement she attempted to share with César, but César simply stared steadily back at her, not a muscle moving on his darkly handsome face.

'How did you find out where I was?' Dixie demanded, still in César's arms and momentarily blinded when the photographer stepped forward to take a flash photo of their entrance.

'You left a forwarding address, darling. And when I showed up at César's house and ran into Brucie, I persuaded him to let me hitch a ride out here with him.'

'Brucie' angled a somewhat weak and apologetic smile in his employer's direction. César sent him a flashing glance that made him tense. 'Congratulations, César,' he managed, nonetheless. 'And Dixie, my very warmest good wishes. I have to confess...I didn't see this development on the horizon.'

'You said it first,' Petra said, rather shrilly. 'But don't you just love weddings? I know *I* do!'

César slowly lowered Dixie to the floor. 'Excuse me, *cara*,' he murmured in a quiet aside. 'I have an urgent call to make.'

Petra crossed the hall and closed an arm round her much smaller stepsister. 'I really have missed having you around,' she confided, while Jasper looked on with warm approval of such sisterly affection.

Surprised by Petra's unusual demonstrativeness, Dixie glowed. 'I've missed you too. How was California?'

As Jasper moved away, Petra dropped her smile and gave a petulant shrug. 'It didn't work out, and then I landed back in London, expecting you to be able to put me up—'

'Oh, *no*!' Dixie was dismayed.

'And then when I realised you were in Spain, with dear old Jasper, I just crossed my fingers and *prayed* there'd be room for an extra house guest!' Petra studied Dixie's concerned and guilty face with cool green eyes. 'As I'm really broke right now, I had no choice.'

'No, *of course*, you didn't,' Dixie agreed fervently, hoping that César and Jasper wouldn't mind Petra staying on while she herself looked forward to an opportunity to catch up with all her sister's news.

César returned to her side, and Dixie noticed that Bruce was now welded to a phone on the far side of the hall.

Although Dixie would have appreciated a few minutes to talk to her sister in private, she could see it wasn't possible when everybody was waiting for their meal. At the table, she had Jasper on one side of her and César on the other. Petra ended up beside Father Navarro, who seemed to be rather heavily into talking about the joys of early matrimony and large families. Unfortunately Petra made several rather inappropriate comments, and then sank into a silence punctuated only by large yawns.

'I'm just so pleased Petra is here,' Dixie shared shyly with César as he put his hand over hers to cut the beautiful wedding cake. 'Obviously she's really tired, and she's not too comfortable with men of the cloth, but isn't she just gorgeous?'

'So that's the shade of blonde hair you hanker after? It wouldn't suit you at all,' César informed her in a charged undertone. 'You're not hankering after the butterfly tattoo and the body piercing as well, are you?'

'Well, I must say—'

'All that stuff hurts like hell. You'd be in real agony,' César interrupted, watching Dixie pale. 'Your stepsister must be very brave.'

'Yes, she is. Things didn't work out for her in California, but she's just taking it on the chin.' Dixie sighed, full of sympathy.

After the meal, Dixie went to the cloakroom to tidy her hair. When she emerged, Petra was pacing the floor outside, an angry look on her face.

'I nearly fell asleep over that meal…I thought the punishment was never going to end!'

Curving a determined hand over her arm, Petra herded Dixie into the nearest empty room. Closing the door, her blonde stepsister rested back against it, widening her cat-green eyes meaningfully. '*You* and César Valverde married?' she questioned with a rather high-pitched laugh. 'I am gob-smacked—and obviously it changes my plans. I can hardly stay here when you've just got hitched!'

Dixie stared at her in surprise. 'Why ever not?'

'Use your brain, Dixie,' Petra said thinly. 'This is Jasper's house, and now you'll be taking off on some extravagant honeymoon trip. I can scarcely plonk myself down here and wait for your return. I wouldn't want to anyway. I've never met so many pontificating old bores in one spot in my entire life!'

'This is actually César's house, Petra. It belonged to his late father, but Jasper has lived here for years.' Disconcerted as she was by such scorn, Dixie couldn't help being relieved that Petra wasn't instantly subjecting her to a barrage of awkward questions as to how she and César had contrived to get together. She really didn't want to lie to her sister. 'And since Jasper hasn't been too well, César and I won't be taking off anywhere.'

'Rather you than me. I can't stick nurse-maiding old folk, but I can see that this time it's paid off *very* well for you!' Sullen resentment flashed in Petra's eyes. 'Look, why don't you do me a favor and just give me a loan so that I can hightail it back out of this rural place and leave you to enjoy the fruits of your stupendously *good* marriage?'

In receipt of that pointedly derisive speech, Dixie frowned in growing bewilderment, wondering what had got into Petra, who was usually the life and soul of every social gathering. 'A...*loan*?'

'You just married an entire bank,' Petra spelt out with a curled lip.

Uneasy colour lit Dixie's cheeks. 'Petra, I couldn't possibly ask César to give you money—'

'Why not? Is the catch of the century tight with his mega-millions?'

'César settled the bills that you overlooked when you flew out to California,' Dixie countered uncomfortably, disturbed that her stepsister had yet to make any reference to the debts she had left behind her.

Petra stiffened. 'So César knows about all that?'

'Yes.'

Petra reddened angrily. 'It wasn't my fault that I got in such a mess!'

'No, I know it wasn't.' But Petra seemed to have a very cavalier attitude to other people's money, and that did trouble Dixie.

Soothed by Dixie's agreement, Petra sniffed. 'Well, if you'll excuse me for saying so, I've got no desire to hang around here playing gooseberry to my kid sister!'

'If you stayed, it wouldn't be like that… I mean…' Dixie floundered '…our marriage isn't like that.'

But as soon as she said that she recalled the heated embrace she and César had shared in the car. She flushed. Had César been acting for Jasper's benefit again? Or was César just not very good at maintaining a platonic relationship? Or was it even remotely possible that César could still be as tempted by her as she was by him? She discounted that third possibility and opted to believe the first. He had just been *acting* passionate.

'What is that supposed to mean?' Petra demanded very drily.

'César only married me to please Jasper. It's really just a pretend marriage to keep Jasper happy until he gets over his coming surgery,' Dixie heard herself confess tautly. 'So there would be no question of you needing to feel like a gooseberry.'

Petra gave her an arrested look, green eyes gleaming with sudden satisfaction. 'Now that does make more sense to me. After all, what the hell would a guy like César Valverde see in a little dowdy dumpling like you? No offence intended,' she added carelessly as Dixie paled, 'but let's face it, you're no oil painting, and he *is*—'

'Yes,' Dixie cut in tightly, really hurt by that 'dumpling' label.

'The guy is absolutely gorgeous,' Petra continued, carefully examining her own striking reflection in a nearby mirror. 'He's a hunk and he's loaded. Much more my type than yours.'

'I guess he is,' Dixie responded not quite evenly, studying the carpet, feeling very round and very small and horribly plain for the first time since César had worked what she had fondly imagined was a transformation of no mean order. You thought a new hairstyle and some fancy clothes could pull off a miracle? a little voice sounding remarkably like Petra's sneered. Are you for real?

'And César has got to be bored witless stuck here with you and that bunch of old fogies! And you really don't count, do you?' Petra said reflectively, as if her thoughts were far away. 'You're quite right. In the circumstances, there's no reason why I shouldn't stay. It might be fun to spend some time with you.'

Dixie focused on her stepsister's exotically embellished navel, shocked and concerned to discover that from the instant Petra had pointed out that she herself was much more César's type she hadn't really wanted her to stay any more. She was appalled by such a mean-minded prompting.

'And...have I got a surprise for you!' Petra continued, digging a hand into her fashionably tiny bag to produce a crumpled envelope.

At that point the door opened, framing César. Tall and dark and smiling. Even so Dixie sensed an oddly charged quality to his stance. His attention immediately went to her troubled face.

'Your ex-landlady passed it on to me.' Petra handed the letter to Dixie and sidestepped César with a vibrant smile to walk out of the room.

'What's that?' César demanded, striding forward.

Dixie's attention fell on the handwriting. 'Oh, my goodness, it's a letter from Scott!'

Eyes glittering like ice shards, César reached out a hand and snatched it from her again.

Dixie gave him an aghast look of complete bewilderment.

'*Dio…*' César scanned the postmark. 'He posted this from the airport!'

Bruce's voice intervened quietly from the doorway. 'Everything's organised, César.'

One of the maids chose that same moment to enter with a tray of coffee.

'Can I h-have my letter back, please?' Dixie stammered.

'Be my guest.' César returned the letter with precise cool and strolled across the room to join Bruce. 'Would you like some coffee? Help yourself. I need somebody really grounded around me at this minute, because whether you realise it or not, the most major event of my bride's day is now taking place. And this thrilling, unexpected joy, so thoughtfully provided by my stepsister-in-law? A letter from Scott.'

'He's never written to me before, César!' Not really listening, believing that he was teasing her again, and Bruce's presence quite passing her by, Dixie was busy tearing open the envelope. 'Oh, *no*!'

'He's dead?'

'Don't be silly, César. Scott wanted me to go round to his flat so that the repair man could fix his washing machine.'

'New York wasn't far enough,' César mused reflectively.

'But he's actually given me his phone number over there!' Dixie shared in genuine surprise. 'Imagine that!'

'The computer's using every line in the house at the minute,' César delivered flatly. 'And it costs a *fortune* to ring New York.'

'You're right. And then there's the time difference,' Dixie muttered vaguely, automatically glancing at César, as if she expected him to clarify that seeming technicality for her.

'Time differences confuse the hell out of me. You'd have to look it up…haven't a clue where. Get the hell out of here, Bruce,' César raked softly to his convulsed executive assistant, who, having emerged from sheer incredulity, was now struggling desperately hard not to laugh.

'I'd really have liked to know how Scott was getting on with his new job,' Dixie sighed, re-reading her three-line letter rather forlornly.

'He'll be having a whale of a time. New York is a very exciting place,' César murmured, evidently in an attempt to be comforting. 'It's full of sophisticated, gorgeous, unattached women.'

'Knowing Scott as I do,' Dixie mused absently, 'he's sure to be making the most of the experience.'

She was lost in her own thoughts. She no longer believed that she was in love with Scott, and was rather embarrassed by that reality now. How could she have known herself so little and contrived to assume so much?

Over the past week or so she had learnt a lot about herself, and grown up a fair bit too. While she'd been nursing her stepmother she simply hadn't had a social life. And when she'd arrived in London men hadn't exactly beaten a path to her door. So she'd developed a crush on Scott, a harmless but rather juvenile infatuation that had given her more pleasure than pain. After all, she'd enjoyed daydreaming about Scott and discussing him endlessly with anybody willing to listen. Not having a boyfriend hadn't seemed to matter while she had Scott to focus on, and goodness knows she had had nothing much else in her life, she conceded ruefully…

In the stretching silence, César watched Dixie like a hawk. Looking pale and unbearably sad as she inwardly acknowledged the end of an era, Dixie crushed the letter slowly between her fingers. For a normally sunny personality, the gesture seemed redolent of real drama.

'OK…you can phone Scott tonight.'

Emerging from her reverie in some surprise, Dixie encountered the full onslaught of César's penetrating dark eyes and struggled not to shiver in reaction. She wondered why he looked so tense, so…*guilty*? She immediately discarded that fleeting impression. What, after all, could César have to feel guilty about, today of all days? Jasper was happy as a sandboy.

'Thanks...I'd like to wish him well,' she admitted.

'I'm afraid we'll have to leave soon. And, beautiful as that dress is, I imagine you'll want to change,' César continued with supreme cool.

That statement certainly grabbed Dixie's attention. 'Leave?' she queried. 'Leave to go where?'

'We'll be spending the next few days at another location.'

'Like...like on a honeymoon?' Dixie prompted in undisguised horror, quick to catch his drift in spite of his avoidance of that emotive label. 'But I assumed that with Jasper unwell—'

'Eduardo Arribas will be staying while we're away. Jasper naturally expects us to *want* to spend time alone together.'

Colliding with César's stunning dark eyes, Dixie reddened and looked away. 'But it's going to be so awkward...being alone, I mean.'

'Pack plenty of books,' César advised bracingly.

While Dixie was getting changed, Petra came upstairs to find her again.

A bright smile suggesting a considerable improvement in her mood, her stepsister breezed into her room and broke straight into speech. 'Since you *are* going away, César's offered me the use of a condo in an exclusive development on the coast! I've decided to take him up on it. He knows it's too quiet here for me.'

Dixie smiled as she slid her feet into shoes. 'That was really kind of him.'

'Kind? Oh, I don't think it was just that—and I'm so relieved you told me the truth about this marriage of yours *because*...' As Petra fulminatingly scrutinised Dixie, in her scarlet designer sundress with its flirty hem, her green eyes sparkled with more than a hint of malice. 'I think César fancies me like mad!'

Dixie's stomach turned over sickly. The colour drained from her face and she turned away to hide her reaction.

'I can always tell when a man wants me,' Petra continued

with conviction. 'When César first saw me downstairs he just froze; he didn't show any reaction at all. Of course he *couldn't*, could he? Not when it was supposed to be his wedding day! And he's clever, isn't he? Good at concealing things…'

'Yes, he is,' Dixie acknowledged gruffly, her throat closing over. And suddenly, with a sinking heart, she knew exactly why she was hurting—but not why she was so shocked by Petra's announcement. After all, most men were attracted to Petra. Her stepsister wasn't just glamorous and sexy; she was a fun person to be with. So why had she got the idea that César was less than impressed by Petra? Had that been wishful thinking?

'In fact, I think César's already regretting getting himself into this crazy charade with you just to keep the old boy content!' Petra opined drily. 'Still, like you said, that'll be over soon, and César will be free to do as he likes…and I'll certainly be free to do it with him!'

CHAPTER NINE

DIXIE never once asked César where they were to spend their brief honeymoon. In a melodramatic mood, new to her experience, her sole concern was getting César away from Petra as fast as possible. She could not have borne the strain of seeing them together, watching her stepsister flirt, watching César cloak his eyes, shutter that lean, dark, fallen-angel face to conceal his desire to respond in kind…

She had never dreamt she could feel so sick with jealousy or be torn by so many deeply unpleasant emotions. Nothing could have prepared her for the shameful knowledge that for a split second she had actually felt she hated Petra, and had wished her stepsister would vanish in a puff of smoke like the wicked fairy!

But within an hour of their departure Dixie's anger was directed solely at herself. She had fallen head over heels in love with César, but she had cravenly refused to confront that reality. Stubborn denial hadn't protected her, it had just left her out of touch with her own emotions and defenceless. The pain she had tried to evade she was feeling now. César was never going to love her back.

Her love had been an accident waiting to happen. His sheer animal sex appeal had overwhelmed her, and then she had started thinking about him and worrying about him and caring about him. All common sense had deserted her and she had ended up in bed with him, foolishly risking pregnancy and even greater heartbreak.

If she had never experienced that incredible intimate closeness with César she would have been less vulnerable. Whereas *now*… Dixie reflected with intense shame, she couldn't even look at that lean, powerful body of his, exquisitely packaged by superb tailoring, without feeling quite sick with longing and desire.

The helicopter delivered them to the airport, where they boarded the jet. Dixie pretended to doze during the flight. Put aboard a second helicopter in Athens, she was merely grateful that conversation was impossible, but was surprised that César had chosen to travel so far afield when a more convenient location would surely have satisfied Jasper's expectations.

When they had made a final landing, César lifted Dixie out of the helicopter. They were only yards away from a golden stretch of sand and surging sparkling blue sea. The pilot loaded their luggage into the beach buggy parked above the quay.

'It's a private island,' César divulged with considerable satisfaction. 'And we have it all to ourselves.'

Of course, Dixie thought without surprise. He wouldn't want other people around. He wouldn't want to have to pretend they were normal honeymooners, all over each other like a rash and deliriously happy. Parting her lips, she said as much before she could think better of it.

'You've got a point,' César agreed, studying her strained profile and the down-curve of her lips. 'Delirious happiness is not a realistic goal at this point in time.'

As Dixie climbed into the beach buggy she flushed guiltily. 'I've been a real drag all the way here, haven't I?'

'No,' César countered steadily. 'You've just been quiet.'

Dixie frowned, trying to recall when she had last really spoken to César. They had been leaving the house. 'You would've found Petra much better company,' she heard herself say tightly now. 'Maybe you should've dropped me at the condo on the coast and brought her here instead. Jasper wouldn't have known any different!'

That outburst took César as much by surprise as it did Dixie. Clamping her hand to her mouth, she stared at him in horror over the top of her fingers. 'Just joking!' she added abruptly.

His brilliant dark gaze narrowed and gleamed as if he had

suddenly struck gold. 'Where did you get the idea that I was interested in your stepsister?'

Dixie stiffened, lashes concealing her stricken gaze. 'Most men are.'

'I'm not most men.'

But he *was*. Long tall blondes with a lot of temperament were his trademark. And for the few minutes it had taken them to say their goodbyes and depart Dixie had carefully observed César's behaviour. He had more or less ignored Petra. Men did not simply ignore Petra when she was smiling and being genuinely amusing. Such a complete lack of re-action had convinced Dixie that César was indeed very much attracted to her stepsister but determined to hide the fact.

In the shimmering silence that rewarded his assurance that he was *not* one of the common herd, César's wide, sensual mouth suddenly clenched hard. Breathing in deep, he sent the buggy up the hill at a roaring pace and drew it to a grinding halt outside an amazing house that was, until the very last bend, all but concealed by a magnificent belt of specimen trees and wild lush planting.

'Oh, this is really lovely,' Dixie whispered shakily, know-ing that men didn't relish comments on their driving skills.

His bronzed profile taut, shimmering eyes veiled, César sprang out, hauled out all their luggage in one go and strode to the door with it, ferocious tension splintering from every movement.

All too well aware that she should have kept quiet about her suspicions, Dixie followed him at a slower pace into the cool tiled hall. What has possessed her? she asked herself miserably. Naturally César would not wish to confess that he was attracted to Petra when he had already more or less ac-cidentally shared a bed with Dixie and there wasn't the slightest chance of him getting together with her stepsister in the near future.

'I had hoped to avoid admitting it,' César breathed in a driven undertone. 'But I disliked Petra on sight. It was in-stantaneous.'

Falling still, Dixie gazed at him in astonishment.

'In fact there is a five-letter word that sums up my exact opinion of your stepsister, who wasn't under my roof an hour before she began causing trouble!' César slung in raw-edged addition.

'A f-five-letter word…?' Dixie stammered.

'But out of respect for your affection for her I would prefer not to use it.'

He couldn't mean… But, absorbing the icy glitter of his eyes, Dixie registered that he did mean exactly that, and she reeled in shock. But out of the shock emerged the most giddy sense of relief she had ever experienced.

'Right now,' César murmured with sudden surprising intensity, 'I don't have another woman in my life, and—'

At that precise moment, his mobile phone buzzed.

With an expressive sound of impatience César answered it, and immediately tensed. Dixie was close enough to recognise the pitch of a woman's voice. Dark colour accentuated César's slashing cheekbones. He glanced around himself like a male in dire need of an escape hatch, and finally strode out through the front door again with something less than his usual cool. 'It's not very convenient for me to talk at this moment,' she heard him confide grittily.

He leant up against the side of the beach buggy, wide shoulders rigid, his entire attention fiercely pinned to Dixie, who was lugging her case noisily upstairs one step at a time.

'Here, let me take that,' César insisted when he caught up with her. 'That was Lisette on the phone. I…I told her I'd got married.'

'I suppose it's as good an excuse as any you'll ever have.' Dixie surveyed him with reproachful eyes. 'But couldn't you have come up with something kinder?'

'Kinder?' César repeated, very much as though he wasn't quite getting the response he had expected.

'What an awful shock for the poor woman! One minute you're having an affair with her, and the next—'

'The relationship hadn't progressed as far as the bedroom…and now it's over, OK?' César cut in, ruthlessly blunt in his exasperation.

Embarrassed, Dixie reddened and averted her eyes. 'I really don't think that's any of my business, César. I'm sorry, I shouldn't have said what I did,' she told him apologetically. 'It's so confusing, this pretending and then not having to pretend...after a while pretending begins to feel like the real thing, and before I know where I am, I'm being too personal again.'

'Maybe we should just keep on pretending. It might be more interesting...' César cast wide the single door off the landing.

Dixie was already puzzled by the absence of any other doors in so apparently spacious a villa. 'Interesting? My goodness!' she gasped after one astonished glimpse at the vast and luxurious bedroom stretching before her.

Maybe there was another bedroom downstairs. She turned round. César had already gone down to get the rest of the luggage. On the ground floor, Dixie discovered an incredibly opulent reception area, an elegant dining room and a superb kitchen with a fridge full of food. She finally accepted that there was only one bed in the entire house.

César rejoined her and helped himself to a rather large brandy. Dixie took a deep breath. 'César, when I was upstairs I just couldn't help...er...noticing that there's only one...'

While she had been speaking César had downed the brandy in one unappreciative gulp. He straightened his shoulders and angled a shuttered look at her. 'I think this would be a good time for you to ring Scott,' he said flatly.

'Oh...yes, right,' Dixie muttered, distracted by that suggestion.

Five minutes later she dialled the number, and was delighted when Scott answered immediately. Scott was surprised to hear from her, but really, really pleased.

'You're homesick? Oh, Scott, how awful!' Dixie sighed with loads of sympathy, while watching César ram back the sliding patio doors with what struck her as quite unnecessary force. 'Tell me about the New York office... But you're really smart too, Scott, don't let people intimidate you,' she urged supportively as César hovered several feet away with the most strange aura of controlled menace, his lean, strong face rigid, bright eyes mere slivers of silver. 'Of course you'll cope. I know you'll be absolutely brilliant. I have every faith in you. I always have had. You can do *anything* you want to do!'

César suddenly strode past her into the kitchen. The door slammed. Dixie flinched. She heard a dulled thud, a muffled oath and then an unholy silence stretched. She stared in real dismay at that closed door. Was César OK? Had he fallen and hurt himself? The door opened a crack again and she relaxed slightly.

'Yes, I'm still here, Scott,' Dixie continued a little weakly.

'You're such a special person, Dixie. I feel better already,' Scott told her gratefully. 'I'll take you out to dinner when I get home.'

'Dinner? Oh I'd love that,' Dixie assured him, rather eager to get off the phone now.

'Can you give me your number?'

'Well, I'm in Greece right now,' Dixie explained uncertainly.

'What are you doing there?' Scott sounded aghast. 'Are you on holiday?'

'A sort of working holiday.' As the kitchen door crashed shut again, Dixie concluded her call.

She sped into the kitchen. Ashen-faced and breathing rapidly, César was leaning back against the units, blood dripping from a cut on his left hand. 'Oh, your poor hand!' Dixie moaned in instant agony for his suffering.

Reaching straight for the first-aid kit prominently displayed, Dixie broke into it. 'Let me get that cleaned up—'

'Don't fuss...it's just a graze!' he grated.

Dixie hauled over a chair and dragged him down into it. He looked as if he was about to faint. It was his thumb, quite a deep slash. 'This might need stitches—'

'Nonsense...it's nothing.'

'How on earth did you do it?'

'I...*bumped* into something on the wall,' César advanced,

with brooding grimness and eyes as unreadable as a black wall.

'Do you feel dizzy?'

'No,' he growled.

Dixie dealt with the cut with great efficiency.

'I suppose you were a girl guide.'

'Yes...' Dixie studied that lean brown hand, so dark against hers, and without the slightest warning was just overcome with strong emotion. He would have submitted to death by torture sooner than admit up-front that the sight of blood seriously challenged his ability to stay upright. Without even thinking about it, she pressed her lips softly to the back of his hand.

César tensed, but when she tried to pull back he held on to her. 'I have a confession to make.'

Drowning in a wave of appalled mortification at the rather revealing liberty she had just taken, Dixie bowed her head.

'*I* had Scott sent to New York.'

'S-sorry?' Dixie stammered with a frown.

'The minute you told me about Scott I was worried that you might be tempted to put being with him ahead of Jasper,' César revealed harshly. 'So I called in a favour with a partner in his firm and arranged to have him sent abroad. All it took was a two-minute phone call.'

Genuinely horrified by that level of cold-blooded calculation, Dixie lifted her head and gazed into fathomless dark eyes.

'And I'd be lying if I said I was sorry,' César completed.

'I'm just...I'm just so shocked by this...' Registering that it didn't seem quite right to still be holding hands with César after such a revelation, Dixie tugged her fingers free with a tearing sense of loss and confusion she despised. 'You are, without doubt, the most dreadfully selfish person,' she told him unsteadily. 'I can only hope that this temporary transfer at least benefits Scott's career, because so far he is not enjoying himself over there!'

'I think I'm beginning to feel sorry,' César remarked

thoughtfully. 'Not sorry I did what I did, but sorry I succumbed to the disastrous desire to confess.'

'That doesn't surprise me in the slightest,' Dixie said unevenly. 'Don't you *ever* think of people as individuals?'

'I'm getting the image of an exceedingly *wet* individual where Scott's concerned,' César shared very drily. 'I hand him the opportunity of a lifetime and he gets homesick after a week in one of the most exciting cities in the world!'

'That's not the point,' Dixie protested. 'People are more than just puppets you can manipulate!'

'Isn't it strange that I always had this sentimental belief that a free confession won an instant pardon?' César drawled as he rose to his feet with controlled grace.

Dixie leapt up, her cheeks colouring at that response. There was a certain truth in that comeback. If César hadn't chosen to tell her what he had done, she would certainly never, ever have found out. She followed him back into the sitting room. 'Yes...well, actually I—'

'I think I'll go down to the beach for a while.' His darkly handsome features shuttered, César murmured drily. 'I need no mystic powers to divine that this is unlikely to be a wedding night to remember!'

Technically, it *was* their wedding night, Dixie recalled numbly. And she guessed that so far César hadn't found it very entertaining. On the trip here she had been a real wet blanket, and not much more fun since their arrival. In less than an hour she had preached at him twice. 'I'm sorry you're bored,' she whispered tightly, just as he reached the doors that led out to the grounds.

César stilled. 'I'm not bored.'

'Are you hungry?' Dixie pressed hopefully, guilty discomfiture and a very strong desire to keep him with her making her powerfully keen to feed him. 'I could make you something to eat.'

Against the backdrop of the magnificent sunset, César shook his arrogant dark head in apparent wonderment at the offer. 'I'm not hungry for food.'

Her brow indented. César turned back to her. Silhouetted

against the strong light, broad shoulders sheathed in the finest pale linen, lean hips and long powerful thighs accentuated by expensive tailoring, he was achingly beautiful. Bronze skin, black hair, glittering dark eyes silvering as he tipped his proud head back. Her tummy twisted and her heart jumped, tension snaking through her as she succumbed to the compulsive need to stare.

'I'm hungry for you...' César murmured.

'For...for me?' Dixie's shaken voice was strained.

'Famished, ravenous, starving,' César extended, not quite levelly, dazzling eyes glinting over her like laser probes.

Her tummy flipped sky-high, her legs turning hollow.

'Just thought I'd mention it... You see, what was an awful mistake for you *wasn't* an awful mistake for me,' César spelt out very carefully.

Dixie couldn't take her eyes off him. She was paralysed to the spot. 'It...wasn't?'

'*I* thought the experience was sensational,' César confided huskily.

Dixie shivered as her full breasts stirred, their rosy peaks swelling into almost painful sensitivity. 'Possibly because you had been drinking—'

'No...and don't do that—don't sell yourself short!' César censured, bright eyes blazingly intent on her bemused face, his mouth twisting. 'A man can't fake his response to the woman he wants.'

And as she stared at him and divined his meaning, and involuntarily lowered her gaze, a soft little sound of sheer surprise escaped her parted lips. His arousal was boldly etched, and as she met his eyes again the devouring hunger there made liquid heat burn up between her slender thighs. In fact, so intense was that physical sensation she stumbled back a step in dismay.

'You couldn't trust me within a yard of that bed with you in it,' César admitted with unashamed candour. 'I would definitely pounce! I'll sleep down here.'

As he swung away, Dixie's face fell a mile. Yes, he really wanted her...well, sexually. The lust bit again. *Sensational?*

A wanton tingle ran down her spine and her legs quivered. He was walking out of the door...why wasn't she stopping him? Sex for the sake of it—what he was used to, *all* he was used to, and the most he had ever required from a woman. But not enough for her. All wrong for her! She loved him too much already, was too vulnerable, too painfully aware that within weeks Jasper's recovery would lead to a complete separation.

But as César disappeared into the lengthening shadows he flung Dixie into emotional turmoil. She was so tempted to snatch at what he offered. What did she have to lose? She wanted him so much. More than pride, more than principle. And at that instant it was César's own ruthlessly cutting drawl which flooded her memory. 'You're so convinced you're going to fail, you won't even bother trying!'

Right, Dixie decided, her adrenalin fairly leaping to that challenge. Just for once she was going to take a risk and break all her own rules. She plucked the magnum of champagne from the ice bucket in the fridge, dug out a corkscrew and started down the hill to the beach, plotting every step of the way. He was scared of commitment, so she would have to set him free at the outset rather than give him the faintest hint that she was hoping for anything other than a casual affair. That way he would relax...

César was on the shore, staring out to sea. Kicking off her shoes, Dixie padded across the sand with a fast-beating heart, wishing he would hear her and turn round, but the soft rush of the surf concealed her approach. She trod right up to him and pressed the champagne bottle into his hand.

He spun with a startled frown.

Dixie planted the corkscrew into his other hand and addressed his chest. 'I thought it was sensational too...and I don't see any reason for you to sleep downstairs on a stupid squashy floral sofa—'

'Scott?' César almost whispered.

'He's in New York!' Dixie responded, quick as a flash. 'He's like—'

'Out of sight…out of mind?' César slotted in with rich cynicism.

'It's not like that, César—'

'*Dio mio*…why am I arguing?' César demanded in a raw undertone as he suddenly dropped both champagne and cork-screw and swept her up into his arms with devastating strength and enthusiasm.

'Absolutely no strings,' Dixie told him breathlessly, the warm, achingly familiar scent of him washing over her as she wrapped her arms round his neck and pushed her face against his shoulder. 'I'm not a committed sort of person,' she added, in case her first statement hadn't been enough to release him from any subconscious anxiety that she might be more clingy than his usual kind of lover.

César lifted her higher and crushed her soft mouth with fierce hunger under his. She went weak from head to toe. Urgently prying her lips apart, he kept on kissing her, but the whole tenor of the embrace changed. He went from pas-sion to unexpected tenderness, running his mouth lightly over her swept down eyelids, her damp cheeks, before recapturing her reddened lips with a sweetness that was almost unbear-able, his breath mingling with hers. And then, very slowly, he slid her down over his powerfully masculine frame until her bare feet hit the sand again.

As she looked up at him with unwittingly enquiring eyes, César framed her hectically flushed cheekbones with two big hands. 'Sand gets everywhere,' he murmured teasingly.

And he knew that. Of course he did. Nine years older than her, he was a lot more than nine years ahead of her in ex-perience. But Dixie discovered that she didn't want to think about the other women César had had in his life, or of how very different she was from those other women. Not glossy, not glamorous, not sophisticated, not even blonde. She didn't fit the mould, and that scared her.

When they arrived in the bedroom she felt horrendously shy. She hadn't had to think about what she was doing the last time, hadn't had to take responsibility. But César reached for her with a knowing light in his beautiful dark eyes and drew her close. With deft hands he unzipped her dress, gently brushed the straps from her shoulders and let the garment fall to her feet.

His burnished gaze gleamed with rich appreciation over the strapless ivory silk bra and matching lace panties she wore. 'You're exquisite, *cara mia*,' he murmured very softly.

'You say all the right things…practice, I suppose,' Dixie conceded tautly.

A wolfish grin illuminated his mobile mouth, brilliant eyes glinting. 'You're so perfect for me. Nothing I do impresses you!'

'Oh, it does…' Dixie contradicted instantly, dark blue eyes anxious that he should think that, even as her susceptible heart lurched beneath the onslaught of that wonderful smile.

Catching her up in his arms, he laid her down on the magnificent canopied bed. Her breasts rising and falling with every shortened breath, she watched him peel off his clothes with fluid cool. Her heart pounded in her ears as the surging tide of longing dug deep, warming her cheeks, clenching her fingers in on her palms. His lithe, sun-darkened body had the balance and flow of a classic statue suddenly cloaked in living flesh and muscle, but no statue had ever been so rampantly male in his arousal.

'I just can't believe this is us,' she whispered, as a mental image flashed into her mind of César as he was at the bank. Ruthlessly cold, remote, reserved. The memory terrified her.

'Believe it,' César urged huskily, surveying her opulently feminine curves with reverent anticipation.

'But it's not really us…it's like time out of time…'

Lacing his fingers possessively into her tumbled hair, César tugged her into his arms. Suddenly she was trembling helplessly, shot through with need, shifting against his lean, hard length with leaping hunger. Moth to a candle-flame, she thought fearfully, and then, as he freed her breasts from their silk confinement and expertly caressed the tormentingly sensitive tips, she gasped, and the glory of simply feeling stopped all thought dead in its tracks.

'*Dio*…I love your body, *cara mia*,' César confessed with

passionate intensity, and as he cupped her ripe curves he bent his dark head and let the tip of his tongue travel down between her proud breasts, licking the perspiration from her skin.

Her tummy contracted, excitement pulling at her. 'I never knew I could feel like this…' she gasped achingly.

His sure hands curved over her hips as he lifted her up to him and kissed her with unrestrained hunger and all-male dominance. Her every sense sang. He traced a slender trembling thigh to its apex, groaned with eloquent appreciation as he discovered the hot dampness even her panties couldn't conceal. He pressed his mouth hotly to the tiny pulse going crazy at her collarbone and gritted feverishly, 'Jasper was right to patrol the courtyard all those endless evenings…never had so many cold showers in my life!'

She kissed the top of his head, loving the silky density of his hair, the smell of him, the smoothness of his cheekbones below her palms, the interesting roughness beyond, and all the time the heat was pooling inside her, driving her increasingly crazy. 'Want you so much,' she moaned.

'How much?' César demanded with sizzling bite.

In the state she was in as he stripped away the silk and lace barrier still separating him from her she couldn't quantify such a thing. At that moment he was everything, the planet around which she spun like a satellite. 'Too much…'

'Not possible, *mi amore.*' He strung an enervating line of darting kisses over her squirmingly restive body, finding erotic places she hadn't known existed before, letting his fingertips smooth through the damp dark curls screening the hot core of her.

And then he relented and traced the silken flesh crying out for his touch, and her breath caught on a rising pant of sensual shock and she threw her head back, spine arching as the shameless pleasure took her in uncontrollable waves. She ached and she needed him with every screaming fibre of her wanton body.

He came over her and she folded round him, exulting in his heat and his hardness and his weight. And when he surged into her with primal force the wild burning excitement of his possession drove her out of her senses. He sent her flying with every thrust, until she reached an incredible peak and the expanding ache inside her could no longer be restrained. Then she cried out in ecstasy with him, her body convulsing beneath his before she drowned in the sweet aftermath of satiation.

Encircled in his arms, she felt so safe, so supremely, crazily happy.

'You're always surprising me, *cara*,' César drawled softly above her head, and yet there was something in that light almost lazy intonation which made her tense. 'I really didn't think you'd share a bed with me again.'

Long, elegant fingers turned her flushed face up to his. 'Didn't you? You're like chocolate fudge cake…I can't resist you,' she muttered ruefully.

'The oddest thing is…I rather respected those principles of yours.'

Feeling suddenly very naked and under attack, Dixie pulled out of his arms and rolled over. She was caught in a trap of her own making. It wasn't the pleasure which had seduced her, it was the love, the hungry, overriding need to be as close to him as his skin, and to take what she could for as long as she could.

'And sex on a no strings basis?' César mused in a suspiciously smooth tone bordering on the sardonic. 'I've got to hand it to you. For a female who was a virgin only a few days ago, you learn fast.'

Dixie dug her hot face into the pillow like a hedgehog going into hibernation.

'And possibly it's my incurably suspicious mind at work again, but does your sudden change of heart relate to the fact that now that we've consummated this marriage of ours we can no longer go for an annulment?'

Slowly Dixie raised her head and turned over, dragging the rumpled sheet defensively round herself. 'I don't understand…'

Eyes as keen as silver daggers held hers by sheer force of

will. 'We'll have to go for a divorce now. You could make a huge alimony claim.'

Her colour evaporating at that suggestion, her dark blue eyes pained, Dixie simply stuffed her head back in the pillow and turned her back on him.

'No comment?' César probed icily.

So now she was a gold-digger, willing to sacrifice her principles and jump into bed with him purely out of greed! Dixie just sagged, deeply hurt and really angry with him. He could be so stupid when it came to the things that really mattered. He couldn't take anything at superficial value. Didn't he know her at all? How could he have possessed her body with such fiery tenderness while that over-developed brain of his was coming up with such a nasty scenario?

'Does everybody try to rip you off?' she whispered.

'Rarely do I put myself at risk.'

Dixie lifted her head, her dark blue gaze gleaming into chilling, dark, formidable eyes that might have belonged to a stranger. That hurt even more, but she rammed back the pain and tilted her chin. 'Stop worrying. Your bank balance is safe...I'm just using you for sex!'

A stunned light flashed in César's intent stare. 'You didn't say that—'

He looked shocked rigid, and somehow that pleased her. 'Oh, I did. And, blunt as it was, it's really all I've got to say on the subject.'

'You don't mean it...' César released a sudden husky laugh. 'Of course you don't. We're married...you're my wife!'

'You wouldn't accuse your wife of sleeping with you for the sake of money...well, maybe you would,' Dixie conceded, his stock being very low in her eyes at that moment. 'In fact you just did.'

César curved his arms round her rigid, resisting body. 'You changed your mind so suddenly. I have a logical mind. I need to know your motivation.'

'I've just explained that, and will you please let go of me?'

'No.' César planted a kiss at the nape of her neck.

'We're not really married and you know we're not,' she murmured heavily. 'I don't like you saying that we are.'

Instantly, he released her. 'Fine…'

He left her alone then, and she didn't like that either, could feel the stormy tension emanating from him in perceptible waves.

'*And* you owe me an apology,' Dixie muttered miserably.

'I don't apologise to one-night stands,' César breathed witheringly.

The silence stretched and stretched.

'OK,' César ground out tautly. 'I should've reserved comment on a potential alimony claim until it actually happened. Since I asked you to marry me, *and* I asked you to share this bed, my suspicions were unreasonable and unjust.'

There was a definite sense of waiting expectation in the silence which followed that admission of fault, but unfortunately, in relieved receipt of that apology, Dixie just fell asleep, worn out by a very long and emotional day.

Hours later, Dixie lay watching César sleep as the dawn light filtered through the slats of the tall shutters that screened the balcony. Having pushed off the bedding, he lay on his stomach in a relaxed sprawl, his blue-shadowed jawline resting on a brown forearm, ebony lashes gleaming above a slightly flushed cheekbone. He looked younger, less intimidating, incredibly sexy, not an inch of that lean, muscular bronzed body out of condition.

Some time during the night they had collided again, and clung and made love with such frantic intensity she blushed just thinking about it. And she wondered, indeed marvelled that César could desire her as much as he evidently did, and still she couldn't begin to understand it. Sex was clearly very important to César, and hadn't he told her that himself? Bed being the one place he let himself go. Oh, she had already divined that when he had said back in London that she had the kind of shape which kept teenage boys awake and fantasising at night he was talking about himself at that age.

But it didn't mean anything, did it? Physical release, fleeting pleasure on his terms. But she wasn't going to think like that, she scolded herself. She was going to live for the moment.

'Magdalena…my mother, she had tremendous charm and I was very fond of her,' César admitted rather tautly as he lay back against the tumbled pillows like a lithe, bronzed pagan. 'But she was a total airhead. I worried more about her than she did about me.'

'Did you ever meet your father?'

'Once. I was ten. He was curious…that was all,' César admitted without a shade of censure.

'And how did it go?' Dixie prompted.

César grimaced. 'I unnerved him, *cara*. I was a real little nerd at that age, and I had a pretty smart mouth. Yet he left me everything he possessed when he died the following year—probably because I was his only child.'

'So how did you end up going into the family bank?' Dixie asked curiously.

'My father was a playboy all his life, but he expected something more from me,' César conceded with wry amusement. 'He stipulated in his will that I could only inherit his shareholding in Valverde Mercantile if I started at the bank at the bottom and worked my way up.'

'Your first serious girlfriend?' Dixie questioned daringly.

'I was eighteen. I found her in bed with my best friend. I think I can safely say that she was my *only* serious girlfriend.' César leant forward to refill her wine glass.

'You must've been so hurt!' Dixie muttered fiercely.

César smiled at her, a surprisingly tender and amused smile. 'I survived. So tell me about Scott,' he invited.

Dixie blinked. 'What about him?'

'I'm just curious.'

'He likes football and cars. He's twenty-two on his next birthday…' César winced without her noticing as she ran an abstracted fingertip round and round the rim of her glass, wondering why on earth he wanted to hear about Scott. 'He's not a smartass,' she said carefully. 'But he would really love to be called one. Everybody he admires at work seems to be like that, so he wears the same clothes and drives an old Porsche he really can't afford.'

'You're describing a very immature personality.'

'Yes…well, you can't expect him to know everything yet.' Her affection for Scott warmed her smile. 'He's really quite sweet.'

Taking her by surprise, César pulled her into his arms and crushed her soft mouth with fierce, almost angry urgency under his, making her world spin on its axis. 'I'm not sweet…'

Feeling giddy, she scanned the lean strong face above hers with a secretive light in her eyes. She found some of the strangest things sweet when she found them in César. His grizzly bear reaction to her walking away down the beach and getting lost in a book for three hours and totally forgetting about him. His energetic need to be *doing* something every second of the day. His sudden bursts of passion at the most inopportune moments…like when she was in the middle of making a meal or trying to change the bed.

In a week of incredible contentment and happiness, Dixie had learnt a lot about César, and had fallen even more deeply in love with the complex male behind that dark fallen-angel face. He could be so incredibly tender, so honestly affectionate, but always in a hit and run fashion, retreating again fast. Her dog, Spike, had been a bit like that at first, she mused. Full of distrust and unease, afraid to respond to her overtures or express affection.

'What are you thinking about?' César probed, at the wrong moment.

Dixie reddened, knowing he absolutely did not want to know that she had been comparing him to a dog who had been mistreated by a cruel owner in his early years.

'No, don't tell me.' César's bronzed features shuttered as if he had thrown away the key and locked her out.

But she knew what to do when that happened now. She closed her arms round him tight and shut her eyes, as if she was too unobservant to read his signals, and kissed him regardless. He tensed, and then with a hungry driven groan he kissed her back with ravishing need.

'We're leaving the day after tomorrow.' Over an hour later, Dixie was still in César's arms. She was anxious about Jasper's coming surgery, but sad that they had to leave the island.

'No, we're leaving tomorrow.'

'But you said we were flying back on the thirty-first.'

'It'll be the thirty-first in less than five minutes,' César informed her wryly. 'You need a calendar. Somewhere you've lost a day.'

And out of nowhere, as Dixie thought about calendars, something that she had tucked right to the back of her mind struck her. She had always had a twenty-six-day cycle, and today her period should have started, but it hadn't...

So she was late. Perhaps her system had been upset by the change in diet and climate, she told herself feverishly. But what if it wasn't that? What if she had conceived César's baby that very first night?

CHAPTER TEN

'I WANTED to gag Jasper when he started telling us what was in his will!' César confessed, pacing the elegant waiting room like a caged lion and shrugging back his sleeve to consult his slim gold Rolex watch for possibly the fourth time in as many minutes. '*Accidenti!* If I ran a merchant bank the way they run the surgical unit here, I'd be a pauper!'

'Jasper will be fine,' Dixie told him with soothing conviction.

'How can you be so calm?' César demanded, almost accusingly.

'My stepmother was in Intensive Care several times towards the end.'

A veil of dark colour accentuated César's spectacular cheekbones. He breathed in deep and swallowed hard. 'The queen of the gentle put-down, *cara mia*,' he murmured with a wryly apologetic twist of his beautiful mouth. 'I walked smack bang into that one, didn't I?'

'Jasper will come through with flying colours. It's a straightforward procedure.'

César flung himself down on the seat beside her, only to fly upright the instant the door opened. It was the surgeon. His reassuring smile told Dixie all she needed to know, but César talked at length to him. Dixie watched César with her heart in her eyes. He was being very Italian, or was it very Spanish? She smiled. Whichever, he was in a volatile, highly expressive mood, his lean hands moving to illustrate his speech. Not a side of his nature he had ever shown at the bank, where formality and reserve as chilling as ice had always ruled him.

And how would César respond if she chose to tell him that she was carrying his child? Probably with ice. Dixie lost colour, her eyes shadowing with strain. After Jasper had checked into the clinic on the busy outskirts of Granada yesterday, Dixie had mentioned that she had some shopping to do and had slipped away for an hour. She had bought a pregnancy testing kit, and early this morning she had used it. Within minutes the simple test had confirmed that she was pregnant. The shock had hit her hard. Had César not been so worried about Jasper's surgery he might well have questioned the extent of her preoccupation.

How on earth *could* she tell César? He wasn't even aware that there had been cause for concern. She had let him assume that she was taking the contraceptive pill, and since the wedding César had ensured that they took not the smallest risk. Regardless of what she had allowed him to believe, he had still chosen to use protection. Such scrupulous care told Dixie that César was determined not to accidentally father any woman's child.

But it had already been too late. She was carrying César's baby and she didn't feel it was his fault; she felt it was all her fault! And when, as had happened throughout the day, rosy images of a little girl or boy with César's eyes had strayed into Dixie's mind, she felt even guiltier, and more foolish than ever for being so happy with César on the island. In spite of reminding him on their wedding night that their marriage wasn't a real marriage, she had ended up behaving as if it was. Yet their brief but intense relationship was already existing on borrowed time, and within a few weeks would end entirely.

They spent the following day at the clinic, quietly taking turns to sit with Jasper. By that evening, however, César was in an ebullient mood. Being a dire pessimist, having feared the very worst might happen either during surgery or in the crucial recovery period which followed, César's relief at his godfather's continuing steady improvement now knew no bounds.

Back in their luxurious hotel suite, he pulled a full-length gold evening gown out of the closet and dropped it on to the bed. 'Dress up. We're going out to celebrate!'

Had Dixie done her own packing she wouldn't even have had a suitable dress to wear, because it would not have occurred to her that they might go out anywhere special while they were staying in Granada.

Emerging from the shower twenty minutes later, a towel wrapped round his narrow hips, César dropped Dixie's wedding and engagement rings down on the dressing table beside her. 'You leave them absolutely everywhere. Every opportunity you get, you take those rings off and forget about them. Sooner or later they'll be lost or stolen!'

'I'll try to be more careful,' Dixie said in a small voice.

'Sometimes it's like you're trying to make some kind of statement with those rings,' César murmured grittily, but the sight of Dixie rising from the stool, clad only in a highly feminine peach lace bra and diminutive panties, set his mind in what was becoming a very predictable direction.

'*Porca miseria!*' he breathed raggedly. 'You look fantastic!'

As she turned round self-consciously, her cheeks warm, she encountered brilliant dark eyes and felt the wicked weakness and heat he could evoke so easily flood through her trembling body.

'*Dio*…how I want you, *cara*!' César loosened his towel and reached for her in practically the same movement.

He crushed her into the hard, muscular heat of him and she shivered violently, every pulse-point reacting instantaneously. But, for the first time in over a week, a new voice in her head screamed no. Momentarily, she stilled in confusion at that negative prompting, but César's power over her wanton body was greater. Snapping free the bra and casting it aside, he raised his hands to shape her achingly responsive flesh and she was lost, moaning helplessly under his hungry, sensual mouth as he backed her down on to the bed.

It was wilder than it had ever been between them. Raw and sexy and frantically exciting, even shocking in its intensity. He didn't have to wait. She was ready for him. And the instant she felt him inside her she was out of control, reaching a height of intolerable excitement so fast she raked her nails down his back in shaken reaction and he had to smother her scream of release with his mouth.

And then it was over and she was in a complete daze and César was gazing down at her with unconcealed satisfaction. 'It gets better every time,' he said with a very male wolfish grin, sliding off her and then hauling her up into his arms to carry her back into the shower with him.

Only somehow this time she felt embarrassed and ashamed. No longer was it possible to pretend that theirs was a normal relationship. It was really just a casual affair, she told herself. But while she stood under the shower, getting her hair wrecked, knowing it would be wildly curly and unmanageable after a second soaking, an even more disturbing thought occurred to Dixie. It wasn't even an affair. The truth was far less presentable. By settling those debts César had bought her, like a can of peas off a supermarket shelf, and here she was *sleeping* with him as well.

César folded her into a big fleecy towel as if she was a small child. 'I keep on forgetting how new to all this you are,' he drawled softly as he surveyed her evasive eyes and tense mouth. 'But at the same time I like that knowledge. It makes everything so special between us—'

'Does it?'

'Of course it does.' He rested his hands on her taut shoulders, ebony brows drawing together in a frown. 'The last forty-eight hours have been very stressful…we just blew away all that tension in bed and it was electrifying. That's nothing to feel awkward about.'

But Dixie was not in the mood to be comforted. She felt like one of those stress-busting toys businessmen kept on their desks for relaxation. And when César turned away she saw long parallel scratches marring his smooth brown back and just about died a thousand deaths on the spot. She scuttled out of the bathroom to get dressed, feeling hot tears burning the back of her eyes, all her emotions in upheaval at once.

She knew why she was upset. What could be more brutally realistic and impossible to overlook than an unplanned pregnancy which would infuriate the man she loved? Her days of closing her eyes to harsh facts were at end. It wasn't possible to live for the moment with new life growing inside her womb.

César took her to a really fancy restaurant for dinner by candlelight. Dixie wondered out loud why people would want to have to squint at the menu. César requested another candle.

Vintage champagne was brought with a flourish. Dixie asked for mineral water.

César translated the entire menu for her. Then she said she just wanted a salad and played with it.

César had pre-ordered chocolate fudge cake as a surprise. She said she wasn't hungry enough to eat it.

He told her the coffee was a speciality. She told him it tasted metallic and funny.

She left her rings on the sink in the cloakroom. This necessitated a return to the restaurant from the very doors of the nightclub they had been about to enter and twenty-five minutes sitting in a traffic jam. Dixie gave the restaurateur a glum smile of apology and put the rings back on again.

César gave her a brooding look of censure. 'I'm amazed that diamond wasn't stolen.'

'I'm not,' Dixie said, without a shred of remorse for all the inconvenience she'd caused. 'It looks like it fell out of a Christmas cracker!'

César's teeth visibly clenched. 'OK...I've finally got the message. You don't like your engagement ring.'

'It's not mine, it's yours...so what does it matter what I think of it?' Dixie snapped pettishly, shocked at herself, indeed shocked at the way she had been behaving all evening, but quite incapable of controlling the stormy promptings of her own flailing insecurity. And hating César, oh, yes, absolutely hating him as the evening had worn on. Hating him for every smile and every woman who stared at him. Hating him for forgetting about precautions the one time he couldn't afford to forget. Hating him for making her love him and not loving her back...

'*Dio!* What is the matter with you?' César suddenly

launched at her halfway back into the limousine. 'Why the hell are you acting like this?'

As she saw his chauffeur swiftly step back in discomfiture, Dixie reddened fiercely and twisted her pounding head away, her true self recoiling from the blunt bewilderment César expressed in spite of his anger.

'You've been like that little girl in the nursery rhyme. You know the one,' César asserted sardonically. 'When she was good, she was very, very good, but when she was bad, she was horrid!'

'I just don't feel like pretending any more.' She wanted to bite down on her tongue but she couldn't; she just couldn't hold the bitterness back.

The silence seemed to scream.

'And what's that cryptic utterance supposed to mean?' César's rich, dark drawl was suddenly cool as ice, and it had been a very long time since he had used that tone with her.

'You're making me feel bad about myself.'

'Using men for sex has its disadvantages,' César incised very drily. 'I thought that was a stupid joke, but now I'm starting to wonder.'

Dixie drew in a breath so deep she was surprised she didn't burst. The bright lights of the city streets flickered in her eyes. 'It's a lot worse than that...'

'Tell me this is a mini-breakdown after all the stress we've had and I'll take a deep breath too and all this bull is going to wash over me while I embrace saint-like restraint!' César shot back at her in a roughened warning.

Dixie desperately wanted to keep quiet, but she couldn't. Now all those feelings had foamed up inside her, she had to let them out. 'What we've got is very sordid—'

'I didn't hear that.'

'You bought the right to tell me what to do when you paid those debts. You said that yourself,' Dixie reminded him shakily. 'And I could just about live with that if we hadn't ended up in bed—'

'When we made that deal there was nothing between us. We've gone way beyond that level since then!'

'Well, I still really hate you for what you've done to me!' Dixie told him wildly. But even as she slung those bitter words she knew that she wanted him to pull her into his arms and tell her she was talking rubbish and make her feel safe again, not just sit there like an insensitive stone watching her tear herself apart!

'OK.' César stared at her, lean, strong face ferociously taut, eyes a bright lambent silver as unreadable as a mirror, and then he lifted the phone to communicate with his chauffeur. Minutes later, the limo drew out of the traffic and purred in at the front of their hotel.

'I'll see you tomorrow at the clinic,' César breathed without inflection, and a moment later the passenger door beside Dixie opened for her to get out.

'*Tomorrow?* Where are you going?' she demanded helplessly.

'I don't think that's anything which need concern you now.'

It had never once occurred to Dixie that César might just walk out on her and the argument she had begun. It felt like the cruellest kind of punishment. Appalled into silence, she climbed out and watched the limo pull back into the flow of traffic.

She already knew she had made a dreadful mistake. She had wrecked the relationship they did have. Getting a grip on her wildly fluctuating emotions, she sat up waiting for César to come back. At that point she was absolutely convinced that in spite of what he had said he would return to the hotel. But at three in the morning she went to bed and fell into an uneasy doze, only to wake up still alone at dawn, and feel very scared.

He had probably just gone back to the hacienda for the night. It was only an hour's drive away, she reminded herself. They were only in a hotel because it was more convenient while they were spending so much time with Jasper.

Experiencing a very real need to talk to someone about the mess she had made of things, Dixie toyed with the idea of ringing Petra, where she was staying on the coast. But the nagging awareness that confiding in her stepsister on her wedding day had given her nothing but grief held her back. And César, who wouldn't dream of confiding anything private in anybody, even under torture, would be furious if she was indiscreet.

So Dixie buttoned up her desire to unburden herself, but ended up succumbing to the temptation to ring Scott for another chat, just to fill in the time until she could go to the clinic and sit with Jasper. Scott was much more cheerful. He had been told that he would be free to return to London within a fortnight. Emboldened by that news, he had ventured out to explore New York, but only got as far as the car showrooms. He spent most of the call talking at length about a car he had fallen in love with.

More clued up about Corvettes than she had ever wanted to be, but relieved Scott was happier, Dixie took a taxi to the clinic around ten. It was distinctly humiliating to arrive with Jasper and discover that although César had not been in touch with her he had already sent a message to his godfather. It did not occur to her that she had stayed on the phone to New York for well over an hour because she hadn't the slightest idea that the call had actually lasted that long.

'Such a shame that you and César have to be separated so soon after the wedding,' Jasper sighed with sympathy.

'Sorry?' Dixie prompted uncertainly.

'This stockmarket crisis…César having to rush back to London,' Jasper filled in gloomily. 'Said he'd call in on the way to the airport. You should go with him. You shouldn't be sitting about here with me.'

Stockmarket crisis? What stockmarket crisis? César was rushing back to London? In receipt of that devastating news, it was a challenge to summon up a sunny reproving smile, but Dixie managed it because she cared so much about the old man anxiously watching for her reaction. 'I *love* sitting about here with you!'

Jasper's forlorn look evaporated. 'I expect César will be far too busy to spend time with you over the next few days anyway,' he conceded. 'He's a terrible workaholic.'

César was returning to London. César was leaving her behind in Spain, just the way it had always been planned, Dixie reminded herself numbly. César had already been away from Valverde Mercantile for more than two weeks. Soon Jasper would be able to go home to convalesce, and she would stay on to keep him company and ensure he didn't try to do too much too soon.

She chatted to Jasper, and only when the sound of answering silence finally penetrated did she appreciate that he had fallen asleep. She couldn't even recall what she had been talking about. Feeling the need to stretch her legs, she slipped out of the room, only to stop dead again.

César was striding down the corridor towards her. In a fabulous light grey pinstripe business suit teamed with a white shirt and silver silk tie, he was no longer the relaxed and smiling male she had come to expect. As he drew to a halt a couple of feet from her he looked cold, distant and unbelievably intimidating.

Meeting those chilling dark deep-set eyes, she felt as she had that very first day she had gone into his office, to be faced with the computer print-out listing Petra's debts. The shock of that realisation made Dixie shiver in disbelief. It was as if everything that had happened between them since then only existed in her own imagination.

'Jasper's asleep,' she muttered unevenly.

'He needs all the rest he can get. I'll call him this evening.'

Dixie breathed in deep and braced herself to say what she knew needed to be said. 'César, I'm really sorry about the way I acted last night—'

'Forget it,' César cut in with dismissive, deflating cool.

Her tension screamed up another notch. It was as if a terrifying wall of impenetrable glass separated him from her. It was as if they had never made love, never laughed together, never shared anything. 'I *can't*…I didn't mean it when I said I hate—'

'I don't want to talk about this.' He was cold as ice, his impatience unhidden.

Involuntarily, Dixie's eyes just filled with tears.

With a soft, succinct expletive, César splayed a hand over her spine to press her another few yards down the corridor into the empty waiting room. He didn't close the door, though. As he walked over to the window a nurse walked past, her footsteps an audible reminder that they didn't have privacy. Then Dixie sensed that César didn't want privacy, didn't want to speak to her in depth, didn't want to be with her one second more than he had to be. The completeness of that rejection savaged her like a physical blow.

And, suddenly feeling dizzy, she sank heavily down into a chair. 'You're dumping me...' She hadn't meant to say that, hadn't even thought of saying that, but somehow that was what emerged from her bloodless lips.

Ferocious tension radiated from every inch of César's rigid back view. He dug coiled fists into the pockets of his well-cut trousers, tightening the fine fabric over his long powerful thighs, but he didn't turn round and he didn't respond.

'Where did you go last night?' Dixie whispered shakily, desperate to talk just to keep him with her, because her whole world felt as if it was shattering around her.

'The beach.'

'Wh-what beach?' she stammered, completely thrown by that admission, as Granada was a long drive from the coast.

'A beach...OK? What does it matter *where* I went?' César gritted in a driven undertone.

'I was worried about you...you told me once not to do that.' Dixie recalled in a sick daze.

'I've settled the hotel bill.' César half turned towards her and then swung back to the window again, but not before she had seen the fierce tautening of his strong profile. 'You'll be more comfortable staying at the hacienda. Jasper's chauffeur will run you back and forth. In a couple of weeks you can come back to London. We'll sort out the rest then.'

If there was a right moment to tell César that she was carrying his baby, Dixie acknowledged painfully, this was definitely not it, here where they could be interrupted at any time or overheard.

César finally spun round. He treated her to a glittering

diamond-hard appraisal, not a revealing muscle moving on his darkly handsome face. Then, slowly elbowing back his superbly tailored jacket, he removed something from the inner pocket. 'You might as well have *this*...' He tossed the tiny item with studied casualness down on her lap. 'I'm never going to give it to anybody else.'

In complete astonishment, Dixie gazed down at the exquisite ruby ring, the sunlight gleaming over the beautiful jewel's rich gleaming density of colour.

'Throughout this whole thing you've been really great.' César hovered uneasily halfway towards the open door, like a male being painfully pulled in two different directions, lines of deep strain engraved between his nose and compressed mouth, brilliant eyes screened. 'I should've told you that first...but I wasn't in the mood. You should sell that ring. Scott may not know it yet, but keeping you in washing machines will probably be more of a challenge than keeping a Porsche on the road!'

Scott? Why was César suddenly talking about Scott? Dixie's brain refused to function. Why was he behaving so unnaturally? Was he reminding her about Scott in the hope that she would pick up on that prompting and stop being so embarrassingly emotional?

'Yes,' Dixie muttered flatly. 'But it won't be a Porsche. It'll be a Corvette.'

'Sorry, am I interrupting?' a bright familiar female voice exclaimed from the doorway.

Dixie's head flew up and she gaped, utterly taken aback by the sight of her stepsister standing there, her sleek brown torso and endless long legs on show in a white lace top and brief flirty skirt. 'Petra...?' she breathed in bewilderment.

'I thought César was going to bring you down to the car to see me, but I got fed up waiting.' Petra flicked back her stunning golden mane of hair, a distinctly petulant look on her lovely face. 'I feel like I've spent the whole morning in that blasted car *waiting*!'

César frowned at Dixie. 'Sorry, I forgot to mention that your sister had decided to fly back to London with me.'

'Forgot?' Petra repeated thinly, but then she plastered a wide, bright smile on her lips and shrugged. 'This guy is just so bad for my ego!'

Dixie just looked through the two of them, refusing to focus on either as she struggled valiantly to conceal the most sick sense of betrayal. So, César had gone to the beach. And who had been staying by that beach? She understood now, wished she didn't. So much for his impressively stated dislike of Petra! Last night César had walked away from her and deliberately sought out her beautiful stepsister's company.

'It's time I got back to Jasper.' Pale as death, Dixie scrambled upright, eager to escape both her companions. 'Have a good trip back to London!'

'Dixie…?' Halfway down the corridor César caught up with her, but he only succeeded in halting her by catching hold of her hand.

Unwillingly, Dixie spun back. *'What?'* she demanded baldly.

César gazed down at her with charged dark eyes, and then very slowly let go of her hand again. 'Nothing…nothing at all!' he breathed fiercely, and strode away.

Dixie leant back against the wall until she had stopped trembling, and as soon as he was out of sight dived into the cloakroom to be ingloriously and horribly sick.

CHAPTER ELEVEN

THREE weeks later, Dixie arrived back in London.

Every evening for those three weeks César had phoned her. After she had given her daily bulletin on Jasper, César had then questioned her in astonishing detail about what she did every day, right down to what she was reading. And every evening she had just talked and talked about nothing in particular, just so that she could keep on hearing the sound of that rich, dark drawl. Not once had either of them referred to their marriage, their once intimate relationship, or the divorce that now had to be on the cards.

Indeed, César's constant calls had utterly bewildered Dixie, until she had belatedly worked out that he was behaving exactly as Jasper would expect a newly married husband to behave when he was separated from his wife. Naturally there would be no necessity for such pretences once she was back in London.

Dixie was a complete bag of nerves by the time César's chauffeur met her off her flight. She hadn't been sleeping well, and keeping up a sunny façade for Jasper had been a strain. And three long endless weeks away from César's enervating presence had forced her to face too many depressing realities.

What they had briefly shared was over. For César, it had been a casual sexual affair. For her, it had been the most wonderful but ultimately the most traumatic experience of her life. And right now she still felt that she was never, ever going to recover. She had known César had a very low tolerance for the kind of scene she had thrown that night in Granada, but she still felt that even he could have practised sufficient consideration not to make it obvious that he was planning to replace her with her own stepsister.

159

But she was equally aware that she couldn't afford to wallow in her squashed ego or her misery. She was pregnant. She was broke. She was unemployed. To save face she would very much have liked to vanish out of César's life with a cheery smile, but as matters now stood that wasn't an option open to her. It was time she told César about the baby. She had been tempted to just blurt the news out on the phone, but had decided that that would be the coward's way out.

It was afternoon when Dixie trekked wearily in the chauffeur's wake towards the limousine parked outside the airport. She wasn't expecting to have to face César before evening. So when the passenger door suddenly opened and César climbed gracefully out she was completely unprepared, and an expression of unconcealed dismay froze her face.

And that dismay merely concealed a whole host of humiliating and all too personal reactions. César looked so impossibly gorgeous. Black hair gleaming in the sunshine, stunning dark eyes just zooming in on her susceptible heart and stealing it back again. Feeling the tarmac literally rock beneath her feet, Dixie came to a halt, just staring endlessly at him, wondering with a deep sense of injustice why he had to look so fantastically sexy and exotic in an incredibly elegant cream designer suit. And here she was, a make-up-free zone, hair curling and wearing the first outfit she had pulled out of the wardrobe.

'I'd have met you off the plane, but Spike doesn't like being left alone in the car...' César began tautly.

'S-Spike?'

An agonised whine sounded from the back seat. César bent down and reached in and emerged with Spike, his little short legs pedalling in the air with excitement, pleading brown eyes prominent.

Dixie just dived at Spike. Reaching him out of César's arms, she scrambled into the car to take part in an ecstatic reunion with her pet. By the time Spike had been restored to order the limo was a long way from the airport, and Dixie was grateful for the distraction.

'I can't believe he came with you.' Dixie watched as Spike

arranged himself between them, like a dog trying to stretch himself to three times his natural length so that he could be in contact with both. 'My goodness, he's not the slightest bit scared of you!'

Spike made that comment somewhat redundant by giving Dixie's hand an apologetic lick, then squirming round and sneaking in the most grovelling fashion imaginable across the back seat to settle down beside César and look up at him with worshipping eyes.

'He's quite friendly,' César conceded in modest under-statement, stroking Spike's tufty ears and reducing the Jack Russell to a mindless heap of bliss.

'I just never thought…I mean, he was so *terrified* of men!' With difficulty, Dixie mastered her astonishment. 'It took me ages to win his trust, but obviously you have the magic touch…only…' She bit her lip anxiously. 'He's going to be very upset if he loses you now.'

'Yes, I feel it could really traumatise him,' César agreed reflectively. 'You'll have to try to detach him from me by easy stages.'

'Yes, of course.'

'I shouldn't think you'll be able to consider moving out of my house in the near future,' César sighed.

Dixie continued to survey Spike with wondering eyes. Welded to César's thigh, he was the very picture of intense doggy devotion. 'I guess not…'

A slow smile nudged at the corners of César's once tense lip-line. 'I have to confess I've spoilt him.'

'He needed spoiling.'

Silence fell. Dixie watched Spike as though her life depended on it. He was a great ice-breaker, she thought ruefully. And she couldn't help but be touched to see César being so kind to her distinctly scruffy little pet. She had really been dreading seeing César again after that emotionally devastating final meeting at the clinic. Unfortunately even Spike wasn't likely to be much use as a diversion once she told César what she had to tell him…

'When we get back to the house,' Dixie began, deciding

that César deserved some warning of what was coming his way, 'we'll have to talk. I'm afraid I've got something really serious and shocking—well, *very* shocking to confess, and you're not going to be very happy about it... In fact, I think you're likely to be really annoyed, and I want to say now in advance that that is understandable—'

'Scott flew out to Spain and you sneaked out and slept with him...' César slotted in rawly.

Dixie's lashes fluttered up on incredulous dark blue eyes. She couldn't have responded to such an outrageous suggestion had her life depended on it.

'*Madre di Dio*...anything of that nature, keep it to yourself, because "annoyed" won't cover it. I'll *kill* him!' César swore in a voice that fractured between visibly clenched teeth.

'What's the matter with you? Have you been drinking...or something?' Dixie enquired tautly.

'No, but I badly need a large shot of alcohol,' César confided jaggedly as he leant forward and wrenched open the drinks cabinet.

'Scott has not been in Spain.' Hot, mortified colour now bloomed in Dixie's cheeks. 'And I can't imagine why you think he would've been, or that I would do what you suggested. Perhaps you think I behaved in a rather impulsive fashion with you, but believe me, I've learnt my lesson.'

César thrust shut the drinks cabinet without succumbing to temptation. He drew in a deep, steadying breath. 'I had nerves of steel until I met you.'

'I was just trying to prepare you for what I have to tell you,' Dixie muttered ruefully.

'Relax. I'm cool as ice,' César informed her with glittering dark eyes of probing enquiry that made it very hard for her to breathe. 'Battle-hardened, unshockable, and ready to cope with anything you want to throw at me.'

The limo drew up outside the house. Dixie smiled at Fisher as he opened the imposing front door.

'Welcome home, Mrs Valverde,' the butler said with immense warmth.

'Oh, no, who told you we were married?' Dixie gasped in dismay, looking worriedly at César. 'It's a really big secret!'

'It's all round the bank too,' César told her apologetically.

Dixie's eyes got even bigger. 'Bruce didn't keep quiet? Oh, how awful for you, César!'

'I'm bearing up surprisingly well. And I wish I could tell you that it was a seven-day wonder, but it's a story set to run and run, and that in itself has created certain problems you may not have foreseen,' César confided, curving a determined arm over her spine and walking her fast towards his study, Spike at their heels.

'Problems?'

'Wedding presents, invitations out as a couple—'

'*Wedding* presents?' Dixie exclaimed in horror.

César slammed shut the door, leant back against it with squared shoulders and breathed. 'OK…give me the really serious, very shocking bad news. Don't keep me in suspense…'

Dazed by the revelation that their marriage was now a matter of public knowledge, and feeling rather light-headed from the effects of stress and tiredness, Dixie surveyed César with open misery.

'I just wish I hadn't been foolish enough to let you think what I let you think… You see, I'm not and I've never been taking the contraceptive pill,' she admitted tightly, and waited for César to leap to the obvious conclusion.

His lush black lashes dropped very low over his fiercely intent eyes. 'What's that got to do with anything?'

A wave of dizziness ran over Dixie. She swayed slightly.

'You've gone white!' Striding forward on that exclamation, César steadied her with two careful hands and backed her down gently on to a leather couch.

'I'm pregnant…' Dixie told him flatly as he dropped down on a level with her.

'Pregnant,' César repeated, as if he had never heard the word before.

'That night Jasper collapsed…' Dixie added in a helpful

whisper, wondering when the awful truth was going to sink in.

'You're pregnant...' César's eyes suddenly silvered and flashed. 'All of a sudden I feel...almost dizzy,' he completed, not quite levelly.

Dixie just couldn't bear to watch his next reaction. She bowed her head over her tightly clasped hands and waited for the storm to break. In the circumstances, he would have to be superhuman not to lament such bad luck.

'You've got my baby inside you...' César framed with audible difficulty, his dark deep drawl roughening.

'After just that one time,' Dixie sighed shakily.

César unlaced her fingers with gentle force and wound them into his palms. '*Dio*...just that one time, *cara mia*,' he swore in the strangest tone.

'You're very shocked. I don't blame you. You were so careful every other time...' Her voice trailed away in embarrassment.

'The hand of fate is definitely operating here,' César remarked, sounding buoyant in what she could only assume to be his evident determination not to hurt her feelings or cause offence in any way. 'But I'm much inclined to think this is only what you call a storm in a teacup—'

'A storm in a teacup?' Dixie parroted in disbelief.

'Obviously you're not looking on the bright side,' César censured silkily. 'We're married—not that anyone would guess that by the ringless state of your hands.'

'I took the rings off as soon as I said goodbye to Jasper. I thought our marriage was to stay a secret,' she explained, mystified by the turn the conversation had taken, still apprehensively fearing a more painful response to the revelation that she had conceived.

Vaulting upright, César bent down and lifted her slowly into his arms. 'You need to lie down. You're very tired.'

'We need to talk about this now.'

'When you're more comfortable.'

Supporting her with one powerful arm, César opened the

door and strode across the hall to mount the stairs. 'This isn't where I sleep,' she protested.

'It's just not the done thing to keep your wife in the servants' quarters.'

'I was very comfortable there...I really don't want to intrude,' Dixie said miserably. 'You've got marvellous self-discipline, haven't you? You still haven't said one thing that I thought you would say.'

'It's a mistake to try and second-guess me. And I don't want to be discouraging, but because your mind works on a different plane from mine you don't read me very well,' César declared ruefully.

He settled her down on a magnificent canopied bed in a spacious room that had a distinctly masculine decor of burgundy and dark green. Several other doors led off from it. It was a truly massive house. Slipping off her shoes, he helped her out of her light jacket, pausing with amusement to scrutinise the price label still attached to the garment.

'So, say what you have to say,' Dixie urged anxiously.

'After you've had a nap, *cara*.' César sank down on the side of the bed, lean bronzed features arranged in an expression of unbelievable calm. 'You came close to fainting downstairs and you're still very pale. We've got plenty of time to talk.'

Dixie pushed her face into a pillow. 'Stop being nice,' she pleaded in a pained voice. 'It just makes me feel more of a nuisance. I know you don't really feel nice...it's just you hide your true feelings better than I do.'

César smoothed one of her curls down, watched it spring back rebelliously and smiled. 'Go to sleep,' he murmured softly. 'If it's any consolation, I used to think I could read you like a book, and then I discovered that there's nothing logical about the way you think. It's all gut reaction and impulses with you, thrills and spills...'

'Not true,' she mumbled, just loving him being there, too exhausted even to despise herself for being that weak. She might as well enjoy it, she thought. He wouldn't be there for much longer.

*   *   *

Dixie slept until almost seven that evening. When she wakened, she went for a shower and thought about César. He had been really kind. Why had she expected anything else? He was too sophisticated and too self-disciplined to react like a scared teenager trying to escape his responsibilities. But would kindness ultimately prove to be any easier to bear?

Fisher came to the door to inform her that dinner would be served at eight. She put on an elegant black sleeveless dress. She had worn it on the island, but the new fullness of her breasts gave the dress a tighter fit. Already her body was changing shape, an ever-present reminder of the tiny life forming inside her.

In the formal dining room, Fisher had set out magnificent silver candelabra and the very best china and crystal. Poor Fisher, Dixie reflected ruefully. He couldn't have a clue how inappropriate the romantic approach was for this particular occasion.

César joined her in the doorway. She turned. Tall, dark and devastatingly attractive, he made her outrageously aware of her own femininity.

'Do you think you can tolerate candlelight for one meal?' César enquired lazily.

Recalling that dreadful evening in Granada, Dixie went pink. 'I was really awful that night, wasn't I?' she groaned. 'I'd just found out I was pregnant and I went into a sort of tailspin—'

César frowned in surprise. 'You knew about the baby that far back?'

Dixie nodded.

'No wonder you were upset,' César settled her down into her chair.

Fisher served their meal. It was delicious, and she was hungry, but she couldn't have said what she ate. Afterwards, they had coffee in the drawing room, and her tension started to rocket again.

'Can we get the rest of this discussion over with?' Dixie asked, rising restively from her seat and beginning to wander aimlessly round the room. 'I don't understand how you can just make conversation as if there's nothing wrong!'

Slumbrous dark eyes rested on her. 'The obvious answer to that is that as far as I'm concerned there *is* nothing wrong. I want this baby,' César countered with incredible cool.

Dixie didn't see that that was necessarily the slightest bit obvious. 'But it was an accident—'

'No, and don't ever use that expression again.' César's mouth twisted as he moved forward to steady a tall lamp which she had brushed past. 'Take it from one who knows, tiny babies grow into adolescents who do not want to live with the news that they are the result of an accidental lapse in birth control!'

Dixie flushed and backed into a chair before setting off in another direction. 'I know that, but—'

'I can't believe that you would want a termination.'

'I don't.' Dixie stiffened defensively. 'But I thought you might.'

'That's not something I need to think about. My father tried to deprive me of the right to be born,' César reminded her with wry distaste. 'I could never feel like that about my own child. I don't just *want* our baby, I also intend to be a good father right from the start.'

Both those sweeping statements of intent left Dixie bereft of breath. Not once had she even hoped for that level of acceptance or commitment from César. 'That'll be difficult when we're living apart…divorced, I mean,' she finally pointed out awkwardly, coming to a halt as she met with another obstacle.

Helpfully, César removed the entire jardinière from her path. 'I'm afraid this is where *you* have to be very brave and self-sacrificing, *cara mia*.' He surveyed her with glittering dark eyes full of expectation.

'I don't understand…'

César spread fluidly expressive hands in a gesture of finality. 'It's goodbye to Scott time.'

'Goodbye to Scott?' Dixie marvelled at the way poor Scott

seemed to intrude in all sorts of places where he didn't belong.

'If we both want to do what is best for our child, we won't even consider getting a divorce now,' César asserted with complete conviction, watching her turn in little circles in the centre of the room.

Wildly disconcerted by that announcement, and giddy at the mere thought of it, Dixie breathed, 'But—'

'So we stay together, but Scott's *out* of our lives,' César stressed tautly. 'You have to accept that.'

'But Scott's just a friend—'

'You spent one hour and forty-two minutes on the phone to New York from our hotel in Granada,' César cited in a low-pitched growl of censure, making no move to protect her from stubbing her toe on the edge of the marble hearth. 'That was at least one hour and thirty minutes of what I call excessive friendship!'

Dixie studied him wide-eyed and then stumbled over the hearth. She righted herself with a bracing hand on the superb fireplace and slowly shook her head. 'Oh, my goodness…was I really on the phone that long? How on earth do you *know* that?'

'I paid the hotel bill before I came to the clinic,' César reminded her grittily.

He really was obsessed with Scott. She couldn't think how she had failed to notice that before. And he was genuinely angry that she had chatted that long to Scott on the phone. Was he jealous? Jealous of Scott? And being Dixie, in the grip of an astounding idea, she instantly asked him outright.

Dark colour accentuated César's fantastic cheekbones, lashes sweeping down on bright slivers of silvered outrage. '*Porca miseria!* Don't be ridiculous!'

Dixie flushed, and now saw no reason to add that she had long since got over her conviction that Scott was ever likely to be anything other than a friend. 'Sorry. I just—'

As she wandered back near the lamp table, César put his hands on her slight shoulders and directed her down on to a sofa. 'You're making me dizzy. Stay put,' he instructed. 'All

I am saying is that there is only room for two people in this marriage. You and I.'

'What about Petra?' Dixie almost whispered, knotting her fingers together.

Strong face clenching, his expressive mouth curled. 'I can put up with her in small doses, but if you could persuade her that covering up a little more flesh would make her look less like a hooker, I'd be grateful.'

Stunned by that sardonic response, Dixie studied him fixedly from below her lashes. 'But you went to see Petra the night you left me at the hotel—'

'No, I did not go to see her. I ran into her…to be exact, she ran into me the following morning,' César contradicted with careful clarity, seemingly quite unaware of Dixie's extreme tension. 'I do own the block of apartments she was staying in. I used one myself that night. Petra saw the limo, invited herself over for breakfast and expressed a desire to return to London with me. I could hardly refuse.'

César drew a perfectly possible scenario. Yet no matter how badly Dixie wanted to believe him, newly learnt cynicism assailed her. César was so clever. Would César tell her a truth that would hurt her now that he was talking about staying married to her? If he had been attracted to her stepsister, if he had followed through on that attraction, it would be very foolish of him to confess it now and drive an uneasy wedge between Dixie and Petra.

All Dixie knew was that she still couldn't quite follow what had been going on with César, either that night or the following morning. He had come to the clinic armed with a fabulous ruby ring as a kind of goodbye gift. Petra had been unusually brittle and awkward, exactly as she might have behaved had she got 'close' to Dixie's supposed temporary husband.

'You created a problem there,' César drawled, as if he could read her mind. 'You should never have told Petra that our marriage was a fake.'

Dixie stiffened. Her second mistake had been stopping short of complete honesty. Had she confided that she and

César were rather more than platonic partners, her stepsister would surely never have admitted or acted on her interest in him. So if anything *had* happened between César and Petra that night on the coast it was partly her own fault, not least for saying all those ghastly things about their relationship and tearing it apart.

'Did she tell you where she'd be staying in London?' Dixie asked uncomfortably.

'No, just that she'd be with a friend.'

'I'm sure she'll be in touch soon.'

'I shouldn't think we've seen the last of her,' César remarked quietly.

Dixie's thoughts were on her stepsister. It made her unhappy to acknowledge that the wedge between herself and Petra already existed, in the form of her own insecurity. And she knew then that she would have to talk to Petra before she could put those secret and undoubtedly quite foolish fears away.

As soon as Dixie had decided that, she was then free to appreciate how very happy she actually was. There wasn't going to be a divorce. César was determined that their child should have the stable background and support he himself had been denied. A little of her happiness ebbed on her next acknowledgement: if she hadn't been pregnant, César would have been discussing their divorce right now.

'I'm not sure you could cope with being married to me for years and years,' Dixie remarked ruefully.

César tensed. 'Why not?'

'You get bored awfully easy.' All her doubts showed in her eyes.

'How could I possibly get bored with you? I never know what you're about to spring on me from one minute to the next!'

'The trouble is, I also know you're not very good at being faithful.'

'Try me! *Dios mio*,' César rhymed, visibly shaking at having that thrown in his teeth. 'You seem so soft and trusting, but when it comes to me you're really tough and suspicious!'

Dixie thought about that and decided it was very true. 'You wouldn't respect anything else,' she pointed out helplessly.

'Tell me, were you like this with Scott?'

'No. He's not very clever and ruthless—'

'I forgot…he was really sweet,' César breathed with derisive bite.

Fisher knocked on the door to mention an urgent call.

After waiting fifteen minutes, and deciding that César might well be absolute ages, Dixie walked back upstairs at a sedate pace. With a gentle hand she shut the bedroom door. Then she took an undignified leap on to the wellsprung bed, punched the pillows with exuberant energy, rolled over again to kick off her shoes and gasped, 'Yes…yes…*yes*!'

The door that led into the connecting sitting room was ajar. Slowly it spread wide to frame César. Lounging back against the doorjamb, an unholy grin slashing his dark features as he absorbed Dixie's paralysed expression of appalled chagrin, he cast aside the cordless phone in his hand.

'So, I must be pretty good at doing something, *cara mia*,' César remarked with sexy sibilant softness. 'Downstairs, I would never have credited that you had the slightest enthusiasm for staying married to me. But here you are celebrating all by yourself. Fancy that.'

'I…I—'

César shimmied his shoulders fluidly out of his jacket and pitched it on a nearby chair. Tugging loose his tie, he surveyed her widening eyes and the colour building in her cheeks.

'Yes, now you *know* when I want you!' César carolled with satisfaction. 'That has to be a step in the right direction.'

And Dixie just couldn't control her response to the atavistic leap of boundless excitement tearing through her. He came down beside her on the bed with a brilliant smile that tore her heart from its moorings. Heat pooled deep inside her and made her tremble, and yet beyond that she was conscious of the most powerful ache of tenderness. Gosh, he just looked so really happy, even happier than he had been on the island.

The first thing she did was hug him tight, straining against him as the last of her tension drained away in the circle of his arms.

'I've really missed you...' he groaned raggedly.

In bed, she translated.

'I've even been thinking about you when I'm at the bank,' he confessed.

Thinking about the frustrating emptiness of the bed, she translated.

He curved his fingers to her cheekbones and kissed her breathless, so much hungry need in his stunning dark eyes she couldn't stop staring, still marvelling at the miracle which had made this elegant, cool, often cold guy seemingly burn with endless desire for her uncool and never elegant self.

'I got used to you being there...now you're here,' he completed, with a wealth of relief in his roughened intonation.

Back in the bed, she translated, but she ached with love for him, and told herself she wasn't going to want any more than he was able to give her. And tomorrow she would put on the ruby ring. Bit of a joke, that, she conceded. César had given her a ring that symbolised *her* passionate love for *him,* just because rubies were the only jewels she had seemed to have no reservations about...

'So I want to see Scott one last time,' Dixie concluded in the simmering silence. One glorious week had passed since her return to London, and this was their first difference of opinion.

'No,' César said flatly.

'Just to explain that I've got married and that that's why I haven't been in touch,' Dixie repeated for the second time.

'I don't want you anywhere near him. I think that's perfectly reasonable,' César drawled.

'Well, I don't,' Dixie muttered ruefully. 'I don't think it's reasonable at all. Nor do I think that you should behave as if I need your permission.'

'You're my wife,' César breathed chillingly, like a domestic tyrant. 'You should *care* about what I think.'

These days Dixie wasn't as easily chilled as she had once been. 'It's not like Scott's an ex-boyfriend or anything. I would understand if you were jealous—'

'I'm *not* jealous!' César gritted with predictable ferocity. 'Jealousy would imply that I regard him as a threat. Why would I consider an immature twenty-two-year-old car fanatic a threat?'

'I used to imagine I was in love with Scott, but I got over that ages ago,' Dixie remarked with studious casualness.

The silence hung there, throbbing with undertones.

'OK.' César flung the *Financial Times* down across the breakfast table and stood up. 'You can meet him somewhere public for an hour.'

'I'll call him today…' Dixie returned to her book and her coffee with an aura of complete tranquillity.

César reached the door at an unusually slow pace, and then swung back. 'I could come too,' he suggested abruptly.

Without lifting her head, Dixie muttered, 'Not much point you meeting him now. Anyway, he'd be so in awe of someone like you he wouldn't be able to relax.'

'I should hate to be a third wheel.'

Dixie laughed at that idea, knowing that César would simply take over.

'Why don't you ring Scott next week, when Jasper's here?' César suggested then, as he hovered by the door. 'I'm sure Jasper would love to meet him.'

'No, I don't want to leave it that long.' Dixie looked up and gave him a sunny smile, finally registering that he was about to leave. 'Will you be home for lunch?'

The brooding look on his lean bronzed face evaporated like magic. 'I'd really love to, but lunch at home exhausts me.'

Dixie coloured.

'Actually, I'm down for a very boring diplomatic do at lunchtime today…I'd much rather be with you,' César murmured, still lingering while she went back to her book.

In bed, she was thinking. Typical. But she warmed up inside with the wonderful safe feeling she was beginning to experience around César now. Sexual desire might have got him involved with her in the first place, but he was turning out to be so surprisingly wonderful in other ways.

According to Fisher, César had gone to fantastic lengths to win Spike's affection. Spike had been lured from his various hiding places with chocolate drops, doggy bones, choice treats from the dining table and toys. With a patience and a determination that had quite dumbfounded his butler, César had inched and pushed his way into Spike's scared little heart. And Dixie was incredibly touched that a male who had never had a pet in his life had made such a big effort. Initially he could only have done it to please her, but now he had been doubly rewarded by Spike's devotion.

Then there was the custom-built pond her goldfish now rejoiced in. César the fish hadn't eaten his companion, Milly, and they swam around together occasionally now. It would be too much to call them inseparable, but who knew what the future might hold?

Indeed, the only thing that troubled Dixie was that César hadn't yet offered to try to help her locate Petra. She still didn't know where her stepsister was staying. She had thrown out loads of hints, but either César hadn't picked up on them or he preferred that her stepsister remain out of touch. And Dixie had worked out that that was either because he genuinely couldn't stand Petra or because possibly something *had* happened between them which he didn't want Dixie to find out about…

But that was the only current cloud on Dixie's horizon. Next week, when Jasper arrived to spend the rest of the summer with them, they were having a belated wedding reception with five hundred guests. Dixie felt married now. Every time she woke up in the morning in César's arms she felt jubilant. It was the little things that mattered. The way he phoned her from the bank on what sometimes seemed the slimmest pretext. The way he had laughed at the sight of Spike trying to drag a bone nearly as big as himself upstairs. The way he talked about the baby, as if he or she was already here and part of their lives.

Dixie rang Scott at work mid-morning and told him she had got married. He reacted as if he was really shocked, and was surprisingly keen to make an arrangement to meet up with her that evening. She had rather thought he mightn't want to bother.

And then, at lunchtime, without the smallest warning, Dixie's world fell apart again. Bruce Gregory phoned to ask her where César was lunching.

She frowned in surprise. 'He mentioned an embassy thing—'

'No, he cancelled that to meet with your stepsister, and he must have his mobile switched off. I assumed he'd be back with you, at the house, but Fisher said not. So, do you know where they are?' Bruce prompted hopefully, quite unconscious of the bombshell he had dropped. 'The chairman of the Osana Corporation wants to speak to César urgently.'

Dixie's lips moved to frame conventional words before she could find her actual voice. 'I'm sorry, I didn't pick up on where they were planning to go.'

Bruce rang off, leaving Dixie sitting there in shock. César was with Petra? All this time César had known where her stepsister was? Well, obviously he had, if he was lunching with her! And yet he hadn't mentioned it to Dixie, even when he knew how worried she was that Petra hadn't been in touch?

Dear heaven, were they having an affair? If Dixie hadn't conceived, their marriage would have been over now. Yet César hadn't been acting like a male trapped in a marriage he didn't want! Or had he been? Had she just been too dumb and too much in love to see the obvious? Although if César was involved with Petra, why was he dragging Dixie off to bed early every night?

Half an hour later, Fisher opened the door of the drawing room. 'Miss Sinclair, madam.'

And before Dixie could even catch her breath, Petra erupted into the room, tear-stained and almost hysterical.

'I've done something dreadful, and you're going to hate me, but you're the only person who can help me!' her stepsister gasped before Fisher even got the door closed behind her.

'Help you?' Dixie was already rising from her seat.

'I made an awful mistake. I tried to blackmail César!' Petra ran a trembling berringed hand through her tumbled blonde tresses and groaned. 'How could you marry a ruthless bastard like that, Dixie?'

Dixie had slumped heavily back into her seat. Blackmail? So she had been right. Something *had* happened that night on the coast.

Her stepsister lit a cigarette with a hand that was still shaking so badly she could hardly get the flame near the tip. 'César said I'd never work again if I stayed in the UK. He said I was a spiteful, nasty harpy and I wasn't fit to polish your shoes, and that if I hurt you he'd be after me like a shark in a feeding frenzy…and the worst thing is…it was *all* true!' Her face crumpling on that final wail, Petra sobbed in very real distress.

'*You slept with César…*' Dixie gulped, feeling as if she had been smacked in the face by a brick, trying to be big enough to come to terms with such a betrayal and finally doggedly forcing herself upright to offer comfort. Whatever Petra had done, César had no business intimidating her to such an extent.

'Slept with César? Chance would be a fine thing!' Petra hissed through her falling tears. 'I threw myself at him that morning in Spain and he told me to *wise up*! He wasn't even tempted. In fact, do you know what the worst thing was?'

Not even tempted? Dixie suddenly found her sympathy gushing a lot more freely and closed her arms round her much taller stepsister to bring her down on to the sofa beside her. 'No…what was the worst thing?'

'César *knew* I was going to make a pass at him and he tried to head me off, and then, when I sort of moved close…' Her stepsister's tremulous voice faltered and she burst back into tears.

'What?'

Petra emerged from her hair, looking pathetic. 'He said he

got this really creepy feeling when I did that, so could I please stop it?' she howled. 'And I just felt so *ugly* and *horrible* then!'

Dixie patted her shoulder soothingly. 'I can understand that…'

'Then he left me sitting in that limo on my own most of the morning…like I was just nobody!' Petra wept. 'First he went into this jeweller's, and I'm sure he was in there an hour, and then he went into the hotel, and he was away even longer, and when he came out he was in this really freezing hostile mood and he ignored me. I was really starting to *hate* him by then—'

Dixie broke into that self-absorbed flood. 'So what did you try to blackmail César about today?'

'I called him up out of the blue this morning and told him he'd be really sorry if he didn't agree to see me,' her stepsister revealed shakily. 'And when he showed up I threatened to tell Jasper Dysart that your marriage was just a big empty nothing!'

Dixie turned pale. 'Oh dear…'

'It was my way of trying to get my own back,' her stepsister whispered shamefacedly. 'I'd never have done it. But if I ripped off some money from César, I thought I would feel better about him humiliating me!'

'I don't think César meant to humiliate you, Petra.'

'It was *very* humiliating when he burst out laughing at my threat and told me that you were pregnant!' Petra protested, shredding a tissue violently between her thin fingers. 'And then he got really cold and heavy and scary and said he'd *pay* just to get me out of your life, and I felt even worse then!'

Trying very hard not to smile, Dixie comforted her distraught stepsister. All Petra's real problems came tumbling out then. How she'd stopped getting modelling assignments in London because she was getting older. How nobody had shown the slightest interest in her bid to become an actress in Los Angeles. And Dixie finally began to see what had really been bothering Petra when she'd arrived in Spain.

'I was just so jealous. I just couldn't credit you had got hitched to this mega-rich, gorgeous guy, and there was me, trying so hard all these years and never even getting close to the altar!' Petra pointed out chokily.

'I encouraged you by telling you that our marriage was a fake—'

'It wouldn't have mattered. I was so desperate to prove myself more fanciable than you I'd *still* have tried to poach him!'

'I know.'

'He said he was going to come straight home now and tell you *everything*…so I had to get here first, because I really don't want to lose you, because you're always there for me…' Petra mumbled tightly. 'Nobody else ever is.'

At that very moment the door flew open. Petra cringed into the sofa. Dixie stood up. César got only one aggressive step into the room.

'I'm really grateful you found Petra for me, César,' Dixie delivered with a determined smile. 'And now that she's told me everything we're mending fences.'

'Mending fences?' César gritted incredulously, a fulminating toughness clenching his darkly handsome features.

'So you're a bit sort of superfluous here at the minute,' Dixie mentioned, very apologetically.

César backed off with extreme reluctance.

Dixie got Petra calmed down and tucked into a taxi.

César was waiting behind the front door for her. 'I should've been straight with you about Petra right from the start,' he announced darkly. 'The minute you said her name the night you explained about those debts, I recognised it. She's notorious! A publicity-grabbing, free-loading, prom—'

'I know,' Dixie interceded gently. 'Did you honestly think I didn't?'

César took an unusual split second to close his mouth again.

'I lived with her for quite a while,' Dixie reminded him. 'But I always try not to judge other people just because they're from a different mould. Petra's always been very in-secure.'

César parted his lips, looked deep into Dixie's reproachful blue eyes and subsided again, like a volcano with a lid suddenly crammed forcibly down on its fiery destructive flow.

'I'm very fond of her and you really don't need to protect me from her. You certainly don't need to bring out any big guns. She'd never have carried out that stupid threat. She's just been going through a rough patch and her self-esteem is very low.' Dixie sighed with compassion. 'She got used to relying on her looks to get her everything she wants. Now she needs support and understanding so that she can make some changes—'

'*Accidenti!* If you think she's going to change—'

'She will, but not overnight.' Quiet confidence backed that assurance from Dixie. 'She really has no choice. She can't run around dressed like a teenage raver for ever. And it's all right. She won't want to visit when you're around,' she told him soothingly. 'She really doesn't fancy you a bit now.'

Dumbfounded by that decidedly upbeat conclusion, César watched Dixie head for the stairs. 'Where are you going?'

'I'm meeting Scott for a drink after he comes out of work.'

César froze.

'You said it was OK.'

'I lied.' He said it so quietly Dixie almost didn't hear him.

Dixie gazed down at him where he stood in the hall.

César strode up to the landing and dug clenched fists into the pockets of his well-cut trousers. He didn't look at her. 'I really don't want you to go,' he breathed in a ferociously taut undertone. 'I'm scared that if you see him again you'll realise you're still crazy about him.'

'I'm scared'. Knowing how much that admission must have cost him, Dixie just melted. 'I'll cancel, then. You didn't need to worry,' she murmured gently. 'I've loved you to bits for weeks now.'

Having dropped that news because she felt he deserved it, Dixie continued on to the bedroom to call and cancel her arrangement with Scott. Would she regret telling César that she loved him later? She didn't think so. It got harder and harder to conceal her own emotions.

César followed her into the room. 'You said you loved me...' he prompted, not quite levelly. 'Does that mean you're just sort of very *fond* of me, or that you're as keen on me as you were on Scott?'

Her heart just overflowed. He sounded so vulnerable. She turned round with a helplessly tender look on her face. 'I was just infatuated with the idea of being in love with Scott. That was only the tiniest shadow of what I feel for you.'

His strained dark eyes blazed into brilliance. 'I thought it was still Scott—'

'You pushed him out, but I didn't want to face that at first...because I didn't think we had any future.'

César reached down and took her hands and drew her to him. 'I've been praying we had a future ever since the night Jasper was taken ill.'

Dixie's eyes rounded. 'That soon? Our very first night together?'

'*Dio!* It was really weird. I just looked down at you outside the bedroom door and it was like being hit with a brick,' César imparted gruffly.

Dixie was hanging on his every word. 'Painful?' she probed worriedly.

'I'd just realised I was in love with you, and I didn't want to let go of you in case you got away,' César revealed, a dark flush emphasising his taut cheekbones. 'And then I felt terrific the next morning, until you shot me down by saying it was a mistake and how Scott was the only one for you—'

'Oh dear...I thought that was what you wanted to hear. I really did.' A sort of heavenly chorus was sounding in Dixie's bemused head at that moment. César *loved* her. He'd felt as if he had been hit with a brick, which suggested a moment of stunning self-revelation. Suddenly those words acquired the hue of a deeply romantic and touching confession.

'What I *wanted* to hear? Are you kidding?' César demanded, a full octave higher, keen to tell her just how wrong she'd been in that assessment. 'I was already sick to death of the guy's name, but that morning I wanted to wipe him off the face of the earth! Every time I turned round there he was, like an invisible presence!'

Dixie stretched up and framed his furious face with two adoring hands. 'I'm sorry I upset you like that. I wouldn't have done it for the world if I'd known how you felt about me.'

Thoroughly consoled, César seemed to recollect himself then. His stunning dark eyes shimmered. He curved his mouth into the centre of one of her palms and then he started kissing her fingers in the most shockingly erotic way, and she got all out of breath and her knees wobbled. With the sense of good timing that always distinguished him, César got the message and lifted her up into his arms.

Later, she didn't remember how they'd got to the bed, and their clothes had sort of melted away. And after they had made wild, passionate love, with the new sweet knowledge that lay between them and joined them closer than ever, they were able to talk again.

'So there I was, feeling very rejected,' César relived feelingly, back on the topic of the morning after their first intimacy.

'And you're not used to feeling rejected,' Dixie slotted in tenderly, stringing a line of little sympathetic kisses across a wide brown shoulder which tensed unexpectedly. 'So it must have really hurt.'

'You're always shooting me down out of the sky.' César turned up her face and smiled with so much love down at her. 'I was really panicking when we went out to join Jasper for lunch—'

'Panicking?' Dixie looked dubious.

'As far as I could see you were still clinging to Scott, and I wasn't going to get another opportunity to change that!' César extended ruefully. 'So when Jasper dropped the news that he was getting organised for our wedding, it was like a last-minute rescue. I reckoned the minute I got a wedding ring on your finger I'd be in a position to stage an all-out war on your affections—'

'You really wanted to marry me?' Dixie gasped, and then she recalled the rough sincerity with which he had persuaded her to go ahead and marry him, and knew she was hearing the absolute truth.

'*Per meraviglia!* Of course I did. I'd never have let Jasper push us that far if I hadn't!' César stressed. 'I could have given him two dozen different reasons why we shouldn't get married that quickly—not the least being that you deserved the chance to have the enjoyment of planning a proper wedding.'

'But it was a lovely wedding,' Dixie assured him. 'And we had a terrific honeymoon.'

'After your stepsister arrived, I couldn't get you away fast enough,' César confided, without a shade of remorse. 'One glance was enough to tell me she was out to cause trouble.'

'I didn't see that until it was too late. She told me she thought you were really attracted to her—'

'In her dreams,' César growled like a grizzly bear.

Dixie told him that Petra wasn't really as bad as he seemed to think. He didn't look madly impressed by the news, but at least he wasn't arguing any more. Some unanswered questions continued to worry at Dixie, and she was eager to make further inroads into César's wonderfully new and welcome willingness to explain his own feelings and motivations.

'So, if you were so fed up with the idea of Scott, why did you encourage me to ring him on our wedding night?'

'You just looked so lost and unhappy after getting that stupid letter he sent…' César grimaced. 'I felt guilty. I felt I didn't have the right to deny you contact with him—'

'Oh, César, if you loved me that was really sweet and unselfish of you…' Dixie's eyes misted over her view of his broodingly handsome and tense features.

'It was a buck stupid impulse!' César countered. 'And when I heard you oozing care and compassion on the phone to him I just wanted him dead and buried! So I went into the kitchen and smashed my fist against the wall and hit the blasted can opener…'

'Oh, d-dear.' Dixie's voice wobbled betrayingly in spite of her attempt to hold back her sudden amusement. 'Your poor thumb.'

'I was just eaten with jealousy.'

He had finally admitted it. She kissed his thumb in reward.

'And then after that I thought I was in with a real chance, because I never believed you were just using me for sex, *mi amore*,' César revealed, curving her close with two posses-sive hands and studying her with even more possessive eyes.

'No, I knew I was in love with you by then, but I didn't want to scare you off…and then I did that anyway, in Granada,' Dixie lamented.

'You really shocked me, *cara mia*,' César agreed. 'I just had to get out of the city and sort everything out in my head. Once I'd done that, I realised that I couldn't really expect you to feel any other way when I hadn't admitted how I felt about you. Then Petra arrived for breakfast and really wound me up.'

'I know…let's forget about that,' Dixie urged.

'I was coming back to the clinic to tell you that I loved you and I bought the ring on the way. I remembered you saying that rubies stood for passionate love… *What's wrong?*'

'I've really misjudged you.' Dixie sighed. 'And now I un-derstand it all. You saw that hotel bill and knew I'd been calling Scott—'

'That shot the ground out from under me, and I was too proud to tell you how I felt then,' César admitted. 'But I'd cooled off by the time I got back to London, and I tried to keep the lines open between us. I also grovelled to Spike to get him on my side. I was ready to do anything it took to hang on to you…'

Such confessions were music to Dixie's ears. 'So the baby really was good news?'

'The *best*!' César grinned at her with wolfish satisfaction and smoothed a rather smug hand over her tummy. 'I really struck gold. I was ready to play a thousand violins about the baby needing a father.'

'I was so happy when you said you didn't want a divorce.' An expression of dismay suddenly crossed Dixie's features. 'Gosh, Bruce was trying to get hold of you to tell you that you had to call the chairman of the Osana Corporation—'

'Relax, I picked him up on the car phone.'

'Oh, no…and I've just stood poor Scott up!' Dixie registered in horror as she realised what time it was.

'Happens to the best of us. You can ask him to our wedding reception, but tell him he must bring a partner. You're very much spoken for,' César reminded her, watching her edge surreptitiously off the bed to let Spike in because he was whining piteously outside the door.

'Just for a little while…he gets awfully lonely.'

'Just like César the fish… A *fish*!' César emphasised without warning as Dixie turned, wearing a gobsmacked look. 'How could you christen a goldfish with my name?'

Sidling back into bed, Dixie breathed, 'Because he was always eating other fish. How did you find out?'

'Fisher couldn't resist letting me know. I didn't think it was really sweet either. There's comparisons and there's comparisons, and a manic goldfish—'

'No, he's got a partner now, and I think he's settling down…and you had that beautiful pond built just for him—'

'I was very tempted to stick him in with a very large and hungry carp to teach him the rules of the jungle!'

'Only you didn't.' Dixie ran an appreciative hand over his magnificent torso, feeling him tense in instantaneous response, revelling in the glow of love in his intense dark eyes, feeling she should have worked out long ago that her warmth would almost inevitably draw him to her. 'You're changing…'

'No, I'm still the cold, critical, inhuman guy you fell madly in love with,' César rushed to assert, somewhat apprehensively. 'I'm not going to change!'

'Spike, get down off this bed!' Dixie called in a shocked

aside. 'He's never been allowed on a bed in his life…what's got into him?'

César looked slightly uneasy.

Dixie surveyed him in mute disbelief.

'He was crying like a baby. He was really missing you. He'd have dug compassion out of a stone!' César protested in his own defence.

Dixie concealed a tender smile against his shoulder. She just loved him to death, and he loved her, and he loved their unborn child, and he even loved her dog and tolerated her goldfish. For a once commitment-shy male, he had made tremendous strides, and she was planning to spend the rest of her life ensuring he never had cause for a single regret.

Modern Romance™
...seduction and
passion guaranteed

Tender Romance™
...love affairs that
last a lifetime

Medical Romance™
...medical drama on
the pulse

Historical Romance™
...rich, vivid and
passionate

Sensual Romance™
...sassy, sexy and seductive

27 new titles every month.

*With all kinds of Romance for
every kind of mood...*

MILLS & BOON®

Makes any time special™

MAT4RS